[Page 52

" 'DON'T YOU KNOW THAT YOU OUGHTN'T TO SAY "NO'M"
AND "YES'M"?' "

RAGGED LADY

A Novel

BY

W. D. HOWELLS

AUTHOR OF "A HAZARD OF NEW FORTUNES"
"THE LANDLORD AT LION'S HEAD" ETC.

ILLUSTRATED
BY A. I. KELLER

The life of a New England girl from childhood to her second marriage. Round her are grouped a variety of Americans, who are nearer to a comic type. Scenes, America and Italy.

NEW YORK AND LONDON
HARPER & BROTHERS PUBLISHERS
1899

Electrotyped by J. A. Howells & Co., Jefferson, Ohio.

ILLUSTRATIONS

RAGGED LADY.

I.

It was their first summer at Middlemount and the Landers did not know the roads. When they came to a place where they had a choice of two, she said that now he must get out of the carry-all and ask at the house standing a little back in the edge of the pine woods, which road they ought to take for South Middlemount. She alleged many cases in which they had met trouble through his perverse reluctance to find out where they were before he pushed rashly forward in their drives. Whilst she urged the facts she reached forward from the back seat where she sat, and held her hand upon the reins to prevent his starting the horse, which was impartially cropping first the sweet fern on one side and then the blueberry bushes on the other side of the narrow wheel-track. She declared at last that if he would not get out and ask she would do it herself, and at this the dry little man jerked the reins in spite of her, and the horse suddenly pulled the carry-all to the right, and seemed about to overset it.

"Oh, what are you doing, Albe't?" Mrs. Lander lamented, falling helpless against the back of her seat. "Haven't I always told you to speak to the hoss fust?"

"He wouldn't have minded my speakin'," said her husband. "I'm goin' to take you up to the dooa so that you can ask for youaself without gettin' out."

This was so well, in view of Mrs. Lander's age and bulk, and the hardship she must have undergone, if she had tried to carry out her threat, that she was obliged to take it in some sort as a favor; and while the vehicle rose and sank over the surface left rough, after building, in front of the house, like a vessel on a chopping sea, she was silent for several seconds.

The house was still in a raw state of unfinish, though it seemed to have been lived in for a year at least. The earth had been banked up at the foundations for warmth in winter, and the sheathing of the walls had been splotched with irregular spaces of weather boarding; there was a good roof over all, but the window-casings had been merely set in their places and the trim left for a future impulse of the builder. A block of wood suggested the intention of steps at the front door, which stood hospitably open, but remained unresponsive for some time after the Landers made their appeal to the house at large by anxious noises in their throats, and by talking loud with each other, and then talking low. They wondered whether there were anybody in the house; and decided that there must be, for there was smoke coming out of the stove pipe piercing the roof of the wing at the rear.

Mr. Lander brought himself under censure by venturing, without his wife's authority, to lean forward and tap on the door-frame with the butt of his whip. At the sound, a shrill voice called instantly from the region of the stove pipe, "Clem! Clementina? Go to the front dooa! The'e's somebody knockin'." The sound of feet, soft and quick, made itself heard within, and in a few moments a slim maid, too large for a little girl, too childlike for a young girl, stood in the open doorway, looking down on the elderly people in the buggy, with a face as glad as a flower's. She had blue eyes, and a smiling mouth, a straight nose, and a pretty chin whose firm jut accented a certain wistfulness of her lips. She had hair of a dull, dark yellow, which sent out from its thick mass light prongs, or tendrils, curving inward again till they delicately touched it. Her tanned face was not very different in color from her hair, and neither were her bare feet, which showed well above her ankles in the calico skirt she wore. At sight of the elders in the buggy she involuntarily stooped a little to lengthen her skirt in effect, and at the same time she pulled it together sidewise, to close a tear in it, but she lost in her anxiety no ray of the joy which the mere presence of the strangers seemed to give her, and she kept smiling sunnily upon them while she waited for them to speak.

"Oh!" Mrs. Lander began with involuntary apology in her tone, "we just wished to know which of these roads went to South Middlemount. We've come from the hotel, and we wa'n't quite ce'tain."

The girl laughed as she said, "Both roads go to South Middlemount'm; they join together again just a little piece farther on."

The girl and the woman in their parlance replaced the letter *r* by vowel sounds almost too obscure to be represented, except where it came last in a word before a word beginning with a vowel; there it was annexed to the vowel by a strong *liaison*, according to the custom universal in rural New England.

"Oh, do they?" said Mrs. Lander.

"Yes'm," answered the girl. "It's a kind of tu'n-out in the wintatime; or I guess that's what made it in the beginning; sometimes folks take one hand side and sometimes the other, and that keeps them separate; but they're really the same road, 'm."

"Thank you," said Mrs. Lander, and she pushed her husband to make him say something, too, but he remained silently intent upon the child's prettiness, which her blue eyes seemed to illumine with a light of their own. She had got hold of the door, now, and was using it as if it was a piece of drapery, to hide not only the tear in her gown, but somehow both her bare feet. She leaned out beyond the edge of it; and then, at moments she vanished altogether behind it.

Since Mr. Lander would not speak, and made no sign of starting up his horse, Mrs. Lander added, "I presume you must be used to havin' people ask about the road, if it's so puzzlin'."

"O, yes'm," returned the girl, gladly. "Almost every day, in the summatime."

"'BOTH ROADS GO TO SOUTH MIDDLEMOUNT'M.'"

"You have got a pretty place for a home, he'e," said Mrs. Lander.

"Well, it will be when it's finished up." Without leaning forward inconveniently Mrs. Lander could see that the partitions of the house within were lathed, but not plastered, and the girl looked round as if to realize its condition and added, "It isn't quite finished inside."

"We wouldn't have troubled you," said Mrs. Lander, "if we had seen anybody to inquire of."

"Yes'm," said the girl. "It a'n't any trouble."

"There are not many otha houses about, very nea', but I don't suppose you get lonesome; young folks are plenty of company for themselves, and if you've got any brothas and sistas"—

"Oh," said the girl, with a tender laugh, "I've got eva so many of *them!*"

There was a stir in the bushes about the carriage, and Mrs. Lander was aware for an instant of children's faces looking through the leaves at her and then flashing out of sight, with gay cries at being seen. A boy, older than the rest, came round in front of the horse and passed out of sight at the corner of the house.

Lander now leaned back and looked over his shoulder at his wife as if he might hopefully suppose she had come to the end of her questions, but she gave no sign of encouraging him to start on their way again.

"That your brotha, too?" she asked the girl.

"Yes'm. He's the oldest of the boys; he's next to me."

"I don't know," said Mrs. Lander thoughtfully,

"as I noticed how many boys there were, or how many girls."

"I've got two sistas, and three brothas, 'm," said the girl, always smiling sweetly. She now emerged from the shelter of the door, and Mrs. Lander perceived that the slight movements of such parts of her person as had been evident beyond its edge were the effects of some endeavor at greater presentableness. She had contrived to get about her an overskirt which covered the rent in her frock, and she had got a pair of shoes on her feet. Stockings were still wanting, but by a mutual concession of her shoe-tops and the border of her skirt, they were almost eliminated from the problem. This happened altogether when the girl sat down on the threshold, and got herself into such foreshortening that the eye of Mrs. Lander in looking down upon her could not detect their absence. Her little head then showed in the dark of the doorway like a painted head against its background.

"You haven't been livin' here a great while, by the looks," said Mrs. Lander. "It don't seem to be clea'ed off very much."

"We've got quite a ga'den-patch back of the house," replied the girl, "and we should have had moa, but fatha wasn't very well, this spring; he's eva so much better than when we fust came he'e."

"It has the name of being a very healthy locality," said Mrs. Lander, somewhat discontentedly, "though I can't see as it's done *me* so very much good, yit. Both your payrints livin'?"

"Yes'm. Oh, yes, indeed!"

"And your mother, is she real rugged? She need to be, with such a flock of little ones!"

"Yes, motha's always well. Fatha was just run down, the doctas said, and ought to keep more in the open aia. That's what he's done since he came he'e. He helped a great deal on the house and he planned it all out himself."

"Is he a ca'penta?" asked Mrs. Lander.

"No'm; but he's— I don't know how to express it—he likes to do every kind of thing."

"But he's got *some* business, ha'n't he?" A shadow of severity crept over Mrs. Lander's tone, in provisional reprehension of possible shiftlessness.

"Yes'm. He was a machinist at the Mills; that's what the doctas thought didn't agree with him. He bought a piece of land he'e, so as to be in the pine woods, and then we built this house."

"*When* did you say you came?"

"Two yea's ago, this summa."

"Well! What did you do befoa you built this house?"

"We camped the first summa."

"You *camped?* In a tent?"

"Well, it was pahtly a tent, and pahtly bahk."

"I should have thought you would have died."

The girl laughed. "Oh, no, we all kept fust-rate. We slept in the tents—we had two—and we cooked in the shanty." She smiled at the notion in adding, "At fust the neighbas thought we we'e Gipsies; and the summa folks thought we were Indians, and wanted to get baskets of us."

Mrs. Lander did not know what to think, and she asked, "But didn't it almost perish you, stayin' through the winter in an unfinished house?"

"Well, it was pretty cold. But it was so dry, the aia was, and the woods kept the wind off nicely."

The same shrill voice in the region of the stovepipe which had sent the girl to the Landers now called her from them. "Clem! Come here a minute!"

The girl said to Mrs. Lander, politely, "You'll have to excuse me, now'm. I've got to go to motha."

"So do!" said Mrs. Lander, and she was so taken by the girl's art and grace in getting to her feet and fading into the background of the hallway without visibly casting any detail of her raiment, that she was not aware of her husband's starting up the horse in time to stop him. They were fairly under way again, when she lamented, "What you doin', Albe't? Whe'e you goin'?"

"I'm goin' to South Middlemount. Didn't you want to?"

"Well, of all *the* men! Drivin' right off without waitin' to say thankye to the child, or take leave, or anything!"

"Seemed to me as if *she* took leave."

"But she was comin' back! And I wanted to ask—"

"*I* guess you asked enough for one while. Ask the rest to-morra."

Mrs. Lander was a woman who could often be thrown aside from an immediate purpose, by the suggestion of some remoter end, which had already, perhaps, intimated itself to her. She said, "That's true," but by the time her husband had driven down one of the roads beyond the woods into open country, she was a quiver of intolerable curiosity. "Well, all I've got to say is that *I* sha'n't rest till I know all about 'em."

"Find out when we get back to the hotel, I guess," said her husband.

"No, I can't wait till I get back to the hotel. I want to know now. I want you should stop at the very fust house we come to. Dea'! The'e don't seem to *be* any houses, any moa." She peered out around the side of the carry-all and scrutinized the landscape. "Hold on! No, yes it is, too! Whoa! Whoa! The'e's a man in that hay-field, *now!*"

She laid hold of the reins and pulled the horse to a stand. Mr. Lander looked round over his shoulder at her. "Hadn't you betta wait till you get within half a mile of the man?"

"Well, I want you should stop when you *do* git to him. Will you? I want to speak to him, and ask him all about those folks."

"I didn't suppose you'd let *me* have much of a chance," said her husband. When he came within easy hail of the man in the hay-field, he pulled up beside the meadow-wall, where the horse began to nibble the blackberry vines that overran it.

Mrs. Lander beckoned and called to the man, who had stopped pitching hay and now stood leaning on the handle of his fork. At the signs and sounds she made, he came actively forward to the road, bringing his fork with him. When he arrived within easy conversational distance, he planted the tines in the ground and braced himself at an opposite incline from the long smooth handle, and waited for Mrs. Lander to begin.

"Will you please tell us who those folks ah', livin' back there in the edge of the woods, in that new unfinished house?"

The man released his fork with one hand to stoop for a head of timothy that had escaped the scythe, and he put the stem of it between his teeth, where it moved up and down, and whipped fantastically about as he talked, before he answerd, "You mean the Claxons?"

"I don't know what thei' name is." Mrs. Lander repeated exactly what she had said.

The farmer said, "Long, red-headed man, kind of sickly-lookin'?"

"We didn't see the man"—

"Little woman, skinny-lookin'; pootty tonguey?"

"We didn't see *her*, eitha; but I guess we hea'd her at the back of the house."

"Lot o' children, about as big as pa'tridges, runnin' round in the bushes?"

"Yes! And a very pretty-appearing girl; about thi'teen or fou'teen, I should think."

The farmer pulled his fork out of the ground, and planted it with his person at new slopes in the figure of a letter A, rather more upright than before. "Yes; it's them," he said. "Ha'n't been in the neighbahood a great while, eitha. Up from down Po'tland way, some'res, I guess. Built that house last summer, as far as it's got, but I don't believe it's goin' to git much fa'tha."

"Why, what's the matta?" demanded Mrs. Lander in an anguish of interest.

The man in the hay-field seemed to think it more dignified to include Lander in this inquiry, and he said with a glimmer of the eye for him, "Hea'd of do-nothin' folks?"

"Seen 'em, too," answered Lander, comprehensively.

"Well, that a'n't Claxon's complaint exactly. He a'n't a do-nothin'; he's a do-everything. I guess it's about as bad." Lander glimmered back at the man, but did not speak.

"Kind of a machinist down at the Mills, where he come from," the farmer began again, and Mrs. Lander, eager not to be left out of the affair for a moment, interrupted:

"Yes, yes! That's what the gul said."

"But he don't seem to think't the i'on agreed with him, and now he's goin' in for wood. Well, he *did* have a kind of a foot-powa tu'nin' lathe, and tu'ned all so'ts o' things; cups, and bowls, and u'ns for fence-posts, and vases, and sleeve-buttons and little knick-knacks; but the place bu'nt down, here, a while back, and he's been huntin' round for wood, the whole winta long, to make canes out of for the summa-folks. Seems to think that the smell o' the wood, whether it's green or it's dry, is goin' to cure him, and he can't git too much of it."

"Well, I believe it's *so*, Albe't!" cried Mrs. Lander, as if her husband had disputed the theory with his taciturn back. He made no other sign of controversy, and the man in the hay-field went on.

"I hea' he's goin' to put up a wind mill, back in an open place he's got, and use the powa for tu'nin', if he eva gits it up. But he don't seem to be in any great of a hurry, and they scrape along somehow. Wife takes in sewin' and the girl wo'ked at the Middlemount House last season. Whole fam'ly's got to tu'n in and help s'po't a man that can do everything."

The farmer appealed with another humorous cast of his eye to Lander; but the old man tacitly refused to take any further part in the talk, which began to flourish apace, in question and answer, between his wife and the man in the hay-field. It seemed that the children had all inherited the father's smartness. The oldest boy could beat the nation at figures, and one of the young ones could draw anything you had a mind to. They were all clear up in their classes at school, and yet you might say they almost ran wild, between times. The oldest girl was a pretty-behaved little thing, but the man in the hay-field guessed there was not very much to her, compared with some of the boys. Any rate, she had not the name of being so smart at school. Good little thing, too, and kind of mothered the young ones.

Mrs. Lander, when she had wrung the last drop of information out of him, let him crawl back to his work, mentally flaccid, and let her husband drive on, but under a fire of conjecture and asseveration that was scarcely intermitted till they reached their hotel.

That night she talked a long time about their afternoon's adventure before she allowed him to go to sleep. She said she must certainly see the child again; that they must drive down there in the morning, and ask her all about herself.

"Albe't," she concluded, "I wish we had her to live with us. Yes, I do! I wonder if we could get her to. You know I always did want to adopt a baby."

"You neva said so," Mr. Lander opened his mouth almost for the first time, since the talk began.

"I didn't suppose you'd like it," said his wife.

"Well, *she* a'n't a baby. I guess you'd find you had your hands full, takin' a half-grown gul like that to bring up."

"I shouldn't be afraid any," the wife declared. "She has just twined herself round my hea't. I can't get her pretty looks out of my eyes. I know she's good."

"We'll see how you feel about it in the monning."

The old man began to wind his watch, and his wife seemed to take this for a sign that the incident was closed, for the present at least. He seldom talked, but there came times when he would not even listen. One of these was the time after he had wound his watch. A minute later he had undressed, with an agility incredible of his years, and was in bed, as effectively blind and deaf to his wife's appeals as if he were already asleep.

II.

When Albert Gallatin Lander (he was named for an early Secretary of the Treasury as a tribute to the statesman's financial policy) went out of business, his wife began to go out of health; and it became the most serious affair of his declining years to provide for her invalid fancies. He would have liked to buy a place in the Boston suburbs (he preferred one of the Newtons) where they could both have had something to do, she inside of the house, and he outside; but she declared that what they both needed was a good long rest, with freedom from care and trouble of every kind. She broke up their establishment in Boston, and stored their furniture, and she would have made him sell the simple old house in which they had always lived, on an unfashionable up-and-down-hill street of the West End, if he had not taken one of his stubborn stands, and let it for a term of years without consulting her. But she had her way about their own movements, and they began that life of hotels, which they had now lived so long that she believed any other impossible. Its luxury and idleness had told upon each of them with diverse effect.

They had both entered upon it in much the same corporal figure, but she had constantly grown in flesh, while he had dwindled away until he was not much more than half the weight of his prime. Their digestion was alike impaired by their joint life, but as they took the same medicines Mrs. Lander was baffled to account for the varying result. She was sure that all the anxiety came upon her, and that logically she was the one who ought to have wasted away. But she had before her the spectacle of a husband who, while he gave his entire attention to her health, did not audibly or visibly worry about it, and yet had lost weight in such measure that upon trying on a pair of his old trousers taken out of storage with some clothes of her own, he found it impossible to use the side pockets which the change in his figure carried so far to the rear when the garment was reduced at the waist. At the same time her own dresses of ten years earlier would not half meet round her; and one of the most corroding cares of a woman who had done everything a woman could to get rid of care, was what to do with those things which they could neither of them ever wear again. She talked the matter over with herself before her husband, till he took the desperate measure of sending them back to storage; and they had been left there in the spring when the Landers came away for the summer.

They always spent the later spring months at a hotel in the suburbs of Boston, where they arrived in May from a fortnight in a hotel at New York, on their way up from hotels in Washington, Ashville, Aiken and St. Augustine. They passed the summer months in the mountains, and early in the autumn they went back to the hotel in the Boston suburbs, where Mrs. Lander considered it essential to make some sojourn before going to a Boston hotel for November and December, and getting ready to go down to Florida in January. She would not on any account have gone directly to the city from the mountains, for people who did that were sure to lose the good of their summer, and to feel the loss all the winter, if they did not actually come down with a fever.

She was by no means aware that she was a selfish or foolish person. She made Mr. Lander subscribe statedly to worthy objects in Boston, which she still regarded as home, because they had not dwelt any where else since they ceased to live there; and she took lavishly of tickets for all the charitable entertainments in the hotels where they stayed. Few if any guests at hotels enjoyed so much honor from porters, bell-boys, waiters, chambermaids and bootblacks as the Landers, for they gave richly in fees for every conceivable service which could be rendered them; they went out of their way to invent debts of gratitude to menials who had done nothing for them. He would make the boy who sold papers at the dining-room door keep the change, when he had been charged a profit of a hundred per cent. already; and she would let no driver who had plundered them according to the carriage tariff escape without something for himself.

A sense of their munificence penetrated the clerks

and proprietors with a just esteem for guests who always wanted the best of everything, and questioned no bill for extras. Mrs. Lander, in fact, who ruled these expenditures, had no knowledge of the value of things, and made her husband pay whatever was asked. Yet when they lived under their own roof they had lived simply, and Lander had got his money in an old-fashioned business way, and not in some delirious speculation such as leaves a man reckless of money afterwards. He had been first of all a tailor, and then he had gone into boys' and youths' clothing in a small way, and finally he had mastered this business and come out at the top, with his hands full. He invested his money so prosperously that the income for two elderly people, who had no children, and only a few outlying relations on his side, was far beyond their wants, or even their whims.

She was a woman, who in spite of her bulk and the jellylike majesty with which she shook in her smoothly casing brown silks, as she entered hotel dining-rooms, and the severity with which she frowned over her fan down the length of the hotel drawing-rooms, betrayed more than her husband the commonness of their origin. She could not help talking, and her accent and her diction gave her away for a middle-class New England person of village birth and unfashionable sojourn in Boston. He, on the contrary, lurked about the hotels where they passed their days in a silence so dignified that when his verbs and nominatives seemed not to agree, you accused your own hearing. He was correctly dressed, as an elderly man should be, in the yesterday of the fashions, and he wore with impressiveness a silk hat whenever such a hat could be worn. A pair of drab cloth gaiters did much to identify him with an old school of gentlemen, not very definite in time or place. He had a full gray beard cut close, and he was in the habit of pursing his mouth a great deal. But he meant nothing by it, and his wife meant nothing by her frowning. They had no wish to subdue or overawe any one, or to pass for persons of social distinction. They really did not know what society was, and they were rather afraid of it than otherwise as they caught sight of it in their journeys and sojourns. They led a life of public seclusion, and dwelling forever amidst crowds, they were all in all to each other, and nothing to the rest of the world, just as they had been when they resided (as they would have said) on Pinckney street. In their own house they had never entertained, though they sometimes had company, in the style of the country town where Mrs. Lander grew up. As soon as she was released to the grandeur of hotel life, she expanded to the full measure of its responsibilities and privileges, but still without seeking to make it the basis of approach to society. Among the people who surrounded her, she had not so much acquaintance as her husband even, who talked so little that he needed none. She sometimes envied his ease in getting on with people when he chose; and his boldness in speaking to fellow guests and fellow travellers, if he really wanted anything. She wanted something of them all the time, she wanted their conversation and their companionship; but in her ignorance of the social arts she was thrown mainly upon the compassion of the chambermaids. She kept these talking as long as she could detain them in her rooms; and often fed them candy (which she ate herself with childish greed) to bribe them to further delays. If she was staying some days in a hotel, she sent for the house-keeper, and made all she could of her as a listener, and as soon as she settled herself for a week, she asked who was the best doctor in the place. With doctors she had no reserves, and she poured out upon them the history of her diseases and symptoms in an inexhaustible flow of statement, conjecture and misgiving, which was by no means affected by her profound and inexpugnable ignorance of the principles of health. From time to time she forgot which side her liver was on, but she had been doctored (as she called it) for all her organs, and she was willing to be doctored for any one of them that happened to be in the place where she fancied a present discomfort. She was not insensible to the claims which her husband's disorders had upon science, and she liked to end the tale of her own sufferings with some such appeal as: "I wish you could do something for Mr. Landa, too, docta." She made him take a little of each medicine that was left for her; but in her presence he always denied that there was anything the matter with him, though he was apt to follow the doctor out of the room, and get a prescription from him for some ailment which he professed not to believe in himself, but wanted to quiet Mrs. Lander's mind about.

He rose early, both from long habit, and from the scant sleep of an elderly man; he could not lie in bed; but his wife always had her breakfast there and remained so long that the chambermaid had done up most of the other rooms and had leisure for talk with her. As soon as he was awake, he stole softly out and was the first in the dining-room for breakfast. He owned to casual acquaintance in moments of expansion that breakfast was his best meal, but he did what he could to make it his worst by beginning with oranges and oatmeal, going forward to beefsteak and fried potatoes, and closing with griddle cakes and syrup, washed down with a cup of cocoa, which his wife decided to be wholesomer than coffee. By the time he had finished such a repast, he crept out of the dining-room in a state of tension little short of anguish, which he confided to the sympathy of the bootblack in the washroom.

He always went from having his shoes polished to get a toothpick at the clerk's desk; and at the Middlemount House, the morning after he had been that drive with Mrs. Lander, he lingered a moment with his elbows beside the register. "How about a buckboa'd?" he asked.

"Something you can drive yourself"—the clerk professionally dropped his eye to the register—"Mr. Lander?"

"Well, no, I guess not, this time," the little man returned, after a moment's reflection. "Know anything of a family named Claxon, down the road, here, a piece?" He twisted his head in the direction he meant.

"This is my first season at Middlemount; but I guess Mr. Atwell will know." The clerk called to the landlord, who was smoking in his private room behind the office, and the landlord came out. The clerk repeated Mr. Lander's questions.

"Pootty good kind of folks, I guess," said the landlord provisionally, through his cigar-smoke. "Man's a kind of univussal genius, but he's got a nice family of children; smaht as traps, all of 'em."

"How about that oldest gul?" asked Mr. Lander.

"Well, the'a," said the landlord, taking the cigar out of his mouth. "*I* think she's about the nicest little thing goin'. We've had her up he'e, to help out in a busy time, last summer, and she's got moa sense than guls twice as old. Takes hold like—lightnin'."

"About how old did you say she was?"

"Well, you've got me the'a, Mr. Landa; I guess I'll ask Mis' Atwell."

"The'e's no hurry," said Lander. "That buckboa'd be round pretty soon?" he asked of the clerk.

"Be right along now, Mr. Lander," said the clerk, soothingly. He stepped out to the platform that the teams drove up to from the stable, and came back to say that it was coming. "I believe you said you wanted something you could drive yourself?"

"No, I didn't, young man," answered the elder sharply. But the next moment he added, "Come to think of it, I guess it's just as well. You needn't get me no driver. I guess I know the way well enough. You put me in a hitchin' strap."

"All right, Mr. Lander," said the clerk, meekly.

The landlord had caught the peremptory note in Lander's voice, and he came out of his room again to see that there was nothing going wrong.

"It's all right," said Lander, and went out and got into his buckboard.

"Same horse you had yesterday," said the young clerk. "You don't need to spare the whip."

"I guess I can look out for myself," said Lander, and he shook the reins and gave the horse a smart cut, as a hint of what he might expect.

The landlord joined the clerk in looking after the brisk start the horse made. "Not the way he set off with the old lady, yesterday," suggested the clerk.

The landlord rolled his cigar round in his tubed lips. "I guess he's used to ridin' after a good hoss." He added gravely to the clerk, "You don't want to make very free with that man, Mr. Fane. He won't stan' it, and he's a class of custom that you want to cata to when it comes in your way. I suspicioned what he was when they came here and took the highest cost rooms without tu'nin' a haia. They're a class of custom that you won't get outside the big hotels in the big reso'ts. Yes, sir," said the landlord taking a fresh start, "they're them kind of folks that live the whole yea' round in hotels; no'th in summa, south in winta, and city hotels between times. They want the best their money can buy, and they got plenty of it. *She*"—he meant Mrs. Lander—"has been tellin' my wife how they do; she likes to talk a little betta than he doos; and I guess when it comes to society, they're away up, and they won't stan' any nonsense."

III.

LANDER came into his wife's room between ten and eleven o'clock, and found her still in bed, but with her half-finished breakfast on a tray before her. As soon as he opened the door she said, "I do wish you would take some of that hea't-tonic of mine, Albe't, that the docta left for me in Boston. You'll find it in the upper right bureau box, the'a; and I know it'll be the very thing for you. It'll relieve you of that suffocatin' feeling that *I* always have, comin' up stai's. Dea'! I don't see why they don't have an elevata; they make you *pay* enough; and I wish you'd get me a little more silva, so's't I can give to the chambamaid and the bell-boy; I do hate to be out of it. I guess you been up and out long ago. They *did* make that polonaise of mine too tight after all I said, and I've been thinkin' how I could get it alt'ed; but I presume there ain't a seamstress to be had around he'e for *love* or money. Well, now, that's right, Albe't; I'm glad to see you doin' it."

Lander had opened the lid of the bureau box, and uncorked a bottle from it, and tilted this to his lips.

"Don't take too much," she cautioned him, "or you'll lose the effects. When I take too much of a medicine, it's wo'se than nothing, as fah's I can make out. When I had that spell in Thomasville spring before last, I believe I should have been over it twice as quick if I had taken just half the medicine I did. You don't *really* feel anyways bad about the hea't, do you, Albe't?"

"I'm all right," said Lander. He put back the bottle in its place and sat down.

Mrs. Lander lifted herself on her elbow and looked over at him. "Show me on the bottle how much you took."

He got the bottle out again and showed her with his thumb nail a point which he chose at random.

"Well, that was just about the dose for you," she said, and she sank down in bed again with the air of having used a final precaution. "You don't want to slow your hea't up too quick."

Lander did not put the bottle back this time. He kept it in his hand, with his thumb on the cork, and rocked it back and forth on his knees as he spoke. "Why don't you get that woman to alter it for you?"

"What woman alta what?"

"Your polonaise. The one whe'e we stopped yestaday."

"Oh! Well, I've been thinkin' about that child, Albe't; I did before I went to sleep; and I don't believe I want to risk anything with her. It would be a ca'e," said Mrs. Lander with a sigh, "and I guess I don't want to take any *moa* ca'e than what I've got now. What makes you think she could alta my polonaise?"

"Said she done dress-makin'," said Lander, doggedly.

"You *ha'n't* been the'a?"

He nodded.

"You *didn't* say anything to her about her daughta?"

"Yes, I did," said Lander.

"Well, you ce'tainly do equal anything," said his wife. She lay still awhile, and then she roused herself with indignant energy. "Well, then, I can tell you what, Albe't Landa: you can go right straight and take back everything you said. I don't want the child, and I won't have her. I've got care enough to worry me now, I should think; and we should have her whole family on our hands, with that shiftless father of hers, and the whole pack of her brothas and sistas. What made you think I wanted you to do such a thing?"

"You wanted me to do it last night. Wouldn't ha'dly let me go to bed."

"Yes! And how many times have I told you neva to go off and do a thing that I wanted you to, unless you asked me if I *did?* Must I *die* befo'e you can find out that there is such a thing as talkin', and such anotha thing as doin'? You wouldn't get yourself into half as many scrapes if you talked more and done less, in this wo'ld." Lander rose.

"Wait! Hold on! What are you going to say to the pooa thing? She'll be *so* disappointed!"

"I don't know as I shall need to say anything myself," answered the little man, at his dryest. "Leave that to you."

"Well, I can tell you," returned his wife, "I'm not goin' nea' them again; and if you think— What did you ask the woman, anyway?"

"I asked her," he said, "if she wanted to let the gul come and see you about some sewing you had to have done, and she said she did."

"And you didn't speak about havin' her come to live with us?"

"No."

"Well, why in the land didn't you say so before, Albe't?"

"You didn't ask me. What do you want I should say to her now?"

"Say to who?"

"The gul. She's down in the pahlor, waitin'."

"Well, of all the *men!*" cried Mrs. Lander. But she seemed to find herself, upon reflection, less able to cope with Lander personally than with the situation generally. "Will you send her up, Albe't?" she asked, very patiently, as if he might be driven to further excesses, if not delicately handled. As soon as he had gone out of the room she wished that she had told him to give her time to dress and have her room put in order, before he sent the child up; but she could only make the best of herself in bed with a cap and a breakfast jacket, arranged with the help of a handglass. She had to get out of bed to put her other clothes away in the closet and she seized the chance to push the breakfast tray out of the door, and smooth up the bed, while she composed her features and her ideas to receive her visitor. Both, from long habit rather than from any cause or reason, were of a querulous cast, and her ordinary tone was a snuffle expressive of deep-seated affliction. She was at once plaintive and voluable, and in moments of excitement her need of freeing her mind was so great that she took herself into her own confidence, and found a more sympathetic listener than when she talked to her husband. As she now whisked about her room in her bed-gown with an activity not predicable of her age and shape, and finally plunged under the covering and drew it up to her chin with one hand while she pressed it out decorously over her person with the other, she kept up a rapid flow of lamentation and conjecture. "I do suppose he'll be right back with her before I'm half ready; and what the man was thinkin' of to do such a thing anyway, *I* don't know. I don't know as she'll notice much, comin' out of such a *lookin'* place as that, and I don't know as I need to care if she did. But if the'e's care anywhe's around, I presume I'm the one to have it. I presume I *did* take a fancy to her, and I guess I shall be glad to see how I like her now; and if he's only told her I want some sewin' done, I can scrape up something to let her carry home with her. It's well I keep my things where I can put my hand on 'em at a time like this, and I don't believe I shall *sca'e* the child, as it is. I do hope Albe't won't hang round half the day before he brings her; I like to have a thing *ova.*"

Lander wandered about looking for the girl through the parlors and the piazzas, and then went to the office to ask what had become of her.

The landlord came out of his room at his question to the clerk. "Oh, I guess she's round in my wife's room, Mr. Landa. She always likes to see Clementina, and I guess they all do. She's a so't o' pet amongst 'em."

"No hurry," said Lander, "I guess my wife ain't quite ready for her yet."

"Well, she'll be right out, in a minute or so," said the landlord.

The old man tilted his hat forward over his eyes, and went to sit on the veranda and look at the landscape while he waited. It was one of the loveliest landscapes in the mountains; the river flowed at the foot of an abrupt slope from the road before the hotel, stealing into and out of the valley, and the mountains, gray in the farther distance, were draped with folds of cloud hanging upon their flanks and tops. But Lander was tired of nearly all kinds of views and prospects, though he put up with them, in his perpetual movement from place to place, in the same resignation that he suffered the limitations of comfort in parlor cars and sleepers, and the unwholesomeness of hotel tables. He was chained to the restless pursuit of an ideal not his own, but doomed to suffer for its impossibility as if he contrived each of his wife's disappointments from it. He did not philosophize his situation, but accepted it as in an order of Providence which it would be useless for him to oppose; though there were moments when he permitted himself to feel a modest doubt of its justice. He was aware that when he had a house of his own he was master in it, after a fashion, and that as long as he was in business he was in some sort of authority. He perceived that now he was a slave to the wishes of a mistress who did not know what she wanted, and that he was never farther from pleasing her than when he tried to do what she asked. He could not have told how all initiative had been taken from him, and he had fallen into the mere follower of a woman guided only by her whims, who had no object in life except to deprive it of all object. He felt no rancor toward her for this; he knew that she had a tender regard for him, and that she believed she was considering him first in her most selfish arrangements. He always hoped that sometime she would get tired of her restlessness, and be willing to settle down again in some stated place; and wherever it was, he meant to get into some kind of business again. Till this should happen he waited with an apathetic patience of which his present abeyance was a detail. He would hardly have thought it anything unfit, and certainly nothing surprising, that the landlady should have taken the young girl away from where he had left her, and then in the pleasure of talking with her, and finding her a centre of interest for the whole domestic force of the hotel, should have forgotten to bring her back.

The Middlemount House had just been organized on the scale of a first class hotel, with prices that had risen a little in anticipation of the other improvements. The landlord had hitherto united in himself the functions of clerk and head waiter, but he had now got a senior, who was working his way through college, to take charge of the dining-room, and had put in the office a youth of a year's experience as under clerk at a city hotel. But he meant to relinquish no more authority than his wife who frankly kept the name as well as duty of house-keeper. It was in making her morning inspection of the dusting that she found Clementina in the parlor where Lander had told her to sit down till he should come for her.

"Why, Clem!" she said, "I didn't know you! You *have* grown so! Youa folks all well? I decla'e you ah' quite a woman now," she added, as the girl stood up in her slender, graceful height. "You look as pretty as a pink in that hat. Make that dress youaself? Well, you do beat the witch! I want you should come to my room with me."

Mrs. Atwell showered other questions and exclamations on the girl, who explained how she happened to be there, and said that she supposed she must stay where she was for fear Mr. Lander should come back and find her gone; but Mrs. Atwell overruled her with the fact that Mrs. Lander's breakfast had just gone up to her; and she made her come out and see the new features of the enlarged house-keeping. In the dining-room there were some of the waitresses who had been there the summer before, and recognitions of more or less dignity passed between them and Clementina. The place was now shut against guests, and the head-waiter was having it put in order for the one o'clock dinner. As they came near him, Mrs. Atwell introduced him to Clementina, and he behaved deferentially, as if she were some young lady visitor whom Mrs. Atwell was showing the improvements, but he seemed harassed and impatient, as if he were anxious about his duties, and eager to get at them again. He was a handsome little fellow, with hair lighter than Clementina's and a sanguine complexion, and the color coming and going.

"He's smaht," said Mrs. Atwell, when they had left him—he held the dining-room door open for them, and bowed them out. "I don't know but he worries almost *too* much. That'll wear off when he gets things runnin' to suit him. He's pretty p'tic'la'. Now I'll show you how they've made the office over, and built in a room for Mr. Atwell behind it."

The landlord welcomed Clementina as if she had been some acceptable class of custom, and when the tall young clerk came in to ask him something, and Mrs. Atwell said, "I want to introduce you to Miss Claxon, Mr. Fane," the clerk smiled down upon her from the height of his smooth, acquiline young face, which he held bent encouragingly upon one side.

"Now, I want you should come in and see where *I* live, a minute," said Mrs. Atwell. She took the girl from the clerk, and led her to the official housekeeper's room which she said had been prepared for her so that folks need not keep running to her in her private room where she wanted to be alone with her children, when she was there. "Why, you a'n't much moa than a child youaself, Clem, and here I be talkin' to you as if you was a mother in Israel. How old *ah'* you, this summa? Time does *go* so!"

"I'm sixteen now," said Clementina, smiling.

"You *be?* Well, I don't see why I say that, eitha! You're full lahge enough for your age, but not seein' you in long dresses before, I didn't realize your age so much. My, but you do all of you know how to do things!"

"I'm about the only one that don't, Mrs. Atwell," said the girl. "If it hadn't been for mother, I don't believe I could have eva finished this dress." She began to laugh at something passing in her mind, and Mrs. Atwell laughed too, in sympathy, though she did not know what at till Clementina said, "Why, Mrs. Atwell, nea'ly the whole family wo'ked on this dress. Jim drew the patte'n of it from the dress of one of the summa boa'das that he took a fancy to at the Centa, and fatha cut it out, and I helped motha make it. I guess every one of the children helped a little."

"Well, it's just as I said, you can all of you do things," said Mrs. Atwell. "But I guess you ah' the one that keeps 'em straight. *What* did you say Mr. Landa said his wife wanted of you?"

"He said some kind of sewing that motha could do."

"Well, I'll tell you what! Now, if she ha'n't really got anything that your motha'll want you to help with, I wish you'd come here again and help me. I tu'ned my foot, here, two-three weeks back, and I feel it, times, and I should like some one to do about half my steppin' for me. I don't want to take you away from her, but *if*. You sha'n't go int' the dinin'-room, or be under anybody's oddas but mine. Now, will you?"

"I'll see, Mrs. Atwell. I don't like to say anything till I know what Mrs. Landa wants."

"Well, that's right. I decla'e, you've got moa judgment! That's what I used to say about you last summa to my husband: she's got *judgment*. Well, what's wanted?" Mrs. Atwell spoke to her husband, who had opened her door and looked in, and she stopped rocking, while she waited his answer.

"I guess you don't want to keep Clementina from Mr. Landa much longa. He's settin' out there on the front piazza waitin' for her."

"Well, the'a!" cried Mrs. Atwell. "Ain't that just like *me*? Why didn't you tell me sooner, Alonzo? Don't you forgit what I said, Clem!"

IV.

Mrs. Lander had taken twice of a specific for what she called her nerve-fag before her husband came with Clementina, and had rehearsed aloud many of the things she meant to say to the girl. In spite of her preparation, they were all driven out of her head when Clementina actually appeared, and gave her a bow like a young birch's obeisance in the wind.

"Take a chaia," said Lander, pushing her one, and the girl tilted over toward him, before she sank into it. He went out of the room, and left Mrs. Lander to deal with the problem alone. She apologized for being in bed, but Clementina said so sweetly, "Mr. Landa told me you were not feeling very well, 'm," that she began to be proud of her ailments, and bragged of them at length, and of the different doctors who had treated her for them. While she talked she missed one thing or another, and Clementina seemed to divine what it was she wanted, and got it for her, with a gentle deference which made the elder feel her age cushioned by the girl's youth. When she grew a little heated from the interest she took in her personal annals, and cast off one of the folds of her bed clothing, Clementina got her a fan, and asked her if she should put up one of the windows a little.

"How you do think of things!" said Mrs. Lander. "I guess I *will* let you. I presume you get used to thinkin' of othas in a lahge family like youas. I don't suppose they could get along without you very well," she suggested.

"I've neva been away except last summa, for a little while."

"And where was you then?"

"I was helping Mrs. Atwell."

"Did you like it?"

"I don't know," said Clementina. "It's pleasant to be whe'e things ah' going on."

"Yes—for young folks," said Mrs. Lander, whom the going on of things had long ceased to bring pleasure.

"It's real nice at home, too," said Clementina. "We have very good times—evenings in the winta; in the summer it's very nice in the woods, around there. It's safe for the children, and they enjoy it, and fatha likes to have them. Motha don't ca'e so much about it. I guess she'd ratha have the house fixed up more, and the place. Fatha's going to do it pretty soon. He thinks the'e's time enough."

"That's the way with men," said Mrs. Lander. "They always think the's time enough; but I like to have things over and done with. What chuhch do you 'tend?"

"Well, there isn't any but the Episcopal," Clementina answered. "I go to that, and some of the children go to the Sunday School. I don't believe fatha ca'es very much for going to chuhch, but he likes Mr. Richling; he's the recta. They take walks in the woods; and they go up the mountains togetha."

"They want," said Mrs. Lander, severely, "to be ca'eful how they drink of them cold brooks when they're heated. Mr. Richling a married man?"

"Oh, yes'm! But they haven't got any family."

"If I could see his wife, I sh'd caution her about lettin' him climb mountains too much. A'n't your father afraid he'll ovado?"

"I don't know. He thinks he can't be too much in the open air on the mountains."

"Well, he *may* not have the same complaint as Mr. Landa; but I know if *I* was to climb a mountain, it would lay me up for a yea'."

The girl did not urge anything against this conviction. She smiled politely and waited patiently for the next turn Mrs. Lander's talk should take, which was oddly enough toward the business Clementina had come upon.

"I declare I most forgot about my polonaise. Mr. Landa said your motha thought she could do something to it for me."

"Yes'm."

"Well, I may as well let you see it. If you'll reach into that fuhthest closet, you'll find it on the last uppa hook on the right hand, and if you'll give it to me, I'll show you what I want done. Don't mind the looks of that closet; I've just tossed my things in, till I could get a little time and stren'th to put 'em in odda."

Clementina brought the polonaise to Mrs. Lander, who sat up and spread it before her on the bed, and had a happy half hour in telling the girl where she had bought the material and where she had it made up, and how it came home just as she was going away, and she did not find out that it was all wrong till a week afterwards when she tried it on. By the end of this time the girl had commended herself so much by judicious and sympathetic assent, that Mrs. Lander learned with a shock of disappointment that her mother expected her to bring the garment home with her, where Mrs. Lander was to come and have it fitted over for the alterations she wanted made.

"But I supposed, from what Mr. Landa said, that your motha would come here and fit me!" she lamented.

"I guess he didn't undastand, 'm. Motha doesn't eva go out to do wo'k," said Clementina gently but firmly.

"Well, I might have known Mr. Landa would mix it up, if it *could* be mixed;" Mrs. Lander's sense of injury was aggravated by her suspicion that he had brought the girl in the hope of pleasing her, and confirming her in the wish to have her with them; she was not a woman who liked to have her way in spite of herself; she wished at every step to realize that she was taking it, and that no one else was taking it for her.

"Well," she said dryly, "I shall have to see about

it. I'm a good deal of an invalid, and I don't know as I could go back and fo'th to try on. I'm moa used to havin' the things brought to me."

"Yes'm," said Clementina. She moved a little from the bed, on her way to the door, to be ready for Mrs. Lander in leave-taking.

"I'm real sorry," said Mrs. Lander. "I presume it's a disappointment for you, too."

"Oh, not at all," answered Clementina. "I'm sorry we can't do the wo'k he'a; but I know motha wouldn't like to. Good-mo'ning, 'm!"

"No, no! Don't go yet a minute! Won't you just give me my hand bag off the bureau the'a?" Mrs. Lander entreated, and when the girl gave her the bag she felt about among the bank-notes which she seemed to have loose in it, and drew out a handful of them without regard to their value. "He'a!" she said, and she tried to put the notes into Clementina's hand, "I want you should get yourself something."

The girl shrank back. "Oh, no'm," she said, with an effect of seeming to know that her refusal would hurt, and with the wish to soften it. "I—couldn't; indeed I couldn't."

"Why couldn't you? Now you must! If I can't let you have the wo'k the way you want, I don't think it's fair, and you ought to have the money for it just the same."

Clementina shook her head smiling. "I don't believe motha would like to have me take it."

"Oh, now, pshaw!" said Mrs. Lander, inadequately. "I want you should take this for youaself; and if you don't want to buy anything to wea', you can get something to fix your room up with. Don't you be afraid of robbin' us. Land! We got moa *money!* Now you take this."

Mrs. Lander reached the money as far toward Clementina as she could and shook it in the vehemence of her desire.

"Thank you, I couldn't take it," Clementina persisted. "I'm afraid I must be going; I guess I must bid you good-mo'ning."

"Why, I believe the child's sca'ed of me! But you needn't be. Don't you suppose I know how you feel? You set down in that chai'a there, and I'll tell you how you feel. I guess we've been pooa, too—I don't mean anything that a'n't exactly right—and I guess I've had the same feelin's. You think it's demeanin' to you to take it. A'n't that it?" Clementina sank provisionally upon the edge of the chair. "Well, it did use to be so consid'ed. But it's all changed, nowadays. We travel pretty nea' the whole while, Mr. Lander and me, and we see folks everywhere, and it a'n't the custom to refuse any moa. Now, a'n't there any little thing for your own room, there in your nice new house? Or something your motha's got her hea't set on? Or one of your brothas? My, if you don't have it, some one else will! Do take it!"

The girl kept slipping toward the door. "I shouldn't know what to tell them, when I got home. They would think I must be—out of my senses."

"I guess you mean they'd think I was. Now, listen to me a minute!" Mrs. Lander persisted.

"You just take this money, and when you get home, you tell your mother every word about it, and if she says to, you bring it right straight back to me. Now, can't you do that?"

"I don't know but I can," Clementina faltered.

"Well, then take it!"

Mrs. Lander put the bills into her hand but she did not release her at once. She pulled Clementina down and herself up till she could lay her other arm on her neck. "I want you should let me kiss you. Will you?"

"Why, certainly," said Clementina, and she kissed the old woman.

"You tell your mother I'm comin' to see her before I go; and I guess," said Mrs. Lander in instant expression of the idea that came into her mind, "we shall be goin' pretty soon, now."

"Yes'm," said Clementina.

She went out, and shortly after Lander came in with a sort of hopeful apathy in his face.

Mrs. Lander turned her head on her pillow, and so confronted him. "Albe't, what made you want me to see that child?"

Lander must have perceived that his wife meant business, and he came to it at once. "I thought you might take a fancy to her, and get her to come and live with us."

"Yes?"

"We're both of us gettin' pretty well *on*, and you'd ought to have somebody to look after you if—I'm not around. You want somebody that can do for you;

and keep you company, and read to you, and talk to you—well, moa like a daughta than a suvvant—somebody that you'd get attached to, maybe"—

"And don't you see," Mrs. Lander broke out severely upon him, "what a *ca'e* that would be? Why, it's got so already that I can't help thinkin' about her the whole while, and if I got attached to her I'd have her on my mind day and night, and the moa she done for me the more I should be tewin' around to do for her. I shouldn't have any peace of my life any moa. Can't you *see* that?"

"I guess if you see it, I don't need to," said Lander.

"Well, then, I want you shouldn't eva mention her to me again. I've had the greatest escape! But I've got her off home, and I've give her money enough—I had a time with her about it—so that they won't feel as if we'd made 'em trouble for nothing, and now I neva want to hear of her again. I don't want we should stay here a great while longer; I shall be frettin' if I'm in reach of her, and I shan't get any good of the ai'a. Will you promise?"

"Yes."

"Well, then!" Mrs. Lander turned her face upon the pillow again in the dramatization of her exhaustion; but she was not so far gone that she was insensible to the possible interest that a light rap at the door suggested. She once more twisted her head in that direction and called, "Come in!"

The door opened and Clementina came in. She advanced to the bedside smiling joyously, and put the money Mrs. Lander had given her down upon the counterpane.

"Why, you haven't been home, child?"

"No'm," said Clementina, breathlessly. "But I couldn't take it. I knew they wouldn't want me to, and I thought you'd like it better if I just brought it back myself. Good-mo'ning." She slipped out of the door. Mrs. Lander swept the bank-notes from the coverlet and pulled it over her head, and sent from beneath it a stifled wail. "Now we *got* to go! And it's all *youa* fault, Albe't."

Lander took the money from the floor, and smoothed each bill out, and then laid them in a neat pile on the corner of the bureau. He sighed profoundly but left the room without an effort to justify himself.

V.

The Landers had been gone a week before Clementina's mother decided that she could spare her to Mrs. Atwell for a while. It was established that she was not to serve either in the dining-room or the carving room; she was not to wash dishes or to do any part of the chamber work, but to carry messages and orders for the landlady, and to save her steps, when she wished to see the head-waiter, or the head-cook; or to make an excuse or a promise to some of the lady-boarders; or to send word to Mr. Atwell about the buying, or to communicate with the clerk about rooms taken or left.

She had a good deal of dignity of her own and such a gravity in the discharge of her duties that the *chef*, who was a middle-aged Yankee with grown girls of his own, liked to pretend that it was Mrs. Atwell herself who was talking with him, and to discover just as she left him that it was Clementina. He called her the Boss when he spoke of her to others in her hearing, and he addressed her as Boss when he feigned to find that it was not Mrs. Atwell. She did not mind that in him, and let the *chef* have his joke as if it were not one. But one day when the clerk called her Boss she merely looked at him without speaking, and made him feel that he had taken a liberty which he must not repeat. He was a young man who much preferred a state of self-satisfaction to humiliation of any sort, and after he had endured Clementina's gaze as long as he could, he said, "Perhaps you don't allow anybody but the *chef* to call you that?"

She did not answer, but repeated the message Mrs. Atwell had given her for him, and went away.

It seemed to him undue that a person who exchanged repartees with the young lady boarders across his desk, when they came many times a day to look at the register, or to ask for letters, should remain snubbed by a girl who still wore her hair in a braid; but he was an amiable youth, and he tried to appease her by little favors and services, instead of trying to bully her.

He was great friends with the head-waiter, whom he respected as a college student, though for the time being he ranked the student socially. He had him in behind the frame of letter-boxes, which formed a sort of little private room for him, and talked with him at such hours of the forenoon and the late evening as the student was off duty. He found comfort in the student's fretful strength, which expressed itself in the pugnacious frown of his hot-looking young face, where a bright sorrel mustache was beginning to blaze on a short upper lip.

Fane thought himself a good-looking fellow, and he regarded his figure with pleasure, as it was set off by the suit of fine gray check that he wore habitually; but he thought Gregory's educational advantages told in his face. His own education had ended at a commercial college, where he acquired a good knowledge of book-keeping, and the fine business hand he wrote, but where it seemed to him sometimes that the earlier learning of the public school had been hermetically sealed within him by several coats of mathematical varnish. He believed that he had once known a number of things that he no longer knew, and that he had not always been so weak in his double letters as he presently found himself.

One night while Gregory sat on a high stool and rested his elbow on the desk before it, with his chin in his hand, looking down upon Fane, who sprawled sadly in his chair, and listening to the last dance playing in the distant parlor, Fane said, "Now, what'll you bet that they won't every one of 'em come and look for a letter in her box before she goes to bed? I tell you, girls are queer, and there's no place like a hotel to study 'em."

"I don't want to study them," said Gregory, harshly.

"Think Greek's more worth your while, or know 'em well enough already?" Fane suggested.

"No, I don't know them at all," said the student.

"I don't *believe*," urged the clerk, as if it were relevant, "that there's a girl in the house that you couldn't marry, if you gave your mind to it."

Gregory twitched irascibly. "I don't want to marry them."

"Pretty cheap lot, you mean? Well, I don't know."

"I don't mean that," retorted the student. "But I've got other things to think of."

"Don't you believe," the clerk modestly urged, "that it is natural for a man—well, a *young* man—to think about girls?"

"I suppose it is."

"And you don't consider it wrong?"

"How, wrong?"

"Well, a waste of time. I don't know as I always think about wanting to marry 'em, or be in love, but I like to let my mind run on 'em. There's something about a girl that, well, you don't know what it is, exactly. Take almost any of 'em," said the clerk, with an air of inductive reasoning. "Take that Claxon girl, now for example, I don't know what it is about *her*. She's good-looking, I don't deny that; and she's got pretty manners, and she's as graceful as a bird. But it a'n't any one of 'em, and it don't seem to be all of 'em put together that makes you want to keep your eyes on her the whole while. Ever noticed what a nice little foot she's got? Or her hands?"

"No," said the student.

"I don't mean that she ever tries to show them off; though I know some girls that would. But she's not that kind. She ain't much more than a child, and yet you got to treat her just like a woman. Noticed the kind of way she's got?"

"No," said the student, with impatience.

The clerk mused with a plaintive air for a moment before he spoke. "Well, it's something as if she'd been trained to it, so that she knew just the right thing to do, every time, and yet I guess it's nature. You know how the *chef* always calls her the Boss? That explains it about as well as anything, and I presume that's what my mind was running on, the other day, when *I* called her Boss. But, my! I can't get anywhere near her since!"

"It serves you right," said Gregory. "You had no business to tease her."

"Now, do *you* think it was teasing? *I* did, at first, and then again it seemed to me that I came out with the word because it seemed the right one. I presume I couldn't explain that to her."

"It wouldn't be easy."

"I look upon her," said Fane, with an effect of argument in the sweetness of his smile, "just as I would upon any other young lady in the house. Do you spell apology with one p or two?"

"One," said the student, and the clerk made a minute on a piece of paper.

"I feel badly for the girl. I don't want her to think I was teasing her or taking any sort of liberty with her. Now, would you apologize to her, if you was in my place, and would you write a note, or just wait your chance and speak to her?"

Gregory got down from his stool with a disdainful laugh, and went out of the place. "You make me sick, Fane," he said.

The last dance was over, and the young ladies who had been waltzing with one another, came out of the parlor with gay cries and laughter, like summer girls who had been at a brilliant hop, and began to stray down the piazzas, and storm into the office. Several of them fluttered up to the desk, as the clerk had foretold, and looked for letters in the boxes bearing their initials. They called him out, and asked if he had not forgotten something for them. He denied it with a sad, wise smile, and then they tried to provoke him to a belated flirtation, in lack of other material, but he met their overtures discreetly, and they presently said, Well, they guessed they must go; and went. Fane turned to encounter Gregory, who had come in by a side door.

"Fane, I want to beg your pardon. I was rude to you just now."

"Oh, no! Oh, no!" the clerk protested. "That's all right. Sit down a while, can't you, and talk with a fellow. It's early, yet."

"No, I can't. I just wanted to say I was sorry I spoke in that way. Good-night. Is there anything in particular?"

"No; good-night. I was just wondering about—that girl."

"Oh!"

VI.

Gregory had an habitual severity with his own behavior which did not stop there, but was always passing on to the behavior of others; and his days went by in alternate offence and reparation to those he had to do with. He had to do chiefly with the dining-room girls, whose susceptibilities were such that they kept about their work bathed in tears or suffused with anger much of the time. He was not only good-looking but he was a college student, and their feelings were ready to bud toward him in tender efflorescence, but he kept them cropped and blighted by his curt words and impatient manner. Some of them loved him for the hurts he did them, and some hated him, but all agreed fondly or furiously that he was too cross for anything. They were mostly young school-mistresses, and whether they were of a soft and amorous make, or of a forbidding temper, they knew enough in spite of their hurts to value a young fellow whose thoughts were not running upon girls all the time. Women, even in their spring-time, like men to treat them as if they had souls as well as hearts, and it was a saving grace in Gregory that he treated them all, the silliest of them, as if they had souls. Very likely they responded more with their hearts than with their souls, but they were aware that this was not his fault.

The girls that waited at table saw that he did not distinguish in manner between them and the girls whom they served. The knot between his brows did not dissolve in the smiling gratitude of the young ladies whom he preceded to their places, and pulled out their chairs for, any more than in the blandishments of a waitress who thanked him for some correction.

They owned when he had been harshest that no one could be kinder if he saw a girl really trying, or more patient with well meaning stupidity, but some things fretted him, and he was as apt to correct a girl in her grammar as in her table service. Out of work hours, if he met any of them, he recognized them with deferential politeness; but he shunned occasions of encounter with them as distinctly as he avoided the ladies among the hotel guests. Some of the table girls pitied his loneliness, and once they proposed that he should read to them on the back piazza in the leisure of their mid-afternoons. He said that he had to keep up with his studies in all the time he could get; he treated their request with grave civility, but they felt his refusal to be final.

He was seen very little about the house outside of his own place and function, and he was scarcely known to consort with anyone but Fane, who celebrated his high sense of the honor to the lady-guests;

but if any of these would have been willing to show Gregory that they considered his work to get an education as something that redeemed itself from discredit through the nobility of its object, he gave them no chance to do so.

The afternoon following their talk about Clementina, Gregory looked in for Fane behind the letter boxes, but did not find him, and the girl herself came round from the front to say that he was out buying, but would be back now, very soon; it was occasionally the clerk's business to forage among the farmers for the lighter supplies, such as eggs, and butter, and poultry, and this was the buying that Clementina meant. "Very well, I'll wait here for him a little while," Gregory answered.

"So do," said Clementina, in a formula which she thought polite; but she saw the frown with which Gregory took a Greek book from his pocket, and she hurried round in front of the boxes again, wondering how she could have displeased him. She put her face in sight a moment to explain, "I have got to be here and give out the lettas till Mr. Fane gets back," and then withdrew it. He tried to lose himself in his book, but her tender voice spoke from time to time beyond the boxes, and Gregory kept listening for Clementina to say, "No'm, there a'n't. Perhaps, the'e'll be something the next mail," and "Yes'm, he'e's one, and I guess this paper is for some of youa folks, too."

Gregory shut his book with a sudden bang at last and jumped to his feet, to go away.

The girl came running round the corner of the boxes. "Oh! I thought something had happened."

"No, nothing has happened," said Gregory, with a sort of violence, which was heightened by a sense of the rings and tendrils of loose hair springing from the mass that defined her pretty head. "Don't you know that you oughtn't to say 'No'm' and 'Yes'm?'" he demanded, bitterly, and then he expected to see the water come into her eyes, or the fire into her cheeks.

Clementina merely looked interested. "Did I say that? I meant to say Yes, ma'am and No, ma'am; but I keep forgetting."

"You oughtn't to say anything!" Gregory answered savagely, "Just say Yes, and No, and let your voice do the rest."

"Oh!" said the girl, with the gentlest abeyance, as if charmed with the novelty of the idea. "I should be afraid it wasn't polite."

Gregory took an even brutal tone. It seemed to him as if he were forced to hurt her feelings. But his words, in spite of his tone, were not brutal; they might have even been thought flattering. "The politeness is in the manner, and you don't need anything but your manner."

"Do you think so, truly?" asked the girl joyously. "I should like to try it once!"

He frowned again. "I've no business to criticise your way of speaking"—

"Oh yes'm—yes, *ma'am ; sir*, I mean; I mean, Oh, yes, indeed! The'a! It does sound just as well, don't it?" Clementina laughed in triumph at the outcome of her efforts, so that a reluctant and provisional smile came upon Gregory's face, too. "And I'm very much obliged to you, Mr. Gregory. I shall always want to do it, if it's the right way."

"It's the right way," said Gregory coldly.

"And don't they," she urged, "don't they really say *Sir* and *Ma'am*, whe'e—whe'e you came from?"

He said gloomily, "Not ladies and gentlemen. Servants do. Waiters—like me." He inflicted this stab to his pride with savage fortitude and he bore with self-scorn the pursuit of her innocent curiosity.

"But I thought— I thought you was a college student."

"Were," Gregory corrected her, involuntarily, and she said, "Were, I *mean*."

"I'm a student at college, and here I'm a servant! It's all right!" he said with a suppressed gritting of the teeth; and he added, "My Master was the servant of the meanest, and I must— I beg your pardon for meddling with your manner of speaking"—

"Oh, I'm very much obliged to you; indeed I am. And I shall not care if you tell me of anything that's out of the way in my talking," said Clementina, generously.

"Thank you; I think I won't wait any longer for Mr. Fane."

"Why, I'm su'a he'll be back very soon, now. I'll try not to disturb you any moa."

Gregory turned from taking some steps towards the door, and said, "I wish you would tell Mr. Fane something."

"For you? Why, suttainly!"

"No. For you. Tell him that it's all right about his calling you Boss."

The indignant color came into Clementina's face. "He had no business to call me that."

"No; and he doesn't think he had, now. He's truly sorry for it."

"I'll see," said Clementina.

She had not seen by the time Fane got back. She received his apologies for being gone so long coldly, and went away to Mrs. Atwell, whom she told what had passed between Gregory and herself.

"Is he truly so proud?" she asked.

"He's a very *good* young man," said Mrs. Atwell, "but I guess he's proud. He can't help it, but you can see he fights against it. If I was you, Clem, I wouldn't say anything to the guls about it."

"Oh, no'm—I mean, no, indeed. I shouldn't think of it. But don't you think that was funny, his bringing in Christ, that way?"

"Well, he's going to be a minister, you know."

"Is he really?" Clementina was a while silent. At last she said, "Don't you think Mr. Gregory has a good many freckles?"

"Well, them red-complected kind is liable to freckle," said Mrs. Atwell, judicially.

After rather a long pause for both of them, Clementina asked, "Do you think it would be nice for me to ask Mr. Gregory about things, when I wasn't suttain?"

"Like what?"

"Oh—wo'ds, and pronunciation; and books to read."

"Why, I presume he'd *love* to have you. He's always correctin' the guls; I see him take up a book one day, that one of 'em was readin', and when she as't him about it, he said it was rubbage. I guess you couldn't have a betta guide."

"Well, that was what I was thinking. I guess I sha'n't do it, though. I sh'd neva have the courage." Clementina laughed and then fell rather seriously silent again.

VII.

One day the shoeman stopped his wagon at the door of the helps' house, and called up at its windows, "Well, guls, any of you want to git a numba foua foot into a numba two shoe, to-day? Now's youa chance, but you got to be quick about it. The'e ha'n't but just so many numba two shoes made, and the wohld's full o' numba foua feet."

The windows filled with laughing faces at the first sound of the shoeman's ironical voice; and at sight of his neat wagon, with its drawers at the rear and sides, and its buggy-hood over the seat where the shoeman lounged lazily holding the reins, the girls flocked down the stairs, and out upon the piazza where the shoe man had handily ranged his vehicle.

They began to ask him if he had not this thing and that, but he said with firmness, "Nothin' but shoes, guls. I did carry a gen'l line, one while, of what you may call ankle-wea', such as spats, and stockin's, and gaitas, but I neva did like to speak of such things befoa ladies, and now I stick ex-clusively to shoes. You know that well enough, guls; what's the use?"

He kept a sober face amidst the giggling that his

words aroused, and let his voice sink into a final note of injury.

"Well, if you don't want any *shoes*, to-day, I guess I must be goin'." He made a feint of jerking his horse's reins, but forebore at the entreaties that went up from the group of girls.

"Yes, we do!" "Let's see them!" "Oh, don't go!" they chorused in an equally histrionic alarm, and the shoeman got down from his perch to show his wares.

"Now, the'a, ladies," he said, pulling out one of the drawers, and dangling a pair of shoes from it by the string that joined their heels, "the'e's a shoe that looks as good as any Sat'd'y-night shoe you eva see. Looks as han'some as if it had a pasteboa'd sole and was split stock all through, like the kind you buy for a dollar at the store, and kick out in the fust walk you take with your fella—or some other gul's fella, I don't ca'e which. And yet that's an honest shoe, made of the best of material all the way through, and in the best manna. Just look at that shoe, ladies; *ex*-amine it; sha'n't cost you a cent, and I'll pay for youa lost time myself, if any complaint is made." He began to toss pairs of the shoes into the crowd of girls, who caught them from each other before they fell, with hysterical laughter, and ran away with them in-doors to try them on. "This is a shoe that I'm intaducin'," the shoeman went on, "and every pair is warranted—warranted numba two; don't make any otha size, because we want to cata to a strictly numba two custom. If any lady *doos* feel 'em a little mite too snug, I'm sorry for her, but I can't do anything to help her in *this* shoe."

"Too *snug!*" came a gay voice from in-doors. "Why my foot feels puffectly lost in this one."

"All right," the shoeman shouted back. "Call it a numba one shoe and then see if you can't find that lost foot in it, some'eres. Or try a little flour, and see if it won't feel more at home. I've hea'd of a shoe that give that sensation of looseness by not goin' on at all."

The girls exulted joyfully together at the defeat of their companion, but the shoeman kept a grave face, while he searched out other sorts of shoes and slippers, and offered them, or responded to some definite demand with something as near like as he could hope to make serve. The tumult of talk and laughter grew till the *chef* put his head out of the kitchen door, and then came sauntering across the grass to the helps' piazza. At the same time the clerk suffered himself to be lured from his post by the excitement. He came and stood beside the *chef*, who listened to the shoeman's flow of banter with a longing to take his chances with him.

"That's a nice hawss," he said. "What'll you take for him?"

"Why, hello!" said the shoeman, with an eye that dwelt upon the *chef's* official white cap and apron, "You talk English, don't you? Fust off, I didn't know but it was one of them foreign dukes come ova he'a to marry some oua poor millionai'es daughtas." The girls cried out for joy, and the *chef* bore their mirth stoically, but not without a personal relish of the shoeman's up-and-comingness. "Want a hawss?" asked the shoeman with an air of business. "What'll you give?"

"I'll give you thutty-seven dollas and a half," said the *chef*.

"Sorry I can't take it. That hawss is sellin' at present for just one hundred and fifty dollas."

"Well," said the *chef*, "I'll raise you a dolla and a quahta. Say thutty-eight and seventy-five."

"Well now, you're gittin' up among the figgas where you're liable to own a hawss. You just keep right on a raisin' me, while I sell these ladies some shoes, and maybe you'll hit it yit, 'fo'e night."

The girls were trying on shoes on every side now, and they had dispensed with the formality of going in-doors for the purpose. More than one put out her foot to the clerk for his opinion of the fit, and the shoeman was mingling with the crowd, testing with his hand, advising from his professional knowledge, suggesting, urging, and in some cases artfully agreeing with the reluctance shown.

"This man," said the *chef*, indicating Fane, "says you can tell moa lies to the square inch than any man out o' Boston."

"Doos he?" asked the shoeman, turning with a pair of high-heeled bronze slippers in his hand from the wagon. "Well, now, if I stood as nea' to him as you do, I believe I sh'd hit him."

"Why, man, I can't *dispute* him!" said the *chef*, and as if he had now at last scored a point, he threw back his head and laughed. When he brought down his head again, it was to perceive the approach of Clementina. "Hello," he said for her to hear, "he'e comes the Boss. Well, I guess I must be goin'," he added, in mock anxiety. "I'm a goin', Boss, I'm a goin'."

Clementina ignored him. "Mr. Atwell wants to see you a moment, Mr. Fane," she said to the clerk.

"All right, Miss Claxon," Fane answered, with the sorrowful respect which he always showed Clementina, now, "I'll be right there." But he waited a moment, either in expression of his personal independence, or from curiosity to know what the shoeman was going to say of the bronze slippers.

Clementina felt the fascination, too; she thought the slippers were beautiful, and her foot thrilled with a mysterious prescience of its fitness for them.

"Now, the'e, ladies, or as I may say guls, if you'll excuse it in one that's moa like a fatha to you than anything else, in his feelings"—the girls tittered, and some one shouted derisively—"It's true!—now there is a shoe, or call it a slippa, that I've rutha hesitated about showin' to you, because I know that you're all rutha serious-minded, I don't ca'e *how* young ye be, or how good-*lookin'* ye be; and I don't presume the'e's one among you that's eva hea'd o' dancin'." In the mirthful hooting and mocking that followed, the shoeman hedged gravely from the extreme position he had taken. "What? Well, maybe you have among some the summa folks, but we all know what *summa* folks ah', and I don't expect you to patte'n by *them*. But what I *will* say is that if any young lady within the sound of my voice,"—he looked round for the applause which did not fail him in his parody of the pulpit style—"should get an invitation to a dance next winta, and should feel it a wo'k of a charity to the young man to go, she'll be sorry—on *his* account, rememba—that she ha'n't got this pair o' slippas. The'a! They're a numba two, and they'll fit any lady here, I don't ca'e *how* small a foot she's got. Don't all speak at once, sistas! Ample time allowed for meals. That's a custom-made shoe, and if it hadn't b'en too small for the lady they was oddid foh, you couldn't 'a' got 'em for less than seven dollas; but now I'm throwin' on 'em away for three."

A groan of dismay went up from the whole circle, and some who had pressed forward for a sight of the slippers, shrank back again.

"Did I hea' just now," asked the shoeman, with a soft insinuation in his voice, and in the glance he suddenly turned upon Clementina, "a party addressed as Boss?" Clementina flushed, but she did not cower; the *chef* walked away with a laugh, and the shoeman pursued him with his voice. "Not that I am goin' to folla the wicked example of a man who tries to make spo't of young ladies; but if *the* young lady addressed as Boss"—

"Miss Claxon," said the clerk with ingratiating reverence.

"Miss Claxon—I *stan'* corrected," pursued the shoeman. "If Miss Claxon will do me the fava just to try on this slippa, I sh'd be able to tell at the next place I stopped just how it looked on a *lady's* foot. I see you a'n't any of you disposed to buy 'em this aftanoon, and I a'n't complainin'; you done pootty well by me, already, and I don't want to uhge you; but I do want to carry away the picture, in my mind's eye—what you may call a mental photograph—of this slipper on the kind of a foot it was made foh, so't I can praise it *truthfully* to my next customer. What do you say, ma'am?" he addressed himself with profound respect to Clementina.

"Oh, *do* let him, Clem!" said one of the girls, and another pleaded, "Just so he needn't tell a story to his next customa," and that made the rest laugh.

Clementina's heart was throbbing, and joyous lights were dancing in her eyes. "I don't care if I do," she said, and she stooped to unlace her shoe, but one of the big girls threw herself on her knees at her feet to prevent her. Clementina remembered too late that there was a hole in her stocking and that her little toe came through it, but she now folded the toe artfully down, and the big girl discovered the hole in time to abet her attempt at concealment. She caught the slipper from the shoeman and hurried it on; she tied the ribbons across the instep, and then put on the other. "Now put out youa foot, Clem! Fust dancin' position!" She leaned back upon her own heels, and Clementina daintily lifted the edge of her skirt a little, and peered over at her feet. The slippers might or might not have been of an imperfect taste, in their imitation of the prevalent fashion, but on Clementina's feet they had distinction.

"Them feet was made for them slippas," said the shoeman devoutly.

The clerk was silent; he put his hand helplessly to his mouth, and then dropped it at his side again.

Gregory came round the corner of the building from the dining-room, and the big girl who was crouching before Clementina, and who boasted that *she* was not afraid of the student, called saucily to him, "Come here, a minute, Mr. Gregory," and as he approached, she tilted aside, to let him see Clementina's slippers.

Clementina beamed up at him with all her happiness in her eyes, but after a faltering instant, his face reddened through its freckles, and he gave her a rebuking frown and passed on.

"Well, I decla'e!" said the big girl. Fane turned uneasily, and said with a sigh, he guessed he must be going, now.

A blight fell upon the gay spirits of the group, and the shoeman asked with an ironical glance after Gregory's retreating figure, "Owna of this propaty?"

"No, just the ea'th," said the big girl, angrily.

The voice of Clementina made itself heard with a cheerfulness which had apparently suffered no chill, but was really a rising rebellion. "How much ah' the slippas?"

"Three dollas," said the shoeman in a surprise which he could not conceal at Clementina's courage.

She laughed, and stooped to untie the slippers. "That's too much for me."

"Let me untie 'em, Clem," said the big girl. "It's a shame for you eva to take 'em off."

"That's right, lady," said the shoeman. "And you don't eva need to," he added, to Clementina, "unless you object to sleepin' in 'em. You pay me what you want to now, and the rest when I come around the latta paht of August."

"Oh keep 'em, Clem!" the big girl urged, passionately, and the rest joined her with their entreaties.

"I guess I betta not," said Clementina, and she completed the work of taking off the slippers in which the big girl could lend her no further aid, such was her affliction of spirit.

"All right, lady," said the shoeman. "Them's youa slippas, and I'll just keep 'em for you till the latta paht of August."

He drove away, and in the woods which he had to pass through on the road to another hotel he overtook the figure of a man pacing rapidly. He easily recognized Gregory, but he bore him no malice. "Like a lift?" he asked, slowing up beside him.

"No, thank you," said Gregory. "I'm out for the walk." He looked round furtively, and then put his hand on the side of the wagon, mechanically, as if to detain it, while he walked on.

"Did you sell the slippers to the young lady?"

"Well, not as you may say *sell*, exactly," returned the shoeman, cautiously.

"Have you—got them yet?" asked the student.

"Guess so," said the man. "Like to see 'em?" He pulled up his horse.

Gregory faltered a moment. Then he said, "I'd like to buy them. Quick!" He looked guiltily about, while the shoeman alertly obeyed, with some delay for a box to put them in. "How much are they?"

"Well, that's a custom made slipper, and the price to the lady that oddid 'em was seven dollas. But I'll let *you* have 'em for three—if you want 'em for a present." The shoeman was far too discreet to permit himself anything so overt as a smile; he merely let a light of intelligence come into his face.

Gregory paid the money. "Please consider this as confidential," he said, and he made swiftly away. Before the shoeman could lock the drawer that had held the slippers, and clamber to his perch under the buggy-hood, Gregory was running back to him again.

"Stop!" he called, and as he came up panting in an excitement which the shoeman might well have mistaken for indignation attending the discovery of some blemish in his purchase. "Do you regard this as in any manner a deception?" he palpitated.

"Why," the shoeman began cautiously, "it wa'n't what you may call a promise, exactly. More of a joke than anything else, I looked on it. I just said I'd keep 'em for her; but"—

"You don't understand. If I seemed to disapprove—if I led any one to suppose, by my manner, or by—anything—that I thought it unwise or unbecoming to buy the shoes, and then bought them myself, do you think it is in the nature of an acted falsehood?"

"Lo'd no!" said the shoeman, and he caught up the slack of his reins to drive on, as if he thought this amusing maniac might also be dangerous.

Gregory stopped him with another question. "And shall—will you—think it necessary to speak of—of this transaction? I leave you free!"

"Well," said the shoeman. "I don't know what you're after, exactly, but if you think I'm so sho't on for subjects that I've got to tell the folks at the next stop that I sold a fellar a pair of slippas for his gul—Go 'long!" he called to his horse, and left Gregory standing in the middle of the road.

VIII.

The people who came to the Middlemount in July were ordinarily the nicest, but that year the August folks were nicer than usual and there were some students among them, and several graduates just going into business, who chose to take their outing there instead of going to the sea-side or the North Woods. This was a chance that might not happen in years again, and it made the house very gay for the young ladies; they ceased to pay court to the clerk, and asked him for letters only at mail-time. Five or six couples were often on the floor together, at the hops, and the young people sat so thick upon the stairs that one could scarcely get up or down.

So many young men made it gay not only for the young ladies, but also for a certain young married lady, when she managed to shirk her rather filial duties to her husband, who was much about the verandas, purblindly feeling his way with a stick, as he walked up and down, or sitting opaque behind the glasses that preserved what was left of his sight, while his wife read to him. She was soon acquainted with a good many more people than he knew, and was in constant request for such occasions as needed a chaperon not averse to mountian climbing, or drives to other hotels for dancing and supper and return by moonlight, or the more boisterous sorts of charades; no sheet and pillow case party was complete without her; for welsh-rarebits her presence was essential. The event of the conflict between these social claims and her duties to her husband was her appeal to Mrs. Atwell on a point which the landlady referred to Clementina.

"She wants somebody to read to her husband, and I don't believe but what *you* could do it, Clem. You're a good reader, as good as I want to hear, and while you may say that you don't put in a great deal of elocution, I guess you can read full well enough. All he wants is just something to keep him occupied, and all *she* wants is a chance to occupy herself with otha folks. Well, she *is* moa their own age. I d'know as the's any hahm in her. And my foot's so much betta, now, that I don't need you the whole while, any moa."

"Did you speak to her about me?" asked the girl.

"Well, I told her I'd tell you. I couldn't say how you'd like."

"Oh, I guess I should *like*," said Clementina, with her eyes shining. "But—I should have to ask motha."

"I don't believe but what your motha'd be willin'," said Mrs. Atwell. "You just go down and see her about it."

The next day Mrs. Milray was able to take leave

of her husband, in setting off to matronize a coaching party, with an exuberance of good conscience that she shared with the spectators. She kissed him with lively affection, and charged him not to let the child read herself to death for him. She cautioned Clementina that Mr. Milray never knew when he was tired, and she had better go by the clock in her reading, and not trust to any sign from him.

Clementina promised, and when the public had followed Mrs. Milray away, to watch her ascent to the topmost seat of the towering coach, by means of the ladder held in place by two porters, and by help of the down-stretched hands of all the young men on the coach, Clementina opened the book at the mark she found in it, and began to read to Mr. Milray.

The book was a metaphysical essay, which he professed to find a lighter sort of reading than fiction; he said most novelists were too seriously employed in preventing the marriage of the lovers, up to a certain point, to be amusing; but you could always trust a metaphysician for entertainment if he was very much in earnest, and most metaphysicians were. He let Clementina read on a good while in her tender voice, which had still so many notes of childhood in it, before he manifested any consciousness of being read to. He kept the smile on his delicate face which had come there when his wife said at parting, "I don't believe I should leave her with you if you could see how prettty she was," and he held his head almost motionlessly at the same poise he had given it in listening to her final charges. It was a fine head, still well covered with soft hair, which lay upon it in little sculpturesque masses, like chiseled silver, and the acquiline profile had a purity of line in the arch of the high nose and the jut of the thin lips and delicate chin, which had not been lost in the change from youth to age. One could never have taken it for the profile of a New York lawyer who had early found New York politics more profitable than law, and after a long time passed in city affairs, had emerged with a name shadowed by certain doubtful transactions. But this was Milray's history, which in the rapid progress of American events, was so far forgotten that you had first to remind people of what he had helped do before you could enjoy their surprise in realizing that this gentle person, with the cast of intellectual refinement which distinguished his face, was the notorious Milray, who was once in all the papers. When he made his game and retired from politics, his family would have sacrificed itself a good deal to reclaim him socially, though they were of a severer social than spiritual conscience, in the decay of some ancestral ideals. But he had rendered their willingness hopeless by marrying, rather late in life, a young girl from the farther West who had come East with a general purpose to get on. She got on very well with Milray, and it was perhaps not altogether her own fault that she did not get on so well with his family, when she began to substitute a society aim for the artistic ambition that had brought her to New York. They might have forgiven him for marrying her, but they could not forgive her for marrying him. They were of New

England origin and they were perhaps a little more critical with her than if they had been New Yorkers of Dutch strain. They said that she was a little Western hoyden, but that the stage would have been a good place for her if she could have got over her Pike county accent; in the hush of family councils they confided to one another the belief that there were phases of the variety business in which her accent would have been no barrier to her success, since it could not have been heard in the dance, and might have been disguised in the song.

"Will you kindly read that passage over again?" Milray asked as Clementina paused at the end of a certain paragraph. She read it, while he listened attentively. "Could you tell me just what you understand by that?" he pursued, as if he really expected Clementina to instruct him.

She hesitated a moment before she answered, "I don't believe I undastand anything at all."

"Do you know," said Milray, "that's exactly my own case? And I've an idea that the author is in the same box," and Clementina perceived she might laugh, and laughed discreetly.

Milray seemed to feel the note of discreetness in her laugh, and he asked, smiling, "How old did you tell me you were?"

"I'm sixteen," said Clementina.

"It's a great age," said Milray. "I remember being sixteen myself; I have never been so old since. But I was very old for my age, then. Do you think you are?"

"I don't believe I am," said Clementina, laughing again, but still very discreetly.

"Then I should like to tell you that you have a very agreeable voice. Do you sing?"

"No'm—no, sir—*no*," said Clementina, "I can't sing at all."

"Ah, that's very interesting," said Milray, "but it's not surprising. I wish I could see your face distinctly; I've a great curiosity about matching voices and faces; I must get Mrs. Milray to tell me how you look. Where did you pick up your pretty knack at reading? In school, here?"

"I don't know," answered Clementina. "Do I read—the way you want?"

"Oh, perfectly. You let the meaning come through—when there is any."

"Sometimes," said Clementina ingenuously, "I read too fast; the children ah' so impatient when I'm reading to them at home, and they hurry me. But I can read a great deal slower if you want me to."

"No, I'm impatient, too," said Milray. "Are there many of them,—the children?"

"There ah' six in all."

"And are you the oldest?"

"Yes," said Clementina. She still felt it very blunt not to say sir, too, but she tried to make her tone imply the sir, as Mr. Gregory had bidden her.

"You've got a very pretty name."

Clementina brightened. "Do you like it? Motha gave it to me; she took it out of a book that fatha was reading to her."

"I like it very much," said Milray. "Are you tall for your age?"

"I guess I am *pretty* tall."

"You're fair, of course. I can tell that by your voice; you've got a light-haired voice. And what are your eyes?"

"Blue!" Clementina laughed at his pursuit.

"Ah, of course! It isn't a gray-eyed blonde voice. Do you think—has anybody ever told you—that you were graceful?"

"I don't know as they have," said Clementina, after thinking.

"And what is your own opinion?" Clementina began to feel her dignity infringed; she did not answer, and now Milray laughed. "I felt the little tilt in your step as you came up. It's all right. Shall we try for our friend's meaning, now?"

Clementina began again, and again Milray stopped her. "You mustn't bear malice. I can hear the grudge in your voice; but I didn't mean to laugh at you. You don't like being made fun of, do you?"

"I don't believe anybody does," said Clementina.

"No, indeed," said Milray. "If I had tried such a thing I should be afraid you would make it uncomfortable for me. But I haven't, have I?"

"I don't know," said Clementina, reluctantly.

Milray laughed gleefully. "Well, you'll forgive me, because I'm an old fellow. If I were young, you wouldn't, would you?"

Clementina thought of the clerk; she had certainly never forgiven him. "Shall I read on?" she asked.

"Yes, yes. Read on," he said, respectfully. Once he interrupted her to say that she pronounced admirable, but he would like now and then to differ with her about a word if she did not mind. She answered, Oh no, indeed; she should like it ever so much, if he would tell her when she was wrong. After that he corrected her, and he amused himself by studying forms of respect so delicate that they should not alarm her pride; Clementina reassured him in terms as fine as his own. She did not accept his instructions implicitly; she meant to bring them to the bar of Gregory's knowledge. If he approved of them, then she would submit.

Milray easily possessed himself of the history of her life and of all its circumstances, and he said he would like to meet her father and make the acquaintance of a man whose mind, as Clementina interpreted it to him, he found so original.

He authorized his wife to arrange with Mrs. Atwell for a monopoly of Clementina's time while he stayed at Middlemount, and neither he nor Mrs. Milray seemed surprised at the good round sum, as the landlady thought it, which she asked in the girl's behalf.

IX.

The Milrays stayed through August, and Mrs. Milray was the ruling spirit of the great holiday of the summer, at Middlemount. It was this year that the landlords of the central mountain region had decided to compete in a coaching parade, and to rival by their common glory the splendor of the East Side and the West Side parades. The boarding-houses were to take part, as well as the hotels; the farms where only three or four summer folks were received, were to send their mountain-wagons, and all were to be decorated with bunting. An arch draped with flags and covered with flowers spanned the entrance to the main street at Middlemount Centre, and every shop in the village was adorned for the event.

Mrs. Milray made the landlord tell her all about coaching parades, and the champions of former years on the East Side and the West Side, and then she said that the Middlemout House must take the prize from them all this year, or she should never come near his house again. He answered, with a dignity and spirit he rarely showed with Mrs. Milray's class of custom, "I'm goin' to drive our hossis myself."

She gave her whole time to imagining and organizing the personal display on the coach. She consulted with the other ladies as to the kind of dresses that were to be worn, but she decided everything herself; and when the time came she had all the young men ravaging the lanes and pastures for the goldenrod and asters which formed the keynote of her decoration for the coach.

She made peace and kept it between factions that declared themselves early in the affair, and of all who could have criticized her for taking the lead perhaps none would have willingly relieved her of the trouble. She freely declared that it was killing her, and she sounded her accents of despair all over the place. When their dresses were finished she made the persons of her drama rehearse it on the coach top in the secret of the barn, where no one but the stable men were suffered to see the effects she aimed at. But on the eve of realizing these in public she was overwhelmed by disaster. The crowning glory of her composition was to be a young girl standing on the highest seat of the coach, in the character of the Spirit of Summer, wreathed and garlanded with flowers, and invisibly sustained by the twelve months of the year, equally divided as to sex, but with the more difficult and painful attitudes assigned to the gentlemen who were to figure as the fall and winter months. It had been all worked out and the actors drilled in their parts, when the Spirit of Summer, who had been chosen for the inoffensiveness of her extreme youth, was taken with mumps, and withdrawn by the doctor's orders. Mrs. Milray had now not only to improvise another Spirit of Summer, but had to choose her from a group of young ladies, with the chance of alienating and embittering those who were not chosen. In her calamity she asked her husband what she should do, without the least hope that he could tell her. But he answered promptly, "Take Clementina; I'll let you have her for the day," and then waited for the storm of her renunciations and denunciations to spend itself.

"To be sure," she said, when this had happened, "it isn't as if she were a servant in the house; and the position can be regarded as a kind of public function, anyhow. I can't say that I've hired her to take the part, but I can give her a present afterwards, and it will be the same thing."

The question of clothes for Clementina Mrs. Milray declared was almost as sweeping in its implication as the question of the child's creation. "She has got to be dressed new from head to foot," she said, "every stitch, and how am I to manage it in twenty-four hours?"

By a succession of miracles with cheese-cloth, and sashes and ribbons, it was managed; and ended in a triumph so great that Mrs. Milray took the girl in her arms and kissed her for looking the Spirit of Summer to a perfection that the victim of the mumps could not have approached. The victory was not lastingly marred by the failure of Clementina's shoes to look the Spirit of Summer as well as the rest of her costume. No shoes at all would have been the very thing, but shoes so shabby and worn down at one side of the heel as Clementina's were very far from the thing. Mrs. Milray decided that another fold of cheese-cloth would add to the statuesque charm of her figure, and give her more height; and she was richly satisfied with the effect when the Middlemount coach drove up to the great veranda the next morning, with all the figures of her picture in position on its roof, and Clementina supreme among them. She herself mounted in simple, undramatized authority to her official seat beside the landlord, who in coachman's dress, with a bouquet of autumnal flowers in his lapel, sat holding his garlanded reins over the backs of his six horses; and then the coach as she intended it to appear in the parade set out as soon as the turnouts of the other houses joined it. They were all to meet at the Middlemount, which was thickly draped and festooned in flags, with knots of evergreen and the first red boughs of the young swamp maples holding them in place over its irregular façade. The coach itself was a mass of foliage and flowers, from which it defined itself as a wheeled vehicle in vague and partial outline; the other wagons and coaches, as they drove tremulously up, with an effect of having been mired in blossoms about their spokes and hubs, had the unwieldiness which seems inseparable from spectacularity. They represented motives in color and design sometimes tasteless enough, and sometimes so nearly very good that Mrs. Milray's heart was a great deal in her mouth, as they arrived, each with its hotel cry roared and shrilled from a score of masculine and feminine throats, and finally spelled for distinctness' sake, with an ultimate yell or growl. But she had not finished giving the lady-representative of a Sunday newspaper the points of her own tableau, before she regained the courage and the faith in which she remained serenely steadfast throughout the parade.

It was when all the equipages of the neighborhood had arrived that she climbed to her place; the ladder was taken away; the landlord spoke to his horses, and the Middlemount coach led the parade, amid the renewed slogans, and the cries and fluttered handkerchiefs of the guests crowding the verandas.

The line of march was by one road to Middlemount Centre, where the prize was to be awarded at the judges' stand, and then the coaches were to escort the triumphant vehicle homeward by another route, so as to pass as many houses on the way as possible. It was a curious expression of the carnival spirit in a region immemorially starved of beauty in the lives of its people; and whatever was the origin of the mountain coaching parade, or from whatever impulse of sentimentality or advertising it came, the effect was of undeniable splendor, and of phantasmagoric strangeness.

Gregory watched its progress from a hill-side pasture as it trailed slowly along the rising and falling road. The songs of the young girls, interrupted by the explosion of hotel slogans and college cries from the young men, floated off to him on the thin breeze of the cloudless August morning, like the hymns and shouts of a saturnalian rout going in holiday processional to sacrifice to their gods. Words of fierce

Hebrew poetry burned in his thought; the warnings and the accusals and the condemnations of the angry prophets; and he stood rapt from his own time and place in a dream of days when the Most High stooped to commune face to face with His ministers, while the young voices of those forgetful or ignorant of Him, called to his own youth, and the garlanded chariots, with their banners and their streamers passed on the road beneath him and out of sight in the shadow of the woods beyond.

When the prize was given to the Middlemount coach at the Center the landlord took the flag, and gallantly transferred it to Mrs. Milray, and Mrs. Milray passed it up to Clementina, and bade her, "Wave it, wave it!"

The village street was thronged with people that cheered, and swung their hats and handkerchiefs to the coach as it left the judges' stand and drove under the triumphal arch, with the other coaches behind it. Then Atwell turned his horses heads homewards, and at the brisker pace with which people always return from festivals or from funerals, he left the village and struck out upon the country road with his long escort before him. The crowd was quick to catch the courteous intention of the victors, and followed them with applause as far beyond the village borders as wind and limb would allow; but the last noisy boy had dropped off breathless before they reached a half-finished house in the edge of some woods. A line of little children was drawn up by the road-side before it, who watched the retinue with grave eagerness, till

"THE MIDDLEMOUNT COACH LED THE PARADE."

the Middlemount coach came in full sight. Then they sprang into the air, and beating their hands together, screamed, "Clem! Clem! Oh it's Clem!" and jumped up and down, and a shabby looking work-worn woman came round the corner of the house and stared up at Clementina waving her banner wildly to the children, and shouting unintelligible words to them. The young people on the coach joined in response to the children, some simply, some ironically, and one of the men caught up a great wreath of flowers which lay at Clementina's feet, and flung it down to them; the shabby woman quickly vanished round the corner of the house again. Mrs. Milray leaned over to ask the landlord, "Who in the world are Clementina's friends?"

"Why don't you know?" he retorted in a bated voice. "Them's her brothas and sistas."

"And that woman"—

"The lady at the conna? That's her motha."

When the event was over, and all the things had been said and said again, and there was nothing more to keep the spring and summer months from going up to their rooms to lie down, and the fall and winter months from trying to get something to eat, Mrs. Milray found herself alone with Clementina.

The child seemed anxious about something, and Mrs. Milray, who wanted to go and lie down, too, asked a little impatiently, "What is it, Clementina?"

"Oh, nothing. Only I was afraid maybe you didn't like my waving to the children, when you saw how *queea* they looked." Clementina's lips quivered.

"Did any of the rest say anything?"

"I know what they *thought*. But I don't care! I should do it right over again!"

Mrs. Milray's happiness in the day's triumph was so great that she could indulge a generous emotion. She caught the girl in her arms. "I want to kiss you; I want to hug you, Clementina!"

X.

The notion of a dance for the following night to celebrate the success of the house in the coaching parade came to Mrs. Milray over a welsh-rarebit which she gave at the close of the evening. The party was in the charge of Gregory, who silently served them at their orgy with an austerity that might have conspired with the viand itself against their dreams, if they had not been so used to the gloom of his ministrations. He would not allow the waitresses to be disturbed in their evening leisure, or kept from their sleep by such belated pleasures; and when he had provided the materials for the rarebit, he stood aloof, and left their combination to Mrs. Milray and her chafing-dish.

She had excluded Clementina on account of her youth, as she said to one of the fall and winter months, who came in late, and noticed Clementina's absence with a "Hello! Anything the matter with the Spirit of Summer?" Clementina had become both a pet and a joke with these months before the parade was over, and now they clamored together, and said they must have her at the dance anyway. They were more tepidly seconded by the spring and summer months, and Mrs. Milray said, "Well, then, you'll have to all subscribe and get her a pair of dancing slippers." They pressed her for her meaning, and she had to explain the fact of Clementina's destitution, which that additional fold of cheese-cloth had hidden so well in the coaching tableau that it had never been suspected. The young men entreated her to let them each buy a pair of slippers for the Spirit of Summer, which she should wear in turn for the dance that she must give each of them; and this made Mrs. Milray declare that, no, the child should not come to the dance at all, and that she was not going to have her spoiled. But, before the party broke up, she promised that she would see what could be done, and she put it very prettily to the child the next day, and waited for her to say, as she knew she must, that she could not go, and why. They agreed that the cheese-cloth draperies of the Spirit of Summer were surpassingly fit for the dance; but they had to agree that this still left the question of slippers untouched. It remained even more hopeless when Clementina tried on all of Mrs. Milray's festive shoes, and none of her razor-points and high heels would avail. She went away disappointed, but not yet disheartened; youth does not so easily renounce a pleasure pressed to the lips; and Clementina had it in her head to ask some of the table girls to help her out. She meant to try first with that big girl who had helped her put on the shoeman's bronze slippers; and she hurried through the office, pushing purblindly past Fane without looking his way, when he called to her in the deference which he now always used with her, "Here's a package here for you, Clementina—Miss Claxon," and he gave her an oblong parcel, addressed in a hand strange to her.

"Who is it from?" she asked, innocently, and Fane replied with the same ingenuousness: "I'm sure I don't know." Afterwards he thought of having retorted, "I haven't opened it," but still without being certain that he would have had the courage to say it.

Clementina did not think of opening it herself, even when she was alone in her little room above Mrs. Atwell's, until she had carefully felt it over, and ascertained that it was a box of pasteboard, three or four inches deep and wide, and eight or ten inches long. She looked at the address again, "Miss Clementina Claxon," and at the narrow notched ribbon which tied it, and noted that the paper it was wrapped in was very white and clean. Then she sighed, and loosed the knot, and the paper slipped off the box, and at the same time the lid fell off, and the shoe man's bronze slippers fell out upon the floor.

Either it must be a dream or it must be a joke; it could not be both real and earnest; somebody was trying to tease her; such flattery of fortune could not be honestly meant. But it went to her head, and she was so giddy with it as she caught the slippers from the floor, and ran down to Mrs. Atwell, that she knocked against the sides of the narrow staircase.

"What is it? What does it mean? Who did it?" she panted, with the slippers in her hand. "Whe'e did they come from?" She poured out the history of her trying on these shoes, and of her present need of them, and of their mysterious coming, to meet her longing after it had almost ceased to be a hope. Mrs. Atwell closed with her in an exultation hardly short of a clapping the hands. Her hair was gray, and the girl's hair still hung in braids down her back, but they were of the same age in their transport, which they referred to Mrs. Milray, and joined with her in glad but fruitless wonder who had sent Clementina the shoes. Mrs. Atwell held that the help who had seen the girl trying them on had clubbed together and got them for her at the time; and had now given them to her for the honor she had done the Middlemount House in the parade. Mrs. Milray argued that the spring and summer months had secretly dispatched some fall and winter month to ransack the stores at Middlemount Centre for them. Clementina believed that they came from the shoe man himself, who had always wanted to send them, in the hope that she would keep them, and had merely happened to send them just then in that moment of extremity when she was helpless against them. Each conjecture involved improbabilities so gross that it left the field free to any opposite theory.

Rumor of the fact could not fail to go through the house, and long before his day's work was done it reached the *chef*, and amused him as a piece of the Boss's luck. He was smoking his evening pipe at the kitchen door after supper, when Clementina passed him on one of the many errands that took her between Mrs. Milray's room and her own, and he called to her: "Boss, what's this I hear about a pair o' glass slippas droppin' out the sky int' youa lap?"

Clementina was so happy that she thought she might trust him for once, and she said, "Oh, yes, Mr. Mahtin! *Who* do you suppose sent them?" she entreated him so sweetly that it would have softened any heart but the heart of a tease.

"I believe I could give a pootty good guess if I had the facts."

Clementina innocently gave them to him, and he listened with a well-affected sympathy.

"Say Fane fust told you about 'em?"

"Yes. 'He'e's a package for you,' he said. Just that way; and he couldn't tell me who left it, or anything."

"Anybody asked him about it since?"

"Oh, yes! Mrs. Milray, and Mrs. Atwell, and Mr. Atwell, and everybody."

"Everybody." The *chef* smiled with a peculiar droop of one eye. "And he didn't know when the slippas got into the landlo'd's box?"

"No. The fust thing he knew, the' they we'e!" Clementina stood expectant, but the *chef* smoked on as if that were all there was to say, and seemed to have forgotten her. "Who do *you* think put them thea, Mr. Mahtin?"

The *chef* looked up as if surprised to find her still there. "Oh! Oh, yes! Who d' I think? Why, I *know*, Boss. But I don't believe I'd betta tell you."

"Oh, do, Mr. Mahtin! If you knew how I felt about it"—

"No, no! I guess I betta not. 'Twouldn't do you any good. I guess I won't say anything moa. But if I was in youa place, and I really wanted to know whe'e them slippas come from "—

"I do—I do indeed"—

The *chef* paused before he added, "I should go at Fane. I guess what he don't know ain't wo'th knowin', and I guess nobody else knows anything. Thea! I don't know but I said mo'n I ought, *now*."

What the *chef* said was of a piece with what had been more than once in Clementina's mind; but she had driven it out, not because it might not be true, but because she would not have it true. Her head drooped; she turned limp and springless away. Even the heart of the tease was touched; he had not known that it would worry her so much, though he knew that she disliked the clerk.

"Mind," he called after her, too late, "I ain't got no proof 't he done it."

She did not answer him, or look round. She went to her room, and sat down in the growing dusk to think, with a hot lump in her throat.

Mrs. Atwell found her there an hour later, when she climbed to the chamber where she thought she ought to have heard Clementina moving about over her own room.

"Didn't know but I could help you do youa dressin'," she began, and then at sight of the dim figure she broke off: "Why, Clem! What's the matta? Ah' you asleep? Ah' you sick? It's half an hour of the time and"—

"I'm not going," Clementina answered, and she did not move.

"Not goin'! Why the land o'—"

"Oh, I can't go, Mrs. Atwell. Don't ask me! Tell Mrs. Milray, please!"

"I will, when I got something to tell," said Mrs. Atwell. "Now, you just say what's happened, Clementina Claxon!" Clementina suffered the woful truth to be drawn from her. "But you don't know whether it's so or not," the landlady protested.

"Yes, yes, I do! It was the fust thing I thought of, and the *chef* wouldn't have said it if he didn't believe it."

"That's just what he *would* done," cried Mrs. Atwell. "And I'll give him such a goin' ova, for his teasin', as he ain't had in *one* while. He just said it *to* tease. What you goin' to say to Mrs. Milray?"

"Oh, tell her I'm not a bit well, Mrs. Atwell! My head does ache, truly."

"Why, listen," said Mrs. Atwell, recklessly. "If you believe he done it—and he no business to—why don't you just go to the dance, in 'em, and then give 'em back to him after it's ova? It would suv him right."

Clementina listened for a moment of temptation, and then shook her head. "It wouldn't do, Mrs. Atwell; you know it wouldn't," she said, and Mrs. Atwell had too little faith in her suggestion to make it prevail. She went away to carry Clementina's message to Mrs. Milray, and her task was greatly eased by the increasing difficulty Mrs. Milray had begun to find, since the way was perfectly smoothed for her, in imagining the management of Clementina at the dance: neither child nor woman, neither servant nor lady, how was she to be carried successfully through it, without sorrow to herself or offence to others? In proportion to the relief she felt, Mrs. Milray protested her irreconcilable grief; but when the simpler Mrs. Atwell proposed her going and reasoning with Clementina, she said, No, no; better let her alone, if she felt as she did; and perhaps after all she was right.

XI.

Clementina listened to the music of the dance, till the last note was played; and she heard the gay shouts and laughter of the dancers as they issued from the ball room and began to disperse about the halls and verandas, and presently to call good night to one another. Then she lighted her lamp, and put the slippers back into the box and wrapped it up in the nice paper it had come in, and tied it with the notched ribbon. She thought how she had meant to put the slippers away so, after the dance, when she had danced her fill in them, and how differently she was doing it all now. She wrote the clerk's name on the parcel, and then she took the box, and descended to the office with it. There seemed to be nobody there, but at the noise of her step Fane came round the case of letter-boxes, and advanced to meet her at the long desk.

"What's wanted, Miss Claxon?" he asked, with his hopeless respectfulness. "Anything I can do for you?"

She did not answer, but looked him solemnly in the

eyes and laid the parcel down on the open register, and then went out.

He looked at the address on the parcel, and when he untied it, the box fell open and the shoes fell out of it, as they had with Clementina. He ran with them behind the letter-box frame, and held them up before Gregory, who was seated there on the stool he usually occupied, gloomily nursing his knee.

"What do you suppose this means, Frank?"

Gregory looked at the shoes frowningly. "They're the slippers she got to-day. She thinks you sent them to her."

"And she wouldn't have them because she thought I sent them! As sure as I'm standing here, I never did it," said the clerk, solemnly.

"I know it," said Gregory. "I sent them."

"You!"

"What's so wonderful?" Gregory retorted. "I saw that she wanted them that day when the shoe peddler was here. I could see it, and you could."

"Yes."

"I went across into the woods, and the man overtook me with his wagon. I was tempted, and I bought the slippers of him. I wanted to give them to her then, but I resisted, and I thought I should never give them. To-day, when I heard that she was going to that dance, I sent them to her anonymously. That's all there is about it."

The clerk had a moment of bitterness. "If she'd known it was you, she wouldn't have given them back."

"That's to be seen. I shall tell her, now. I never meant her to know, but she must, because she's doing you wrong in her ignorance."

Gregory was silent, and Fane was trying to measure the extent of his own suffering, and to get the whole bearing of the incident in his mind. In the end his attempt was a failure. He asked Gregory, "And do you think *you've* done just right by me?"

"I've done right by nobody," said Gregory, "not even by myself; and I can see that it was my own pleasure I had in mind. I must tell her the truth, and then I must leave this place."

"I suppose you want I should keep it quiet," said Fane.

"I don't ask anything of you."

"And she wouldn't," said Fane, after reflection. "But I know she'd be glad of it, and I sha'n't say anything. Of course, she never can care for me; and —there's my hand with my word, if you want it." Gregory silently took the hand stretched toward him and Fane added: "All I'll ask is that you'll tell her I wouldn't have presumed to send her the shoes. She wouldn't be mad at *you* for it."

Gregory took the box, and after some efforts to speak, he went away. It was an old trouble, an old error, an old folly; he had yielded to impulse at every step, and at every step he had sinned against another or against himself. What pain he had now given the simple soul of Fane; what pain he had given that poor child who had so mistaken and punished the simple soul! With Fane it was over now, but with Clementina the worst was perhaps to come yet. He could not hope to see the girl before morning, and then, what should he say to her? At sight of a lamp burning in Mrs. Atwell's room, which was on a level with the veranda where he was walking, it came to him that first of all he ought to go to her, and confess the whole affair; if her husband were with her, he ought to confess before him; they were there in the place of the child's father and mother, and it was due to them. As he pressed rapidly toward the light he framed in his thought the things he should say, and he did not notice, as he turned to enter the private hallway leading to Mrs. Atwell's apartment, a figure at the door. It shrank back from his contact, and he recognized Clementina. His purpose instantly changed, and he said, "Is that you, Miss Claxon? I want to speak with you. Will you come a moment where I can?"

"I—I don't know as I'd betta," she faltered. But she saw the box under his arm, and she thought that he wished to speak to her about that, and she wanted to hear what he would say. She had been waiting at the door there, because she could not bear to go to her room without having something more happen.

"You needn't be afraid. I shall not keep you—Come with me a moment. There is something I must tell you at once. You have made a mistake. And it is my fault. Come!"

Clementina stepped out into the moonlight with him, and they walked across the grass that sloped between the hotel and the river. There were still people about, late smokers singly and in groups along the piazzas, and young couples, like themselves, strolling in the dry air, under the pure sky.

Gregory made several failures in trying to begin, before he said: "I have to tell you that you are mistaken about Mr. Fane. I was there behind the letter boxes when you came in, and I know that you left these shoes because you thought he sent them to you. He didn't send them." Clementina did not say anything, and Gregory was forced to ask: "Do you wish to know who sent them? I won't tell you unless you do wish it."

"I think I ought to know," she said, and she asked, "Don't you?"

"Yes; for you must blame some one else now, for what you thought Fane did. *I* sent them to you."

Clementina's heart gave a leap in her breast, and she could not say anything. He went on.

"I saw that you wanted them that day, and when the peddler happened to overtake me in the woods where I was walking, after I left you, I acted on a sudden impulse, and I bought them for you. I meant to send them to you anonymously, then. I had committed one error in acting upon impulse—my rashness is my besetting sin—and I wished to add a species of deceit to that. But I was kept from it until—to-day. I hoped you would like to wear them to the dance to-night, and I put them in the post-office for you myself. Mr. Fane didn't know anything about it. That is all. I am to blame, and no one else."

He waited for her to speak, but Clementina could only say, "I don't know what to say."

"You can't say anything that would be punishment enough for me. I have acted foolishly, cruelly."

Clementina did not think so. She was not indignant, as she was when she thought Fane had taken this liberty with her, but if Mr. Gregory thought it was so very bad, it must be something much more serious than she had imagined. She said, "I don't see why you wanted to do it," hoping that he would be able to tell her something that would make his behavior seem less dreadful than he appeared to think it was.

"There is only one thing that could justify it, and that is something that I cannot justify." It was very mysterious, but youth loves mystery, and Clementina was very young. "I did it," said Gregory solemnly, and he felt that now he was acting from no impulse, but from a wisely considered decision which he might not fail in without culpability, "because I love you."

"Oh!" said Clementina, and she started away from him.

"I knew that it would make me detestable!" he cried, bitterly. "I had to tell you, to explain what I did. I couldn't help doing it. But now if you can forget it, and never think of me again, I can go away, and try to atone for it somehow. I shall be guided."

Clementina did not know why she ought to feel affronted or injured by what he had said to her; but if Mr. Gregory thought it was wrong for him to have spoken so, it must be wrong. She did not wish him to feel badly, even if he had done wrong, but she had to take his view of what he had done. "Why, suttainly, Mr. Gregory," she answered. "You mustn't mind it."

"But I do mind it. I have been very, very selfish, very thoughtless. We are both too young. I can't ask you to wait for me till I could marry"—

The word really frightened Clementina. She said, "I don't believe I betta promise."

"Oh, I know it!" said Gregory. "I am going away from here. I am going to-morrow as soon as I can arrange—as soon as I can get away. Good-night —I"—Clementina in her agitation put her hands up to her face. "Oh, don't cry—I can't bear to have you cry."

She took down her hands. "I'm not crying! But I wish I had neva seen those slippas."

They had come to the bank of the river, whose current quivered at that point in a scaly ripple in the moonlight. At her words Gregory suddenly pulled the box from under his arm, and flung it into the stream as far as he could. It caught upon a shallow of the ripple, hung there a moment, then loosed itself, and swam swiftly down the stream.

"Oh!" Clementina moaned.

"Do you want them back?" he demanded. "I will go in for them!"

"No, no! No. But it seemed such a—waste!"

"Yes, that is a sin, too." They climbed silently to the hotel. At Mrs. Atwell's door, he spoke. "Try to forget what I said, and forgive me, if you can."

"Yes—yes, I will, Mr. Gregory. You mustn't think of it any moa."

XII.

Clementina did not sleep till well toward morning, and she was still sleeping when Mrs. Atwell knocked and called in to her that her brother Jim wanted to see her. She hurried down, and in the confusion of mind left over from the night before she cooed sweetly at Jim as if he had been Mr. Gregory, "What is it, Jim? What do you want me for?"

The boy answered with the disgust a sister's company manners always rouse in a brother. "Motha wants you. Says she's wo'ked down, and she wants you to come and help." Then he went his way.

Mrs. Atwell was used to having help snatched from her by their families at a moment's notice. "I presume you've got to go, Clem," she said.

"Oh, yes, I've got to go," Clementina assented, with a note of relief which mystified Mrs. Atwell.

"You ti'ed readin' to Mr. Milray?"

"Oh, no'm—no, I mean. But I guess I betta go home. I guess I've been away long enough."

"Well, you're a good gul, Clem. I presume your motha's got a right to have you home if she wants you." Clementina said nothing to this, but turned briskly, and started upstairs toward her room again. The landlady called after her, "Shall you speak to Mis' Milray, or do you want I should?"

Clementina looked back at her over her shoulder to warble, "Why, if *you* would, Mrs. Atwell," and kept on to her room.

Mrs. Milray was not wholly sorry to have her go; she was going herself very soon, and Clementina's earlier departure simplified the question of getting rid of her; but she overwhelmed her with reproaches which Clementina received with such sweet sincerity that another than Mrs. Milray might have blamed herself for having abused her ingenuousness.

The Atwells could very well have let the girl walk home, but they sent her in a buckboard, with one of the stablemen to drive her. The landlord put her neat bundle under the seat of the buckboard with his own hand. There was something in the child's bearing, her dignity and her amiability, which made people offer her, half in fun, and half in earnest, the deference paid to age and state.

She did not know whether Gregory would try to see her before she went. She thought he must have known she was going, but since he neither came to take leave of her, nor sent her any message, she decided that she had not expected him to do so. About the third week of September she heard that he had left Middlemount and gone back to college.

She kept at her work in the house and helped her mother, and looked after the little ones; she followed her father in the woods, in his quest of stuff for walking-sticks, and advised with both concerning the taste of summer folks in dress and in canes. The winter came, and she read many books in its long leisure, mostly novels, out of the rector's library. He had a whole set of Miss Edgeworth, and nearly all of Miss Austen and Miss Burney, and he gave of them to Clementina, as the best thing for her mind as well as her morals; he believed nothing could be better for any one than these old English novels, which he had nearly forgotten in their details. She colored the faded English life of the stories afresh from her Yankee circumstance; and it seemed the consensus of their testimony that she had really been made love to, and not so very much too soon, at her age of sixteen, for most of their heroines were not much older. The terms of Gregory's declaraction and of its withdrawal were mystifying, but not more mystifying than many such things, and from what happened in the novels she read, the affair might be trusted to come out all right of itself in time. She was rather thoughtfuller for it, and once her mother asked her what was the matter with her. "Oh, I guess I'm getting old, motha," she said, and turned the question off. She would not have minded telling her mother about Gregory, but it would not have been the custom; and her mother would have worried, and would have blamed him. Clementina could have more easily trusted her father with the case, but so far as she knew fathers never were trusted with anything of the kind. She would have been willing that accident should bring it to the knowledge of Mrs. Richling; but the moment never came when she could voluntarily confide in her, though she was a great deal with her that winter. She was Mrs. Richling's lieutenant in the social affairs of the parish, which the rector's wife took under her care. She helped her get up entertainments of the kind that could be given in the church parlor, and they managed together some dances which had to be exiled to the town hall. They contrived to make the young people of the village feel that they were having a gay time, and Clementina did not herself feel that it was a dull one. She taught them some of the new steps and figures which the help used to pick up from the summer folks at the Middlemount, and practise together; she liked doing that; her mother said the child would rather dance than eat, any time. She was never sad, but so much dignity got into her sweetness that the rector now and then complained of feeling put down by her.

She did not know whether she expected Gregory to write to her or not; but when no letters came she decided that she had not expected them. She wondered if he would come back to the Middlemount the next summer; but when the summer came, she heard that they had another student in his place. She heard that they had a new clerk, and that the boarders were not so pleasant. Another year passed, and towards the end of the season Mrs. Atwell wished her to come and help her again, and Clementina went over to the hotel to soften her refusal. She explained that her mother had so much sewing now that she could not spare her; and Mrs. Atwell said: Well, that was right, and that she must be the greatest kind of dependence for her mother. "You ah' going on seventeen this year, ain't you?"

"I was nineteen the last day of August," said Clementina, and Mrs. Atwell sighed, and said, How the time did fly.

It was the second week of September, but Mrs. Atwell said they were going to keep the house open till the middle of October, if they could, for the autumnal foliage, which there was getting to be quite a class of custom for.

"I presume you knew Mr. Landa was dead," she added, and at Clementina's look of astonishment, she said with a natural satisfaction, "Mm! died the thutteenth day of August. I presumed somehow you'd know it, though you didn't see a great deal of 'em, come to think of it. I guess he was a good man; too good for *her*, I guess," she concluded, in the New England necessity of blaming some one. "She sent us the papah."

There was an early frost; and people said there was going to be a hard winter, but it was not this that made Clementina's father set to work finishing his house. His turning business was well started, now, and he had got together money enough to pay for the work. He had lately enlarged the scope of his industry by turning gate-posts and urns for the tops of them, which had become very popular, for the front yards of the farm and village houses in a wide stretch of country. They sold more steadily than the smaller wares, the cups, and tops, and little vases and platters which had once been the output of his lathe; after the first season the interest of the summer folks in these fell off; but the gate posts and the urns appealed to a lasting taste in the natives.

Claxon wished to put the finishing touches on the house himself, and he was willing to suspend more profitable labors to do so. After some attempts at plastering he was forced to leave that to the plasterers, but he managed the clap-boarding, with Clementina to hand him boards and nails, and to keep him supplied with the hammer he was apt to drop at critical moments. They talked pretty constantly at their labors, and in their leisure, which they spent on the brown needles under the pines at the side of the house. Sometimes the hammering or the talking would be interrupted by a voice calling, from a passing vehicle in the hidden roadway, something about urns. Claxon would answer, without troubling himself to verify the inquirer, or moving from his place, that he would get round to them, and then would hammer on, or talk on with Clementina.

One day in October a carriage drove up to the door, after the work on the house had been carried as far as Claxon's mood and money allowed, and he and Clementina were picking up the litter of his carpentering. He had replaced the block of wood which once served at the front door by some steps under an arbor of rustic work; but this was still so novel that the younger children had not outgrown their pride in it and were playing at house-keeping there. Clementina ran around to the back door and out through the front entry in time to save the visitor and the children from the misunderstanding they began to fall into, and met her with a smile of hospitable brilliancy, and a recognition full of compassionate welcome.

Mrs. Lander gave way to her tears as she broke out, "Oh, it ain't the way it was the last time I was he'a! You hea'd that he—that Mr. Landa"—

"Mrs. Atwell told me," said Clementina. "Won't you come in, and sit down?"

"Why, yes." Mrs. Lander pushed in through the narrow door of what was to be the parlor. Her crapes swept about her and exhaled a strong scent of their dyes. Her veil softened her heavy face; but she had not grown thinner in her bereavement.

"I just got to the Middlemount last night," she said, "and I wanted to see you and your payrents, both, Miss Claxon. It *doos* bring him back so! You won't neva know how much he thought of you, and you'll all think I'm crazy. I wouldn't come as long as he was with me, and now I have to come without him; I held out ag'inst him as long as I had him *to* hold out ag'inst. Not that he was eva one to push, and I don't know as he so much as spoke of it, afta we left the hotel two yea's ago; but I presume it wa'n't out of his mind a single minute. Time and time again I'd say to him, 'Now, Albe't, do you feel about it just the way you done?' and he'd say, 'I ha'n't had any call to change my mind about it,' and then I'd begin tryin' to ahgue him out of it, and keep a hectorin', till he'd say, 'Well, I'm not askin' you to do it,' and that's all I could get out of him. But I see all the while 't he wanted me to do it, whateva he asked, and now I've got to do it when it can't give *him* any pleasure." Mrs. Lander put up her black-bordered handkerchief and sobbed into it, and Clementina waited till her grief had spent itself; then she gave her a fan, and Mrs. Lander gratefully cooled her hot wet face. The children had found the noises of her affliction and the turbid tones of her monologue annoying, and had gone off to play in the woods; Claxon kept incuriously about the work that Clementina had left him to; his wife maintained the confidence which she always felt in Clementina's ability to treat with the world when it presented itself, and though she was curious enough, she did not offer to interrupt the girl's interview with Mrs. Lander; Clementina would know how to behave.

Mrs. Lander, when she had refreshed herself with the fan, seemed to get a fresh grip of her theme, and she told Clementina all about Mr. Lander's last sickness. It had been so short that it gave her no time to try the climate of Colorado upon him, which she now felt sure would have brought him right up; and she had remembered, when too late, to give him a liver-medicine of her own, though it did not appear that it was his liver which was affected; that was the strange part of it. But, brief as his sickness was, he had felt that it was to be his last, and had solemnly talked over her future with her, which he seemed to think would be lonely. He had not named Clementina, but Mrs. Lander had known well enough what he meant; and now she wished to ask her, and her father and mother, how they would all like Clementina to come and spend the winter with her at Boston first, and then further South, and wherever she should happen to go. She apologized for not having come sooner upon this errand; she had resolved upon it as soon as Mr. Lander was gone, but she had been sick herself, and had only just now got out of bed.

Clementina was too young to feel the pathos of the case fully, or perhaps even to follow the tortuous course of Mrs. Lander's motives, but she was moved by her grief; and she could not help a thrill of pleasure in the vague splendor of the future outlined by Mrs. Lander's proposal. For a time she had thought that Mrs. Milray was going to ask her to visit her in New York; Mrs. Milray had thrown out a hint of something of the kind at parting, but that was the last of it; and now she at once made up her mind that she would like to go with Mrs. Lander, while discreetly saying that she would ask her father and mother to come and talk with her.

XIII.

Her parents objected to leaving their work; each suggested that the other had better go; but they both came at Clementina's urgence. Her father laughed and her mother frowned when she told them what Mrs. Lander wanted, from the same misgiving of her sanity. They partly abandoned this theory for a conviction of Mrs. Lander's mere folly when she began to talk, and this slowly yielded to the perception that she had some streaks of sense. It was sense in the first place to want to have Clementina with her, and though it might not be sense to suppose that they would be anxious to let her go, they did not find so much want of it as Mrs. Lander talked on. It was one of her necessities to talk away her emotions before arriving at her ideas, which were often found in a tangle, but were not without a certain propriety. She was now, after her interview with Clementina, in the immediate presence of these, and it was her ideas that she began to produce for the girl's father and mother. She said, frankly, that she had more money than she knew what to do with, and they must not think she supposed she was doing a favor, for she was really asking one.

She was alone in the world, without near connections of her own, or relatives of her husband's, and it would be a mercy if they could let their daughter come and visit her; she would not call it more than a visit; that would be the best thing on both sides; she told of her great fancy for Clementina the first time she saw her, and of her husband's wish that she would come and visit with them then for the winter. As for that money she had tried to make the child take, she presumed that they knew about it, and she wished to say that she did it because she was afraid Mr. Lander had said so much about the sewing, that they would be disappointed. She gave way to her tears at the recollection, and confessed that she wanted the child to have the money anyway. She ended by asking Mrs. Claxon if she would please to let her have a drink of water; and she looked about the room, and said that they had got it finished up a great deal, now, had not they? She made other remarks upon it, so apt that Mrs. Claxon gave her a sort of permissive invitation to look about the whole lower floor, ending with the kitchen.

Mrs. Lander sat down there while Mrs. Claxon drew from the pipes a glass of water, which she proudly explained was pumped all over the house by the wind mill that supplied the power for her husband's turning lathes.

"Well, I wish *my* husband could have tasted that wata," said Mrs. Lander, as if reminded of husbands by the word, and by the action of putting down the glass. "He was always such a great hand for good, cold wata. My! He'd 'a liked youa kitchen, Mrs Claxon. He always was such a home-body, and he did get so ti'ed of hotels. For all he had such an appearance, when you see him, of bein'—well!—stiff and proud, he was fah moa common in his tastes—I don't mean common, exactly, eitha—than what I was; and many a time when we'd be drivin' through the country, and we'd pass some o' them long-strung-out houses, don't you know, with the kitchen next to the wood shed, and then an ahchway befoa you get to the stable, Mr. Landa he'd get out, and make an urrand, just so's to look in at the kitchen dooa; he said it made him think of his own motha's kitchen. We was both brought up in the country, that's a fact, and I guess if the truth was known we both expected to settle down and die thea, some time; but now he's gone, and I don't know what'll become o' me, and sometimes I don't much care. I guess if Mr. Landa 'd 'a seen youa kitchen, it wouldn't 'a' been so easy to git him out of it; and I do believe if he's livin' anywhe' now he takes as much comfo't in my settin' here as what I do. I presume I shall settle down somewhe's before a great while, and if you could make up youa mind to let your daughta come to me for a little visit till spring, you couldn't do a thing that 'd please Mr. Landa moa."

Mrs. Claxon said that she would talk it over with the child's father; and then Mrs. Lander pressed her to let her take Clementina back to the Middlemount with her for supper, if they wouldn't let her stay the night. After Clementina had driven away, Mrs. Claxon accused herself to her husband of being the greatest fool in the State, but he said that the carriage was one of the Middlemount rigs, and he guessed it was all right. He could see that Clem was wild to go, and he didn't see why she shouldn't.

"Well, *I* do, then," his wife retorted. "We don't know anything about the woman, or *who* she is."

"I guess no harm'll come to Clem for *one* night," said Claxon, and Mrs. Claxon was forced back upon the larger question for the maintenance of her anxiety. She asked what he was going to do about letting Clem go the whole winter with a perfect stranger; and he answered that he had not got round to that yet, and that there were a good many things to be thought of first. He got round to see the rector before dark, and in the light of his larger horizon, was better able to orient Mrs. Lander and her motives than he had been before.

When she came back with the girl the next morning, she had thought of something in the nature of credentials. It was the letter from her church in Boston, which she took whenever she left home, so that if she wished she might unite with the church in any place where she happened to be stopping. It did not make a great impression upon the Claxons, who were of no religion, though they allowed their children to go to the Episcopal church and Sunday-school, and always meant to go themselves. They said they would like to talk the matter over with the rector, if Mrs. Lander did not object; she offered to send her carriage for him, and the rector was brought at once.

"THEY SAID THEY WOULD LIKE TO TALK THE MATTER OVER."

He was one of those men who have, in the breaking down of the old Puritanical faith, and the dying out of the later Unitarian rationalism, advanced and established the Anglican church so notably in the New England hill-country, by a wise conformity to the necessities and exactions of the native temperament. On the ecclesiastical side he was conscientiously uncompromising, but personally he was as simple-mannered as he was simple-hearted. He was a tall lean man in rusty black, with a clerical waistcoat that buttoned high, and scholarly glasses, but with a belated straw hat that had counted more than one summer, and a farmer's tan on his face and hands. He pronounced the church-letter, though quite outside of his own church, a document of the highest respectability, and he listened with patient deference to the autobiography which Mrs. Lander poured out upon him, and her identifications, through reference to this or that person in Boston whom he knew either at first or second hand. He had not to pronounce upon her syntax, or her social quality; it was enough for him, in behalf of the Claxons, to find her what she professed to be.

"You must think," he said, laughing, "that we are over-particular; but the fact is that we value Clementina rather highly, and we wish to be sure that your hospitable offer will be for her real good."

"Of cou'se," said Mrs. Lander. "I should be just so myself about her."

"I don't know," he continued, "that I've ever said how much we think of her, Mrs. Richling and I, but this seems a good opportunity, as she is not present.

She is not perfect, but she comes as near being a thoroughly good girl as she can without knowing it. She has a great deal of common-sense, and we all want her to have the best chance."

"Well, that's just the way I feel about her, and that's just what I mean to give her," said Mrs. Lander.

"I am not sure that I make myself quite clear," said the rector. "I mean, a chance to prove how useful and helpful she can be. Do you think you can make life hard for her occasionally? Can you be peevish and exacting, and unreasonable? Can you do something to make her value superfluity and luxury at their true worth?"

Mrs. Lander looked a little alarmed and a little offended. "I don't know as I undastand what you mean, exactly," she said, frowning rather with perplexity than resentment. "But the child sha'n't have a care, and her own motha couldn't be betta to her than me. There a'n't anything money can buy that she sha'n't have, if she wants it, and all I'll ask of her is 't she'll enjoy herself as much as she knows how. I want her with me because I should love to have her round; and we did from the very fust minute she spoke, Mr. Lander and me, both. She shall have her own money, and spend it for anything she pleases, and she needn't do a stitch o' work from mohnin' till night. But if you're afraid I shall *put* upon her"—

"No, no," said the rector, and he threw back his head with a laugh.

When it was all arranged, a few days later, after

the verification of certain of Mrs. Lander's references by letters to Boston, he said to Clementina's father and mother, "There's only one danger, now, and that is that she will spoil Clementina; but there's a reasonable hope that she won't know how." He found the Claxons struggling with a fresh misgiving, which Claxon expressed. "The way I look at it is like this. I don't want that woman should eva think Clem was after her money. On the face of it there a'n't very much to her that would make anybody think but what we *was* after it; and I should want it pootty well undastood that we wa'n't that *kind*. But I don't seem to see any way of tellin' her."

"No," said the rector, with a sympathetic twinkle, "that would be difficult."

"It's plain to be seen," Mrs. Claxon interposed, "that she thinks a good deal of her money; and I d' know but what she'd think she was doin' Clem most too much of a favor anyway. If it can't be a puffectly even thing, all round, I d' know as I should want it to be at all."

"You're quite right, Mrs. Claxon, quite right. But I believe Mrs. Lander may be safely left to look out for her own interests. After all, she has merely asked Clementina to pass the winter with her. It will be a good opportunity for her to see something of the world; and perhaps it may bring her the chance of placing herself in life. We have got to consider these things with reference to a young girl."

Mrs. Claxon said, "Of cou'se," but Claxon did not assent so readily.

"I don't feel as if I should want Clem to look at it in that light. If the chance don't come to her, I don't want she should go huntin' round for it."

"I thoroughly agree with you," said the rector. "But I was thinking that there was not only no chance worthy of her in Middlemount, but there is no chance at all."

"I guess that's so," Claxon owned with a laugh. "Well, I guess we can leave it to Clem to do what's right and proper everyway. As you *say*, she's got lots of sense."

From that moment he emptied his mind of care concerning the matter; but husband and wife are never both quite free of care on the same point of common interest, and Mrs. Claxon assumed more and more of the anxieties which he had abandoned. She fretted under the load, and expressed an exasperated tenderness for Clementina when the girl seemed forgetful of any of the little steps to be taken before the great one in getting her clothes ready for leaving home. She said finally that she presumed they were doing a wild thing, and that it looked crazier and crazier the more she thought of it; but all was, if Clem didn't like, she could come home. By this time her husband was in something of that insensate eagerness to have the affair over that people feel in a house where there is a funeral.

At the station, when Clementina started for Boston with Mrs. Lander, her father and mother, with the rector and his wife, came to see her off. Other friends mistakenly made themselves of the party, and kept her talking vacuities when her heart was full, till the train drew up. Her father went with her into the parlor car, where the porter of the Middlemount House set down Mrs. Lander's hand baggage and took the final fee she thrust upon him. When Claxon came out he was not so satisfactory about the car as he might have been to his wife, who had never been inside a parlor car, and who had remained proudly in the background, where she could not see into it from the outside. He said that he had felt so bad about Clem that he did not notice what the car was like. But he was able to report that she looked as well as any of the folks in it, and that, if there were any better dressed, he did not see them. He owned that she cried some, when he said good-bye to her.

"I guess," said his wife, grimly, "we're a passel o' fools to let her go. Even if she don't like, the'a, with that crazy-head, she won't be the same Clem when she comes back."

They were too heavy-hearted to dispute much, and were mostly silent as they drove home behind Claxon's self-broken colt: a creature that had taken voluntarily to harness almost from its birth, and was an example to its kind in sobriety and industry.

The children ran out from the house to meet them, with a story of having seen Clem at a point in the woods where the train always slowed up before a crossing, and where they had all gone to wait for her. She had seen them through the car-window, and had come out on the car platform, and waved her handkerchief, as she passed, and called something to them, but they could not hear what it was, they were all cheering so.

At this their mother broke down, and went crying into the house. Not to have had the last words of the child whom she should never see the same again if she ever saw her at all, was more, she said, than heart could bear.

The rector's wife arrived home with her husband in a mood of mounting hopefulness, which soared to tops commanding a view of perhaps more of this world's kingdoms than a clergyman's wife ought ever to see, even for another. She decided that Clementina's chances of making a splendid match, somewhere, were about of the nature of certainties, and she contended that she would adorn any station, with experience, and with her native tact, especially if it were a very high station in Europe, where Mrs. Lander would now be sure to take her. If she did not take her to Europe, however, she would be sure to leave her all her money, and this would serve the same end, though more indirectly.

Mr. Richling scoffed at this ideal of Clementina's future with a contempt which was as little becoming to his cloth. He made his wife reflect that, with all her inherent grace and charm, Clementina was an ignorant little country girl, who had neither the hardness of heart nor the greediness of soul, which gets people on in the world, and repair for them the disadvantages of birth and education. He represented that even if favorable chances for success in society showed themselves to the girl, the intense and inexpugnable vulgarity of Mrs. Lander would spoil them; and he was glad of this, he said, for he believed that the best thing which could happen to the child would be to come home as sweet and good as she had gone away; he added this was what they ought both to pray for.

His wife admitted this, but she retorted by asking if he thought such a thing was possible, and he was obliged to own that it was not possible. He marred the effect of his concession by subjoining that it was no more possible than her making a brilliant and triumphant social figure in society, either at home or in Europe.

XIV.

So far from embarking at once for Europe, Mrs. Lander went to that hotel in a suburb of Boston, where she had the habit of passing the late autumn months, in order to fortify herself for the climate of the early winter months in the city. She was a little puzzled how to provide for Clementina, with respect to herself, but she decided that the best thing would be to have her sleep in a room opening out of her own, with a folding bed in it, so that it could be used as a sort of parlor for both of them during the day, and be within easy reach, for conversation, at all times.

On her part, Clementina began by looking after Mrs. Lander's comforts, large and little, like a daughter, to her own conception and to that of Mrs. Lander, but to other eyes, like a servant. Mrs. Lander shyly shrank from acquaintance among the other ladies, and in the absence of this, she could not introduce Clementina, who went down to an early breakfast alone, and sat apart with her at lunch and dinner, ministering to her in public as she did in private. She ran back to their rooms to fetch her shawl, or her handkerchief, or whichever drops or powders she happened to be taking with her meals, and adjusted with closer care the hassock which the head waiter had officially placed at her feet. They seldom sat in the parlor where the ladies met, after dinner; they talked only to each other; and there, as elsewhere, the girl kept her filial care of the old woman. The question of her relation to Mrs. Lander became so pressing among several of the guests that, after Clementina had watched over the banisters, with throbbing heart and feet, a little dance one night which the other girls had got up among themselves, and had fled back to her room at the approach of one of the kindlier and bolder of them, the landlord felt forced to learn from Mrs. Lander how Miss Claxon was to be regarded. He managed delicately, by saying he would give the Sunday paper she had ordered to her nurse, "Or, I beg your pardon," he added, as if he had made a mistake.

"Why, she a'n't my *nuhse*," Mrs. Lander explained, simply, neither annoyed nor amused; "she's just a young lady that's visiting me, as you may say," and this put an end to the misgiving among the ladies. But it suggested something to Mrs. Lander, and a few days afterwards, when they came out from Boston where they had been shopping, and she had been lavishing a bewildering waste of gloves, hats, shoes, capes and gowns upon Clementina, she said, "I'll tell you what. We've got to have a maid."

"A maid?" cried the girl.

"It isn't me, or my things I want her for," said

Mrs. Lander. "It's you and these dresses of youas. I presume you could look afta them, come to give youa mind to it; but I don't want to have you tied up to a lot of clothes; and I presume we should find her a comfo't in moa ways than one, both of us. I don't know what we shall want her to do, exactly; but I guess *she* will, if she undastands her business, and I want you should go in with me, to-morror, and find one. I'll speak to some of the ladies, and find out whe's the best place to go, and we'll get the best there is."

A lady whom Mrs. Lander spoke to entered into the affair with zeal born of a lurking sense of the wrong she had helped do Clementina in the common doubt whether she was not herself Mrs. Lander's maid. She offered to go into Boston with them to an intelligence office, where you could get nice girls of all kinds; but she ended by giving Mrs. Lander the address, and instructions as to what she was to require in a maid. She was chiefly to get an English maid, if at all possible, for the qualifications would more or less naturally follow from her nationality. There proved to be no English maid, but there was a Swedish one who had received a rigid training in an English family living on the Continent, and had come immediately from that service to seek her first place in America. The manager of the office pronounced her character, as set down in writing, faultless, and Mrs. Lander engaged her. "You want to look afta this young lady," she said, indicating Clementina. "I can look afta myself," but Ellida took charge of them both on the train out from Boston with prompt intelligence.

"We got to get used to it, I guess," Mrs. Lander confided at the first chance of whispering to Clementina.

Within a month after washing the faces and combing the hair of all her brothers and sisters who would suffer it at her hands, Clementina's own head was under the brush of a lady's maid, who was of as great a discreetness in her own way as Clementina herself. She supplied the defects of Mrs. Lander's elementary habits by simply asking if she should get this thing and that thing for the toilet, without criticising its absence, and then asking whether she should get the same things for her young lady. She appeared to let Mrs. Lander decide between having her brushes in ivory or silver, but there was really no choice for her, and they came in silver. She knew not only her own place, but the places of her two ladies, and she presently had them in such training that they were as proficient in what they might and might not do for themselves and for each other, as if making these distinctions were the custom of their lives.

Their hearts would both have gone out to Ellida, but Ellida kept them at a distance with the smooth respectfulness of the iron hand in the glove of velvet; and Clementina first learned from her to imagine the impassable gulf between mistress and maid.

At the end of her month she gave them, out of a clear sky, a week's warning. She professed no grievance, and was not moved by Mrs. Lander's appeal to say what wages she wanted. She would only say that she was going to take a place on Commonwealth Avenue, where a friend of hers was living, and when the week was up, she went, and left her late mistresses feeling rather blank. "I presume we shall have to get anotha," said Mrs. Lander.

"Oh, not right away!" Clementina pleaded.

"Well, not right away," Mrs. Lander assented; and provisionally they each took the other into her keeping, and were much freer and happier together.

Soon after Clementina was startled one morning, as she was going in to breakfast, by seeing Mr. Fane at the clerk's desk. He did not see her; he was looking down at the hotel register, to compute the bill of a departing guest; but when she passed out she found him watching for her, with some letters.

"I didn't know you were with us," he said, with his pensive smile, "till I found your letters here, addressed to Mrs. Lander's care; and then I put two and two together. It only shows how small the world is, don't you think so? I've just got back from my vacation; I prefer to take it in the fall of the year, because it's so much pleasanter to travel, then. I suppose you didn't know I was here?"

"No, I didn't," said Clementina. "I never dreamed of such a thing."

"To be sure; why should you?" Fane reflected. "I've been here ever since last spring. But I'll say this, Miss Claxon, that if it's the least unpleasant to you, or the least disagreeable, or awakens any kind of associations"—

"Oh, no!" Clementina protested, and Fane was spared the pain of saying what he would do if it were.

He bowed, and she said sweetly, "It's pleasant to meet any one I've seen before. I suppose you don't know how much it's changed at Middlemount since you we'e thea." Fane answered blankly, while he felt in his breast pocket, Oh, he presumed so; and she added: "Ha'dly any of the same guests came back this summer, and they had more in July than they had in August, Mrs. Atwell said. Mr. Mahtin, the *chef*, is gone, and nea'ly all the help is different."

Fane kept feeling in one pocket and then slapped himself over the other pockets. "No," he said, "I haven't got it with me. I must have left it in my room. I just received a letter from Frank—Mr. Gregory, you know, I always call him Frank—and I thought I had it with me. He was asking about Middlemount; and I wanted to read you what he said. But I'll find it upstairs. He's out of college, now, and he's begun his studies in the divinity school. He's at Andover. I don't know what to make of Frank, oftentimes," the clerk continued, confidentially. "I tell him he's a kind of a survival, in religion; he's so aesthetic." It seemed to Fane that he had not meant aesthetic, exactly, but he could not ask Clementina what the word was. He went on to say, "He's a grand good fellow, Frank is, but he don't make enough allowance for human nature. He's more like one of those old fashioned orthodox. I go in for having a good time, so long as you don't do anybody else any hurt."

He left her, and went to receive the commands of a lady who was leaning over the desk, and saying severely, "My mail, if you please," and Clementina could not wait for him to come back; she had to go to Mrs. Lander, and get her ready for breakfast; Ellida had taught Mrs. Lander a luxury of helplessness in which she persisted after the maid's help was withdrawn.

Clementina went about the whole day with the wonder what Gregory had said about Middlemount filling her mind. It must have had something to do with her; he could not have forgotten the words he had asked her to forget. She remembered them now with a curiosity, which had no rancor in it, to know why he really took them back. She had never blamed him, and she had outlived the hurt she had felt at not hearing from him. But she had never lost the hope of hearing from him, or rather the expectation, and now she found that she was eager for his message; she decided that it must be something like a message, although it could not be anything direct. No one else had come to his place in her fancy, and she was willing to try what they would think of each other now, to measure her own obligation to the past by a knowledge of his. There was scarcely more than this in her heart when she allowed herself to drift near Fane's place that night, that he might speak to her, and tell her what Gregory had said. But he had apparently forgotten about his letter, and only wished to talk about himself. He wished to analyze himself, to tell her what sort of person he was. He dealt impartially with the subject; he did not spare some faults of his; and after a week, he proposed a correspondence with her, in a letter of carefully studied spelling, as a means of mutual improvement as well as further acquaintance.

It cost Clementina a good deal of trouble to answer him as she wished and not hurt his feelings. She declined in terms she thought so cold that they must offend him beyond the point of speaking to her again; but he sought her out, as soon after as he could, and thanked her for her kindness, and begged her pardon. He said he knew that she was a very busy person, with all the lessons she was taking, and that she had no time for carrying on a correspondence. He regretted that he could not write French, because then the correspondence would have been good practice for her. Clementina had begun taking French lessons, of a teacher who came out from Boston. She lunched three times a week with her and Mrs. Lander, and spoke the language with Clementina, whose accent she praised for its purity; purity of accent was characteristic of all this lady's pupils; but what was really extraordinary in Mademoiselle Claxon was her sense of grammatical structure; she wrote the language even more perfectly than she spoke it; but beautifully, but wonderfully; her exercises were something marvellous.

Mrs. Lander would have liked Clementina to take all the lessons that she heard any of the other young ladies in the hotel were taking. One of them went in town every day, and studied drawing at an art-school, and she wanted Clementina to do that, too. But

Clementina would not do that; she had tried often enough at home, when her brother Jim was drawing, and her father was designing the patterns of his woodwork; she knew that she never could do it, and the time would be wasted. She decided against piano lessons and singing lessons, too; she did not care for either, and she pleaded that it would be a waste to study them; but she suggested dancing lessons, and her gift for dancing won greater praise, and perhaps sincerer, than her accent won from Mademoiselle Blanc, though Mrs. Lander said that she would not have believed any one could be more complimentary. She learned the new steps and figures in all the fashionable dances; she mastered some fancy dances, which society was then beginning to borrow from the stage; and she gave these before Mrs. Lander with a success which she felt herself.

"I believe I could teach dancing," she said.

"Well, you won't eva haf to, child," returned Mrs. Lander, with an eye on the side of the case that seldom escaped her.

In spite of his wish to respect these preoccupations, Fane could not keep from offering Clementina attentions, which took the form of persecution when they changed from flowers for Mrs. Lander's table to letters for herself. He apologized for his letters whenever he met her; but at last one of them came to her before breakfast with a special delivery stamp from Boston. He had withdrawn to the city to write it, and he said that if she could not make him a favorable answer, he should not come back to Woodlake.

She had to show this letter to Mrs. Lander, who asked: "You want he should come back?"

"*No*, indeed! I don't want eva to see him again."

"Well, then, I guess you'll know how to tell him so."

The girl went into her own room to write, and when she brought her answer to show it to Mrs. Lander she found her in frowning thought. "I don't know but you'll have to go back and write it all over again, Clementina," she said, "if you've told *him* not to come. I've been thinkin', if you don't want to have anything to do with him, we betta go ouaselves."

"Yes," answered Clementina, "that's what I've said."

"You *have?* Well, the witch is *in* it! How came you to"—

"I just wanted to talk with you about it. But I thought maybe you'd like to go. Or at least *I* should. I should like to go home, Mrs. Landa."

"Home!" retorted Mrs. Lander. "The'e's plenty of places where you can be safe from the fella besides home, though I'll take you back the'a this minute if you *say* so. But you needn't to feel wo'ked up about it."

"Oh, I'm not," said Clementina, but with a gulp which betrayed her nervousness.

"I did think," Mrs. Lander went on, "that I should go into the Vonndome, for December and January, but just as likely as not he'd come pesterin' the'a, too, and I wouldn't go, now, if you was to give me the whole city of Boston. Why shouldn't we go to Florida?"

When Mrs. Lander had once imagined the move, the nomadic impulse mounted irresistably in her. She spoke of hotels in the South, where they could renew the summer, and she mapped out a campaign which she put into instant action so far as to advance upon New York.

XV.

Mrs. Lander went to a hotel in New York where she had been in the habit of staying with her husband, on their way South or North. The clerk knew her, and shook hands with her across the register, and said she could have her old rooms if she wanted them; the bell-boy who took up their hand-baggage recalled himself to her; the elevator-boy welcomed her with a smile of remembrance.

Since she was already up, from coming off the sleeping-car, she had no excuse for not going to breakfast like other people; and she went with Clementina to the dining-room, where the head-waiter, who found them places, spoke with an outlandish accent, and the waiter who served them had a parlance that seemed superficially English, but was inwardly something else; there was even a touch in the cooking of the familiar dishes, that needed translation for the girl's inexperienced palate. She was finding a refuge in the strangeness of everything, when she was startled by the sound of a familiar voice calling, "Clementina Claxon! Well, I was sure all along it was you, and I determined I wouldn't stand it another minute. Why, child, how you *have* changed! Why, I declare you are quite a woman! When did you come? How pretty you are!"

Mrs. Milray took Clementina in her arms and kissed her in proof of her admiration before the whole breakfast room. She was very nice to Mrs. Lander, too, who, when Clementina introduced them, made haste to say that Clementina was there on a visit with her. Mrs. Milray answered that she envied her such a visitor as Miss Claxon, and protested that she should steal her away for a visit to herself, if Mr. Milray was not so much in love with her that it made her jealous. "Mr. Milray has to have his breakfast in his room," she explained to Clementina. "He's not been so well, since he lost his mother. Yes," she said, with decorous solemnity, "I'm still in mourning for her," and Clementina saw that she was in a tempered black. "She died last year, and now I'm taking Mr. Milray abroad to see if it won't cheer him up a little. Are you going South for the winter?" she inquired, politely, of Mrs. Lander. "I wish I was going," she said, when Mrs. Lander guessed they should go, later on. "Well, you must come in and see me all you can, Clementina; and I shall have the pleasure of calling upon you," she added to Mrs. Lander with state that was lost in the soubrette-like volatility of her flight from them the next moment. "Goodness, I forgot all about Mr. Milray's breakfast!" She ran back to the table she had left on the other side of the room.

"Who is that, Clementina?" asked Mrs. Lander, on their way to their rooms. Clementina explained as well as she could, and Mrs. Lander summed up her feeling in the verdict, "Well, she's a *lady*, if ever I saw a lady; and you don't see many of 'em, nowadays."

The girl remembered how Mrs. Milray had once before seemed very fond of her, and had afterwards forgotten the pretty promises and professions she had made her. But she went with Mrs. Lander to see her, and she saw Mr. Milray, too, for a little while. He seemed glad of their meeting, but still depressed by the bereavement which Mrs. Milray supported almost with gayety. When he left them she explained that he was a good deal away from her, with his family, as she approved of his being, though she had apparently no wish to join him in all the steps of the reconciliation which the mother's death had brought about among them. Sometimes his sisters came to the hotel to see her, but she amused herself perfectly without them, and she gave much more of her leisure to Clementina and Mrs. Lander.

She soon knew the whole history of the relation between them, and the first time that Clementina found her alone with Mrs. Lander she could have divined that Mrs. Lander had been telling her of the Fane affair, even if Mrs. Milray had not at once called out to her, "I know all about it; and I'll tell you what, Clementina, I'm going to take you over with me and marry you to an English Duke. Mrs. Lander and I have been planning it all out, and I'm going to send down to the steamer office, and engage your passage. It's all settled!"

When she was gone, Mrs. Lander asked, "What do you s'pose your folks *would* say to your goin' to Europe, anyway, Clementina?" as if the matter had been already debated between them.

Clementina hesitated. "I should want to be su'a Mrs. Milray really wanted me to go ova with her."

"Why, didn't you hear her *say* so?" demanded Mrs. Lander.

"Yes," sighed Clementina. "Mrs. Lander, I think Mrs. Milray means what she says, at the time, but she is one that seems to forget."

"She thinks the wo'ld of you," Mrs. Lander urged.

"She was very nice to me that summer at Middlemount. I guess maybe she would like to have us go with her," the girl relented.

"I guess we'll wait and see," said Mrs. Lander. "I shouldn't want she should change her mind when it was too late, as you *say*." They were both silent for a time, and then Mrs. Lander resumed, "But I presume she ha'n't got the only steama that's crossin'. What should you say about goin' over on some otha steama? I been South a good many wintas, and I should feel kind of lonesome goin' round to the places where I been with Mr. Landa. I felt it since I been here in this hotel, some, and I can't seem to want to go ova the same ground again, well, not right away."

Clementina said, "Why, of cou'se, Mrs. Landa."

"Should you be willin'," asked Mrs. Lander, after another little pause, "if your folks was willin', to go ova the'a, to some of them European countries, to spend the winta?"

"Oh yes, indeed!" said Clementina.

They discussed the matter in one of the full talks they both liked. At the end Mrs. Lander said, "Well, I guess you betta write home, and ask your motha whetha you can go, so't if we take the notion we can go any time. Tell her to telegraph, if she'll let you, and do write all the ifs and ands, so't she'll know just how to answa, without havin' to have you write again."

That evening Mrs. Milray came to their table from where she had been dining alone, and asked in banter: "Well, have you made up your minds to go over with me?"

Mrs. Lander said bluntly, "We can't ha'dly believe you really want us to, Mrs. Milray."

"*I* don't want you? Who put such an idea into your head! Oh, *I* know!" She threatened Clementina with the door-key, which she was carrying in her hand. "It was *you*, was it? What an artful, suspicious thing! What's got into you, child? Do you hate me?" She did not give Clementina time to protest. "Well, now, I can just tell you I *do* want you, and I'll be quite heart-broken if you don't come."

"Well, she wrote to her friends this mohning," Mrs. Lander said, "but I guess she won't git an answa in time for *youa* steamer, even if they do let her go."

"Oh, yes she will," Mrs. Milray protested. "It's all right, now; you've got to go, and there's no use trying to get out of it."

She came to them whenever she could find them in the dining-room, and she knocked daily at their door till she knew that Clementina had heard from home. The girl's mother wrote, without a punctuation mark in her letter, but with a great deal of sense, that such a thing as her going to Europe could not be settled by telegraph. She did not think it worth while to report all the facts of a consultation with the rector which they had held upon getting Clementina's request, and which had renewed all the original question of her relations with Mrs. Lander in an intensified form. He had disposed of this upon much the same terms as before; and they had yielded more readily because the experiment had so far succeeded. Clementina had apparently no complaint to make of Mrs. Lander; she was eager to go, and the rector and his wife, who had been invited to be of the council, were both of the opinion that a course of European travel would be of the greatest advantage to the girl, if she wished to fit herself for teaching. It was an opportunity that they must not think of throwing away. If Mrs. Lander went to Florence, as it seemed from Clementina's letter she thought of doing, the girl would pass a delightful winter in study of one of the most interesting cities in the world, and she would learn things which would enable her to do better for herself when she came home than she could ever hope to do otherwise. She might never marry, Mr. Richling suggested, and it was only right and fair that she should be equipped with as much culture as possible for the struggle of life; Mrs. Richling agreed with this rather vague theory, but she was sure that Clementina would get married to greater advantage in

Florence than anywhere else. They neither of them really knew anything at first hand about Florence; the rector's opinion was grounded on the thought of the joy that a sojourn in Italy would have been to him; his wife derived her hope of a Florentine marriage for Clementina from several romances in which love and travel had gone hand in hand, to the lasting credit of triumphant American girlhood.

The Claxons were not able to enter into their view of the case, but if Mrs. Lander wanted to go to Florence instead of Florida they did not see why Clementina should not go with her to one place as well as the other. They were not without a sense of flattery from the fact that their daughter was going to Europe; but they put that as far from them as they could, the mother severely and the father ironically, as something too silly, and they tried not to let it weigh with them in making up their mind, but to consider only Clementina's best good, and not even to regard her pleasure. Her mother put before her the most crucial questions she could think of, in her letter, and then gave her full leave from her father as well as herself to go if she wished.

Clementina had rather it had been too late to go with the Milrays, but she felt bound to own her decision when she reached it; and Mrs. Milray, whatever her real wish was, made it a point of honor to help get Mrs. Lander berths on her steamer. It did not require much effort; there are plenty of berths for the latest-comers on a winter passage, and Clementina found herself the fellow passenger of Mrs. Milray.

XVI.

As soon as Mrs. Lander could make her way to her state-room, she got into her berth, and began to take the different remedies for sea-sickness which she had brought with her. Mrs. Milray said that was nice, and that now she and Clementina could have a good time. But before it came to that she had taken pity on a number of lonely young men whom she found on board. She cheered them up by walking round the ship with them; but if any of them continued dull in spite of this, she dropped him, and took another; and before she had been two days out she had gone through with nearly all the lonely young men on the list of cabin passengers. She introduced some of them to Clementina, but at such times as she had them in charge; and for the most part she left her to Milray. Once, as the girl sat beside him in her steamer-chair, Mrs. Milray shed a wrap on his knees in whirring by on the arm of one of her young men, with some laughed and shouted charge about it.

"What did she say?" he asked Clementina, slanting the down-pulled brim of his soft hat purblindly toward her.

She said she had not understood, and then Milray asked, "What sort of person is that Boston youth of Mrs. Milray's? Is he a donkey or a lamb?"

Clementina said ingenuously, "Oh, she's walking with that English gentleman now—that lo'd."

"Ah, yes," said Milray. "He's not very much to look at, I hear."

"Well, not *very* much," Clementina admitted; she did not like to talk against people.

"Lords are sometimes disappointing, Clementina," Milray said, "but then, so are other great men. I've seen politicians on our side who were disappointing, and there are clergymen and gamblers who don't look it." He laughed sadly. "That's the way people talk who are a little disappointing themselves. I hope you don't expect too much of yourself, Clementina?"

"I don't know what you mean," she said, stiffening with a suspicion that he might be going to make fun of her.

He laughed more gayly. "Well, I mean we must hold the other fellows up to their duty, or we can't do our own. We need their example. Charity may begin at home, but duty certainly begins abroad." He went on, as if it were a branch of the same inquiry, "Did you ever meet my sisters? They came to the hotel in New York to see Mrs. Milray."

"Yes, I was in the room once when they came in."

"Did you like them?"

"Yes—I sca'cely spoke to them—I only stayed a moment."

"Would you like to see any more of the family?"

"Why, of cou'se!" Clementina was amused at his asking, but he seemed in earnest.

"One of my sisters lives in Florence, and Mrs. Milray says you think of going there, too."

"Mrs. Landa thought it would be a good place to spend the winter. Is it a pleasant place?"

"Oh, delightful! Do you know much about Italy?"

"Not very much, I don't believe."

"Well, my sister has lived a good while in Florence. I should like to give you a letter to her."

"Oh, thank you!" said Clementina.

Milray smiled at her spare acknowledgment, but inquired gravely: "What do you expect to do in Florence?"

"Why, I presume, whateva Mrs. Landa wants to do."

"Do you think Mrs. Lander will want to go into society?"

This question had not occurred to Clementina. "I don't believe she will," she said, thoughtfully.

"Shall you?"

Clementina laughed, "Why, do you think," she ventured, "that society would want me to?"

"Yes, I think it would, if you're as charming as you've tried to make me believe. Oh, I don't mean, to your own knowledge; but some people have ways of being charming without knowing it. If Mrs. Lander isn't going into society, and there should be a way found for you to go, don't refuse, will you?"

"I shall wait and see if I'm asked, fust."

"Yes, that will be best," said Milray. "But I

shall give you a letter to my sister. She and I used to be famous cronies, and we went to a great many parties together when we were young people. We thought the world was a fine thing, then. But it changes."

He fell into a muse, and they were both sitting quite silent when Mrs. Milray came round the corner of the music room in the course of her twentieth or thirtieth compass of the deck, and introduced her lord to her husband and to Clementina. He promptly ignored Milray, and devoted himself to the girl, leaning over her with his hand against the bulkhead behind her and talking down upon her.

Lord Lioncourt must have been about thirty, but he had the heated and broken complexion of a man who has taken more than is good for him in twice that number of years. This was one of the wrongs nature had done him in apparent resentment of the social advantages he was born to, for he was rather abstemious, as Englishmen go. He looked a very shy person till he spoke, and then you found that he was not in the least shy. He looked so English that you would have expected a strong English accent of him, but his speech was more that of an American, without the nasality. This was not apparently because he had been much in America; he was returning from his first visit to the States, which had been spent chiefly in the Territories; after a brief interval of Newport he had preferred the West; he liked rather to hunt than to be hunted, though even in the West his main business had been to kill time, which he found more plentiful there than other game. The natives, everywhere, were much the same thing to him; if he distinguished it was in favor of those who did not suppose themselves cultivated. If again he had a choice it was for the females; they seemed to him more amusing than the males, who struck him as having an exaggerated reputation for humor. He did not care much for Clementina's past, as he knew it from Mrs. Milray, and if it did not touch his fancy, it certainly did not offend his taste. A real artistocracy is above social prejudice, when it will; he had known some of his order choose the mothers of their heirs from the music halls, and when it came to a question of distinctions among Americans, he could not feel them. They might be richer or poorer; but they could not be more patrician or more plebeian.

The passengers, he told Clementina, were getting up, at this point of the ship's run, an entertainment for the benefit of the seaman's hospital in Liverpool, that well-known convention of ocean-travel, which is sure at some time or other, to enlist all the talent on board every English steamer in some sort of public appeal. He was not very clear how he came to be on the committee for drumming up talent for the occasion; his distinction seemed to have been conferred by a popular vote in the smoking room, as nearly as he could make out; but here he was, and he was counting upon Miss Claxon to help him out. He said Mrs. Milray had told him about that charming affair they had got up in the mountains, and he was sure they could have something of the kind again. "Perhaps not a coaching party; that mightn't be so easy to manage at sea. But isn't there something else—some tableaux or something? If we couldn't have the months of the year we might have the points of the compass, and you could take your choice."

He tried to get something out of the notion, but nothing came of it that Mrs. Milray thought possible. She said, across her husband, on whose further side she had sunk into a chair, that they must have something very informal; everybody must do what they could, separately. "I know you can do anything you like, Clementina. Can't you play something, or sing?" At Clementina's look of utter denial, she added, desperately, "Or *dance* something?" A light came into the girl's face at which she caught. "I *know* you can dance something! Why, of course! Now, what is it?"

Clementina smiled at her vehemence. "Why, it's nothing. And I don't know whether I should like to."

"Oh, yes," urged Lord Lioncourt. "Such a good cause, you know."

"What is it?" Mrs. Milray insisted. "Is it something you could do alone?"

"It's just a dance that I learned at Woodlake. The teacha said that all the young ladies we'e lea'ning it. It's a skut-dance"—

"The very thing!" Mrs. Milray shouted. "It'll be the hit of the evening."

"But I've never done it before any one," Clementina faltered.

"They'll all be doing their turns," the Englishman said. "Speaking, and singing, and playing."

Clementina felt herself giving way, and she pleaded in final reluctance, "But I haven't got a pleated skut in my steama trunk."

"No matter! We can manage that." Mrs. Milray jumped to her feet and took Lord Lioncourt's arm. "Now we must go and drum up somebody else." He did not seem eager to go, but he started. "Then that's all settled," she shouted over her shoulder to Clementina.

"No, no, Mrs. Milray!" Clementina called after her. "The ship tilts so"—

"Nonsense! It's the smoothest run she ever made in December. And I'll engage to have the sea as steady as a rock for you. Remember, now, you've promised."

Mrs. Milray whirled her Englishman away, and left Clementina sitting beside her husband.

"Did you want to dance for them, Clementina?" he asked.

"I don't know," she said, with the vague smile of one to whom a pleasant hope has occurred.

"I thought perhaps you were letting Mrs. Milray bully you into it. She's a frightful tyrant."

"Oh, I guess I should like to do it, if you think it would be—nice."

"I dare say it will be the nicest thing at their ridiculous show." Milray laughed as if her willingness to do the dance had defeated a sentimental sympathy in him.

"I don't believe it will be that," said Clementina, beaming joyously. "But I guess I shall try it, if I can find the right kind of a dress."

"Is a pleated skirt absolutely necessary," asked Milray, gravely.

"I don't see how I could get on without it," said Clementina.

She was so serious still when she went down to her state-room that Mrs. Lander was distracted from her potential ailments to ask: "What is it, Clementina?"

"Oh, nothing. Mrs. Milray has got me to say that I would do something at a concert they ah' going to have on the ship." She explained, "It's that skut dance I learnt at Woodlake of Miss Wilson."

"Well, I guess if you're worryin' about that you needn't to."

"Oh, I'm not worrying about the dance. I was just thinking what I should wear. If I could only get at the trunks!"

"It won't make any matta what you wear," said Mrs. Lander. "It'll be the greatest *thing;* and if 't wa'n't for this sea-sickness that I have to keep fightin' off he'a, night and day, I should come up and see you myself. You ah' just lovely in that dance, Clementina."

"Do you think so, Mrs. Landa?" asked the girl, gratefully. "Well, Mr. Milray didn't seem to think that I need to have a pleated skut. Any rate, I'm going to look over my things, and see if I can't make something else do."

XVII.

THE entertainment was to be the second night after that, and Mrs. Milray at first took the whole affair into her own hands. She was willing to let the others consult with her, but she made all the decisions, and she became so prepotent that she drove Lord Lioncourt to rebellion in the case of some theatrical people whom he wanted in the programme. He wished her to let them feel that they were favoring rather than favored, and she insisted that it should be quite the other way. She professed a scruple against having theatrical people in the programme at all, which she might not have felt if her own past had been different, and she spoke with an abhorrence of the stage which he could by no means tolerate in the case. She submitted with dignity when she could not help it. Perhaps she submitted with too much dignity. Her concession verged upon hauteur; and in her arrogant meekness she went back to another of her young men, whom she began to post again as the companion of her promenades.

He had rather an anxious air in the enjoyment of the honor, but the Englishman seemed unconscious of its loss, or else he chose to ignore it. He frankly gave his leisure to Clementina, and she thought he was very pleasant. There was something different in his way from that of any of the other men she had met; something very natural and simple, a way of being easy in what he was, and not caring whether he was like others or not; he was not ashamed of being ignorant of anything he did not know, and she was able to instruct him on some points. He took her quite seriously when she told him about Middlemount, and how her family came to settle there, and then how she came to be going to Europe with Mrs. Lander. He said Mrs. Milray had spoken about it; but he had not understood quite how it was before; and he hoped Mrs. Lander was coming to the entertainment.

He did not seem aware that Mrs. Milray was leaving the affair more and more to him. He went forward with it and was as amiable with her as she would allow. He was so amiable with everybody that he reconciled many true Americans to his leadership, who felt that as nearly all the passengers were Americans, the chief patron of the entertainment ought to have been some distinguished American. The want of an American who was very distinguished did something to pacify them; but the behavior of an English lord who put on no airs was the main agency. When the night came they filled the large music room of the *Asia Minor*, and stood about in front of the sofas and chairs so many deep that it was hard to see or hear through them.

They each paid a shilling admittance; they were prepared to give munificently besides when the hat came round; and after the first burst of blundering from Lord Lioncourt, they led the magnanimous applause. He said he never minded making a bad speech in a good cause, and he made as bad a one as very well could be. He closed it by telling Mark Twain's whistling story so that those who knew it by heart missed the point; but that might have been because he hurried it, to get himself out of the way of the others following. When he had done, one of the most ardent of the Americans proposed three cheers for him.

The actress whom he had secured in spite of Mrs. Milray appeared in woman's dress contrary to her inveterate professional habit, and followed him with great acceptance in her favorite variety-stage song; and then her husband gave imitations of Sir Henry Irving, and of Miss Maggie Kline in "T'row him down, McCloskey," with a cockney accent. A frightened little girl, whose mother had volunteered her talent, gasped a ballad to her mother's accompaniment, and two young girls played a duet on the mandolin and guitar. A gentleman of cosmopolitan military tradition, who sold the pools in the smoking-room, and was the friend of all the men present, and the acquaintance of several, gave selections of his autobiography prefatory to bellowing in a deep bass voice, "They're hanging Danny Deaver," and then a lady interpolated herself into the programme with a kindness which Lord Lioncourt acknowledged, in saying "The more the merrier," and sang Bonnie Dundee, thumping the piano out of all proportion to her size and apparent strength.

Some advances which Clementina had made for Mrs. Milray's help about the dress she should wear in her dance met with bewildering indifference, and she had fallen back upon her own devices. She did not think of taking back her promise, and she had come to look forward to her part with a happiness which the good weather and the even sway of the ship encouraged. But her pulses fluttered, as she glided into the music room, and sank into a chair next Mrs. Milray. She had on an accordion skirt which she had been able to get out of her trunk in the hold, and she felt that the glance of Mrs. Milray did not refuse it approval.

"That will do nicely, Clementina," she said. She added, in careless acknowledgement of her own failure to direct her choice, "I see you didn't need my help after all," and the thorny point which Clementina felt in her praise was rankling, when Lord Lioncourt began to introduce her.

He made rather a mess of it, but as soon as he came to an end of his well-meant blunders, she stood up and began her poses and paces. It was all very innocent, with something courageous as well as appealing. She had a kind of tender dignity in her dance, and the delicate beauty of her face translated itself into the grace of her movements. It was not impersonal; there was her own quality of sylvan, of elegant in it; but it was unconscious, and so far it was typical, it was classic; Mrs. Milray's Bostonian achieved a snub from her by saying it was like a Botticelli; and in fact it was merely the skirt-dance which society had borrowed from the stage at that period, leaving behind the footlights its more acrobatic phases, but keeping its pretty turns and bows and bends. Clementina did it not only with tender dignity, but when she was fairly launched in it, with a passion to which her sense of Mrs. Milray's strange unkindness lent defiance. The dance was still so new a thing then, that it had a surprise to which the girl's gentleness lent a curious charm, and it had some adventitious fascinations from the necessity she was in of weaving it in and out among the stationary armchairs and sofas which still further cramped the narrow space where she gave it. Her own delight in it shone from her smiling face, which was appealingly happy. Just before it should have ended, one of those wandering waves that roam the smoothest sea struck the ship, and Clementina caught herself skilfully from falling, and reeled to her seat, while the room rang with the applause and sympathetic laughter for the mischance she had baffled. There was a storm of encores, but Clementina called out, "The ship tilts so!" and her *naïveté* won her another burst of favor, which was at its height when Lord Lioncourt had an inspiration.

He jumped up and said, "Miss Claxon is going to oblige us with a little bit of dramatics, now, and I'm sure you'll all enjoy that quite as much as her beautiful dancing. She's going to take the principal part in the laughable after-piece of *Passing round the Hat*, and I hope the audience will—a—a—a—do the rest. She's consented on this occasion to use a hat—or cap, rather—of her own, the charming Tam O'Shanter in which we've all seen her, and—a—admired her about the ship for the week past."

He caught up the flat woolen steamer-cap which Clementina had left in her seat beside Mrs. Milray when she rose to dance, and held it aloft. Some one called out, "Chorus! For he's a jolly good fellow," and led off in his praise. Lord Lioncourt shouted through the uproar the announcement that while Miss Claxon was taking up the collection, Mr. Ewins, of Boston, would sing one of the student songs of Cambridge—no! *Harvard*—University; the music being his own.

Everyone wanted to make some joke or some compliment to Clementina about the cap which grew momently heavier under the sovereigns and half sovereigns, half crowns and half dollars, shillings, quarters, greenbacks and every fraction of English and American silver; and the actor who had given the imitations, made bold, as he said, to ask his lordship if the audience might not hope, before they dispersed, for something more from Miss Claxon. He was sure she could do something more; he for one would be glad of anything; and Clementina turned from putting her cap into Mrs. Milray's lap, to find Lord Lioncourt bowing at her elbow, and offering her his arm to lead her to the spot where she had stood in dancing.

The joy of her triumph went to her head; she wished to retrieve herself from any shadow of defeat.

She stood panting a moment, and then, if she had had the professional instinct, she would have given her admirers the surprise of something altogether different from what had pleased them before. That was what the actor would have done, but Clementina thought of how her dance had been brought to an untimely close by the rolling of the ship; she burned to do it all as she knew it, no matter how the sea behaved, and in another moment she struck into it again. This time the sea behaved perfectly, and the dance ended with just the swoop and swirl she had meant it to have at first. The spectators went generously wild over her; they cheered and clapped her, and crowded upon her to tell how lovely it was; but she escaped from them, and ran back to the place where she had left Mrs. Milray. She was not there, and Clementina's cap full of alms lay abandoned on the chair. Lord Lioncourt said he would take charge of the money, if she would lend him her cap to carry it in to the purser, and she made her way into the saloon. In a distant corner she saw Mrs. Milray with Mr. Ewins.

She advanced in a vague dismay toward them, and as she came near Mrs. Milray said to Mr. Ewins, "I don't like this place. Let's go over yonder." She rose and rushed him to the other end of the saloon.

Lord Lioncourt came in looking about. "Ah, have you found her?" he asked, gayly. "There were twenty pounds in your cap, and two hundred dollars."

"Yes," said Clementina, "she's over the'a." She pointed, and then shrank and slipped away.

XVIII.

At breakfast Mrs. Milray would not meet Clementina's eye; she talked to the people across the table in a loud, lively voice, and then suddenly rose, and swept past her out of the saloon.

The girl did not see her again till Mrs. Milray came up on the promenade at the hour when people who have eaten too much breakfast begin to spoil their appetite for luncheon with the tea and bouillon of the deckstewards. She looked fiercely about, and saw Clementina seated in her usual place, but with Lord Lioncourt in her own chair next her husband, and Ewins on foot before her. They were both talking to Clementina, whom Lord Lioncourt was accusing of being in low spirits unworthy of her last night's triumphs. He jumped up, and offered his place, "I've got your chair, Mrs. Milray."

"Oh, no," she said, coldly, "I was just coming to look after Mr. Milray. But I see he's in good hands."

She turned away, as if to make the round of the deck, and Ewins hurried after her. He came back directly, and said that Mrs. Milray had gone into the library to write letters. He stayed, uneasily, trying to talk, but with the air of a man who has been snubbed, and has not got back his composure.

Lord Lioncourt talked on until he had used up the incidents of the night before, and the probabilities of their getting into Queenstown before morning; then he and Mr. Ewins went to the smoking-room together, and Clementina was left alone with Milray.

"Clementina," he said, gently, "I don't see everything; but isn't there some trouble between you and Mrs. Milray?"

"Why, I don't know what it can be," answered the girl, with trembling lips. "I've been trying to find out, and I can't undastand it."

"Ah, those things are often very obscure," said Milray, with a patient smile.

Clementina wanted to ask him if Mrs. Milray had said anything to him about her, but she could not, and he did not speak again till he heard her stir in rising from her chair. Then he said, "I haven't forgotten that letter to my sister, Clementina. I will give it to you before we leave the steamer. Are you going to stay in Liverpool, over night, or shall you go up to London at once?"

"I don't know. It will depend upon how Mrs. Landa feels."

"Well, we shall see each other again. Don't be worried." He looked up at her with a smile, and he could not see how forlornly she returned it.

As the day passed, Mrs. Milray's angry eyes seemed to search her out for scorn whenever Clementina found herself the centre of her last night's celebrity. Many people came up and spoke to her, at first with a certain expectation of knowingness in her, which her simplicity baffled. Then they either dropped her, and went away, or stayed and tried to make friends with her because of this; an elderly English clergyman and his wife were at first compassionately anxious about her, and then affectionately attentive to her in her obvious isolation. Clementina's simple-hearted response to their advances appeared to win while it puzzled them; and they seemed trying to divine her in the strange double character she wore to their more single civilization. The theatrical people thought none the worse of her for her simple-heartedness, apparently; they were both very sweet to her, and wanted her to promise to come and see them in their little box in St. John's Wood. Once, indeed, Clementina thought she saw relenting in Mrs. Milray's glance, but it hardened again as Lord Lioncourt and Mr. Ewins came up to her, and began to talk with her. She could not go to her chair beside Milray, for his wife was now keeping guard of him on the other side with unexampled devotion. Lord Lioncourt asked her to walk with him and she consented. She thought that Mr. Ewins would go and sit by Mrs. Milray, of course, but when she came round in her tour of the ship, Mrs. Milray was sitting alone beside her husband.

After dinner she went to the library and got a book, but she could not read there; every chair was taken by people writing letters to send back from Queenstown in the morning; and she strayed into the ladies' sitting room, where no ladies seemed ever to sit, and lost herself in a miserable muse over her open page.

Some one looked in at the door, and then advanced within and came straight to Clementina; she knew without looking up that it was Mrs. Milray. "I have been hunting for you, Miss Claxon," she said, in a voice frostily fierce, and with a bearing furiously formal. "I have a letter to Miss Milray that my husband wished me to write for you, and give you with his compliments."

"Thank you," said Clementina. She rose mechanically to her feet, and at the same time Mrs. Milray sat down.

"You will find Miss Milray," she continued, with the same glacial hauteur, "a very agreeable and cultivated lady."

Clementina said nothing; and Mrs. Milray added, "And I hope she may have the happiness of being more useful to you than I have."

"What do you mean, Mrs. Milray?" Clementina asked with unexpected spirit and courage.

"I mean simply this, that I have not succeeded in putting you on your guard against your love of admiration—especially the admiration of gentlemen. A young girl can't be too careful how she accepts the attentions of gentlemen, and if she seems to invite them"—

"Mrs. Milray!" cried Clementina. "How can you say such a thing to me?"

"How? I shall have to be plain with you, I see.

Perhaps I have not considered that, after all, you know nothing about life and are not to blame for things that a person born and bred *in* the world would understand from childhood. If you don't know already, I can tell you that the way you have behaved with Lord Lioncourt during the last two or three days, and the way you showed your pleasure the other night in his ridiculous flatteries of you, was enough to make you the talk of the whole steamer. I advise you for your own sake to take my warning in time. You are very young, and inexperienced and ignorant, but that will not save you in the eyes of the world if you keep on." Mrs. Milray rose. "And now I will leave you to think of what I have said. Here is the letter for Miss Milray"—

Clementina shook her head. "I don't want it."

"You don't *want* it? But I have written it at Mr. Milray's request, and I shall certainly leave it with you"—

"If you do," said Clementina, "I shall not take it!"

"And what shall I say to Mr. Milray?"

"What you have just said to me."

"What have I said to you?"

"That I'm a bold girl, and that I've tried to make men admi'a me."

Mrs. Milray stopped as if suddenly daunted by a fact that had not occurred to her before. "Did I say that?"

"The same as that."

"I didn't mean that—I—merely meant to put you

on your guard. It may be because you are so innocent yourself, that you can't imagine what others think, and—I did it out of my regard for you."

Clementina did not answer.

Mrs. Milray went on, "That was why I was so provoked with you. I think that for a young girl to stand up and dance alone before a whole steamer full of strangers"— Clementina looked at her without speaking, and Mrs. Milray hastened to say, "To be sure I advised you to do it, but I certainly was surprised that you should give an encore. But no matter, now. This letter"—

"I can't take it, Mrs. Milray," said Clementina, with a swelling heart.

"Now, listen!" urged Mrs. Milray. "You think I'm just saying it because, if you don't take it I shall have to tell Mr. Milray I was so hateful to you, you couldn't. Well, I *should* hate to tell him that; but that isn't the reason. There!" She tore the letter in pieces, and threw it on the floor. Clementina did not make any sign of seeing this, and Mrs. Milray dropped upon her chair again. "Oh, how hard you are! Can't you say something to me?"

Clementina did not lift her eyes. "I don't feel like saying anything just now."

Mrs. Milray was silent a moment. Then she sighed. "Well, you may hate me, but I shall always be your friend. What hotel are you going to in Liverpool?"

"I don't know," said Clementina.

"You had better come to the one where we go. I'm afraid Mrs. Lander won't know how to manage

"SHE TORE THE LETTER IN PIECES, AND THREW IT ON THE FLOOR."

very well, and we've been in Liverpool so often. May I speak to her about it?"

"If you want to," Clementina coldly assented.

"I see!" said Mrs. Milray. "You don't want to be under the same roof with me. Well, you needn't! But I'll tell you a good hotel: the one that the trains start out of; and I'll send you that letter for Miss Milray." Clementina was silent. "Well, I'll send it, anyway."

Mrs. Milray went away in sudden tears, but the girl remained dry-eyed.

XIX.

Mrs. Lander realized when the ship came to anchor in the stream at Liverpool that she had not been seasick a moment during the voyage. In the brisk cold of the winter morning, as they came ashore in the tug, she fancied a property of health in the European atmosphere, which she was sure would bring her right up, if she stayed long enough; and a regret that she had never tried it with Mr. Lander mingled with her new hopes for herself.

But Clementina looked with home-sick eyes at the strangeness of the alien scene: the pale, low heaven which seemed not to be clouded and yet was so dim; the flat shores with the little railroad trains running in and out over them; the grimy bulks of the city, and the shipping in the river, sparse and sombre after the gay forest of sails and stacks at New York.

She did not see the Milrays after she left the tug, in the rapid dispersal of the steamer's passengers. They both took leave of her at the dock, and Mrs. Milray whispered with penitence in her voice and eyes, "I will write," but the girl did not answer.

Before Mrs. Lander's trunks and her own were

passed, she saw Lord Lioncourt going away with his heavily laden man at his heels. Mr. Ewins came up to see if he could help her through the customs, but she believed that he had come at Mrs. Milray's bidding, and she thanked him so prohibitively that he could not insist. The English clergyman who had spoken to her the morning after the charity entertainment left his wife with Mrs. Lander, and came to her help, and then Mr. Ewins went his way.

The clergyman, who appeared to feel the friendlessness of the young girl and the old woman a charge laid upon him, bestowed a sort of fatherly protection upon them both. He advised them to stop at a hotel for a few hours and take the later train for London that he and his wife were going up by; they drove to the hotel together, where Mrs. Lander could not be kept from paying the omnibus, and made them have luncheon with her. She allowed the clergyman to get her tickets, and she could not believe that he had taken second class tickets for himself and his wife. She said that she had never heard of anyone travelling second class before, and she assured him that they never did it in America. She begged him to let her pay the difference, and bring his wife into her compartment, which the guard had reserved for her. She urged that the money was nothing to her, compared with the comfort of being with some one you knew; and the clergyman had to promise that as they should be neighbors, he would look in upon her, whenever the train stopped long enough.

Before it began to move, Clementina thought she

saw Lord Lioncourt hurrying past their carriage-window. At Rugby the clergyman appeared, but almost before he could speak, Lord Lioncourt's little red face showed at his elbow. He asked Clementina to present him to Mrs. Lander, who pressed him to get into her compartment; the clergyman vanished, and Lord Lioncourt yielded.

Mrs. Lander found him able to tell her the best way to get to Florence, whose situation he seemed to know perfectly; he confessed that he had been there rather often. He made out a little itinerary for going straight through by sleeping-car as soon as you crossed the Channel; she had said that she always liked a through train when she could get it, and the less stops the better. She bade Clementina take charge of the plan and not lose it; without it she did not see what they could do. She conceived of him as a friend of Clementina's, and she lost in the strange environment the shyness she had with most people. She told him how Mr. Lander had made his money, and from what beginnings he rose to be ignorant of what he really was worth when he died. She dwelt upon the diseases they had suffered, and at the thought of his death, so unnecessary in view of the good that the air was already doing her in Europe, she shed tears.

Lord Lioncourt was very polite, but there was no resumption of the ship's comradery in his manner. Clementina could not know how quickly this always drops from people who have been fellow-passengers; and she wondered if he were guarding himself from her because she had danced at the charity entertainment. The poison which Mrs. Milray had instilled worked in her thoughts while she could not help seeing how patient he was with all Mrs. Lander's questions; he answered them with a simplicity of his own, or laughed and put them by, when they were quite impossible. Many of them related to the comparative merits of English and American railroads, and what he thought himself of these. Mrs. Lander noted the difference of the English stations; but she did not see much in the landscape to examine him upon. She required him to tell her why the rooks they saw were not crows, and she was not satisfied that he should say the country seat she pointed out was a castle when it was plainly deficient in battlements. She based upon his immovable confidence in respect to it an inquiry into the structure of English society, and she made him tell her what a lord was, and a commoner, and how the royal family differed from both. She asked him how he came to be a lord, and when he said that it was a peerage of George the Third's creation, she remembered that George III. was the one we took up arms against. She found that Lord Lioncourt knew of our revolution generally, but was ignorant of such particulars as the Battle of Bunker Hill, and the Surrender of Cornwallis, as well as the throwing of the Tea into Boston Harbor; he was much struck by this incident, and said, And quite right, he was sure.

He told Clementina that her friends the Milrays had taken the steamer for London in the morning. He believed they were going to Egypt for the winter.

Cairo, he said, was great fun, and he advised Mrs. Lander, if she found Florence a bit dull, to push on there. She asked if it was an easy place to get to, and he assured her that it was very easy from Italy.

Mrs. Lander was again at home in her world of railroads and hotels; but she confessed, after he left them at the next station, that she should have felt more at home if he had been going on to London with them. She philosophized him to the disadvantage of her own countrymen as much less offish than a great many New York and Boston people. He had given her a good opinion of the whole English nation; and the clergyman, who had been so nice to them at Liverpool, confirmed her friendly impressions of England by getting her a small omnibus at the station in London before he got a cab for himself and his wife, and drove away to complete his own journey on another road. She celebrated the omnibus as if it were an effect of his goodness in her behalf. She admired its capacity for receiving all their trunks, and saving the trouble and delay of the express, which always vexed her so much in New York, and which had nearly failed in getting her baggage to the steamer in time.

The omnibus remained her chief association with London, for she decided to take the first through train for Italy in the morning. She wished to be settled, by which she meant placed in a Florentine hotel for the winter. That lord, as she now began and always continued to call Lioncourt, had first given her the name of the best little hotel in Florence, but as it had neither elevator nor furnace heat in it, he agreed in the end that it would not do for her, and mentioned the most modern and expensive house on the Lungarno. He told her he did not think she need telegraph for rooms; but she took this precaution before leaving London, and was able to secure them at a price which seemed to her quite as much as she would have had to pay for the same rooms at a first class hotel on the Back Bay.

The manager had reserved for her one of the best suites, which had just been vacated by a Russian princess. "I guess you better cable to your folks where you ah', Clementina," she said. "Because if you're satisfied, I am, and I presume we sha'n't want to change as long as we stay in Florence. My, but it's sightly!" She joined Clementina a moment at the windows looking upon the Arno, and the hills beyond it. "I guess you'll spend most of your time settin' at this winder, and I sha'n't blame you."

They had arrived late in the dull, soft winter afternoon. The landlord led the way himself to their apartment, and asked if they would have fire; a *facchino* came in and kindled roaring blazes on the hearths; at the same time a servant lighted all the candles on the tables and mantels. They both gracefully accepted the fees that Mrs. Lander made Clementina give them; the facchino kissed the girl's hand. "My!" said Mrs. Lander. "I guess you never had your hand kissed before."

The hotel developed advantages which, if not those she was used to, were still advantages. The halls were warmed by a furnace, and she came to like the little logs burning in her rooms. In the care of her own fire, she went back to the simple time of her life in the country, and chose to kindle it herself when it died out, with the fagots of broom that blazed up so briskly.

In the first days of her stay she made inquiry for the best American doctor in Florence; and she found him so intelligent that she at once put her liver in his charge, with a history of her diseases and symptoms of every kind. She told him that she was sure that he could have cured Mr. Lander, if he had only had him in time; she exacted a new prescription from him for herself, and made him order some quinine pills for Clementina against the event of her feeling debilitated by the air of Florence.

XX.

In these first days a letter came to Clementina from Mrs. Lander's banker, enclosing the introduction which Mrs. Milray had promised to her sister-in-law. It was from Mr. Milray, as before, and it was in Mrs. Milray's handwriting; but no message from her came with it. To Clementina it explained itself, but she had to explain it to Mrs. Lander. She had to tell her of Mrs. Milray's behavior after the entertainment on the steamer, and Mrs. Lander said that Clementina had done just exactly right; and they both decided, against some impulses of curiosity in Clementina's heart, that she should not make use of the introduction.

The Hotel des Financières was mainly frequented by rich Americans full of ready money, and by rich Russians of large credit. Better Americans and worse, went, like the English, to smaller and cheaper hotels; and Clementina's acquaintance was confined to mothers as shy and ungrammatical as Mrs. Lander herself, and daughters blankly indifferent to her. Mrs. Lander drove out every day when it did not rain, and she took Clementina with her, because the doctor said it would do them both good; but otherwise the girl remained pent in their apartment. The doctor found her a teacher, and she kept on with her French, and began to take lessons in Italian; she spoke with no one but her teacher, except when the doctor came. At the *table d'hôte* she heard talk of the things that people seemed to come to Florence for: pictures, statues, palaces, famous places; and it made her ashamed of not knowing about them. But she could not go to see these things alone, and Mrs. Lander, in the content she felt with all her circumstances, seemed not to suppose that Clementina could care for anything but the comfort of the hotel and the doctor's visits. When the girl began to get letters from home in answer to the first she had written back, boasting how beautiful Florence was, they assumed that she was very gay, and demanded full accounts of her pleasures. Her brother Jim gave something of the village news, but he said he supposed that she would not care for that, and she would probably be too proud to speak to them when she came home. The Richlings had called in to share the family satisfaction in Clementina's first experiences, and Mrs. Richling wrote her very sweetly of their happiness in them. She charged her from the rector not to forget any chance of self-improvement in the allurements of society, but to make the most of her rare opportunities. She said that they had got a guide-book to Florence, with a plan of the city, and were following her in the expeditions they decided she must be making every day; they were reading up the Florentine history in Sismondi's Italian Republics, and she bade Clementina be sure and see all the scenes of Savonarola's martyrdom, so that they could talk them over together when she returned.

Clementina wondered what Mrs. Richling would think if she told her that all she knew of Florence was what she overheard in the talk of the girls in the hotel, who spoke before her of their dances and afternoon teas, and evenings at the opera, and drives in the Cascine, and parties to Fiesole, as if she were not by.

The days and weeks passed, until Carnival was half gone, and Mrs. Lander noticed one day that Clementina appeared dull. "You don't seem to get much acquainted?" she suggested.

"Oh, the'e's plenty of time," said Clementina.

"I wish the'e was somebody you could go round with, and see the place. Shouldn't you like to see the place?" Mrs. Lander pursued.

"There's no hurry about it, Mrs. Lander. It will stay as long as we do."

Mrs. Lander was thoughtfully silent. Then she said, "I declare, I've got half a mind to make you send that letta to Miss Milray, after all. What difference if Mrs. Milray *did* act so ugly to you? *He* never did, and she's *his* sista."

"Oh, I don't want to send it, Mrs. Landa; you mustn't ask me to. I shall get along," said Clementina. The recognition of her forlornness deepened it, but she was cheerfuller, for no reason, the next morning; and that afternoon, the doctor unexpectedly came upon a call which he made haste to say was not professional.

"I've just come from another patient of mine, and I promised to ask if you had not crossed on the same ship with a brother of hers,—Mr. Milray."

Clementina and Mrs. Lander looked guiltily at each other. "I guess we did," Mrs. Lander owned at last, with a reluctant sigh.

"Then, she says you have a letter for her."

The doctor spoke to both, but his looks confessed that he was not ignorant of the fact when Mrs. Lander admitted, "Well Clementina, he'e, has."

"She wants to know why you haven't delivered it," the doctor blurted out.

Mrs. Lander looked at Clementina. "I guess she ha'n't quite got round to it yet, have you, Clementina?"

The doctor put in: "Well, Miss Milray is rather a dangerous person to keep waiting. If you don't deliver it pretty soon, I shouldn't be surprised if she came to get it." Dr. Welwright was a young man in the early thirties, with a laugh that a great many ladies said had done more than any one thing for them, and he now prescribed it for Clementina. But it did not seem to help her in the trouble her face betrayed.

Mrs. Lander took the word, "Well, I wouldn't say it to everybody. But you're our doctor, and I guess you won't mind it. We don't like the way Mrs. Milray acted to Clementina, in the ship, and we don't want to be beholden to any of her folks. I don't know as Clementina wants me to tell you just what it was, and I won't; but that's the long and sho't of it."

"I'm sorry," the doctor said. "I've never met Mrs. Milray, but Miss Milray has such a pleasant house, and likes to get young people about her. There are a good many young people in your hotel, though, and I suppose you all have a very good time here together." He ended by speaking to Clementina, and now he said he had done his errand, and must be going.

When he was gone, Mrs. Lander faltered, "I don't know but what we made a mistake, Clementina."

"It's too late to worry about it now," said the girl.

"We ha'n't bound to stay in Florence," said Mrs. Lander, thoughtfully. "I only took the rooms by the week, and we can go, any time, Clementina, if you are uncomf'table bein' here on Miss Milray's account. We could go to Rome; they say Rome's a nice place; or to Egypt."

"Mrs. Milray's in Egypt," Clementina suggested.

"That's true," Mrs. Lander admitted, with a sigh. After a while she went on, "I don't know as we've got any right to keep the letter. It *belongs* to her, don't it?"

"I guess it belongs to me, as much as it does to her," said Clementina. "If it's *to her*, it's *for me*. I am not going to send it, Mrs. Landa."

They were still in this conclusion when early in the following afternoon Miss Milray's cards were brought up for Mrs. Lander and Miss Claxon.

"Well, I decla'e!" cried Mrs. Lander. "That

docta must have gone straight and told her what we said."

"He had no right to," said Clementina, but neither of them was displeased, and after it was over, Mrs. Lander said that any one would have thought the call was for her, instead of Clementina, from the way Miss Milray kept talking to her. She formed a high opinion of her; and Miss Milray put Clementina in mind of Mr. Milray; she had the same hair of chiseled silver, and the same smile; she moved like him, and talked like him; but with a greater liveliness. She asked fondly after him, and made Clementina tell her if he seemed quite well, and in good spirits; she was civilly interested in Mrs. Milray's health. At the embarrassment which showed itself in the girl, she laughed and said, "Don't imagine I don't know all about it, Miss Claxon! My sister-in-law has owned up very handsomely; she isn't half bad, as the English say, and I think she likes owning up if she can do it safely."

"And you don't think," asked Mrs. Lander, "that Clementina done wrong to dance that way?"

Clementina blushed, and Miss Milray laughed again. "If you'll let Miss Claxon come to a little party I'm giving she may do her dance at my house; but she sha'n't be obliged to do it, or anything she doesn't like. Don't say she hasn't a gown ready, or something of that kind! You don't know the resources of Florence, and how the dress makers here doat upon doing impossible things in no time at all, and being ready before they promise. If you'll put Miss Claxon in my hands, I'll see that she's dressed for my dance. I live out on one of the hills over there, that you see from your windows"—she nodded toward them—"in a beautiful villa, too cold for winter, and too hot for summer, but I think Miss Claxon can endure its discomfort for a day, if you can spare her, and she will consent to leave you to the tender mercies of your maid, and"—

Miss Milray paused at the kind of unresponsive blank to which she found herself talking, and put up her lorgnette, to glance from Mrs. Lander to Clementina. The girl said, with embarrassment, "I don't think I ought to leave Mrs. Landa, just now. She isn't very well, and I shouldn't like to leave her alone."

"But we're just as much obliged to you as if she could come," Mrs. Lander interrupted; "and later on, maybe she can. You see, we ha'n't got any maid, *yit*. Well, we *did* have one at Woodlake, but she made us do so many things for her, that we thought we should like to do a few things for ouaselves, awhile."

If Miss Milray perhaps did not conceive the situation, exactly, she said, Oh, they were quite right in that; but she might count upon Miss Claxon for her dance, might not she; and might not she do anything in her power for them? She rose to go, but Mrs. Lander took her at her word, so far as to say, Why, yes, if she could tell Clementina the best place to get a dress she guessed the child would be glad enough to come to the dance.

"Tell her!" Miss Milray cried. "I'll *take* her! Put on your hat, my dear," she said to Clementina, "and come with me now. My carriage is at your door."

Clementina looked at Mrs. Lander, who said, "Go, of cou'se, child. I wish I could go, too."

"Do come, too," Miss Milray entreated.

"No, no," said Mrs. Lander, flattered. "I a'n't feeling very well, to-day. I guess I'm better off at home. But don't you hurry back on my account, Clementina." While the girl was gone to put on her hat she talked on about her. "She's the best gul in the wo'ld, and she won't be one of the poorest; and I shall feel that I'm doin' just what Mr. Landa would have wanted I should. He picked her out himself, moa than three yea's ago, when we was drivin' past her house at Middlemount, and it was to humor him afta he was gone, moa than anything else, that I took her. Well, she wa'n't so very easy to *git*, either, I can tell you." She cut short her history of the affair to say when Clementina came back, "I want you should do the odderin' yourself, Miss Milray, and not let her scrimp with the money. She wants to git some visitin' cahds; and if you miss anything about her that she'd ought to have, or that any otha young lady's got, won't you just git it for her?"

XXI.

As soon as she imagined the case, Miss Milray set herself to overcome Mrs. Lander's reluctance from a maid. She prevailed with her to try the Italian woman whom she sent her, and in a day the genial Maddalena had effaced the whole tradition of the bleak Ellida. It was not essential to the understanding which instantly established itself between them that they should have any language in common. They babbled at each other, Mrs. Lander in her Bostonized Yankee, and Maddalena in her gutteral Florentine, and Mrs. Lander was flattered to find how well she knew Italian.

Miss Milray had begun being nice to Clementina in fealty to her brother, who so seldom made any proof of her devotion to him, and to whom she had remained passionately true through his shady past. She was eager to humor his whim for the little country girl who had taken his fancy, because it was his whim, and not because she had any hopes that Clementina would justify it. She had made Dr. Welwright tell her all he knew about her, and his report of her grace and beauty had piqued her curiosity; his account of the forlorn dullness of her life with Mrs. Lander in their hotel had touched her heart. But she was still skeptical when she went to get her letter of introduction; when she brought Clementina home from the dressmaker's she asked if she might kiss her, and said she was already in love with her.

Her love might have made her wish to do everything for her that she now began to do, but it simplified the situation to account for her to the world as the ward of Mrs. Lander, who was as rich as she was vulgar, and it was with Clementina in this character that Miss Milray began to make the round of afternoon teas, and inspired invitations for her at pleasant houses, by giving a young ladies' lunch for her at her own. Before the night of her little dance, she had lost any misgiving she had felt at first, in the delight of seeing Clementina take the world as if she had thought it would always behave as amiably as that, and as if she had forgotten her unkind experiences to the contrary. She knew from Mrs. Lander how the girls at their hotel had left her out, but Miss Milray could not see that Clementina met them with rancor, when her authority brought them together. If the child was humiliated by her past in the gross lonely luxury of Mrs. Lander's life or the unconscious poverty of her own home, she did not show it in the presence of the world that now opened its arms to her. She remained so tranquil in the midst of all the novel differences, that it made her friend feel rather vulgar in her anxieties for her, and it was not always enough to find that she had not gone wrong simply because she had held still, and had the gift of waiting for things to happen. Sometimes when Miss Milray had almost decided that her passivity was the calm of a savage, she betrayed so sweet and grateful a sense of all that was done for her, that her benefactress decided that she was not rustic, but was sylvan in a way of her own, and not so much ignorant as innocent. She discovered that she was not ignorant even of books, but with no literary effect from them she had transmitted her reading into the substance of her native gentleness, and had both ideas and convictions. When Clementina most affected her as an untried wilderness in the conventional things she most felt her equality to any social fortune that might befall her, and then she would have liked to see her married to a title, and taking the glory of this world with an unconsciousness that experience would never wholly penetrate. But then again she felt that this would be somehow a profanation, and she wanted to pack her up and get her back to Middlemount before anything of the kind should happen. She gave Milray these impressions of Clementina in the letter she wrote to thank him for her, and to scold him for sending the girl to her. She accused him of wishing to get off on her a riddle which he could not read himself; but she owned that the charm of Clementina's mystery was worth a thousand times the fatigue of trying to guess her out and that she was more and more infatuated with her every day.

In the meantime, Miss Milray's little dance grew upon her till it became a very large one that filled her villa to overflowing when the time came for it. She lived on one of the fine avenues of the Oltrarno region, laid out in the brief period of prosperity which Florence enjoyed as the capital of Italy. The villa was built at that time, and it was much newer than the house on Seventeenth street in New York, where she spent the girlhood that had since prolonged itself beyond middle life with her. She had first lived abroad in the Paris of the Second Empire, and she had been one winter in Rome, but she had settled definitely in Florence before London became an American colony, so that her friends were chiefly Americans, though she had a wide international acquaintance. Perhaps her habit of taking her brother's part, when he was a black sheep, inclined her to mercy with people who had not been so blameless in their morals as they were in their minds and manners. She exacted that they should be interesting and agreeable, and not too threadbare; but if they had something that decently buttoned over the frayed places, she did not frown upon their poverty. Bohemians of all kinds liked her; Philistines liked her too; and in such a place as Florence, where the Philistines themselves are a little Bohemian, she might be said to be very popular. You met persons whom you did not quite wish to meet at her house, but if these did not meet you there, it was your loss.

On the night of the dance the line of private carriages, remises and cabs, lined the Viale Ariosto for a mile up and down before her gates, where young artists of both sexes arrived on foot. By this time her passion for Clementina was at its height. She had Maddalena bring her out early in the evening, and made her dress under her own eye and her French maid's, while Maddalena went back to comfort Mrs. Lander.

"I hated to leave her," said Clementina. "I don't believe she's very well."

"Isn't she always ill?" demanded Miss Milray. She embraced the girl again, as if once were not enough. "Clementina, if Mrs. Lander won't give you to me, I'm going to steal you. Do you know what I want you to do to-night? I want you to stand up with me, and receive, till the dancing begins, as if it were your coming-out. I mean to introduce everybody to you. You'll be easily the prettiest girl, there, and you'll have the nicest gown, and I don't mean that any of your charms shall be thrown away. You won't be frightened?"

"No, I don't believe I shall," said Clementina. "You can tell me what to do."

The dress she wore was of pale green, like the light seen in thin woods; out of it shone her white shoulders, and her young face, as if rising through the verdurous light. The artists, to a man and woman, wished to paint her, and severally told her so, during the evening which lasted till morning. She was not surprised when Lord Lioncourt appeared, toward midnight, and astonished Miss Milray by claiming acquaintance with Clementina. He asked about Mrs. Lander, and whether she had got to Florence without losing the way; he laughed but he seemed really to care. He took Clementina out to supper, when the time came; and she would have topped him by half a head as she leaned on his arm, if she had not considerately drooped and trailed a little after him.

She could not know what a triumph he was making for her; and it was merely part of the magic of the time that Mr. Ewins should come in presently with one of the ladies. He had arrived in Florence that day, and had to be brought unasked. He put on the effect of an old friend with her; but Clementina's curiosity was chiefly taken with a tall American, whom she thought very handsome. His light yellow hair was brushed smooth across his forehead like a well-behaving boy's; he was dressed like the other men, but he seemed not quite happy in his evening coat, and his gloves which he smote together uneasily from time to time. He appeared to think that somehow the radiant Clementina would know how he felt; he did not dance, and he professed to have found himself at the party by a species of accident. He told her that he was out in Europe looking after a patent right that he had just taken hold of, and was having only a middling good time. He pretended surprise to hear her say that she was having a first-rate time, and he tried to reason her out of it. He confessed that from the moment he came into the room he had made up his mind to take her to supper, and had never been so disgusted in his life as when he saw that little lord toddling off with her, and trying to look as large as life. He asked her what a lord was like, anyway, and he made her laugh all the time.

He told her his name, G. W. Hinkle, and asked whether she would be likely to remember it if they ever met again.

Another man who interested her very much was a young Russian, with curling hair and neat, small features who spoke better English than she did, and said he was going to be a writer, but had not yet decided whether to write in Russian or French; she supposed he had wanted her advice, but he did not wait for it, or seem to expect it. He was very much in earnest, while he fanned her, and his earnestness amused her as much as the American's irony. He asked which city of America she came from, and when she said none, he asked which part of America. She answered New England, and he said, "Oh, yes, that is where they have the conscience." She did not know what he meant, and he put before her the ideal of New England girlhood which he had evolved from reading American novels. "Are you like that?" he demanded.

She laughed, and said, "Not a bit," and asked him if he had ever met such an American girl, and he said, frankly, No; the American girls were all mercenary, and cared for nothing but money, or marrying titles. He added that he had a title, but he would not wear it.

Clementina said she did not believe she cared for titles, and then he said, "But you care for money." She denied it, but as if she had confessed it, he went on: "The only American that I have seen with that conscience was a man. I will tell you of him, if you wish."

He did not wait for her answer. "It was in Naples—at Pompeii. I saw at the first glance that he was different from other Americans, and I resolved to know him. He was there in company with a stupid boy, whose tutor he was; and he told me that he was studying to be a minister of the Protestant church. Next year he will go home to be consecrated. He promised to pass through Florence in the spring, and he will keep his word. Every act, every word, every thought of his is regulated by conscience. It is terrible, but it is beautiful." All the time, the Russian was fanning Clementina, with every outward appearance of flirtation. "Will you dance again? No? I should like to draw such a character as his in a romance."

XXII.

It was six o'clock in the morning before Miss Milray sent Clementina home in her carriage. She would have kept her to breakfast, but Clementina said she ought to go on Mrs. Lander's account, and she wished to go on her own.

She thought she would steal to bed without waking her, but she was stopped by the sound of groans when she entered their apartment; the light gushed from Mrs. Lander's door. Maddalena came out, and blessed the name of her Latin deity (so much more familiar and approachable than the Anglo-Saxon divinity) that Clementina had come at last, and poured upon her the story of a night of suffering for Mrs. Lander. Through her story came the sound of Mrs. Lander's voice plaintively reproachful, summoning Clementina to her bedside. "Oh, how could you go away and leave me? I've been in such misery the whole night long, and the docta didn't do a thing for me. I'm puffectly wohn out, and I couldn't make my wants known with that Italian crazy-head. If it hadn't been for the portyary comin' in and interpretin', when the docta left, I don't know what I should have done. I want you should give him a twenty-leary note just as quick as you see him; and oh, isn't the docta comin'?"

Clementina set about helping Maddalena put the room, which was in an impassioned disorder, to rights; and she made Mrs. Lander a cup of her own tea, which she had brought from S. S. Pierce's in passing through Boston; it was the first thing, the sufferer said, that had saved her life. Clementina comforted her, and promised her that the doctor should be there very soon; and before Mrs. Lander fell away to sleep, she was so far out of danger as to be able to ask how Clementina had enjoyed herself, and to be glad that she had such a good time.

The doctor would not wake her when he came; he said that she had been through a pretty sharp gastric attack, which would not recur, if she ate less of the most unwholesome things she could get, and went more into the air, and walked a little. He did not seem alarmed, and he made Clementina tell him about the dance, which he had been called from to Mrs. Lander's bed of pain. He joked her for not having missed him; in the midst of their fun, she caught herself in the act of yawning, and the doctor laughed, and went away.

Maddalena had to call her, just before dinner, when Mrs. Lander had been awake long enough to have sent for the doctor to explain the sort of *gone* feeling which she was now the victim of. It proved, when he came, to be hunger, and he prescribed tea and toast and a small bit of steak. Before he came she had wished to arrange for going home at once, and dying in her own country. But his opinion so far prevailed with her that she consented not to telegraph for berths. "I presume," she said, "it'll do, any time before the icebugs begin to run. But I d' know, afta this, Clementina, as I can let you leave me quite as you be'n doin'. There was a lot of flowas come for you, this aftanoon, but I made Maddalena put 'em on the balcony, for I don't want you should get poisoned with 'em in your sleep; I always hea'd they was dangerous in a person's bed room. I d' know as they are, eitha."

Maddalena seemed to know that Mrs. Lander was speaking of the flowers. She got them and gave them to Clementina, who found they were from some of the men she had danced with. Mr. Hinkle had sent a vast bunch of violets, which presently began to give out their sweetness in the warmth of the room, and the odor brought him before her with his yellow hair, scrupulously parted at the side, and smoothly brushed, showing his forehead very high up. Most of the gentlemen wore their hair parted in the middle, or falling in a fringe over their brows; the Russian's was too curly to part, and Lord Lioncourt had none except at the sides.

She laughed, and Mrs. Lander said, "Tell about it, Clementina," and she began with Mr. Hinkle, and kept coming back to him from the others. Mrs. Lander wished most to know how that lord had got down to Florence; and Clementina told her that he had said he was coming to see her.

"Well, I hope to goodness he won't come to-day, *I* a'n't fit to see anybody."

"Oh, I guess he won't come till to-morrow," said Clementina; she repeated some of the compliments she had got, and she told of all Miss Milray's kindness to her, but Mrs. Lander said, "Well, the next time, I'll thank her not to keep you so late." She was astonished to hear that Mr. Ewins was there, and "Any of the nasty things out of the hotel the'e?" she asked.

"Yes," Clementina said, "the'e we'e, and some of them we'e very nice. They wanted to know if I wouldn't join them, and have an aftanoon of our own here in the hotel, so that people could come to us all at once."

She went back to the party, and described the rest of it. When she came to the part about the Russian, she told what he had said of American girls being fond of money, and wanting to marry foreign noblemen.

Mrs. Lander said, "Well, I hope you a'n't a going to get married in a hurry, anyway, and when you do I hope you'll pick out a nice American."

"Oh, yes," said Clementina.

Mrs. Lander had their dinner brought to their apartment. She cheered up, and she was in some danger of eating too much, but with Clementina's help she denied herself. Their short evening was one of the gayest; Clementina declared she was not the least sleepy, but she went to bed at nine, and slept till nine the next day.

Mrs. Lander, the doctor confessed, the second morning, was more shaken up by her little attack than he had expected; but she decided to see the gentleman who had asked to call on Clementina. Lord Lioncourt did not come quite so soon as she was afraid he might, and when he came he talked mostly to Clementina. He did not get to Mrs. Lander until just before he was going. She hospitably asked him what his hurry was, and then he said that he was off for Rome, that evening at seven. He was nice about hoping she was comfortable in the hotel, and he sympathized with her in her wish that there was a set-bowl in her room; she told him that she always tried to have one, and he agreed that it must be very convenient where any one was, as she said, sick so much.

Mr. Hinkle came a day later; and then it appeared that he had a mother whose complaints almost exactly matched Mrs. Lander's. He had her photograph with him, and showed it; he said if you had no wife to carry round a photograph of, you had better carry your mother's; and Mrs. Lander praised him for being a good son. A good son, she added, always made a good husband; and he said that was just what he told the young ladies himself, but it did not seem to make much impression on them. He kept Clementina laughing; and he pretended that he was going to bring a diagram of his patent right for her to see, because she would be interested in a gleaner like that; and he said he wished her father could see it, for it would be sure to interest the kind of man Mrs. Lander described him to be. "I'll be along up there just about the time you get home, Miss Clementina. *When* did you say it would be?"

"I don't know; pretty ea'ly in the spring, I guess."

She looked at Mrs. Lander, who said, "Well, it depends upon how I git up my health. I couldn't bea' the voyage now."

Mr. Hinkle said, "No, best look out for your health, if it takes all summer. I shouldn't want you to hurry on my account. Your time is my time. All I want is for Miss Clementina, here, to personally conduct me to her father. If I could get him to take hold of my gleaner in New England, we could make the blueberry crop worth twice what it is."

Mrs. Lander perceived that he was joking; and she asked what he wanted to run away for when the young Russian's card came up. He said, "Oh, give every man a chance," and he promised that he would look in every few days, and see how she was getting along. He opened the door after he had gone out, and put his head in to say in confidence to Mrs. Lander, but so loud that Clementina could hear, "I suppose she's told you who the belle of the ball was, the other night? Went out to supper with a lord!" He seemed to think a lord was such a good joke that if you mentioned one you had to laugh.

The Russian's card bore the name Baron Belsky, with the baron crossed out in pencil, and he began to attack in Mrs. Lander the demerits of the American character, as he had divined them. He instructed her that her countrymen existed chiefly to make money; that they were more shopkeepers than the English and worse snobs; that their women were trivial and their men sordid; that their ambition was to unite their families with the European aristocracies; and their doctrine of liberty and equality was a shameless hypocrisy. This followed hard upon her asking, as she did very promptly, why he had scratched out the title on his card. He told her that he wished to be known solely as an artist, and he had to explain to her that he was not a painter, but was going to be a novelist. She taxed him with never having been in America, but he contended that as all America came to Europe he had the materials for a study of the national character at hand, without the trouble of crossing the ocean. In return she told him that she had not been the least sea-sick during the voyage, and that it was no trouble at all; then he abruptly left her and went over to beg a cup of tea from Clementina, who sat behind the kettle by the window.

"I have heard this morning from that American I met in Pompeii" he began. "He is coming northward, and I am going down to meet him in Rome."

Mrs. Lander caught the word, and called across the room, "Why, a'n't that whe'e that lo'd's gone?"

Clementina said yes, and while the kettle boiled, she asked if Baron Belsky were going soon.

"Oh, in a week or ten days, perhaps. I shall know when he arrives. Then I shall go. We write to each other every day." He drew a letter from his breast pocket. "This will give you the idea of his character," and he read, "If we believe that the hand of God directs all our actions, how can we set up our theories of conduct against what we feel to be his inspiration ?"

"What do you think of that ?" he demanded.

"I don't believe that God directs our wrong actions," said Clementina.

"How! Is there anything outside of God ?"

"I don't know whether there is or not. But there is something that tempts me to do wrong, sometimes, and I don't believe that is God."

The Russian seemed struck. "I will write that to him!"

"No," said Clementina, "I don't want you to say anything about me to him."

"No, no!" said Baron Belsky, waving his hand reassuringly. "I would not mention your name!"

Mr. Ewins came in, and the Russian said he must go. Mrs. Lander tried to detain him, too, as she had tried to keep Mr. Hinkle, but he was inexorable. Mr. Ewins looked at the door when it had closed upon him. Mrs. Lander said, "That is one of the gentlemen that Clementina met the otha night at the dance. He is a baron, but he scratches it out. You'd ought to hea'd him go on about Americans."

"Yes," said Mr. Ewins coldly. "He's at our hotel, and he airs his peculiar opinions at the table d'hôte pretty freely. He's a revolutionist of some kind, I fancy." He pronounced the epithet with an abhorrence befitting the citizen of a state born of revolution and a city that had cradled the revolt. "He's a Nihilist, I believe."

Mrs. Lander wished to know what that was, and he explained that it was a Russian who wanted to overthrow the Czar, and set up a government of the people, when they were not prepared for liberty.

"Then, maybe he isn't a baron at all," said Mrs. Lander.

"Oh, I believe he has a right to his title," Ewins answered. "It's a German one."

He said he thought that sort of man was all the more mischievous on account of his sincerity. He instanced a Russian whom a friend of his knew in Berlin, a man of rank like this fellow: he got to brooding upon the condition of working people and that kind of thing, till he renounced his title and fortune and went to work in an iron foundry.

Mr. Ewins also spoke critically of Mrs. Milray. He had met her in Egypt; but you soon exhausted the interest of that kind of woman. He professed a great concern that Clementina should see Florence in just the right way, and he offered his services in showing her the place.

The Russian came the next day, and almost daily after that, in the interest with which Clementina's novel difference from other American girls seemed to inspire him. His imagination had transmuted her simple Yankee facts into something appreciable to a Slav of his temperament. He conceived of her as the daughter of a peasant, whose beauty had charmed the widow of a rich citizen, and who was to inherit the wealth of her adoptive mother. He imagined that the adoption had taken place at a much earlier period than the time when Clementina's visit to Mrs. Lander actually began, and that all which could be done had been done to efface her real character by indulgence and luxury.

His curiosity concerning her childhood, her home, her father and mother, her brothers and sisters, and his misunderstanding of everything she told him, amused her. But she liked him, and she tried to give him some notion of the things he wished so much to know. It always ended in a dissatisfaction, more or less vehement, with the outcome of American conditions as he conceived them.

"But you," he urged one day, "you who are a daughter of the fields and woods, why should you forsake that pure life, and come to waste yourself here?"

"Why, don't you think it's very nice in Florence?" she asked, with eyes of innocent interest.

"Nice! Nice! Do we live for what is nice? Is it enough that you have what you Americans call a nice time?"

Clementina reflected. "I wasn't doing much of anything at home, and I thought I might as well come with Mrs. Lander, if she wanted me so much." She thought in a certain way, that he was meddling with what was not his affair, but she believed that he was sincere in his zeal for the ideal life he wished her to lead, and there were some things she had heard about him that made her pity and respect him; his self-exile and his renunciation of home and country for his principles, whatever they were; she did not understand exactly. She would not have liked never being able to go back to Middlemount, or to be cut off from all her friends as this poor young Nihilist was, and she said, now, "I didn't expect that it was going to be anything but a visit, and I always supposed we should go back in the spring; but now Mrs. Lander is beginning to think she won't be well enough till fall."

"And why need you stay with her?"

"Because she's not very well," answered Clementina, and she smiled, a little triumphantly as well as tolerantly.

"She could hire nurses and doctors, all she wants with her money."

"I don't believe it would be the same thing, exactly, and what should I do if I went back?"

"Do? Teach! Uplift the lives about you."

"But you say it is better for people to live simply, and not read and think so much."

"Then labor in the fields with them."

Clementina laughed outright. "I guess if anyone saw me wo'king in the fields they would think I was a disgrace to the neighbahood."

Belsky gave her a stupified glare through his spectacles. "I cannot undertand you Americans."

"Well, you must come ova to America, then, Mr. Belsky"—he had asked her not to call him by his title—"and then you would."

"No, I could not endure the disappointment. You have the great opportunity of the earth. You could be equal and just, and simple and kind. There is nothing to hinder you. But all you try to do is to get more and more money."

"Now, that isn't faia, Mr. Belsky, and you know it."

"Well, then, you joke, joke—always joke. Like that Mr. Hinkle. He wants to make money with his patent of a gleaner, that will take the last grain of wheat from the poor, and he wants to joke—joke!'

Clementina said, "I won't let you say that about Mr. Hinkle. You don't know him, or you wouldn't. If he jokes, why shouldn't he?"

Belsky made a gesture of rejection. "Oh, you are an American, too."

She had not grown less American, certainly, since she had left home; even the little conformities to Europe that she practiced were traits of Americanism. Clementina was not becoming sophisticated, but perhaps she was becoming more conventionalized. The knowledge of good and evil in things that had all seemed indifferently good to her once, had crept upon her, and she distinguished in her actions. She sinned as little as any young lady in Florence against the superstitions of society; but though she would not now have done a skirt-dance before a shipful of people, she did not afflict herself about her past errors. She put on the world, but she wore it simply and in most matters unconsciously. Some things were imparted to her without her asking or wishing, and merely in virtue of her youth and impressionability. She took them from her environment without knowing it, and in this way she was coming by an English manner and an English tone; she was only the less American for being rather English without trying,

"BELSKY GAVE HER A STUPEFIED GLARE THROUGH HIS SPECTACLES."

when other Americans tried so hard. In the region of harsh nasals, Clementina had never spoken through her nose, and she was now as unaffected in these alien inflections as in the tender cooings which used to rouse the misgivings of her brother Jim. When she was with English people she employed them involuntarily, and when she was with Americans she measurably lost them, so that after half an hour with Mr. Hinkle, she had scarcely a trace of them, and with Mrs. Lander she always spoke with her native accent.

XXIII.

One Sunday night, toward the end of Lent, Mrs. Lander had another of her attacks; she now began to call them so as if she had established an ownership in them. It came on from her cumulative over-eating, again, but the doctor was not so smiling as he had been with regard to the first. Clementina had got ready to drive out to Miss Milray's for one of her Sunday teas, but she put off her things, and prepared to spend the night at Mrs. Lander's bedside. "Well, I should think you would want to," said the sufferer. "I'm goin' to do everything for you, and you'd ought to be willing to give up one of youa junketin's for me. I'm sure I don't know what you see in 'em, anyway."

"Oh, I *am* willing, Mrs. Lander; I'm glad I hadn't stahted before it began." Clementina busied herself with the pillows under Mrs. Lander's dishevelled head, and the bedclothes disordered by her throes, while Mrs. Lander went on.

"I don't see what's the use of so much gaddin', anyway. I don't see as anything comes of it, but just to get a passal of wo'thless fellas afta you that think you'a going to have money. There's such a thing as two sides to everything, and if the favas is goin' to be all on one side I guess there'd betta be a clear undastandin' about it. I think I got a right to a *little* attention, as well as them that ha'n't done anything; and if I'm goin' to be left alone he'e to die among strangers every time one of my attacks comes on"—

The doctor interposed, "I don't think you're going to have a very bad attack, this time, Mrs. Lander."

"Oh, thank you, thank you, docta! But you can undastand, can't you, how I shall want to have somebody around that can undastand a *little* English?"

The doctor said, "Oh yes. And Miss Claxon and I can understand a good deal, between us, and we're going to stay, and see how a little morphine behaves with you."

Mrs. Lander protested, "Oh, I can't bea' mo'phine, docta."

"Did you ever try it?" he asked, preparing his little instrument to imbibe the solution.

"No; but Mr. Landa did, and it 'most killed him; it made him sick."

"Well, you're about as sick as you can be, now, Mrs. Lander, and if you don't die of this pin-prick" —he pushed the needle-point under the skin of her massive fore-arm—"I guess you'll live through it."

She shrieked, but as the pain began to abate, she gathered courage, and broke forth joyfully. "Why, it's beautiful, a'n't it? I declare it wo'ks like a cha'm.

Well, I shall always keep mo'phine around after this, and when I feel one of these attacks comin' on"—

"Send for a physician, Mrs. Lander," said Dr. Welwright, "and he'll know what to do."

"I a'n't so sure of that," returned Mrs. Lander fondly. "He would if you was the one. I declare I believe I could get up and walk right off, I feel so well."

"That's good. If you'll take a walk day after to-morrow it will help you a great deal more."

"Well, I shall always say that you've saved my life, this time, doctor; and Clementina she's stood by, nobly; I'll say that for her." She twisted her big head round on the pillow to get sight of the girl. "I'm all right, now; and don't you mind what I said. It's just my misery talkin'; I don't know what I *did* say; I felt so bad. But I'm fustrate, now, and I believe I could drop off to sleep, this minute. Why don't you go to your tea? You can, just as well as not!"

"Oh, I don't want to go, now, Mrs. Lander; I'd ratha stay."

"But there a'n't any more danger now, is the'e, docta?" Mrs. Lander appealed.

"No. There wasn't any danger before. But when you're quite yourself, I want to have a little talk with you, Mrs. Lander, about your diet. We must look after that."

"Why, docta, that's what I do do, now. I eat all the healthy things I lay my hands on, don't I, Clementina? And ha'n't you always at me about it?"

Clementina did not answer, and the doctor laughed. "Well, I should like to know what more I could do!"

"Perhaps you could do less. We'll see about that. Better go to sleep, now, if you feel like it."

"Well, I will, if you'll make this silly child go to her tea. I s'pose she won't because I scolded her. She's an awful hand to lay anything up against you. You know you ah', Clementina! But I can say this, doctor: a betta child don't breathe, and I just couldn't live without her. Come he'e, Clementina, I want to kiss you once, before I go to sleep, so's to make su'a you don't bea' malice." She pulled Clementina down to kiss her, and babbled on affectionately and optimistically, till her talk became the voice of her dreams, and then ceased altogether.

"You *could* go, perfectly well, Miss Claxon," said the doctor.

"No, I don't ca'e to go," answered Clementina. "I'd ratha stay. If she should wake"—

"She won't wake, until long after you've got back; I'll answer for that. I'm going to stay here awhile. Go! I'll take the responsibility."

Clementina's face brightened. She wanted very much to go. She should meet some pleasant people; she always did, at Miss Milray's. Then the light died out of her gay eyes, and she set her lips. "No, I told her I shouldn't go."

"I didn't hear you," said Dr. Welwright. "A doctor has no eyes and ears except for the symptoms of his patients."

"Oh, I know," said Clementina. She had liked

Dr. Welwright from the first, and she thought it was very nice of him to stay on, after he left Mrs. Lander's bedside, and help to make her lonesome evening pass pleasantly in the parlor. He jumped up finally, and looked at his watch. "Bless my soul!" he said, and he went in for another look at Mrs. Lander. When he came back, he said, "She's all right. But you've made me break an engagement, Miss Claxon. I was going to tea at Miss Milray's. She promised me I should meet *you* there."

It seemed a great joke; and Clementina offered to carry his excuses to Miss Milray, when she went to make her own.

She went the next morning. Mrs. Lander insisted that she should go; she said that she was not going to have Miss Milray thinking that she wanted to keep her all to herself.

Miss Milray kissed the girl in full forgiveness, but she asked, "Did Dr. Welwright think it a very bad attack?"

"Has he been he'a?" returned Clementina.

Miss Milray laughed. "Doctors don't betray their patients—good doctors. No, he hasn't been here, if that will help you. I wish it would help me, but it won't, quite. I don't like to think of that old woman using you up, Clementina."

"Oh, she doesn't, Miss Milray. You mustn't think so. You don't know how good she is to me."

"Does she ever remind you of it?"

Clementina's eyes fell. "She isn't like herself when she doesn't feel well."

"I knew it!" Miss Milray triumphed. "I always knew that she was a dreadful old tabby. I wish you were safely out of her clutches. Come and live with me, my dear, when Mrs. Lander gets tired of you. But she'll never get tired of you. You're just the kind of helpless mouse that such an old tabby would make her natural prey. But she sha'n't, even if another sort of cat has to get you! I'm sorry you couldn't come last night. Your little Russian was here, and went away early and very bitterly because you didn't come. He seemed to think there was nobody, and said so, in everything but words."

"Oh!" said Clementina. "Don't you think he's very nice, Miss Milray?"

"He's very mystical, or else so very simple that he seems so. I hope you can make him out."

"Don't you think he's very much in ea'nest?"

"Oh, as the grave, or the asylum. I shouldn't like him to be in earnest about me, if I were you."

"But that's just what he is!" Clementina told how the Russian had lectured her, and wished her to go back to the country and work in the fields.

"Oh, if that's all!" cried Miss Milray. "I was afraid it was another kind of earnestness: the kind I shouldn't like if I were you."

"There's no danger of that, I guess." Clementina laughed, and Miss Milray went on:

"Another of your admirers was here; but he was not so inconsolable, or else he found consolation in staying on and talking about you, or joking."

"Oh, yes; Mr. Hinkle," cried Clementina with the

smile that the thought of him always brought. "He's lovely."

"Lovely? Well, I don't know why it isn't the word. It suits him a great deal better than some insipid girls that people give it to. Yes, I could really fall in love with Mr. Hinkle. He's the only man I ever saw who would know how to break the fall!"

It was lunch-time before their talk had begun to run low, and it swelled again over the meal. Miss Milray returned to Mrs. Lander, and she made Clementina confess that she was a little trying sometimes. But she insisted that she was always good, and in remorse she went away as soon as Miss Milray rose from table.

She found Mrs. Lander very much better, and willing to have had her stay the whole afternoon with Miss Milray. "I don't want she should have anything to say against me, to you, Clementina; she'd be glad enough to. But I guess it's just as well you'a back. That scratched-out baron has been he'e twice, and he's waitin' for you in the pahla', now. I presume he'll keep comin' till you do see him. I guess you betta have it ova; whatever it is."

"I guess you're right, Mrs. Lander."

Clementina found the Russian walking up and down the room, and as soon as their greeting was over, he asked leave to continue his promenade, but he stopped abruptly before her when she had sunk upon a sofa.

"I have come to tell you a strange story," he said.

"It is the story of that American friend of mine. I tell it to you because I think you can understand, and will know what to advise, what to do."

He turned upon his heel, and walked the length of the room and back before he spoke again.

"Since several years," he said, growing a little less idiomatic in his English as his excitement mounted, "he met a young girl, a child, when he was still not a man's full age. It was in the country, in the mountains of America, and—he loved her. Both were very poor; he, a student, earning the means to complete his education in the university. He had dedicated himself to his church, and with the temperament of the Puritans, he forbade himself all thoughts of love. But he was of a passionate and impulsive nature, and in a moment of abandon he confessed his love. The child was bewildered, frightened; she shrank from his avowal, and he, filled with remorse for his self-betrayal, bade her let it be as if it had not been; he bade her think of him no more."

Clementina sat as if powerless to move, staring at Belsky. He paused in his walk, and allowed an impressive silence to ensue upon his words.

"Time passed: days, months, years; and he did not see her again. He pursued his studies in the university; at their completion, he entered upon the course of divinity, and he is soon to be a minister of his church. In all that time the image of the young girl has remained in his heart, and has held him true to the only love he has ever known. He will know no other while he lives."

Again he stopped in front of Clementina; she looked helplessly up at him, and he resumed his walk.

"He, with his dreams of renunciation, of abnegation, had thought some day to return to her and ask her to be his. He believed her capable of equal sacrifice with himself, and he hoped to win her not for himself alone, but for the religion which he put before himself. He would have invited her to join her fate with his that they might go together on some mission to the pagan—in the South Seas, in the heart of Africa, in the jungle of India. He had always thought of her as gay but good, unworldly in soul, and exalted in spirit. She has remained with him a vision of angelic loveliness, as he had seen her last in the moonlight, on the banks of a mountain torrent. But he believes that he has disgraced himself before her; that the very scruple for her youth, her ignorance, which made him entreat her to forget him, must have made her doubt and despise him. He has never had the courage to write to her one word since all those years, but he maintains himself bound to her forever." He stopped short before Clementina and seized her hands. "If you knew such a girl, what would you have her do? Should she bid him hope again? Would you have her say to him that she, too, had been faithful to their dream, and that she too"—

"Let me go, Mr. Belsky, let me go, I say!" Clementina wrenched her hands from him, and ran out of the room. Belsky hesitated, then he found his hat, and after a glance at his face in the mirror, left the house.

XXIV.

The tide of travel began to set northward in April. Many English, many Americans appeared in Florence from Naples and Rome; many who had wintered in Florence went on to Venice and the towns of northern Italy, on their way to Switzerland and France and Germany.

The spring was cold and rainy, and the irresolute Italian railroads were interrupted by the floods. A tawny deluge rolled down from the mountains through the bed of the Arno, and kept the Florentine fire-department on the alert night and day. "It is a curious thing about this country," said Mr. Hinkle, encountering Baron Belsky on the Ponte Trinità, "that the only thing they ever have here for a fire company to put out is a freshet. If they had a real conflagration once, I reckon they would want to bring their life-preservers."

The Russian was looking down over the parapet at the boiling river. He lifted his head as if he had not heard the American, and stared at him a moment before he spoke. "It is said that the railway to Rome is broken at Grossetto."

"Well, *I'm* not going to Rome," said Hinkle, easily. "Are you?"

"I was to meet a friend there; but he wrote to me that he was starting to Florence, and now"—

"He's resting on the way? Well, he'll get here about as quick as he would in the ordinary course of travel. One good thing about Italy is, you don't *want* to hurry; if you did, you'd get left."

Belsky stared at him in the stupefaction to which the American humor commonly reduced him. "If he gets left on the Grossetto line, he can go back and come up by Orvieto, no?"

"He can, if he isn't in a hurry," Hinkle assented. "It's a good way, if you've got time to burn."

Belsky did not attempt to explore the American's meaning. "Do you know," he asked, "whether Mrs. Lander and her young friend are still in Florence?"

"I guess they are."

"It was said they were going to Venice for the summer."

"That's what the doctor advised for the old lady. But they don't start for a week or two yet."

"Oh!"

"Are you going to Miss Milray's, Sunday night? Last of the season, I believe."

Belsky seemed to recall himself from a distance. "No—no," he said, and he moved away, forgetful of the ceremonious salutation which he commonly used at meeting and parting. Hinkle looked after him with the impression people have of a difference in the appearance and behavior of some one whose appearance and behavior do not particularly concern them.

The day that followed, Belsky haunted the hotel where Gregory was to arrive with his pupil, and where the pupil's family were waiting for them. That night, long after their belated train was due, they came; the pupil was with his father and mother, and Gregory was alone, when Belsky asked for him, the fourth or fifth time.

"You are not well," he said, as they shook hands. "You are fevered!"

"I'm tired," said Gregory. "We've had a bad time getting through."

"I come inconveniently! You have not dined, perhaps?"

"Yes, yes. I've had dinner. Sit down. How have you been yourself?"

"Oh, always well." Belsky sat down, and the friends stared at each other. "I have strange news for you."

"For me?"

"You. *She* is here."

"She?"

"Yes. The young girl of whom you told me. If I had not forbidden myself by my loyalty to you—if I had not said to myself every moment in her presence, 'No, it is for your friend alone that she is beautiful and good!'—But you will have nothing to reproach me in that regard."

"What do you mean?" demanded Gregory.

"I mean that Miss Claxon is in Florence, with her protectress, the rich Mrs. Lander. The most admired young lady in society, going everywhere, and everywhere courted and welcomed; the favorite of the fashionable Miss Milray. But why should this surprise you?"

"You said nothing about it in your letters. You"—

"I was not sure it was she; you never told me her name. When I had divined the fact, I was so soon to see you, that I thought best to keep it till we met."

Gregory tried to speak, but he let Belsky go on.

"If you think that the world has spoiled her, that she will be different from what she was in her home among your mountains, let me reassure you. In her you will find the miracle of a woman whom no flattery can turn the head. I have watched her in your interest; I have tested her. She is what you saw her last."

"Surely," asked Gregory, in an anguish for what he now dreaded, "you haven't spoken to her of me?"

"Not by name, no. I could not have that indiscretion"—

"The name is nothing. Have you said that you knew me— Of course not! But have you hinted at any knowledge— Because"—

"You will hear!" said Belsky; and he poured out upon Gregory the story of what he had done. "She did not deny anything. She was greatly moved, but she did not refuse to let me bid you hope"—

"Oh!" Gregory took his head between his hands. "You have spoiled my life!"

"Spoiled!" Belsky stopped aghast.

"I told you my story in a moment of despicable weakness—of impulsive folly. But how could I dream that you would ever meet her? How could I imagine that you would speak to her as you have done?" He groaned, and began to creep giddily about the room in his misery. "Oh, oh, oh! *What* shall I do?"

"But I do not understand!" Belsky began. "If I have committed an error"—

"Oh, an error that never could be put right in all eternity!"

"Then let me go to her—let me tell her"—

"Keep away from her!" shouted Gregory. "Do you hear? Never go near her again!"

"Gregory!"

"Ah, I beg your pardon! I don't know what I'm doing—saying. What will she think—what will she think of *me!*" He had ceased to speak to Belsky; he collapsed into a chair, and hid his face in his arms stretched out on the table before him.

Belsky watched him in the stupefaction which the artistic nature feels when life proves sentient under its hand, and not the mere material of situations and effects. He could not conceive the full measure of the disaster he had wrought, the outrage of his own behavior had been lost to him in his preoccupation with the romantic end to be accomplished. He had meant to be the friend, the prophet, to these American lovers, whom he was reconciling and interpreting to each other; but in some point he must have misunderstood. Yet the error was not inexpiable; and in his expiation he could put the seal to his devotion. He left the room, where Gregory made no effort to keep him.

He walked down the street from the hotel to the Arno, and in a few moments he stood on the bridge, where he had talked with that joker in the morning, as they looked down together on the boiling river. He had a strange wish that the joker might have been with him again, to learn that there were some things which could not be joked away.

The night was blustering, and the wind that blew the ragged clouds across the face of the moon, swooped in sudden gusts upon the bridge, and the deluge rolling under it and hoarsely washing against its piers. Belsky leaned over the parapet and looked down into the eddies and currents as the fitful light revealed them. He had a fantastic pleasure in studying them, and choosing the moment when he should leap the parapet and be lost in them. The incident could not be used in any novel of his, and no one else could do such perfect justice to the situation, but perhaps afterwards, when the facts leading to his death should be known through the remorse of the lovers whom he had sought to serve, some other artist-nature could distil their subtlest meaning in a memoir delicate as the aroma of a faded flower.

He was willing to make this sacrifice, too, and he stepped back a pace from the parapet when the fitful blast caught his hat from his head, and whirled it along the bridge. The whole current of his purpose changed, and as if it had been impossible to drown himself in his bare head, he set out in chase of his hat, which rolled and gamboled away, and escaped from his clutch whenever he stooped for it, till a final whiff of wind flung it up and tossed it over the bridge into the river, where he helplessly watched it floating down the flood, till it was carried out of sight.

XXV.

Gregory did not sleep, and he did not find peace in the prayers he put up for guidance. He tried to think of some one with whom he might take counsel; but he knew no one in Florence except the parents of his pupil, and they were impossible. He felt himself abandoned to the impulse which he dreaded, in going to Clementina, and he went without hope, willing to suffer whatever penalty she should visit upon him, after he had disavowed Belsky's action, and claimed the responsibility for it.

He was prepared for her refusal to see him; he had imagined her wounded and pathetic; he had fancied her insulted and indignant; but she met him eagerly and with a mystifying appeal in her welcome. He began at once, without attempting to bridge the time since they had met with any formalities.

"I have come to speak to you about—that—Russian, about Baron Belsky"—

"Yes, yes!" she returned, anxiously. "Then you have hea'd"—

"He came to me last night, and—I want to say that I feel myself to blame for what he has done."

"*You?*"

"Yes; I. I never spoke of you by name to him; I didn't dream of his ever seeing you, or that he would dare to speak to you of what I told him. But I believe he meant no wrong; and it was I who did the harm, whether I authorized it or not."

"Yes, yes!" she returned, with the effect of putting his words aside as something of no moment. "Have they hea'd anything more?"

"How, anything more?" he returned, in a daze.

"Then, don't you know? About his falling into the river? I *know* he didn't drown himself."

Gregory shook his head. "When—what makes them think"— He stopped and stared at her.

"Why, they know that he went down to the Ponte Trinità last night; somebody saw him going. And then that peasant found his hat with his name in it in the drift-wood below the Cascine"—

"Yes," said Gregory, lifelessly. He let his arms drop forward, and his helpless hands hang over his knees; his gaze fell from her face to the floor.

Neither spoke for a time that seemed long, and then it was Clementina who spoke. "But it isn't true!"

"Oh, yes, it is," said Gregory, as before.

"Mr. Hinkle doesn't believe it is," she urged.

"Mr. Hinkle?"

"He's an American who's staying in Florence. He came this mo'ning to tell me about it. Even if he's drowned Mr. Hinkle believes he didn't mean to; he must have just fallen in."

"What does it matter?" demanded Gregory, lifting

his heavy eyes. "Whether he meant it or not, I caused it. I drove him to it."

"You drove him?"

"Yes. He told me what he had said to you, and I said that he had spoiled my life—I don't know!"

"Well, he had no right to do it; but I didn't blame you," Clementina began, compassionately.

"It's too late. It can't be helped now." Gregory turned from the mercy that could no longer save him. He rose dizzily, and tried to get himself away.

"You mustn't go!" she interposed. "I don't believe you made him do it. Mr. Hinkle will be back soon, and he will"—

"If he should bring word that it was true?" Gregory asked.

"Well," said Clementina, "then we should have to bear it."

A sense of something finer than the surface meaning of her words pierced his morbid egotism. "I'm ashamed," he said. "Will you let me stay?"

"Why, yes, you must," she said, and if there was any censure of him at the bottom of her heart, she kept it there, and tried to talk him away from his remorse, which was in his temperament, perhaps, rather than his conscience; she made the time pass till there came a knock at the door, and she opened it to Hinkle.

"I didn't send up my name; I thought I wouldn't stand upon ceremony just now," he said.

"Oh, no!" she returned. "Mr. Hinkle, this is Mr. Gregory. Mr. Gregory knew Mr. Belsky, and he thinks"—

She turned to Gregory for prompting, and he managed to say, "I don't believe he was quite the sort of person to— And yet he might—he was in trouble"—

"Money trouble?" asked Hinkle. "They say these Russians have a perfect genius for debt. I had a little inspiration, since I saw you, but there doesn't seem to be anything in it, so far." He addressed himself to Clementina, but he included Gregory in what he said. "It struck me that he might have been running his board, and had used this drowning episode as a blind. But I've been around to his hotel, and he's settled up, all fair and square enough. The landlord tried to think of something he hadn't paid, but he couldn't; and I never saw a man try harder, either." Clementina smiled; she put her hand to her mouth to keep from laughing; but Gregory frowned his distress in the untimely drolling.

"I don't give up my theory that it's a fake of some kind, though. He could leave behind a good many creditors besides his landlord. The authorities have sealed up his effects, and they've done everything but call out the fire department; that's on duty looking after the freshet, and it couldn't be spared. I'll go out now and slop round a little more in the cause,"—Hinkle looked down at his shoes and his drabbled trousers, and wiped the perspiration from his face,—"but I thought I'd drop in, and tell you not to worry about it, Miss Clementina. I would stake anything you pleased on Mr. Belsky's safety. Mr. Gregory, here, looks like he would be willing to take odds," he suggested.

Gregory commanded himself from his misery to say, "I wish I could believe—I mean"—

"Of course, we don't want to think that the man's a fraud, any more than that he's dead. Perhaps we might hit upon some middle course. At any rate, it's worth trying."

"May I—do you object to my joining you?" Gregory asked.

"Why, come!" Hinkle hospitably assented. "Glad to have you. I'll be back again, Miss Clementina!"

Gregory was going away without any form of leave-taking; but he turned back to ask, "Will you let me come back, too?"

"Why, suttainly, Mr. Gregory," said Clementina, and she went to find Mrs. Lander, whom she found in bed.

"I thought I'd lay down," she explained. "I don't believe I'm goin' to be sick, but it's one of my pooa days, and I might just as well be in bed as not." Clementina agreed with her, and Mrs. Lander asked: "You hea'd anything moa?"

"No. Mr. Hinkle has just been he'a, but he hadn't any news."

Mrs. Lander turned her face toward the wall. "Next thing, *he'll* be drownin' himself. I neva wanted you should have anything to do with the fellas that go to that woman's. There ain't any of 'em to be depended on."

It was the first time that her growing jealousy of Miss Milray had openly declared itself; but Clementina had felt it before, without knowing how to meet it. As an escape from it now she was almost willing to say, "Mrs. Lander, I want to tell you that Mr. Gregory has just been he'a, too."

"Mr. Gregory?"

"Yes. Don't you remember? At the Middlemount? The first summa? He was the headwaita —that student."

Mrs. Lander jerked her head round on the pillow. "Well, of all the—What does *he* want, over he'a?"

"Nothing. That is—he's travelling with a pupil that he's preparing for college, and—he came to see us"—

"D'you tell him *I* couldn't see him?"

"Yes"—

"I guess he'd think I was a pretty changed pusson! Now, I want you should stay with me, Clementina, and if anybody else comes"—

Maddalena entered the room with a card which she gave to the girl.

"Who is it?" Mrs. Lander demanded.

"Miss Milray."

"Of cou'se! Well, you may just send wo'd that you can't— Or, no; you must! She'd have it all ova the place, by night, that I wouldn't let you see her. But don't you make any excuse for *me!* If she asks after me, don't you say I'm sick! You say I'm not at home."

"I've come about that little wretch," Miss Milray began, after kissing Clementina. "I didn't know but you had heard something I hadn't, or I had heard something you hadn't. You know I belong to the

Hinkle persuasion: I think Belsky's run his board—as Mr. Hinkle calls it."

Clementina explained how this part of the Hinkle theory had failed, and then Miss Milray devolved upon the belief that he had run his tailor's bill or his shoemaker's. "They are delightful, those Russians, but they're born insolvent. I don't believe he's drowned himself. How," she broke off to ask, in a burlesque whisper, "is—the—old—tabby?" She laughed, for answer to her own question, and then with another sudden diversion she demanded of a look in Clementina's face which would not be laughed away, "Well, my dear, what is it?"

"Miss Milray," said the girl, "should you think me very silly, if I told you something—silly?"

"Not in the least!" cried Miss Milray, joyously. "It's the final proof of your wisdom that I've been waiting for?"

"It's because Mr. Belsky is all mixed up in it," said Clementina, as if some excuse were necessary, and then she told the story of her love affair with Gregory. Miss Milray punctuated the several facts with vivid nods, but at the end she did not ask her anything, and the girl somehow felt the freer to add: "I believe I will tell you his name. It is Mr. Gregory—Frank Gregory"—

"And he's been in Egypt?"

"Yes, the whole winta."

"Then he's the one that my sister-in-law has been writing me about!"

"Oh, did he meet her the'a?"

"I should think so! And he'll meet her *here*, very soon. She's coming, with my poor brother. I meant to tell you, but this ridiculous Belsky business drove it out of my head."

"And do you think," Clementina entreated, "that he was to blame?"

"Why, I don't believe he's done it, you know."

"Oh, I didn't mean Mr. Belsky. I meant—Mr. Gregory. For telling Mr. Belsky?"

"Certainly not. Men always tell those things to some one, I suppose. Nobody was to blame but Belsky, for his meddling."

Miss Milray rose and shook out her plumes for flight, as if she were rather eager for flight, but at the little sigh with which Clementina said, "Yes, that is what I thought," she faltered.

"I was going to run away, for I shouldn't like to mix myself up in your affair—it's certainly a very strange one—unless I was sure I could help you. But if you think I can"—

Clementina shook her head. "I don't believe you can," she said, with a candor so wistful that Miss Milray stopped quite short. "How does Mr. Gregory take this Belsky business?" she asked.

"I guess he feels it moa than I do," said the girl.

"He shows his feeling more?"

"Yes—no— He believes he drove him to it."

Miss Milray took her hand, for parting, but did not kiss her. "I won't advise you, my dear. In fact, you haven't asked me to. You'll know what to do, if you haven't done it already; girls usually have, when they want advice. Was there something you were going to say?"

"Oh, no. Nothing. Do you think," she hesitated, appealingly, "do you think we are—engaged?"

"If he's anything of a man at all, he must think *he* is."

"Yes," said Clementina, wistfully, "I guess he does."

Miss Milray looked sharply at her. "And does he think *you* are?"

"I don't know—he didn't say."

"Well," said Miss Milray, rather dryly, "then it's something for you to think over pretty carefully."

XXVI.

Hinkle came back in the afternoon to make a hopeful report of his failure to learn anything more of Belsky, but Gregory did not come with him. He came the next morning long before Clementina expected visitors, and he was walking nervously up and down the room when she appeared. As if he could not speak, he held toward her without speaking a telegram in English, dated that day in Rome:

"*Deny report of my death. Have written.*

"*Belsky.*"

She looked up at Gregory from the paper, when she had read it, with joyful eyes. "Oh, I am so glad for you! I am so glad he is alive."

He took the dispatch from her hand. "I brought it to you as soon as it came."

"Yes, yes! Of cou'se!"

"I must go now and do what he says— I don't know how yet." He stopped, and then went on from a different impulse. "Clementina, it isn't a question now of that wretch's life and death, and I wish I need never speak of him again. But what he told you was true." He looked steadfastly at her, and she realized how handsome he was, and how well dressed. His thick red hair seemed to have grown darker above his forehead; his moustache was heavier, and it curved in at the corners of his mouth; he bore himself with a sort of self-disdain that enhanced his splendor. "I have never changed toward you; I don't say it to make favor with you; I don't expect to do that now; but it is true. That night, there at Middlemount, I tried to take back what I said, because I believed that I ought."

"Oh, yes, I knew that," said Clementina, in the pause he made.

"We were both too young; I had no prospect in life; I saw, the instant after I had spoken, that I had no right to let you promise anything. I tried to forget you; I couldn't. I tried to make you forget me." He faltered, and she did not speak, but her head drooped a little. "I won't ask how far I succeeded. I always hoped that the time would come when I could speak to you again. When I heard from Fane that you were at Woodlake, I wished to come out and see you, but I hadn't the courage, I hadn't the right. I've had to come to you without either, now. Did he speak to you about me?"

"I thought he was beginning to, once; but he neva did."

"It didn't matter; it could only have made bad worse. It can't help me to say that somehow I was wishing and trying to do what was right; but I was."

"Oh, I know that, Mr. Gregory," said Clementina, generously.

"Then you didn't doubt me, in spite of all?"

"I thought you would know what to do. No, I didn't doubt you, exactly."

"I didn't deserve your trust!" he cried. "How came that man to mention me?" he demanded, abruptly, after a moment's silence.

"Mr. Belsky? It was the first night I saw him, and we were talking about Americans, and he began to tell me about an American friend of his, who was very conscientious. I thought it must be you the fust moment," said Clementina, smiling with an impersonal pleasure in the fact.

"From the conscientiousness?" he asked, in bitter self-irony.

"Why, yes," she returned, simply. "That was what made me think of you. And the last time when he began to talk about you, I couldn't stop him, although I knew he had no right to."

"He had no right. But I gave him the power to do it! He meant no harm, but I enabled him to do all the harm."

"Oh, if he's only alive, now, there *is* no harm!"

He looked into her eyes with a misgiving from which he burst impetuously. "Then you do care for me still, after all that I have done to make you detest me?" He started toward her, but she shrank back.

"I didn't mean that," she hesitated.

"You know that I love *you*,—that I have always loved you?"

"Yes," she assented. "But you might be sorry again that you had said it." It sounded like coquetry, but he knew it was not coquetry.

"Never! I've wished to say it again, ever since that night at Middlemount; I have always felt bound by what I said then, though I took back my words for your sake. But the promise was always there, and my life was in it. You believe that?"

"Why, I always believed what you said, Mr. Gregory."

"Well?"

Clementina paused, with her head seriously on one side. "I should want to think about it before I said anything."

"You are right," he submitted, dropping his outstretched arms to his side. "I have been thinking only of myself, as usual."

"No," she protested, compassionately. "But doesn't it seem as if we ought to be su'a, this time? I did ca'e for you then, but I was very young, and I don't know yet— I thought I had always felt just as you did, but now— Don't you think we had both betta wait a little while till we ah' moa suttain?"

They stood looking at each other, and he said, with a kind of passionate self-denial, "Yes, think it over for me, too. I will come back, if you will let me."

"Oh, thank you!" she cried after him, gratefully, as if his forbearance were the greatest favor.

When he was gone she tried to release herself from the kind of abeyance in which she seemed to have gone back and been as subject to him as in the first days when he had awed her and charmed her with his superiority at Middlemount, and be again older and freer as she had grown since.

He came back late in the afternoon, looking jaded and distraught. Hinkle, who looked neither, was with him. "Well," he began, "this is the greatest thing in my experience. Belsky's not only alive and well, but Mr. Gregory and I are both at large. I did think, one time, that the police would take us into custody on account of our morbid interest in the thing, and I don't believe we should have got off, if the Consul hadn't gone bail for us, so to speak. I thought we had better take the Consul in, on our way, and it was lucky we did."

Clementina did not understand all the implications, but she was willing to take Mr. Hinkle's fun on trust. "I don't believe you'll convince Mrs. Landa that Mr. Belsky's alive and well, till you bring him back to say so."

"Is that so!" said Hinkle. "Well, we must have him brought back by the authorities, then. Perhaps they'll bring him, anyway. They can't try him for suicide, but as I understand the police, here, a man can't lose his hat over a bridge in Florence with impunity, especially in a time of high water. Anyway, they're identifying Belsky by due process of law in Rome, now, and I guess Mr. Gregory"—he nodded toward Gregory, who sat silent and absent—"will be kept under surveillance till the whole mystery is cleared up."

Clementina responded gayly still, but with less and less sincerity, and she let Hinkle go at last with the feeling that he knew she wished him to go. He made a brave show of not seeing this, and when he was gone, she remembered that she had not thanked him for the trouble he had taken on her account, and her heart ached after him with a sense of his sweetness and goodness, which she had felt from the first through his quaint drolling. It was as if the door which closed upon him shut her out of the life she had been living of late, and into the life of the past where she was subject again to the spell of Gregory's mood; it was hardly his will.

He began at once: "I wished to make you say something this morning that I have no right to hear you say, yet; and I have been trying ever since to think how I could ask you whether you could share my life with me, and yet not ask you to do it. But I can't do anything without knowing— You may not care for what my life is to be, at all!"

Clementina's head drooped a little, but she answered distinctly, "I do ca'e, Mr. Gregory."

"Thank you for that much; I don't count upon more than you have said. Clementina, I am going to be a missionary. I think I shall ask to be sent to China; I've not decided yet. My life will be hard; it will be full of danger and privation; it will be exile. You will have to think of sharing such a life if you think"—

He stopped; the time had come for her to speak, and she said, "I knew you wanted to be a missionary."

"And—and—you would go with me? You would"—He started toward her, and she did not shrink from him, now; but he checked himself. "But you mustn't, you know, for *my* sake."

"'AND—AND—YOU WOULD GO WITH ME?'"

"I don't believe I quite undastand," she faltered.

"You must not do it for me, but for what makes me do it. Without that our life, our work, could have no consecration."

She gazed at him in patient, faintly smiling bewilderment, as if it were something he would unriddle for her when he chose.

"We mustn't err in this; it would be worse than error; it would be sin." He took a turn about the room, and then stopped before her. "Will you—will you join me in a prayer for guidance, Clementina?"

"I—I don't know," she hesitated. "I will, but—do you think I had betta?"

He began, "Why, surely"— After a moment he asked gravely, "You believe that our actions will be guided aright, if we seek help?"

"Oh, yes—yes"—

"And that if we do not, we shall stumble in our ignorance?"

"I don't know. I never thought of that."

"Never thought of it?"

"We never did it in our family. Father always said that if we really wanted to do right we could find the way." Gregory looked daunted, and then he frowned darkly. "Are you provoked with me? Do you think what I have said is wrong?"

"No, no! You must say what you believe. It would be double hypocrisy in me if I prevented you."

"But I would do it, if you wanted me to," she said.

"Oh, for me, for *me!*" he protested. "I will try to tell you what I mean, and why you must not, for that very reason." But he had to speak of himself, of the miracle of finding her again by the means which should have lost her to him forever; and of the significance of this. Then it appeared to him that he could not reject such a leading without error, without sin. "Such a thing could not have merely happened."

It seemed so to Clementina, too; she eagerly consented that this was something they must think of, as well. But the light waned, the dark thickened in the room before he left her to do so. Then he said fervently, "We must not doubt that everything will come right," and his words seemed an effect of inspiration to them both.

XXVII.

After Gregory was gone a misgiving began in Clementina's mind, which grew more distinct, through all the difficulties of accounting to Mrs. Lander for his long stay. The girl could see that it was with an obscure jealousy that she pushed her questions, and said at last, "That Mr. Hinkle is about the best of the lot. He's the only one that's eva had the mannas to ask after me, except that lo'd. *He* did."

Clementina could not pretend that Gregory had asked, but she could not blame him for a forgetfulness of Mrs. Lander which she had shared with him. This helped somehow to deepen the misgiving which followed her from Mrs. Lander's bed to her own, and haunted her far into the night. She could escape from it only by promising herself to deal with it the first thing in the morning. She did this in terms much briefer than she thought she could have commanded. She supposed she would have to write a very long letter, but she came to the end of all she need say, in a very few lines.

"Dear Mr. Gregory:

"I have been thinking about what you said yesterday, and I have to tell you something. Then you can do what is right for both of us; you will know better than I can. But I want you to understand that if I go with you in your missionary life, I shall do it *for you*, and not for anything else. I would go anywhere and live anyhow for you, but it would be *for you;* I do not believe that I am religious, and I know that *I should not do it for religion.*

"That is all; but I could not get any peace till I let you know just how I felt.

"CLEMENTINA CLAXON."

The letter went early in the morning, though not so early but it was put in Gregory's hand as he was leaving his hotel to go to Mrs. Lander's. He tore it open, and read it on the way, and for the first moment it seemed as if it were Providence leading him that he might lighten Clementina's heart of its doubts with the least delay. He had reasoned that if she would share for his sake the life that he should live for righteousness' sake they would be equally blest in it, and it would be equally consecrated in both. But this luminous conclusion faded in his thought as he hurried on, and he found himself in her presence with something like a hope that she would be inspired to help him.

His soul lifted at the sound of the gay voice in which she asked, "Did you get my letta?" and it seemed for the instant as if there could be no trouble that their love could not overcome.

"Yes," he said, and he put his arms around her, but with a provisionality in his embrace which she subtly perceived.

"And what did you think of it?" she asked. "Did you think I was silly?"

He was aware that she had trusted him to do away her misgiving. "No, no," he answered, guiltily. "Wiser than I am, always. I—I want to talk with you about it, Clementina. I want *you* to advise *me*."

He felt her shrink from him, and with a pang he opened his arms to free her. But it was right; he must. She had been expecting him to say that there was nothing in her misgiving, and he could not say it.

"Clementina," he entreated, "why do you think you are not religious?"

"Why, I have never belonged to chu'ch," she answered simply. He looked so daunted, that she tried to soften the blow after she had dealt it. "Of course, I always *went* to chu'ch, though father and motha didn't. I went to the Episcopal—to Mr. Richling's. But I neva was confirmed."

"But—you believe in God?"

"Why, certainly!"

"And in the Bible?"

"Why, of cou'se!"

"And that it is our duty to bear the truth to those who have never heard of it?"

"I know that is the way you feel about it; but I am not certain that I should feel so myself if you didn't want me to. That's what I got to thinking about last night." She added hopefully, "But perhaps it isn't so great a thing as I"—

"It's a very great thing," he said, and from standing in front of her, he now sat down beyond a little table before her sofa. "How can I ask you to share my life if you don't share my faith?"

"Why, I should try to believe everything that you do, of cou'se."

"Because I do?"

"Well—yes."

"You wring my heart! Are you willing to study—to look into these questions—to—to"— It all seemed very hopeless, very absurd, but she answered seriously:

"Yes, but I believe it would all come back to just where it is, now."

"What you say, Clementina, makes me so happy; but it ought to make me—miserable! And you would do all this, be all this for *me*, a wretched and erring creature of the dust, and yet not do it for—God?"

Clementina could only say, "Perhaps if He meant me to do it for Him, He would have made me want to. He made you."

"Yes," said Gregory, and for a long time he could not say any more. He sat with his elbow on the table, and his head against his lifted hand.

"You see," she began, gently, "I got to thinking that even if I eva came to believe what you wanted me to, I should be doing it after all, because you wanted me to"—

"Yes, yes," he answered, desolately. "There is no way out of it. If you only hated me, Clementina, despised me—I don't mean that. But if you were not so good, I could have more hope for you—for myself. It's because you are so good that I can't make myself wish to change you, and yet I know—I am afraid that if you told me my life and objects were wrong, I should turn from them, and be whatever you said. Do you tell me that?"

"*No*, indeed!" cried Clementina, with abhorrence. "Then I *should* despise you."

He seemed not to heed her. He moved his lips as if he were talking to himself, and he pleaded, "What shall we do?"

"We must try to think it out, and if we can't—if you can't let me give up to you unless I do it for the same reason that you do; and if I can't let you give up for me, and I know I could neva do that; then—we mustn't!"

"Do you mean, we must part? Not see each other again?"

"What use would it be?"

"None," he owned. She had risen, and he stood up perforce. "May I—may I come back to tell you?"

"Tell me what?" she asked.

"You are right! If I can't make it right, I won't come. But I won't say good bye. I—can't."

She let him go, and Maddalena came in at the door. "Signorina," she said, "the signora is not well. Shall I send for the doctor?"

"Yes, yes, Maddalena. Run!" cried Clementina, distractedly. She hurried to Mrs. Lander's room, where she found her too sick for reproaches, for anything but appeals for help and pity. The girl had not to wait for Doctor Welwright's coming to understand that the attack was severer than any before.

It lasted through the day, and she could see that he was troubled. It had not followed upon any imprudence, as Mrs. Lander pathetically called Clementina to witness when her pain had been so far quelled that she could talk of her seizure.

He found her greatly weakened by it the next day, and he sat looking thoughtfully at her before he said that she needed toning up. She caught at the notion. "Yes, yes! That's what I need, docta! Toning up! That's what I need."

He suggested, "How would you like to try the sea-air, and the baths—at Venice?"

"Oh, anything, anywhere, to get out of this dreadful hole! I ha'n't had a well minute since I came. And Clementina," the sick woman whimpered, "is so taken up all the time, he'a, that I can't get the right attention."

The doctor looked compassionately away from the girl, and said, "Well, we must arrange about getting you off, then."

"But I want you should go with me, doctor, and see me settled all right. You can, can't you? I sha'n't ca'e how much it costs?"

The doctor said gravely he thought he could manage it and he ignored the long unconscious sigh of relief that Clementina drew.

In all her confusing anxieties for Mrs. Lander, Gregory remained at the bottom of her heart a dumb ache. When the pressure of her fears was taken from her she began to suffer for him consciously· then a letter came from him:

"I cannot make it right. It is where it was, and I feel that I must not see you again. I am trying to do right, but with the fear that I am wrong. Send some word to help me before I go away to-morrow.
F. G."

It was what she had expected, she knew now, but it was none the less to be borne because of her expectation. She wrote back:

"I believe you are doing the best you can, and I shall always believe that. C. C."

Her note brought back a long letter from him. He said that whatever he did, or wherever he went, he should try to be true to her ideal of him. If they renounced their love now for the sake of what seemed higher than their love, they might suffer, but they could not choose but do as they were doing.

Clementina was trying to make what she could of this when Miss Milray's name came up, and Miss Milray followed it.

"I wanted to ask after Mrs. Lander, and I want you to tell her I did. Will you? Dr. Welwright says he's going to take her to Venice. Well, I'm sorry—sorry for your going, Clementina, and I'm truly sorry for the cause of it. I shall miss you, my dear, I shall indeed. You know I always wanted to steal you, but you'll do me the justice to say I never did, and I won't try, now."

"Perhaps I wasn't worth stealing," Clementina suggested, with a ruefulness in her smile that went to Miss Milray's heart.

She put her arms round her and kissed her. "I wasn't very kind to you, the other day, Clementina, was I?"

"I don't know," Clementina faltered, with half averted face.

"Yes, you do! I was trying to make-believe that I didn't want to meddle with your affairs; but I was really vexed that you hadn't told me your story before. It hasn't taken me all this time to reflect that you couldn't, but it has to make myself come and confess that I had been dry and cold with you." She hesitated. "It's come out all right, hasn't it, Clementina?" she asked, tenderly. "You see I *want* to meddle, now."

"We ah' trying to think so," sighed the girl.

"Tell me about it!" Miss Milray pulled her down on the sofa with her, and modified her embrace to a clasp of Clementina's hands.

"Why, there isn't much to tell," she began, but she told what there was, and Miss Milray kept her countenance concerning the scruple that had parted Clementina and her lover. "Perhaps he wouldn't have thought of it," she said, in a final self-reproach, "if I hadn't put it into his head."

"Well, then, I'm not sorry you put it into his head," cried Miss Milray. "Clementina, may I say what *I* think of Mr. Gregory's performance?"

"Why, certainly, Miss Milray!"

"I think he's not merely a gloomy little bigot, but a very hard-hearted little wretch, and I'm glad you're rid of him. No, stop! Let me go on! You said I might!" she persisted, at a protest which imparted itself from Clementina's restive hands. "It was selfish and cruel of him to let you believe that he had forgotten you. It doesn't make it right now, when an accident has forced him to tell you that he cared for you all along."

"Why, do you look at it that way, Miss Milray? If he was doing it on my account"—

"He may *think* he was doing it on your account, but *I* think he was doing it on his own. In such a thing as that, a man is bound by his mistakes, if he has made any. He can't go back of them by simply ignoring them. It didn't make it the same for you when he decided for your sake that he would act as if he had never spoken to you."

"I presume he thought that it would come right, sometime," Clementina urged. "I did."

"Yes, that was very well for you, but it wasn't at all well for him. He behaved cruelly; there's no other word for it."

"I don't believe he meant to be cruel, Miss Milray," said Clementina.

"You're not sorry you've broken with him?" demanded Miss Milray, severely, and she let go of Clementina's hands.

"I shouldn't want him to think I hadn't been fai'a."

"I don't understand what you mean by not being fair," said Miss Milray, after a study of the girl's eyes.

"I mean," Clementina explained, "that if I let him

think the religion was all the'e was, it wouldn't have been fai'a."

"Why, weren't you sincere about that?"

"Of cou'se I was!" returned the girl, almost indignantly. "But if the'e was anything else, I ought to have told him that, too; and I couldn't."

"Then you can't tell me, of course?" Miss Milray rose in a little pique.

"Perhaps some day I will," the girl entreated. "And perhaps that *was* all."

Miss Milray laughed. "Well, if that was enough to end it, I'm satisfied, and I'll let you keep your mystery—if it is one—till we meet in Venice; I shall be there early in June. Good bye, dear, and say good bye to Mrs. Lander for me."

XXVIII.

Dr. Welwright got his patient a lodging on the Grand Canal in Venice, and decided to stay long enough to note the first effect of the air and the baths, and to look up a doctor to leave her with.

This took something more than a week, which could not all be spent in Mrs. Lander's company, much as she wished it. There were hours which he gave to going about in a gondola with Clementina, whom he forbade to be always at the invalid's side. He tried to reassure her as to Mrs. Lander's health, when he found her rather mute and absent, while they drifted in the silvery sun of the late April weather, just beginning to be warm, but not warm enough yet for the tent of the open gondola. He asked her about Mrs. Lander's family, and Clementina could only tell him that she had always said she had none. She told him the story of her own relation to her, and he said, "Yes, I heard something of that from Miss Milray." After a moment of silence, during which he looked curiously into the girl's eyes, "Do you think you can bear a little more care, Miss Claxon?"

"I think I can," said Clementina, not very courageously, but patiently.

"It's only this, and I wouldn't tell you if I hadn't thought you equal to it. Mrs. Lander's case puzzles me. But I shall leave Dr. Tradonico watching it, and if it takes the turn that there's a chance it *may* take, he will tell you, and you'd better find out about her friends, and—let them know. That's all."

"Yes," said Clementina, as if it were not quite enough. Perhaps she did not fully realize all that the doctor had intended; life alone is credible to the young; life and the expectation of it.

The night before he was to return to Florence there was a full moon; and when he had got Mrs. Lander to sleep he asked Clementina if she would not go out on the lagoon with him. He assigned no peculiar virtue to the moonlight, and he had no new charge to give her concerning his patient when they were embarked. He seemed to wish her to talk about herself, and when she strayed from the topic, he prompted her return. Then he wished to know how she liked Florence, as compared with Venice, and all the other cities she had seen, and when she said she had not seen any but Boston and New York, and London for one night, he wished to know whether she liked Florence as well. She said she liked it best of all, and he told her he was very glad, for he liked it himself better than any place he had ever seen. He spoke of his family in America, which was formed of grown-up brothers and sisters, so that he had none of the closest and tenderest ties obliging him to return;

there was no reason why he should not spend all his days in Florence, except for some brief visits home. It would be another thing with such a place as Venice; he could never have the same settled feeling there: it was beautiful, but it was unreal; it would be like spending one's life at the opera. Did not she think so?

She thought so, oh, yes; she never could have the home-feeling at Venice that she had at Florence.

"Exactly; that's what I meant—a home-feeling; I'm glad you had it." He let the gondola dip and slide forward almost a minute before he added, with an effect of pulling a voice up out of his throat somewhere, "How would you like to live there—with me—as my wife?"

"Why, what do you mean, Dr. Welwright?" asked Clementina, with a vague laugh.

Dr. Welwright laughed, too; but not vaguely; there was a mounting cheerfulness in his laugh. "What I say. I hope it isn't very surprising."

"No; but I never thought of such a thing."

"Perhaps you will think of it now."

"But you're not in ea'nest!"

"I'm thoroughly in earnest," said the doctor, and he seemed very much amused at her incredulity.

"Then, I'm sorry," she answered. "I couldn't."

"No?" he said, still with amusement, or with a courage that took that form. "Why not?"

"Because I am—not free."

For an interval they were so silent that they could hear each other breathe. Then, after he had quietly bidden the gondolier go back to their hotel, he asked, "If you had been free you might have answered me differently?"

"I don't know," said Clementina, candidly. "I never thought of it."

"It isn't because you disliked me?"

"Oh, *no!*"

"Then I must get what comfort I can out of that. I hope, with all my heart, that you may be happy."

"Why, Dr. Welwright!" said Clementina. "Don't you suppose that I should be glad to do it, if I could? Any one would!"

"It doesn't seem very probable, just now," he answered, humbly. "But I'll believe it if you say so."

"I do say so, and I always shall."

"Thank you."

Dr. Welwright professed himself ready for his departure, at breakfast next morning and he must have made his preparations very late or very early. He was explicit in his charges to Clementina concerning Mrs. Lander, and at the end of them, he said, "She will not know when she is asking too much of you, but you will, and you must act upon your knowledge. And remember, if you are in need of help, of any kind, you're to let me know. Will you?"

"Yes, I will, Dr. Welwright."

"People will be going away soon, and I shall not be so busy. I can come back if Dr. Tradonico thinks it necessary."

He left Mrs. Lander full of resolutions to look after her own welfare in every way, and she went out in her gondola the same morning. She was not only to take the air as much as possible, but she was to amuse herself, and she decided that she would have her second breakfast at the Caffé Florian. Venice was beginning to fill up with arrivals from the south, and it need not have been so surprising to find Mr. Hinkle there over a cup of coffee. He said he had just that moment been thinking of her, and meaning to look her up at the hotel. He said that he had stopped at Venice because it was such a splendid place to introduce his gleaner; he invited Mrs. Lander to become a partner in the enterprise; he promised her a return of fifty per cent. on her investment. If he could once introduce his gleaner in Venice, he should be a made man. He asked Mrs. Lander, with real feeling, how she was; as for Miss Clementina, he need not ask.

"Oh, indeed, the docta thinks she wants a little lookin' after, too," said Mrs. Lander.

"Well, about as much as you do, Mrs. Lander," Hinkle allowed, tolerantly. "I don't know how it affects you, ma'am, such a meeting of friends in these strange waters, but it's building *me* right *up*. It's made another man of me, already, and I've got the other man's appetite, too. Mind my letting him have his breakfast here with me at your table?" He bade the waiter just fetch his plate. He attached himself to them; he spent the day with them. Mrs. Lander asked him to dinner at her lodgings, and left him to Clementina over the coffee.

"She's looking fine, doesn't the doctor think? This air will do everything for her."

"Oh, yes; she's a great deal betta than she was befo'e we came."

"That's right. Well, now, you've got me here, you must let me make myself useful any way I can. I've got a spare month that I can put in here in Venice, just as well as not; I sha'n't want to push north till the frost's out of the ground. They wouldn't have a chance to try my gleaner, on the other side of the Alps much before September, anyway. Now, in Ohio, the part I come from, we cut our wheat in June. When is your wheat harvest at Middlemount?"

Clementina laughed. "I don't believe we've got any. I guess it's all grass."

"I wish you could see our country out there, once."

"Is it nice?"

"Nice? We're right in the centre of the state, measuring from north to south, on the old National Road." Clementina had never heard of this road, but she did not say so. "About five miles back from the Ohio River, where the coal comes up out of the ground, because there's so much of it there's no room for it below. Our farm's in a valley, along a creek bottom, what you Yankees call an intervale; we've got three hundred acres. My grandfather took up the land, and then he went back to Pennsylvania to get the girl he'd left there—we were Pennsylvania Dutch; that's where I got my romantic name—they drove all the way out to Ohio again in his buggy, and when he came in sight of our valley with his bride, he stood up in his buggy and pointed with his whip. 'There! As far as the sky is blue, it's all *ours!*'"

Clementina owned the charm of his story as he seemed to expect, but when he said, "Yes, I want you to see that country, some day," she answered cautiously.

"It must be lovely. But I don't expect to go West, eva."

"I like your Eastern way of saying everr," said Hinkle, and he said it in his Western way. "I like New England folks."

Clementina smiled discreetly. "They have their faults like everybody else, I presume."

"Ah, that's a regular Yankee word: presume," said Hinkle. "Our teacher, my first one, always said presume. She was from your State, too."

XXIX.

In the time of provisional quiet that followed for Clementina, she was held from the remorses and misgivings that had troubled her before Hinkle came. She still thought that she had let Dr. Welwright go away believing that she had not cared enough for the offér which had surprised her so much, and she blamed herself for not telling him how doubly bound she was to Gregory; though when she tried to put her sense of this in words to herself she could not make out that she was any more bound to him than she had been before they met in Florence, unless she wished to be so. Yet somehow in this time of respite, neither the regret for Dr. Welwright nor the question of Gregory persisted very strongly, and there were whole days when she realized before she slept that she had not thought of either.

She was in full favor again with Mrs. Lander, whom there was no one to embitter in her jealous affection. Hinkle formed their whole social world, and Mrs. Lander made the most of him. She was always having him to the dinners which her landlord served her from a restaurant in her apartment, and taking him out with Clementina in her gondola. He came into a kind of authority with them both which was as involuntary with him as with them, and was like an effect of his constant wish to be doing something for them.

One morning when they were all going out in Mrs. Lander's gondola, she sent Clementina back three times to their rooms for outer garments of differing density. When she brought the last Mrs. Lander frowned.

"This won't do. I've got to have something else—something lighter and warma."

"I can't go back any moa, Mrs. Landa," cried the girl, from the exasperation of her own nerves.

"Then I will go back myself," said Mrs. Lander with dignity, "and we sha'n't need the gondoler any more this mo'ning," she added, "unless you and Mr. Hinkle wants to ride."

She got ponderously out of the boat with the help of the gondolier's elbow, and marched into the house again, while Clementina followed her. She did not offer to help her up the stairs; Hinkle had to do it, and he met the girl slowly coming up as he returned from delivering Mrs. Lander over to Maddalena.

"She's all right, now," he ventured to say, tentatively.

"Is she?" Clementina coldly answered.

In spite of her repellant air, he persisted, "She's a pretty sick woman, isn't she?"

"The docta doesn't say."

"Well, I think it would be safe to act on that supposition. Miss Clementina—I think she wants to see you."

"I'm going to her directly."

Hinkle paused, rather daunted. "She wants me to go for the doctor."

"She's always wanting the docta." Clementina lifted her eyes and looked very coldly at him.

"If I were you I'd go up right away," he said, boldly.

She felt that she ought to resent his interference, but the mild entreaty of his pale blue eyes, or the elder-brotherly injunction of his smile, forbade her. "Did she ask for me?"

"No."

"I'll go to her," she said, and she kept herself from smiling at the long sigh of relief he gave as she passed him on the stairs.

Mrs. Lander began as soon as she entered her room, "Well, I was just wonderin' if you was goin' to leave me here all day alone, while you staid down the'e, carryin' on with that simpleton. I don't know what's got into the men."

"Mr. Hinkle has gone for the docta," said Clementina, trying to get into her voice the kindness she was trying to feel.

"Well, if I have one of my attacks, now, you'll have yourself to thank for it."

By the time Dr. Tradonico appeared Mrs. Lander was so much better that in her revulsion of feeling she was all day rather tryingly affectionate in her indirect appeals for Clementina's sympathy.

"I don't want you should mind what I say, when I a'n't feelin' just right," she began that evening, after she had gone to bed, and Clementina sat looking out of the open window, on the moonlit lagoon.

"Oh, no," the girl answered, wearily.

Mrs. Lander humbled herself farther. "I'm real sorry I plagued you so, to-day, and I know Mr. Hinkle thought I was dreadful, but I couldn't help it. I should like to talk with you, Clementina, about something that's worryin' me, if you a'n't busy."

"I'm not busy, now, Mrs. Lander," said Clementina, a little coldly, and relaxing the clasp of her hands; to knit her fingers together had been her sole business, and she put even this away.

She did not come nearer the bed, and Mrs. Lander was obliged to speak without the advantage of noting the effect of her words upon her in her face. "It's like this: What am I agoin' to do for them relations of Mr. Landa's out in Michigan?"

"I don't know. What relations?"

"I told you about 'em: the only ones he's got: his half-sista's children. He neva saw 'em, and he neva wanted to; but they're his kin, and it was *his* money. It don't seem right to pass 'em ova. Do you think it would yourself, Clementina?"

"Why, of cou'se not, Mrs. Lander. It wouldn't be right at all."

Mrs. Lander looked relieved, and she said, as if a little surprised, "I'm glad you feel that way; I should feel just so, myself. I mean to do by you just what I always said I should. I sha'n't forget you, but whe'e the'e's so much I got to thinkin' the'e'd ought to some of it go to his folks, whetha he ca'ed for 'em or not. It's worried me some, and I guess if anything it's that that's made me wo'se lately."

"Why Mrs. Landa," said the girl, "why don't you give it all to them?"

"You don't know what you'a talkin' about," said Mrs. Lander, severely. "I guess if I give 'em five thousand or so amongst 'em, it's full moa than they eva thought of havin', and it's moa than they got any right to. Well, that's all right, then; and we don't need to talk about it any moa. Yes," she resumed, after a moment, "that's what I shall do. I ha'n't eva felt just satisfied with that last will I got made, and I guess I shall tear it up, and get the fust American lawyer that comes along to make me a new one. The prop'ty's all goin' to you, but I guess I shall leave five thousand apiece to the two families out the'e. You won't miss it, any, and I presume it's what Mr. Landa would expect I should do; though why he didn't do it himself, I can't undastand, unless it was to show his confidence in me."

She began to ask Clementina how she felt about staying in Venice all summer; she said she had got so much better there already that she believed she should be well by fall if she stayed on. She was certain that it would put her all back if she were to travel now, and in Europe, where it was so hard to know how to get to places, she did not see how they could pick out any that would suit them as well as Venice did.

Clementina agreed to it all, more or less absent-mindedly, as she sat looking into the moonlight, and the day that had begun so stormily ended in kindness between them.

The next morning Mrs. Lander did not wish to go out, and she sent Clementina and Hinkle together as a proof that they were all on good terms again. She did not spare the girl this explanation in his presence, and when they were in the gondola he felt that he had to say, "I was afraid you might think I was rather meddlesome yesterday."

"Oh, no," she answered. "I was glad you did."

"Yes," he returned, "I thought you would be—afterwards." He looked at her wistfully with his slanted eyes and his odd twisted smile and they both gave way in the same conscious laugh. "What I like," he explained further, "is to be understood when I've said something that doesn't mean anything, don't you? You know anybody can understand you if you really mean something; but most of the time you don't, and that's when a friend is useful. I wish you'd call on me if you're ever in that fix."

"Oh, I *will*, Mr. Hinkle," Clementina promised, gayly.

"Thank you," he said, and her gayety seemed to turn him graver. "Miss Clementina, might I go a little further in this direction, without danger?"

"What direction?" she added, with a flush of sudden alarm.

"Mrs. Lander."

"Why, suttainly!" she answered, in quick relief.

"I wish you'd let me do some of the worrying about her for you, while I'm here. You know I haven't got anything else to do!"

"Why, I don't believe I worry much. I'm afraid I fo'get about her when I'm not with her. That's the wo'st of it."

"No, no," he entreated, "that's the best of it. But I want to do the worrying for you even when you're with her. Will you let me?"

"Why, if you want to so very much."

"Then it's settled," he said, dismissing the subject.

But she recurred to it with a lingering compunction. "I presume that I don't remember how sick she is because I've neva been sick at all, myself."

"Well," he returned, "you needn't be sorry for that altogether. There are worse things than being well, though sick people don't always think so. I've wasted a good deal of time the other way, though I've reformed, now."

They went on to talk about themselves; sometimes they talked about others, in excursions which were more or less perfunctory, and were merely in the way of illustration or instance. She got so far in one of these as to speak of her family, and he seemed to understand them. He asked about them all, and he said he believed in her father's unworldly theory of life. He asked her if they thought at home that she was like her father, and he added, as if it followed, "I'm the worldling of *my* family. I was the youngest child, and the only boy in a flock of girls. That always spoils a boy."

"Are you spoiled?" she asked.

"Well, I'm afraid they'd be surprised if I didn't come to grief somehow—all but mother; she expects I'll be kept from harm."

"Is she religious?"

"Yes, she's a Moravian. Did you ever hear of them?" Clementina shook her head. "They're something like the Quakers, and something like the Methodists. They don't believe in war; but they have bishops."

"And do you belong to her church?"

"No," said the young man. "I wish I did, for her sake. I don't belong to any. Do you?"

"No, I go to the Episcopal, at home. Perhaps I shall belong sometime. But I think that is something everyone must do for themselves." He looked a little alarmed at the note of severity in her voice, and she explained. "I mean that if you try to be religious for anything besides religion, it isn't being religious; —and no one else has any right to ask you to be."

"Oh, that's what I believe, too," he said, with comic relief. "I didn't know but I'd been trying to convert you without knowing it." They both laughed, and were then rather seriously silent.

He asked, after a moment, in a fresh beginning, "Have you heard from Miss Milray since you left Florence?"

"Oh, yes, didn't I tell you? She's coming here in June."

"Well, she won't have the pleasure of seeing me, then. I'm going the last of May."

"I thought you were going to stay a month!" she protested.

"That will be a month; and more, too."

"So it will," she owned.

"I'm glad it doesn't seem any longer—say a year—Miss Clementina!"

"Oh, not at all," she returned. "Miss Milray's brother and his wife are coming with her. They've been in Egypt."

"I never saw them," said Hinkle. He paused, before he added, "Well, it *would* seem rather crowded after they get here, I suppose," and he laughed, while Clementina said nothing.

XXX.

Hinkle came every morning now, to smoothe out the doubts and difficulties that had accumulated in Mrs. Lander's mind over night, and incidentally to propose some pleasure for Clementina, who could feel that he was pitying her in her slavery to the sick woman's whims, and yet somehow entreating her to bear them. He saw them together in what Mrs. Lander called her well days; but there were other days when he saw Clementina alone, and then she brought him word from Mrs. Lander, and reported his talk to her after he went away. On one of these she sent him a cheerfuller message than usual, and charged the girl to explain that she was ever so much better, but had not got up because she felt that every minute in bed was doing her good. Clementina carried back his regrets and congratulation, and then told Mrs. Lander that he had asked her to go out with him to see a church, which he was sorry Mrs. Lander could not see too. He professed to be very particular about his churches, for he said he had noticed that they neither of them had any great gift for sights, and he had it on his conscience to get the best for them. He told Clementina that the church he had for them now could not be better if it had been built expressly for them, instead of having been used as a place of worship for eight or ten generations of Venetians before they came. She gave his invitation to Mrs. Lander, who could not always be trusted with his jokes, and she received it in the best part.

"Well, you go!" she said. "Maddalena can look after me, I guess. He's the only one of the fellas, except that lo'd, that I'd give a cent for." She added, with a sudden lapse from her pleasure in Hinkle to her severity with Clementina, "But you want to be ca'eful what you' doin'."

"Ca'eful?"

"Yes! About Mr. Hinkle. I a'n't agoin' to have you lead him on, and then say you didn't know where he was goin'. I can't keep runnin' away everywhe'e, fo' you, the way I done at Woodlake."

Clementina's heart gave a leap, whether joyful or woeful; but she answered indignantly, "How can you say such a thing to me, Mrs. Lander. I'm *not* leading him on!"

"I don't know what you call it. You're round with him in the gondoler, night and day, and when he's he'e, you'a settin' with him half the time on the balcony, and it's talk, talk, the whole while." Clementina took in the fact with silent recognition, and Mrs. Lander went on. "I ain't sayin' anything against it. He's the only one I don't believe is afta the money he thinks you'a goin' to have; but if you don't want him, you want to look what you're about."

The girl returned to Hinkle in the embarrassment which she was helpless to hide, and without the excuse which she could not invent for refusing to go with him. "Is Mrs. Lander worse—or anything?" he asked.

"Oh, no. She's quite well," said Clementina; but she left it for him to break the constraint in which they set out. He tried to do so at different points, but it seemed to close upon them the more inflexibly. At last he asked, as they were drawing near the church, "Have you ever seen anything of Mr. Belsky since you left Florence?"

"No," she said, with a nervous start. "What makes you ask?"

"I don't know. But you see nearly everybody again that you meet in your travels. That friend of his—that Mr. Gregory—he seems to have dropped out, too. I believe you told me you used to know him in America."

"Yes," she answered, briefly; she could not say more; and Hinkle went on. "It seemed to me, that as far as I could make him out, he was about as much of a crank in his way as the Russian. It's curious, but when you were talking about religion, the other day, you made me think of him!" The blood went to Clementina's heart. "I don't suppose you had him in mind, but what you said fitted him more than anyone I know of. I could have almost believed that he had been trying to convert *you!*" She stared at him, and he laughed. "He tackled *me* one day there in Florence all of a sudden, and I didn't know what to say, exactly. Of course, I respected his earnestness; but I couldn't accept his view of things and I tried to tell him so. I had to say just where I stood, and why, and I mentioned some books that helped to get me there. He said he never read anything that went counter to his faith; and I saw that he didn't want to save me, so much as he wanted to convince me. He didn't know it, and I didn't tell him that I knew it, but I got him to let me drop the subject. He seems to have been left over from a time when people didn't reason about their beliefs, but only argued. I didn't think there was a man like that to be found so late in the century, especially a young man. But that was just where I was mistaken. If there was to be a man of that kind at all, it would have to be a young one. He'll be a good deal opener-minded when he's older. He was conscientious; I could see that; and he did take the Russian's death to heart as long as he *was* dead. But I'd like to talk with him ten years from now; he wouldn't be where he is."

Clementina was still silent, and she walked up the church steps from the gondola without the power to speak. She made no show of interest in the pictures and statues; she never had really cared much for such things, and now his attempts to make her look at them failed miserably. When they got back again into the boat he began, "Miss Clementina, I'm afraid I oughtn't to have spoken as I did of that Mr. Gregory. If he is a friend of yours"—

"He is," she made herself answer.

"'HAVE YOU EVER SEEN ANYTHING OF MR. BELSKY SINCE YOU LEFT FLORENCE?'"

"I didn't mean anything against him. I hope you don't think I wanted to be unfair?"

"You were not unfair. But I oughtn't to have let you say it, Mr. Hinkle. I want to tell you something —I mean, I must"— She found herself panting and breathless. "You ought to know it— Mr. Gregory is— I mean we are"—

She stopped and she saw that she need not say more.

In the days that followed before the time that Hinkle had fixed to leave Venice, he tried to come as he had been coming, to see Mrs. Lander, but he evaded her when she wished to send him out with Clementina. His quaintness had a heartache in it for her; and he was boyishly simple in his failure to hide his suffering. He had no explicit right to suffer, for he had asked nothing and been denied nothing, but perhaps for this reason she suffered the more keenly for him.

A senseless resentment against Gregory for spoiling their happiness crept into her heart; and she wished to show Hinkle how much she valued his friendship at any risk and any cost. When this led her too far she took herself to task with a severity which hurt him too. In the midst of the impulses on which she acted, there were times when she had a confused longing to appeal to him for counsel as to how she ought to behave toward him.

There was no one else whom she could appeal to. Mrs. Lander, after her first warning, had not spoken of him again, though Clementina could feel in the grimness with which she regarded her variable treatment of him that she was silently hoarding up a sum of inculpation which would crush her under its weight when it should fall upon her. She seemed to be growing constantly better, now, and as the interval since her last attack widened behind her, she began to indulge her appetite with a recklessness which Clementina, in a sense of her own unworthiness, was helpless to deal with. When she ventured to ask her once whether she ought to eat of something that was very unwholesome for her, Mrs. Lander answered that she had taken her case into her own hands, now, for she knew more about it than all the doctors. She would thank Clementina not to bother about her; she added that she was at least not hurting anybody but herself, and she hoped Clementina would always be able to say as much.

Clementina wished that Hinkle would go away, but not before she had righted herself with him, and he lingered his month out, and seemed as little able to go as she to let him. She had often to be cheerful for both, when she found it too much to be cheerful for herself. In his absense she feigned free and open talks with him, and explained everything, and experienced a kind of ghostly comfort in his imagined approval and forgiveness, but in his presence, nothing really happened except the alternation of her kindness and unkindness, in which she was too kind and then too unkind.

The morning of the day he was at last to leave Venice, he came to say good bye. He did not ask for Mrs. Lander, when the girl received him, and he did not give himself time to lose courage before he began, "Miss Clementina, I don't know whether I ought to speak to you after what I understood you to mean about Mr. Gregory." He looked steadfastly at her but she did not answer, and he went on. "There's just one chance in a million, though, that I didn't understand you rightly, and I've made up my mind that I want to take that chance. May I?" She tried to speak, but she could not. "If I was wrong—if there was nothing between you and him—*could* there ever be anything beween you and me?"

His pleading looks entreated her even more than his words.

"There was something," she answered, "with him."

"And I mustn't know what," the young man said patiently.

"Yes—yes!" she returned eagerly. "Oh, yes! I want you to know—I want to tell you. I was only sixteen yea's old, and he said that he oughtn't to have spoken; we were both too young. But last winta he spoke again. He said that he had always felt bound"— She stopped, and he got infirmly to his feet. "I wanted to tell you from the fust, but"—

"How could you? You couldn't. I haven't anything more to say, if you are bound to him."

"He is going to be a missionary and he wanted me to say that I would believe just as he did; and I couldn't. But I thought that it would come right; and—yes, I felt bound to him, too. That is all—I can't explain it!"

"Oh, I understand!" he returned, listlessly.

"And do you blame me for not telling before?" She made an involuntary movement toward him, a pathetic gesture which both entreated and compassionated.

"There's nobody to blame. You have tried to do just right by me, as well as him. Well, I've got my answer. Mrs. Lander—can I"—

"Why, she isn't up yet, Mr. Hinkle." Clementina put all her pain for him into the expression of their regret.

"Then I'll have to leave my good-bye for her with you. I don't believe I can come back again." He looked round as if he were dizzy. "Good-bye," he said, and offered his hand. It was cold as clay.

When he was gone, Clementina went into Mrs. Lander's room, and gave her his message.

"Couldn't he have come back this aftanoon to see me, if he ain't goin' till five?" she demanded jealously.

"He said he couldn't come back," Clementina answered sadly.

The woman turned her head on her pillow and looked at the girl's face. "Oh!" she said for all comment.

XXXI.

The Milrays came a month later, to seek a milder sun than they had left burning in Florence. The husband and wife had been sojourning there since their arrival from Egypt, but they had not been his sister's guests, and she did not now pretend to be of their party, though the same train, even the same carriage, had brought her to Venice with them. They went to a hotel, and Miss Milray took lodgings where she always spent her Junes, before going to the Tyrol for the summer.

"You are wonderfully improved, every way," Mrs. Milray said to Clementina when they met. "I knew you would be, if Miss Milray took you in hand; and I can see she *has*. What she doesn't know about the world isn't worth knowing! I hope she hasn't made you *too* worldly? But if she has, she's taught you how to keep from showing it; you're just as innocent-looking as ever, and that's the main thing; you oughtn't to lose *that*. You wouldn't dance a skirt dance now before a ship's company, but if you did, no one would suspect that you knew any better. Have you forgiven me, yet? Well, I *didn't* use you very well, Clementina, and I never pretended I did. I've eaten a lot of humble pie for that, my dear. Did Miss Milray tell you that I wrote to her about it? Of course you won't say *how* she told you; but she ought to have done me the justice to say that I tried to be a friend at court with her for you. If she didn't, she wasn't fair."

"She neva said anything against you, Mrs. Milray," Clementina answered.

"Discreet as ever, my dear! I understand! And I hope *you* understand about that old affair, too, by this time. It was a complication. I had to get back at Lioncourt *some*how; and I don't honestly think *now* that his admiration for a young girl was a very wholesome thing for her. But never mind. You had that Boston goose in Florence, too, last winter, and I suppose he gobbled up what little Miss Milray had left of me. But she's charming. I could go down on my knees to her art when she really tries to finish any one."

Clementina noticed that Mrs. Milray had got a new way of talking. She had a chirpiness, and a lift in her inflections, which if it was not exactly English was no longer Western American. Clementina herself in her association with Hinkle had worn off her English rhythm, and in her long confinement to the conversation of Mrs. Lander, she had reverted to her clipped Yankee accent. Mrs. Milray professed to like it, and said it brought back so delightfully those pleasant days at Middlemount, when Clementina really *was* a child. "I met somebody at Cairo, who seemed very glad to hear about you, though he tried to seem not. Can you guess who it was? I see that you never could, in the world! We got quite chummy one day, when we were going out to the pyramids together, and he gave himself away, finely. He's a simple soul! But when they're in love they're all so! It was a little queer, colloguing with the ex-headwaiter on society terms; but the headwaitership was merely an episode, and the main thing is that he is very talented, and is going to be a minister. It's a pity he's so devoted to his crazy missionary scheme. Some one ought to get hold of him, and point him in the direction of a rich New York congregation. He'd find heathen enough among *them*, and he could do the greatest amount of good with their money; I tried to talk it into him. I suppose you saw him in Florence, this spring?" she suddenly asked.

"Yes," Clementina answered briefly.

"And you didn't make it up together. I got *that* much out of Miss Milray. Well, if *he* were here, I should find out *why*. But I don't suppose *you* would tell me." She waited a moment to see if Clementina would, and then she said, "It's a pity, for I've a notion I could help you, and I think I owe you a good turn, for the way I behaved about your dance. But if you don't want my help, you don't."

"I would say so if I did, Mrs. Milray," said Clementina. "I *was* hu't, at the time; but I don't care anything for it, now. I hope you won't think about it any more."

"Thank you," said Mrs. Milray, "I'll try not to,"

and she laughed. "But I should like to do something to prove my repentance."

Clementina perceived that for some reason she would rather have more than less cause for regret; and that she was mocking her; but she was without the wish or the power to retaliate, and she did not try to fathom Mrs. Milray's motives. Most motives in life, even bad motives, lie nearer the surface than most people commonly pretend, and she might not have had to dig deeper into Mrs. Milray's nature for hers than that layer of her consciousness where she was aware that Clementina was a pet of her sister-in-law. For no better reason she herself made a pet of Mrs. Lander, whose dislike of Miss Milray was not hard to divine, and whose willingness to punish her through Clementina was akin to her own. The sick woman was easily flattered back into her first belief in Mrs. Milray and accepted her large civilities and small services as proof of her virtues. She began to talk them into Clementina, and to contrast them with the wicked principles and actions of Miss Milray.

The girl had forgiven Mrs. Milray, but she could not go back to any trust in her; and she could only passively assent to her praise. When Mrs. Lander pressed her for anything more explicit she said what she thought, and then Mrs. Lander accused her of hating Mrs. Milray, who was more her friend than some that flattered her up for everything, and tried to make a fool of her.

"I undastand now," she said one day, "what that recta meant by wantin' me to make life ha'd for you;

he saw how easy you was to spoil. Miss Milray is one to praise you to your face, and disgrace you behind your back, and so I tell you. When Mrs. Milray thought you done wrong she come and said so; and you can't forgive her."

Clementina did not answer. She had mastered the art of reticence in her relations with Mrs. Lander, and even when Miss Milray tempted her one day to give way, she still had strength to resist. But she could not deny that Mrs. Lander did things at times to worry her, though she ended compassionately with the reflection: "She's sick."

"I don't think she's very sick, now," retorted her friend.

"No; that's the reason she's so worrying. When she's really sick, she's betta."

"Because she's frightened, I suppose. And how long do you propose to stand it?"

"I don't know," Clementina listlessly answered. "She couldn't get along without me. I guess I can stand it till we go home; she says she is going home in the fall."

Miss Milray sat looking at the girl a moment. "Shall you be glad to go home?"

"Oh yes, indeed!"

"To that place in the woods?"

"Why, yes! What makes you ask?"

"Nothing. But Clementina, sometimes I think you don't quite understand yourself. Don't you know that you are very pretty and very charming? I've told you that often enough! But shouldn't you like to be a great success in the world? Haven't you ever thought of that? Don't you care for society?"

The girl sighed. "Yes, I think that's all very nice I did ca'e, one while, there in Florence, last winter!"

"My dear, you don't *know* how much you were admired. I used to tell you, because I saw there was no spoiling you; but I never told you half. If you had only had the time for it you could have been the greatest sort of success; you were formed for it. It wasn't your beauty alone; lots of pretty girls don't make anything of their beauty; it was your temperament. You took things easily and naturally, and that's what the world likes. It doesn't like your being afraid of it, and you were not afraid, and you were not bold; you were just right." Miss Milray grew more and more exhaustive in her analysis, and enjoyed refining upon it. "All that you needed was a little hard-heartedness, and that would have come in time; you would have learned how to hold your own, but the chance was snatched from you by that old cat! I could weep over you when I think how you have been wasted on her, and now you're actually willing to go back and lose yourself in the woods!"

"I shouldn't call it being lost, Miss Milray."

"I don't mean that, and you must excuse me, my dear. But surely your people—your father and mother—would want to have you get on in the world—to make a brilliant match"—

Clementina smiled to think how far such a thing was from their imaginations. "I don't believe they would ca'e. You don't undastand about them, and I couldn't make you. Fatha neva liked the notion of my being with such a rich woman as Mrs. Lander, because it would look as if we wanted her money."

"I never could have imagined that of *you*, Clementina!"

"I didn't think you could," said the girl gratefully. "But now, if I left her when she was sick and depended on me, it would look wohse, yet—as if I did it because she was going to give her money to Mr. Landa's family. She wants to do that, and I told her to; I think that would be right; don't you?"

"It would be right for you, Clementina, if you preferred it—and *I* should prefer it. But it wouldn't be right for her. She has given you hopes—she has made promises—she has talked to everybody."

"I don't ca'e for that. I shouldn't like to feel beholden to any one, and I think it really belongs to his relations; it was *his*."

Miss Milray did not say anything to this. She asked, "And if you went back, what would you do there? Labor in the fields, as poor little Belsky advised?"

Clementina laughed. "No; but I expect you'll think it's almost as crazy. You know how much I like dancing? Well, I think I could give dancing lessons at the Middlemount. There are always a good many children, and girls that have not grown up, and I guess I could get pupils enough, as long as the summa lasted; and come winter, I'm not afraid but what I could get them among the young folks at the Center. I used to teach them before I left home."

Miss Milray sat looking at her. "I don't know about such things; but it sounds sensible—like everything about you, my dear. It *sounds* queer, perhaps because you're talking of such a White Mountain scheme here in Venice."

"Yes, don't it?" said Clementina sympathetically. "I was thinking of that, myself. But I know I could do it. I could go round to different hotels, different days. Yes, I should like to go home, and they would be glad to have me. You can't think how pleasantly we live; and we're company enough for each other. I presume I should miss the things I've got used to ova here, at fust; but I don't believe I should care a great while. I don't deny but what the wo'ld is nice; but you have to pay for it; I don't mean that *you* would make me"—

"No, no! We understand each other. Go on!" Miss Milray leaned towards her and pressed the girl's arm reassuringly.

As often happens with people when they are told to go on, Clementina found that she had not much more to say. "I think I could get along in the wo'ld, well enough. Yes, I believe I could do it. But I wasn't bohn to it, and it would be a great deal of trouble—a great deal moa than if I had been bohn to it. I think it would be too much trouble. I would rather give it up and go home, when Mrs. Landa wants to go back."

Miss Milray did not speak for a time. "I know that you are serious, Clementina; and you're wise always, and good"—

"It isn't that, exactly," said Clementina. "But is it—I don't know how to express it very well—is it wo'th while?"

Miss Milray looked at her as if she doubted the girl's sincerity. Even when the world, in return for our making it our whole life, disappoints and defeats us with its prizes, we still question the truth of those who question the value of these prizes; we think they must be hopeless of them, or must be governed by some interest momentarily superior.

Clementina pursued, "I know that you have had all you wanted of the wo'ld"—

"Oh, *no!*" the woman broke out, almost in anguish. "*Not* what I *wanted!* What I *tried for.* It *never* gave me what I wanted. It couldn't!"

"Well?"

"It isn't worth while in that sense. But if you can't have what you want,—if there's been a hollow left in your life—why the world goes a great way towards filling up the aching void." The tone of the last words was lighter than their meaning, but Clementina weighed them aright.

"Miss Milray," she said, pinching the edge of the table by which she sat, a little nervously, and hanging her head a little, "I think I can have what I want."

"Then, give the whole world for it, child!"

"There is something I should like to tell you."

"Yes!"

"For you to advise me about."

"I will, my dear, gladly and truly!"

"He was here before you came. He asked me"—

Miss Milray gave a start of alarm. She said, to gain time: "How did he get here? I supposed he was in Germany with his"—

"No; he was here the whole of May"

"Mr. Gregory!"

"Mr. Gregory?" Clementina's face flushed and drooped still lower. "I meant Mr. Hinkle. But if you think I oughtn't"—

"I don't think *anything*; I'm so glad! I supposed from what you said about the world, that it must be—But if it isn't, all the better. If it's Mr. Hinkle that you can have"—

"I'm not *sure* I can. I should like to tell you just how it is, and then you will know." It needed fewer words for this than she expected, and then Clementina took a letter from her pocket, and gave it to Miss Milray. "He wrote it on the train, going away, and it's not very plain; but I guess you can make it out."

Miss Milray received the penciled leaves, which seemed to be pages torn out of a note-book. They were dated the day Hinkle left Venice, and the envelope bore the postmark of Verona. They were not addressed, but began abruptly: "I believe I have made a mistake; I ought not to have given you up till I knew something that no one but you can tell me. You are not bound to any body unless you *wish* to be so. That is what I see now, and I will not give you up if I can help it. Even if you had made a promise, and then changed your mind, you would not be bound in such a thing as this. I say this, and I know you will not believe I say it because I want you. I do want you, but I would not urge you to break your faith. I only ask you to realize that if you kept your word when your heart had gone out of it, you would be breaking your faith; and if you broke your word you would be keeping your faith. But if your heart is still in your word, I have no more to say. Nobody knows but you. I would get out and take the first train back to Venice if it were not for two things. I know it would be hard on me; and I am afraid it might be hard on you. But if you will write me a line at Milan, when you get this, or if you will write to me at London before July; or at New York at any time—for I expect to wait as long as I live"—

The letter ended here in the local addresses which the writer gave.

Miss Milray handed the leaves back to Clementina, who put them into her pocket, and apparently waited for her questions.

"And have you written?"

"No," said the girl, slowly and thoughtfully, "I haven't. I wanted to, at fust; and then, I thought that if he truly meant what he said he would be willing to wait."

"And why did *you* want to wait?"

Clementina replied with a question of her own. "Miss Milray, what do you think about Mr. Gregory?"

"Oh, you mustn't ask me that, my dear! I was afraid I had told you too plainly, the last time."

"I don't mean about his letting me think he didn't ca'e for me, so long. But don't you think he *wants* to do what is right! Mr. Gregory, I mean."

"Well, if you put me on my honor, I'm afraid I do.'

"You see," Clementina resumed. "He was the *fust* one, and I did ca'e for him a great deal; and I might have gone on caring for him, if— When I found out that I didn't care any longer, or so much, it seemed to me as if it must be wrong. Do you think it was?"

"No—no."

"When I got to thinking about some one else—at fust it was only *not* thinking about *him*—I was ashamed. Then I tried to make out that I was too young in the fust place, to know whether I really ca'ed for any one in the right way; but after I made out that I was, I couldn't feel exactly easy; and I've been wanting to ask you, Miss Milray"—

"Ask me anything you like, my dear!"

"Why, it's only whether a person ought eva to change"—

"We change whether we ought, or not. It isn't a matter of duty, one way or another."

"Yes, but ought we to stop caring for somebody, when perhaps we shouldn't if somebody else hadn't come between? That is the question."

"No," Miss Milray retorted, "that isn't at all the question. The question is which you want and whether you could get him. Whichever you want most it is right for you to have."

"Do you truly think so?"

"I do, indeed. This is the one thing in life where one may choose safest what one likes best; I mean if there is nothing bad in the man himself."

"I was afraid it would be wrong! That was what I meant by wanting to be fai'a with Mr. Gregory when I told you about him there in Florence. I don't believe but what it had begun then."

"What had begun?"

"About Mr. Hinkle."

Miss Milray burst into a laugh. "Clementina, you're delicious!" The girl looked hurt, and Miss Milray asked seriously, "Why do you like Mr. Hinkle best—if you *do?*"

Clementina sighed. "Oh, I don't know. He's so *resting.*"

"Then that settles it. From first to last, what we poor women want is *rest.* It would be a wicked thing for you to throw your life away on some one who would worry you out of it. I don't wish to say anything against Mr. Gregory. I dare say he *is* good and conscientious; but life is a struggle, at the best, and it's your duty to take the best chance for resting."

Clementina did not look altogether convinced, whether it was Miss Milray's logic or her morality that failed to convince her. She said, after a moment, "I should like to see Mr. Gregory again."

"What good would that do?"

"Why, then I should know."

"Know what?"

"Whether I didn't really ca'e for him any more—or so much."

"Clementina," said Miss Milray, "you mustn't make me lose patience with you!"

"No. But I thought you said that it was my duty to do what I wished."

"Well, yes. That is what I said," Miss Milray consented. "But I supposed that you knew already."

"No," said Clementina, candidly, "I don't believe I do."

"And what if you don't see him?"

"I guess I shall have to wait till I do. The'e will be time enough."

Miss Milray sighed, and then she laughed. "You *are* young!"

XXXII.

Miss Milray went from Clementina to call upon her sister-in-law, and found her brother, which was perhaps what she hoped might happen.

"Do you know," she said, "that that old wretch is going to defraud that poor thing, after all, and leave her money to her husband's half-sister's children?"

"You wish me to infer the Mrs. Lander-Clementina situation?" Milray returned.

"Yes!"

"I'm glad you put it in terms that are not actionable, then; for your words are decidedly libellous."

"What do you mean?"

"I've just been writing Mrs. Lander's will for her, and she's left all her property to Clementina, except five thousand apiece to the half-sister's three children."

"I can't believe it!"

"Well," said Milray, with his gentle smile, "I think that's safe ground for you. Mrs. Lander will probably have time enough to change her will as well as her mind several times yet before she dies. The half-sister's children may get their rights yet."

"I wish they might!" said Miss Milray, with an

impassioned sigh. "Then perhaps *I* should get Clementina—for a while."

Her brother laughed. "Isn't there somebody else wants Clementina?"

"Oh, plenty. But she's not sure she wants anybody else."

"Does she want you?"

"No, I can't say she does. She wants to go home."

"That's not a bad scheme. I should like to go home myself if I had one. What would you have done with Clementina if you had got her, Jenny?"

"What would any one have done with her? Married her brilliantly, of course."

"But you say she isn't sure she wishes to be married at all?"

Miss Milray stated the case of Clementina's divided mind, and her belief that she would take Hinkle in the end, together with the fear that she might take Gregory. "She's very odd," Miss Milray concluded. "She puzzles me. Why did you ever send her to me?"

Milray laughed. "I don't know. I thought she would amuse you, and I thought it would be a pleasure to her."

They began to talk of some affairs of their own, from which Miss Milray returned to Clementina with the ache of an imperfectly satisfied intention. If she had meant to urge her brother to seek justice for the girl from Mrs. Lander, she was not so well pleased to have found justice done already. But the will had been duly signed and witnessed before the American vice-consul, and she must get what good she could out of an accomplished fact. It was at least a consolation to know that it put an end to her sister-in-law's patronage of the girl, and it would be interesting to see Mrs. Milray adapt her behavior to Clementina's fortunes. She did not really dislike her sister-in-law enough to do her a wrong; she was only willing that she should do herself a wrong.

But one of the most disappointing things in all hostile operations is that you never can know what the enemy would be at; and Mrs. Milray's manœuvres were sometimes dictated by such impulses that her strategy was peculiarly baffling. The thought of her past unkindness to Clementina may still have rankled in her, or she may simply have felt the need of outdoing Miss Milray by an unapproachable benefaction. It is certain that when Baron Belsky came to Venice a few weeks after her own arrival, they began to pose at each other with reference to Clementina; she with a measure of consciousness, he with the singleness of a nature that was all pose. In his forbearance to win Clementina from Gregory he had enjoyed the distinction of an unique suffering; and in allowing the fact to impart itself to Mrs. Milray, he bathed in the warmth of her flattering sympathy. Before she withdrew this, as she must when she got tired of him, she learned from him where Gregory was; for it seemed that Gregory had so far forgiven the past that they had again written to each other.

During the fortnight of Belsky's stay in Venice Mrs. Lander was much worse, and Clementina met him only once, very briefly. She felt that he had behaved like a very silly person, but that was all over now, and she had no wish to punish him for it. At the end of his fortnight he went northward into the Austrian Tyrol, and a few days later Gregory came down from the Dolomites to Venice.

It was in his favor with Clementina that he yielded to the impulse he had to come directly to her; and that he let her know with the first words that he had acted upon hopes given him through Belsky from Mrs. Milray. He owned that he doubted the authority of either to give him these hopes, but he said he could not abandon them without a last effort to see her, and learn from her whether they were true or false.

If she recognized the design of a magnificent reparation in what Mrs. Milray had done, she did not give it much thought. Her mind was upon distant things as she followed Gregory's explanation of his presence, and in the muse in which she listened she seemed hardly to know when he ceased speaking.

"I know it must seem to take something for granted which I've no right to take for granted. I don't believe you could think that I cared for anything but you, or at all for what Mrs. Lander has done for you."

"Do you mean her leaving me her money?" asked Clementina, with that boldness her sex enjoys concerning matters of finance and affection.

"Yes," said Gregory, blushing for her. "As far as I should ever have a right to care, I could wish there were no money. It could bring no blessing to our life. We could do no good with it; nothing but the sacrifice of ourselves in poverty could be blessed to us."

"That is what I thought, too," Clementina replied.

"Oh, then you did think"—

"But afterwards," she added, "I changed my mind. If she wants to give me her money I shall take it."

Gregory was blankly silent again.

"I shouldn't know how to refuse, and I don't know as I should have any right to." Gregory shrank a little from her reyankeefied English, as well as from the apparent cynicism of her speech; but he shrank in silence still. She startled him by asking with a kindness that was almost tenderness, "Mr. Gregory, how do you think anything has changed?"

"Changed?"

"You know how it was when you went away from Florence. Do you think differently now? I don't. I don't think I ought to do something for you, and pretend that I was doing it for religion. I don't believe the way you do; and I know I neva shall. Do you want me to go with you, afta that? Do you want me, in spite of my saying that I can neva help you in your wo'k because I believe in it?"

"But if you believe in me"—

She shook her head compassionately. "You know we ahgued that out before. We are just whe'e we were. I am sorry. Nobody had any right to tell you to come he'e. But I am glad you came." She saw the hope that lighted up his face, but she went on unrelentingly. "I think we had betta be free."

"Free?"

"Yes, from each other. I don't know how you have felt, but I have not felt free. It has seemed to me that I promised you something. If I did, I want to take my promise back and be free."

Her frankness appealed to his own. "You are free. I never held you bound to me in my fondest hopes. You have always done right."

"I *have* tried to. And I am not going to let you go away thinking that the reason I said is the only reason. It isn't. I wish to be free because—*there is some one else*, now." It was hard to tell him this, but she knew that she must not do less; and the train that carried him from Venice that night bore a letter from her to Hinkle.

XXXIII.

Clementina told Miss Milray what had happened, but with Mrs. Milray the girl left the sudden departure of Gregory to account for itself.

They all went a week later, and Mrs. Milray having now done her whole duty to Clementina had the easiest mind concerning her. Miss Milray felt that she was leaving her to greater trials than ever with Mrs. Lander; but since there was nothing else, she submitted, as people always do with the trials of others, and when she was once away she began to forget her.

By this time, however, it was really better for her. With no one to suspect of tampering with her allegiance, Mrs. Lander returned to her former fondness for the girl, and they were more peaceful if not happier together again. They had long talks, such as they used to have, and in the first of these Clementina told her how and why she had written to Mr. Hinkle. Mrs. Lander said that it suited her exactly.

"There ha'n't but just two men in Europe behaved like gentlemen to me, and one is Mr. Hinkle, and the other is that lo'd; and between the two I ratha you'd have Mr. Hinkle; I don't know as I believe much in American guls marryin' lo'ds, the best of 'em."

Clementina laughed. "Why, Mrs. Landa, Lo'd Lioncou't never thought of me in the wo'ld!"

"You can't eva know. Mrs. Milray was tellin' that he's what they call a pooa lo'd, and that he was carryin' on with the American girls like everything down there in Egypt last winta. I guess if it comes to money you'd have enough to buy him and sell him again."

The mention of money cast a chill upon their talk; and Mrs. Lander said gloomily, "I don't know as I ca'e so much for that will Mr. Milray made for me, after all. I did want to say ten thousand apiece for Mr. Landa's relations; but I hated to befo'e him; I'd told the whole kit of 'em so much about you, and I knew what they would think."

She looked at Clementina with recurring grudge, and the girl could not bear it.

"Then why don't you tear it up, and make another? I don't want anything, unless you want me to have it; and I'd ratha not have anything."

"Yes, and what would folks say, afta youa takin' care of me?"

"Do you think I do it fo' that?"

"What do you do it fo'?"

"What did you want me to come with you fo'?"

"That's true." Mrs. Lander brightened and warmed again. "I guess it's all right. I guess I done right, and I got to be satisfied. I presume I could get the consul to make me a will any time."

Clementina did not relent so easily. "Mrs. Landa, whateva you do I don't ca'e to know it; and if you talk to me again about this I shall go home. I would stay with you as long as you needed me, but I can't if you keep bringing this up."

"I suppose you think you don't need *me* any moa! Betta not be too su'a."

The girl jumped to her feet, and Mrs. Lander interposed. "Well, the'a! I didn't mean anything, and I won't pesta you about it any moa. But I think it's pretty ha'd. Who am I going to talk it ova with, then?"

"You can talk it ova with the vice-consul," said Clementina, at random.

"Well, that's so." Mrs. Lander let Clementina get her ready for the night, in sign of returning amity; when she was angry with her she always refused her help, and made her send Maddalena.

The summer heat increased, and the sick woman suffered from it, but she could not be persuaded that she had strength to get away, though the vice-consul, whom she advised with, used all his logic with her. He was a gaunt and weary widower, who described himself as being officially between hay and grass; the consul who appointed him had resigned after going home, and a new consul had not yet been sent out to remove him. On what she called her well days Mrs. Lander went to visit him, and she did not mind his being in his shirt-sleeves, in the bit of garden where she commonly found him, with his collar and cravat off, and clouded in his own smoke; when she was sick she sent for him, to visit her. He made excuses as often as he could, and if he saw Mrs. Lander's gondola coming down the Grand Canal to his house he hurried on his cast clothing, and escaped to the Piazza, at whatever discomfort and risk from the heat.

"I don't know how *you* stand it, Miss Claxon," he complained to Clementina, as soon as he learned that she was not a blood relation of Mrs. Lander's, and divined that she had her own reservations concerning her. "But that woman will be the death of me if she keeps this up. What does she think I'm here for? If this goes on much longer I'll resign. The salary won't begin to pay for it. What am I going to do? I don't want to hurt her feelings, or not to help her; but I know ten times as much about Mrs. Lander's liver as I do about my own, *now*."

He treated Clementina as a person of mature judgment and a sage discretion, and he accepted what comfort she could offer him when she explained that it was everything for Mrs. Lander to have him to talk with. "She gets ti'ed of talking to me," she urged, "and there's nobody else, now."

"Why don't she hire a *valet de place*, and talk to him? I'd hire one myself for her. It would be a good deal cheaper for me. It's as much as I can do to stand this weather as it is."

The vice-consul laughed forlornly in his exasperation, but he agreed with Clementina when she said, in further excuse, that Mrs. Lander was really very sick. He pushed back his hat, and scratched his head with a grimace.

"Of course, we've got to remember she's sick, and I shall need a little sympathy myself if she keeps on at me this way. I believe I'll tell her about *my* liver next time, and see how she likes it. Look here, Miss Claxon! Couldn't we get her off to some of those German watering places that are good for her complaints? I believe it would be the best thing for her —not to mention me."

Mrs. Lander was moved by the suggestion which he made in person afterwards; it appealed to her old nomadic instinct; but when the consul was gone she gave it up. "We couldn't git the'e, Clementina. I got to stay he'e till I git up my stren'th. I suppose you'd be glad enough to have me sta't, now the'e's nobody he'e but me," she added, suspiciously. "You git this scheme up, or him?"

Clementina did not defend herself, and Mrs. Lander presently came to her defence. "I don't believe but what he meant it fo' the best—or you, whichever it was, and I appreciate it; but all is I couldn't git off. I guess this aia will do me as much good as anything, come to have it a little coola."

They went every afternoon to the Lido, where a wheeled chair met them, and Mrs. Lander was trundled across the narrow island to the beach. In the evenings they went to the Piazza, where their faces and figures had become known, and the Venetians gossipped them down to the last fact of their relation with an accuracy creditable to their ingenuity in the affairs of others. To them Mrs. Lander was the sick American, very rich, and Clementina was her adoptive daughter, who would have her millions after her. Neither knew the character they bore to the amiable and inquisitive public of the Piazza, or cared for the fine eyes that aimed their steadfast gaze at them along the tubes of straw-barreled Virginia cigars, or across little cups of coffee. Mrs. Lander merely remarked that the Venetians seemed great for gaping, and Clementina was for the most part innocent of their stare.

She rested in the choice she had made in a content which was qualified by no misgiving. She was sorry for Gregory, when she remembered him; but her thought was filled with some one else, and she waited in faith and patience for the answer which should come to the letter she had written. She did not know where her letter would find him, or when she should hear from him; she believed that she should hear, and that was enough. She said to herself that she would not lose hope if no answer came for months; but in her heart she fixed a date for the answer by letter, and an earlier date for some word by cable; but she feigned that she did not depend upon this; and when no word came she convinced herself that she had not expected any.

It was nearing the end of the term which she had tacitly given her lover to make the first sign by letter, when one morning Mrs. Lander woke her. She wished to say that she had got the strength to leave Venice at last, and she was going as soon as their trunks could be packed. She had dressed herself, and she moved about restless and excited. Clementina tried to reason her out of her haste; but she irritated her, and fixed her in her determination. "I want to get away, I tell you; I want to get away," she answered all persuasion, and there seemed something in her like the wish to escape from more than the oppressive environment, though she spoke of nothing but the heat and the smell of the canal. "I believe it's that, moa than any one thing, that's kept me sick he'e," she said. "I tell you it's the malariar, and you'll be down, too, if you stay."

She made Clementina go to the banker's, and get money to pay their landlord's bill, and she gave him notice that they were going that afternoon. Clementina wished to delay till they had seen the vice-consul and the doctor; but Mrs. Lander broke out, "I don't want to see 'em, either of 'em. The docta wants to keep me he'e and make money out of me; I undastand him; and I don't believe that consul's a bit too good to take a pussentage. Now, don't you say a wo'd to either of 'em. If you don't do exactly what I tell you I'll go away and leave you he'e. Now, will you?"

Clementina promised, and broke her word. She went to the vice-consul and told him she had broken it, and she agreed with him that he had better not come unless Mrs. Lander sent for him. The doctor promptly imagined the situation and said he would come in casually during the morning, so as not to alarm the invalid's suspicions. He owned that Mrs. Lander was getting no good from remaining in Venice, and if it were possible for her to go, he said she had better go somewhere into cooler and higher air.

His opinion restored him to Mrs. Lander's esteem, when it was expressed to her, and as she was left to fix the sum of her debt to him, she made it handsomer than anything he had dreamed of. She held out against seeing the vice-consul till the landlord sent in his account. This was for the whole month which she had just entered upon, and it included fantastic charges for things hitherto included in the rent, not only for the current month, but for the months past when, the landlord explained, he had forgotten to note them. Mrs. Lander refused to pay these demands, for they touched her in some of those economies which the gross rich practice amidst their profusion. The landlord replied that she could not leave his house, either with or without her effects, until she had paid. He declared Clementina his prisoner, too, and he would not send for the vice-consul at Mrs. Lander's bidding. How far he was within his rights in all this they could not know, but he was perhaps himself doubtful, and he consented to let them send for the doctor, who, when he came, behaved like anything but the steadfast friend that Mrs. Lander supposed she had bought in him. He advised paying the account without regard to its justice, as the shortest and simplest way out of the trouble; but Mrs. Lander, who saw him talking amicably and even respectfully with the landlord, when he ought to have treated him as an extortionate scamp, returned to her former ill opinion of him; and the vice-consul now appeared the friend that Doctor Tradonico had falsely seemed. The doctor consented, in leaving her to her contempt of him, to carry a message to the vice-consul, though he came back, with his finger at the side of his nose, to charge her by no means to betray his bold championship to the landlord.

The vice-consul made none of those shows of authority which Mrs. Lander had expected of him. She saw him even exchanging the common decencies with the landlord, when they met; but in fact it was not hard to treat the smiling and courteous rogue well. In all their disagreement he had looked as constantly to the comfort of his captives as if they had been his chosen guests. He sent Mrs. Lander a much needed refreshment at the stormiest moment of her indignation, and he deprecated without retort the denunciations aimed at him in Italian which did not perhaps carry so far as his conscience. The consul talked with him in a calm scarcely less shameful than that of Dr. Tradonico; and at the end of their parley which she had insisted upon witnessing, he said:

"Well, Mrs. Lander, you've got to stand this gouge or you've got to stand a law suit. I think the gouge would be cheaper in the end. You see, he's got a right to his month's rent."

"It ain't the rent I ca'e for: it's the candles, and the suvvice, and the things he says we broke. It was undastood that everything was to be in the rent, and his two old chaias went to pieces of themselves when we tried to pull 'em out from the wall; and I'll neva pay for 'em in the wo'ld."

"Why," the vice-consul pleaded, "it's only about forty francs for the whole thing"—

"I don't care if it's only fotty cents. And I must say, Mr. Bennam, you're about the strangest vice-consul, to want me to do it, that *I* eva saw."

The vice-consul laughed unresentfully. "Well, shall I send you a lawyer?"

"No!" Mrs. Lander retorted; and after a moment's reflection she added, "I'm goin' to stay my month, and so you may tell him, and then I'll see whetha he can make me pay for that breakage and the candles and suvvice. I'm all wore out, as it is, and I ain't fit to travel, now, and I don't know when I *shall* be. Clementina, you can go and tell Maddalena to stop packin'. Or, no! *I'll* do it."

She left the room without further notice of the consul, who said ruefully to Clementina, "Well, I've missed my chance, Miss Claxon, but I guess she's done the wisest thing for herself."

"Oh, yes, she's not fit to go. She must stay, now, till it's coola. Will you tell the landlo'd, or shall"—

"I'll tell him," said the vice-consul, and he had in the landlord. He received her message with the pleasure of a host whose cherished guests have consented to remain a while longer, and in the rush of his good feeling he offered, if the charge for breakage seemed unjust to the vice-consul, to abate it; and since the signora had not understood that she was to pay extra for the other things, he would allow the vice-consul to adjust the differences between them; it was a trifle, and he wished above all things to content the signora, for whom he professed a cordial esteem both on his own part and the part of all his family.

"Then that lets me out for the present," said the vice-consul, when Clementina repeated Mrs. Lander's acquiescence in the landlord's proposals, and he took his straw hat, and called a gondola from the nearest *traghetto*, and bargained at an expense consistent with his salary, to have himself rowed back to his own garden-gate.

The rest of the day was an era of better feeling between Mrs. Lander and her host than they had ever known, and at dinner he brought in with his own hand a dish which he said he had caused to be specially made for her. It was so tempting in odor and complexion that Mrs. Lander declared she must taste it, though as she justly said, she had eaten too much already; when she had once tasted it she ate it all, against Clementina's protestations; she announced at the end that every bite had done her good, and that she never felt better in her life. She passed a happy evening, with renewed faith in the air of the lagoon; her sole regret now was that Mr. Lander had not lived to try it with her, for if he had she was sure he would have been alive at that moment.

She allowed herself to be got to bed rather earlier than usual; before Clementina dropped asleep she heard her breathing with long, easy, quiet respirations, and she lost the fear of the landlord's dish which had haunted her through the evening. She was awakened in the morning by a touch on her shoulder. Maddalena hung over her with a frightened face, and implored her to come and look at the signora, who seemed not at all well. Clementina ran into her room, and found her dead. She must have died some hours before without a struggle, for the face was that of sleep, and it had a dignity and beauty which it had not worn in her life of self-indulgent wilfulness for so many years that the girl had never seen it look so before.

XXXIV.

The vice-consul was not sure how far his powers went in the situation with which Mrs. Lander had finally embarrassed him. But he met the new difficulties with patience, and he agreed with Clementina that they ought to see if Mrs. Lander had left any written expression of her wishes concerning the event. She had never spoken of such a chance, but had always looked forward to getting well and going home, so far as the girl knew, and the most careful search now brought to light nothing that bore upon it. In the absence of instructions to the contrary, they did what they must, and the body, emptied of its life of senseless worry and greedy care, was laid to rest in the island cemetery of Venice.

When all was over, the vice-consul ventured an observation which he had hitherto delicately withheld. The question of Mrs. Lander's kindred had already been discussed between him and Clementina, and he now felt that another question had duly presented itself. "You didn't notice," he suggested, "anything like a will when we went over the papers?" He had looked carefully for it, expecting that there might have been some expression of Mrs. Lander's wishes in it. "Because," he added, "I happen to know that Mr. Milray drew one up for her; I witnessed it."

"No," said Clementina, "I didn't see anything of it. She told me she had made a will; but she didn't quite like it, and sometimes she thought she would change it. She spoke of getting you to do it; I didn't know but she had."

The vice-consul shook his nead. "No. And these relations of her husband's up in Michigan; you don't know where they live, exactly?"

"No. She neva told me; she wouldn't; she didn't like to talk about them; I don't even know their names."

The vice-consul thoughtfully scratched a corner of his chin through his beard. "If there isn't any will, they're the heirs. I used to be a sort of wild-cat lawyer, and I know that much law."

"Yes," said Clementina. "She left them five thousand dollas apiece. She said she wished she had made it ten."

"I guess she's made it a good deal more, if she's made it anything. Miss Claxon, don't you understand that if no will turns up, they come in for *all* her money?"

"Well, that's what I thought they ought to do," said Clementina.

"And do you understand that if that's so, *you* don't come in for anything? You must excuse me for mentioning it; but she's told everybody that you were to have it, and if there's no will"—

He stopped and bent an eye of lack-lustre compassion on the girl, who replied, "Oh, yes. I know that; it's what I always told her to do. I didn't want it."

"You didn't *want* it?"

"No."

"Well!" The vice-consul stared at her, but he forbore the comment that her indifference inspired. He said after a pause, "Then what we've got to do is to advertise for the Michigan relations, and let 'em take any action they want to."

"That's the only thing we could do, I presume."

This gave the vice-consul another pause. At the end of it he got to his feet. "Is there anything I can do for *you*, Miss Claxon?"

She went to her portfolio and produced Mrs. Lander's letter of credit. It had been made out for three thousand pounds, in Clementina's name as well as her own; but she had lived wastefully since she had come abroad, and little money remained to be taken up. With the letter Clementina handed the vice-consul the roll of Italian and Austrian bank-notes which she had drawn when Mrs. Lander decided to leave Venice; they were to the amount of several thousand *lire* and *gulden*. She offered them with the insensibility to the quality of money which so many women have, and which is always so astonishing to men. "What must I do with these?" she asked.

"Why, keep them!" returned the vice-consul on the spur of his surprise.

"I don't know as I should have any right to," said Clementina. "They were hers."

"Why, but"— The vice-consul began his protest, but he could not end it logically, and he did not end it at all. He insisted with Clementina that she had a right to some money which Mrs. Lander had given her during her life; he took charge of the bank-notes in the interest of the possible heirs, and gave her his receipt for them. In the meantime he felt that he ought to ask her what she expected to do.

"I think," she said, "I will stay in Venice awhile."

The vice-consul suppressed any surprise he might have felt at a decision given with mystifying cheerfulness. He answered, Well, that was right; and for the second time he asked her if there was anything he could do for her.

"Why, yes," she returned. "I should like to stay on in the house here, if you could speak for me to the padrone."

"I don't see why you shouldn't, if we can make the padrone understand it's different."

"You mean about the price?" The vice-consul nodded. "That's what I want you should speak to him about, Mr. Bennam, if you would. Tell him that I haven't got but a little money now, and he would have to make it very reasonable. That is, if you think it would be right for me to stay, afta the way he tried to treat Mrs. Lander."

The vice-consul gave the point some thought, and decided that the attempted extortion need not make any difference with Clementina, if she could get the right terms. He said he did not believe the padrone was a bad fellow, but he liked to take advantage of a stranger when he could; we all did. When he came to talk with him he found him a man of heart if not of conscience. He entered into the case with the prompt intelligence and vivid sympathy of his race, and he made it easy for Clementina to stay till she had heard from her friends in America. For himself and for his wife, he professed that she could not stay too long, and they proposed that if it would content the signorina still further they would employ Maddalena as chambermaid till she wished to return to Florence; she had offered to remain if the signorina stayed.

"Then that is settled," said Clementina with a sigh of relief; and she thanked the vice-consul for his offer to write to the Milrays for her, and said that she would rather write herself.

She meant to write as soon as she heard from Mr. Hinkle, which could not be long now, for then she could be independent of the offers of help which she dreaded from Miss Milray, even more than from Mrs. Milray; it would be harder to refuse them; and she entered upon a passage of her life which a nature less simple would have found much more trying. But she had the power of taking everything as if it were as much to be expected as anything else. If nothing at all happened she accepted the situation with implicit resignation, and with a gayety of heart which availed her long, and never wholly left her.

While the suspense lasted she could not write home as frankly as before, and she sent off letters to Middlemount which treated of her delay in Venice with helpless reticence. They would have set another sort of household intolerably wondering and suspecting, but she had the comfort of knowing that her father would probably settle the whole matter by saying that she would tell what she meant when she got round to it; and apart from this she had mainly the comfort of the vice-consul's society. He had little to do besides looking after her, and he employed himself about this in daily visits which the padrone and his wife regarded as official, and promoted with a serious respect for the vice-consular dignity. If the visits ended, as they often did, in a turn on the Grand Canal, and an ice in the Piazza, they appealed to the imagination of more sophisticated witnesses, who decided that the young American girl had inherited the millions of the sick lady, and become the betrothed of the vice-consul, and that they were thus passing the days of their engagement in conformity to the American custom, however much at variance with that of other civilizations.

This view of the affair was known to Maddalena, but not to Clementina, who in those days went back in many things to the tradition of her life at Middlemount. The vice-consul was of a tradition almost as simple, and his longer experience set no very wide interval between them. It quickly came to his telling her all about his dead wife and his married daughters, and how, after his home was broken up, he thought he would travel a little and see what that would do for him. He confessed that it had not done much; he was always homesick, and he was ready to go as soon as the President sent out a consul to take his job off his hands. He said that he had not enjoyed himself so much since he came to Venice as he was doing now, and that he did not know what he should do if Clementina first got her call home. He betrayed no curiosity as to the peculiar circumstances of her stay, but affected to regard it as something quite normal, and he watched over her in every way with a fatherly as well as an official vigilance which never degenerated into the semblance of any other feeling.

Clementina rested in his care in entire security. The world had quite fallen from her, or so much of it as she had seen at Florence, and in her indifference she lapsed into life as it was in the time before that with a tender renewal of her allegiance to it. There was nothing in the conversation of the vice-consul to distract her from this; and she said and did the things at Venice that she used to do at Middlemount, as nearly as she could; to make the days of waiting pass more quickly, she tried to serve herself in ways that scandalized the proud affection of Maddalena. It was not fit for the signorina to make her bed or sweep her room; she might sew and knit if she would; but these other things were for servants like herself. She continued in the faith of Clementina's gentility, and saw her always as she had seen her first in the brief hour of her social splendor in Florence. Clementina tried to make her understand how she lived at Middlemount, but she only brought before Maddalena the humiliating image of a contadina, which she rejected not only in Clementina's behalf, but that of Miss Milray. She told her that she was laughing at her, and she was fixed in her belief when the girl laughed at that notion. Her poverty she easily conceived of; plenty of signorine in Italy were poor; and she protected her in it with the duty she did not divide quite evenly between her and the padrone.

The date which Clementina had fixed for hearing from Hinkle by cable had long passed, and the time when she first hoped to hear from him by letter had come and gone. Her address was with the vice-consul as Mrs. Lander's had been, and he could not be ignorant of her disappointment when he brought her letters which she said were from home. On the surface of things it could only be from home that she wished to hear, but beneath the surface he read an anxiety which mounted with each gratification of this wish. He had not seen much of the girl while Hinkle was in Venice; Mrs. Lander had not begun to make such constant use of him until Hinkle had gone; Mrs. Milray had told him of Clementina's earlier romance, and it was to Gregory that the vice-consul related the anxiety which he knew as little in its nature as in its object.

Clementina never doubted the good faith or constancy of her lover; but her heart misgave her as to his well-being when it sank at each failure of the vice-consul to bring her a letter from him. Something must have happened to him, and it must have been something very serious to keep him from writing; or there was some mistake of the post-office. The vice-consul indulged himself in personal inquiries to make sure that the mistake was not in the Venetian post-office; but he saw that he brought her greater distress in ascertaining the fact. He got to dreading a look of resolute cheerfulness that came into her face, when he shook his head in sign that there were no letters, and he suffered from the covert eagerness with which she glanced at the superscriptions of those he brought and failed to find the hoped-for letter among them. Ordeal for ordeal, he was beginning to regret his trials under Mrs. Lander. In them he could at least demand Clementina's sympathy, but against herself this was impossible. Once she noted his mute distress at hers, and broke into a little laugh that he found very harrowing.

"I guess you hate it almost as much as I do, Mr. Bennam."

"I guess I do. I've half a mind to write the letter you want, myself."

"I've half a mind to let you—or the letter *I'd* like to write."

It had come to her thinking she would write again to Hinkle; but she could not bring herself to do it. She often imagined doing it; she had every word of such a letter in her mind; and she dramatized every fact concerning it from the time she should put pen to paper, to the time when she should get back the answer that cleared the mystery of his silence away. Her fond reveries helped her to bear her suspense; they helped to make the days go by, to ease the doubt with which she lay down at night, and the heartsick hope with which she rose up in the morning.

One day, at the hour of his wonted visit, she saw

the vice-consul from her balcony coming, as it seemed to her, with another figure in his gondola, and a thousand conjectures whirled through her mind, and then centred upon one idea. After the first glance she kept her eyes down, and would not look again while she told herself incessantly that it could not be, and that she was a fool and a goose and a perfect coot, to think of such a thing for a single moment. When she allowed herself, or forced herself, to look a second time, as the boat drew near, she had to cling to the balcony parapet for support, in her disappointment.

The person whom the vice-consul helped out of the gondola was an elderly man like himself, and she took a last refuge in the chance that he might be Hinkle's father, sent to bring her to him because he could not come to her; or to soften some terrible news to her. Then her fancy fluttered and fell, and she waited patiently for the fact to reveal itself. There was something countrified in the figure of the man, and something clerical in his face, though there was nothing in his uncouth best clothes that confirmed this impression. In both face and figure there was a vague resemblance to some one she had seen before, when the vice-consul said:

"Miss Claxon, I want to introduce the Rev. Mr. James B. Orson, of Michigan." Mr. Orson took Clementina's hand into a dry, rough grasp, while he peered into her face with small, shy eyes. The vice-consul added with a kind of official formality, "Mr. Orson is the half-nephew of Mr. Lander," and then

"ONE DAY SHE SAW THE VICE-CONSUL FROM HER BALCONY."

Clementina now knew whom it was that he resembled. "He has come to Venice," continued the vice-consul, "at the request of Mrs. Lander; and he did not know of her death until I informed him of the fact. I should have said that Mr. Orson is the son of Mr. Lander's half-sister. He can tell you the balance himself." The vice-consul pronounced the concluding word with a certain distaste, and the effect of gladly retiring into the background.

"Won't you sit down?" said Clementina, and she added with one of the remnants of her Middlemount breeding, "Won't you let me take your hat?"

Mr. Orson in trying to comply with both her invitations, knocked his well worn silk hat from the hand that held it, and sent it rolling across the room, where Clementina pursued it and put it on the table.

"I may as well say at once," he began in a flat irresonant voice, "that I am the representative of Mrs. Lander's heirs, and that I have a letter from her enclosing her last will and testament, which I have shown to the consul here"—

"Vice-consul," the dignitary interrupted with an effect of rejecting any part in the affair.

"Vice-consul, I *should* say,—and I wish to lay them both before you, in order that"—

"Oh, that is all right," said Clementina sweetly. "I'm glad there is a will. I was afraid there wasn't any at all. Mr. Bennam and I looked for it everywhe'e." She smiled upon the Rev. Mr. Orson, who silently handed her a paper. It was the will which Milray had written for Mrs. Lander, and which, with whatever crazy motive, she had sent to her husband's kindred. It provided that each of them should be given five thousand dollars out of the estate, and that then all should go to Clementina. It was the will Mrs. Lander told her she had made, but she had never seen the paper before, and the legal forms hid the meaning from her so that she was glad to have the vice-consul make it clear. Then she said tranquilly, "Yes, that is the way I supposed it was."

Mr. Orson by no means shared her calm. He did not lift his voice, but on the level it had taken it became agitated. "Mrs. Lander gave me the address of her lawyer in Boston when she sent me the will, and I made a point of calling on him when I went East, to sail. I don't know why she wished me to come out to her, but being sick, I presume she naturally wished to see *some* of her own family."

He looked at Clementina as if he thought she might dispute this, but she consented at her sweetest, "Oh, yes, indeed," and he went on:

"I found her affairs in a very different condition from what she seemed to think. The estate was mostly in securities which had not been properly looked after, and they had depreciated until they were some of them not worth the paper they were printed on. The house in Boston is mortgaged up to its full value, I should say; and I should say that Mrs. Lander did not know where she stood. She seemed to think that she was a very rich woman, but she lived high, and her lawyer said he never could make her understand how the money was going. Mr. Lander seemed to lose his grip, the year he died, and engaged in some very unfortunate speculations; I don't know whether he told her. I might enter into details"—

"Oh, that is not necessary," said Clementina, politely, witless of the disastrous quality of the facts which Mr. Orson was imparting.

"But the sum and substance of it all is that there will not be more than enough to pay the bequests to her own family, if there is that."

Clementina looked with smiling innocence at the vice-consul.

"That is to say," he explained, "there won't be anything at all for you, Miss Claxon."

"Well, that's what I always told Mrs. Lander I ratha, when she brought it up. I told her she ought to give it to his family," said Clementina, with a satisfaction in the event which the vice-consul seemed unable to share, for he remained gloomily silent. "There is that last money I drew on the letter of credit, you can give that to Mr. Osson."

"I have told him about that money," said the vice-consul, dryly. "It will be handed over to him when the estate is settled, if there isn't enough to pay the bequests without it."

"And the money which Mrs. Landa gave me before that," she pursued, eagerly. Mr. Orson had the effect of pricking up his ears, though it was in fact merely a gleam of light that came into his eyes.

"That's *yours*," said the vice-consul, sourly, almost savagely. "She didn't give it to you without she wanted you to have it, and she didn't expect you to pay her bequests with it. In my opinion," he burst out, in a wrathful recollection of his own sufferings from Mrs. Lander, "she didn't give you a millionth part of your due for all the trouble she made you; and I want Mr. Orson to understand that, right here."

Clementina turned her impartial gaze upon Mr. Orson as if to verify the impression of this extreme opinion upon him; he looked as if he neither accepted nor rejected it, and she concluded the sentence which the vice-consul had interrupted. "Because I ratha not keep it, if there isn't enough without it."

The vice-consul gave way to violence. "It's none of your business whether there's enough or not. What *you've* got to do is to keep what belongs to you, and I'm going to see that you do. That's what I'm here for." If this assumption of official authority did not awe Clementina, at least it put a check upon her headlong self-sacrifice. The vice-consul strengthened his hold upon her by asking, "What would you do. I should like to know, if you gave that up?"

"Oh, I should get along," she returned, light-heartedly, but upon questioning herself whether she should turn to Miss Milray for help, or appeal to the vice-consul himself, she was daunted a little, and she added, "But just as you *say*, Mr. Bennam."

"I say, keep what fairly belongs to you. It's only two or three hundred dollars at the outside," he explained to Mr. Orson's hungry eyes; but perhaps the sum did not affect the country minister's imagination as trifling; his yearly salary must sometimes have been little more.

The whole interview left the vice-consul out of humor with both parties to the affair; and as to Clementina, between the ideals of a perfect little saint, and a perfect little simpleton he remained for the present unable to class her.

XXXV.

Clementina and the vice-consul afterwards agreed that Mrs. Lander must have sent the will to Mr. Orson in one of those moments of suspicion when she distrusted everyone about her, or in that trouble concerning her husband's kindred which had grown upon her more and more, as a means of assuring them that they were provided for.

"But even then," the vice-consul concluded, "I don't see why she wanted this man to come out here. The only explanation is that she was a little off her base towards the last. That's the charitable supposition."

"I don't think she was herself, some of the time," Clementina assented in acceptance of the kindly construction.

The vice-consul modified his good will toward Mrs. Lander's memory so far as to say, "Well, if she'd been somebody else *most* of the time, it would have been an improvement."

The talk turned upon Mr. Orson, and what he would probably do. The vice-consul had found him a cheap lodging, at his request, and he seemed to have settled down at Venice either without the will or without the power to go home, but the vice-consul did not know where he ate, or what he did with himself except at the times when he came for letters. Once or twice when he looked him up he found him writing, and then the minister explained that he had promised to "correspond" for an organ of his sect in the Northwest; but he owned that there was no money in it. He was otherwise reticent and even furtive in his manner. He did not seem to go much about the city, but kept to his own room; and if he was writing of Venice it must have been chiefly from his acquaintance with the little court into which his windows looked. He affected the vice-consul as forlorn and helpless, and he pitied him and rather liked him as a fellow-victim of Mrs. Lander.

One morning Mr. Orson came to see Clementina, and after a brief passage of opinion upon the weather, he fell into an embarrassed silence from which he pulled himself at last with a visible effort. "I hardly know how to lay before you what I have to say, Miss Claxon," he began, "and I must ask you to put the best construction upon it. I have never been reduced to a similar distress before. You would naturally think that I would turn to the vice-consul, on such an occasion; but I feel, through our relation to the—to Mrs. Lander—ah—somewhat more at home with you."

He stopped, as if he wished to be asked his business, and she entreated him, "Why, what is it, Mr. Osson? Is there something I can do? There isn't anything I wouldn't!"

A gleam, watery and faint, which still could not be quite winked away, came into his small eyes. "Why, the fact is, could you—ah—advance me about five dollars?"

"Why, Mr. Osson!" she began, and he seemed to think she wished to withdraw her offer of help, for he interposed.

"I will repay it as soon as I get an expected remittance from home. I came out on the invitation of Mrs. Lander, and as her guest, and I supposed"—

"Oh, don't say a wo'd!" cried Clementina, but now that he had begun he was powerless to stop.

"I would not ask, but my landlady has pressed me for her rent—I suppose she needs it—and I have been reduced to the last copper"—

The girl whose eyes the tears of self pity so rarely visited, broke into a sob that seemed to surprise her visitor. But she checked herself as with a quick inspiration: "Have you been to breakfast?"

"Well—ah—not *this* morning," Mr. Orson admitted, as if to imply that having breakfasted some other morning might be supposed to serve the purpose.

She left him and ran to the door. "Maddalena, Maddalena!" she called; and Maddalena responded with a frightened voice from the direction of the kitchen:

"Vengo subito!"

She hurried out with the coffee-pot in her hand, as if she had just taken it up when Clementina called; and she halted for the whispered colloquy between them which took place before she set it down on the table already laid for breakfast; then she hurried out of the room again. She came back with a cantaloupe and grapes, and cold ham, and put them before Clementina and her guest, who both ignored the hunger with which he swept everything before him. When his famine had left nothing, he said, in decorous compliment:

"That is very good coffee,—I should think the genuine berry, though I am told that they adulterate coffee a great deal in Europe."

"Do they?" asked Clementina. "I didn't know it."

She left him still sitting before the table, and came back with some bank-notes in her hand. "Are you sure you hadn't betta take moa?" she asked.

"I think that five dollars will be all that I shall require," he answered, with dignity. "I should be unwilling to accept more. I shall undoubtedly receive some remittances soon."

"Oh, I know you will," Clementina returned, and she added, "I am waiting for lettas myself; I don't think any one ought to give up."

The preacher ignored the appeal which was in her tone rather than her words, and went on to explain at length the circumstances of his having come to Europe so unprovided against chances. When he wished to excuse his imprudence, she cried out, "Oh, don't say a wo'd! It's just like my *own* fatha," and she told him some things of her home which apparently did not interest him very much. He had a kind of dull, cold self-absorption in which he was indeed so little like her father that only her kindness for the lonely man could have justified her in thinking there was any resemblance.

She did not see him again for a week, and meantime she did not tell the vice-consul of what had happened. But an anxiety for the minister began to mingle with her anxieties for herself; she constantly wondered why she did not hear from her lover, and she occasionally wondered whether Mr. Orson were not falling into want again. She had decided to betray his condition to the vice-consul, when he came, bringing the money she had lent him. He had received a remittance from an unexpected source, and he hoped she would excuse his delay in repaying her loan. She wished not to take the money, at least till he was quite sure he should not want it, but he insisted.

"I have enough to keep me, now, till I hear from other sources, with the means for returning home. I see no object in continuing here, under the circumstances."

In the relief which she felt for him Clementina's heart throbbed with a pain which was all for herself. Why should she wait any longer either? For that instant she abandoned the hope which had kept her up so long; a wave of homesickness overwhelmed her.

"I should like to go back, too," she said. "I don't see why I'm staying. Mr. Osson, why can't you let me"—she was going to say—"go home with you?" But she really said what was also in her heart, "Why can't you let me give you the money to go home? It is all Mrs. Landa's money, anyway."

"There is certainly that view of the matter," he assented with a promptness that might have suggested a lurking grudge for the vice-consul's decision that she ought to keep the money Mrs. Lander had given her.

But Clementina urged unsuspiciously: "Oh, yes, indeed! And I shall feel better if you take it. I only wish I could go home, too!"

The minister was silent while he was revolving, with whatever scruple or reluctance, a compromise suitable to the occasion. Then he said, "Why should we not return together?"

"Would you *take* me?" she entreated.

"That should be as you wished. I am not much acquainted with the usages in such matters, but I presume that it would be entirely practicable. We could ask the vice-consul."

"Yes"—

"He must have had considerable experience in cases of the kind. Would your friends meet you in New York, or"—

"I don't know," said Clementina with a pang for the thought of a meeting she had sometimes fancied there, when her lover had come out for her, and her father had been told to come and receive them. "No," she sighed, "the'e wouldn't be time to let them know. But it wouldn't make any difference. I could get home from New Yo'k alone," she added, listlessly. Her spirits had fallen again. She saw that she could not leave Venice till she had heard in some sort from the letter she had written. "Perhaps it couldn't be done, after all. But I will see Mr. Bennam about it, Mr. Osson; and I know he will want you to have that much of the money. He will be coming he'e, soon."

He rose upon what he must have thought her hint, and said, "I should not wish to have him swayed against his judgment."

The vice-consul came not long after the minister had left her, and she began upon what she wished to do for him.

The vice-consul was against it. "I would rather lend him the money out of my own pocket. How are you going to get along yourself, if you let him have so much?"

She did not answer at once. Then she said, hopelessly, "I've a great mind to go home with him. I don't believe there's any use waiting here any longa." The vice-consul could not say anything to this. She added, "Yes, I believe I will go home. We we'e talking about it, the other day, and he is willing to let me go with him."

"I should think he would be," the vice-consul retorted in his indignation for her. "Did you *offer* to pay for his passage?"

"Yes," she owned, "I did," and again the vice-consul could say nothing. "If I went, it wouldn't make any difference whether it took it all or not. I should have plenty to get home from New York with."

"Well," the vice-consul assented, dryly, "it's for you to say."

"I know you don't want me to do it!"

"Well, I shall miss you," he answered, evasively.

"And I shall miss you, too, Mr. Bennam. Don't you believe it? But if I don't take this chance to get home, I don't know when I shall eva have anotha. And there isn't any use waiting—no, there isn't!"

The vice-consul laughed at the sort of imperative despair in her tone. "How are you going? Which way, I mean."

They counted up Clementina's debts and assets, and they found that if she took the next steamer from Genoa, which was to sail in four days, she would have enough to pay her own way and Mr. Orson's to New York, and still have some thirty dollars over, for her expenses home to Middlemount. They allowed for a second cabin-passage, which the vice-consul said was perfectly good on the Genoa steamers. He rather urged the gentility and comfort of the second cabin-passage, but his reasons in favor of it were wasted upon Clementina's indifference; she wished to get home, now, and she did not care how. She asked the vice-consul to see the minister for her, and if he were ready and willing, to telegraph for their tickets. He transacted the business so promptly that he was able to tell her when he came in the evening that everything was in train. He excused his coming; he said that now she was going so soon, he wanted to see all he could of her. He offered no excuse when he came the next morning; but he said he had got a letter for her and thought she might want to have it at once.

He took it out of his hat and gave it to her. It was addressed in Hinkle's writing; her answer had come at last; she stood trembling with it in her hand.

The vice-consul smiled. "Is that the one?"

"Yes," she whispered back.

"All right." He took his hat, and set it on the back of his head before he left her without other salutation.

Then Clementina opened her letter. It was in a woman's hand, and the writer made haste to explain at the beginning that she was George W. Hinkle's sister, and that she was writing for him; for though he was now out of danger, he was still very weak, and they had all been anxious about him. A month before, he had been hurt in a railroad collision, and had come home from the West, where the accident happened, suffering mainly from shock, as his doctor thought; he had taken to his bed at once, and had not risen from it since. He had been out of his head a great part of the time, and had been forbidden everything that could distress or excite him. His sister said that she was writing for him now as soon as he had seen Clementina's letter; it had been forwarded from one address to another, and had at last found him there at his home in Ohio. He wished to say that he would come out for Clementina as soon as he was allowed to undertake the journey, and in the meantime she must let him know constantly where she was. The letter closed with a few words of love in his own handwriting.

Clementina rose from reading it, and put on her hat in a bewildered impulse to go to him at once; she knew, in spite of all the cautions and reserves of the letter that he must still be very sick. When she came out of her daze she found that she could only go to the vice-consul. She put the letter in his hands to let it explain itself. "You'll undastand, now," she said. "What shall I do?"

When he had read it, he smiled and answered, "I guess I understood pretty well before, though I wasn't posted on names. Well, I suppose you'll want to lay out most of your capital on cables, now?"

"Yes," she laughed, and then she suddenly lamented, "*Why* didn't they telegraph?"

"Well, I guess he hadn't the head for it," said the vice-consul, "and the rest wouldn't think of it. They wouldn't, in the country."

Clementina laughed again, in joyous recognition of the fact, "No, *my* fatha wouldn't, eitha!"

The vice-consul reached for his hat, and he led the way to Clementina's gondola at his garden gate, in greater haste than she. At the telegraph office he framed a dispatch which for expansive fullness and precision was apparently unexampled in the experience of the clerk who took it and spelt over its English with them. It asked an answer in the vice-consul's care, and, "I'll tell you what, Miss Claxon," he said with a husky weakness in his voice, "I wish you'd let this be my treat."

She understood. "Do you really, Mr. Bennam?"

"I do indeed."

"Well, then, I will," she said, but when he wished to include in his treat the dispatch she sent home to her father announcing her coming, she would not let him.

He looked at his watch, as they rowed away. "It's eight o'clock here, now, and it will reach Ohio about six hours earlier; but you can't expect an answer to-night, you know."

"No"— She had expected it though, he could see that.

"But whenever it comes, I'll bring it right round to you. Now it's all going to be straight, don't you be afraid, and you're going home the quickest way you can get there. I've been looking up the sailings, and this Genoa boat will get you to New York about as soon as any could from Liverpool. Besides there's always a chance of missing connections and losing time between here and England. I should stick to the Genoa boat."

"Oh I shall," said Clementina, far less fidgetted than he. She was, in fact, resting securely again in the faith which had never really deserted her, and had only seemed for a little time to waver from her when her hope went. Now that she had telegraphed, her heart was at peace, and she even laughed as she answered the anxious vice-consul.

XXXVI.

The next morning Clementina watched for the vice-consul from her balcony. She knew he would not send; she knew he would come; but it was nearly noon before she saw him coming. They caught sight of each other almost at the same moment, and he stood up in his boat, and waved something white in his hand, which must be a dispatch for her.

It acknowledged her telegram and reported George still improving; his father would meet her steamer in New York. It was very reassuring, it was everything hopeful; but when she had read it she gave it to the vice-consul for encouragement.

"It's all right, Miss Claxon," he said, stoutly. "Don't you be troubled about Mr. Hinkle's not coming to meet you himself. He can't keep too quiet for a while yet."

"Oh, yes," said Clementina, patiently.

"If you really *want* somebody to worry about, you can help Mr. Orson to worry about himself!" the vice-consul went on, with the grimness he had formerly used in speaking of Mrs. Lander. "He's sick, or he thinks he's going to be. He sent round for me this morning, and I found him in bed. You *may* have to go home alone. But I guess he's more scared than hurt."

Her heart sank, and then rose in revolt against the mere idea of delay. "I wonder if I ought to go and see him," she said.

"Well, it would be a kindness," returned the vice-consul, with a promptness that unmasked the apprehension he felt for the sick man.

He did not offer to go with her, and she took Maddalena. She found the minister seated in his chair beside his bed. A three days' beard heightened the gauntness of his face; he did not move when his padrona announced her.

"I am not any better," he answered when she said that she was glad to see him up. "I am merely resting; the bed is hard. I regret to say," he added, with a sort of formal impersonality, "that I shall be unable to accompany you home, Miss Claxon. That is, if you still think of taking the steamer this week."

Her whole being had set homeward in a tide that already seemed to drift the vessel from its moorings. "What—what do you mean?" she gasped.

"I didn't know," he returned, "but that in view of the circumstances—all the circumstances—you might be intending to defer your departure to some later steamer."

"No, no, no! I must go, now. I couldn't wait a day, an hour, a minute after the first chance of going. You don't know what you are saying! He might die if I told him I was not coming; and then what should

I do?" This was what Clementina said to herself; but what she said to Mr. Orson, with an inspiration from her terror at his suggestion was, "Don't you think a little chicken broth would do you good, Mr. Osson? *I* don't believe but what it would."

A wistful gleam came into the preacher's eyes. "It might," he admitted, and then she knew what must be his malady. She sent Maddalena to a *trattoria* for the soup, and she did not leave him, even after she had seen its effect upon him. It was not hard to persuade him that he had better come home with her; and she had him there, tucked away with his few poor belongings, in the most comfortable room the padrone could imagine, when the vice-consul came in the evening.

"He says he thinks he can go, now," she ended, when she had told the vice-consul. "And I *know* he can. It wasn't anything but pooa living."

"It looks more like *no* living," said the vice-consul. "Why didn't the old fool let some one know that he was short of money?" He went on with a partial transfer of his contempt of the preacher to her, "I suppose if he'd been sick instead of hungry, you'd have waited over till the next steamer for him."

She cast down her eyes. "I don't know what you'll think of me. I should have been sorry for him, and I should have wanted to stay." She lifted her eyes and looked the vice-consul defiantly in the face. "But he hadn't the fust claim on me, and I should have *gone*—I couldn't have helped it!—I should have *gone*, if he had been *dying!*"

"Well, you've got more horse-sense," said the vice-consul, "than any ten men I ever saw," and he testified his admiration of her by putting his arms round her, where she stood before him, and kissing her. "Don't you mind," he explained. "If my youngest girl had lived, she would have been about your age."

"Oh, it's all right, Mr. Bennam," said Clementina.

When the time came for them to leave Venice, Mr. Orson was even eager to go. The vice-consul would have gone with them in contempt of the official responsibilities which he felt to be such a thankless burden, but there was really no need of his going, and he and Clementina treated the question with the matter-of-fact impartiality which they liked in each other. He saw her off at the station where Maddalena had come to take the train for Florence in token of her devotion to the signorina, whom she would not outstay in Venice. She wept long and loud upon Clementina's neck, so that even Clementina was once moved to put her handkerchief to her tearless eyes.

At the last moment she had a question which she referred to the vice-consul. "Should you tell him?" she asked.

"Tell who what?" he retorted.

"Mr. Osson—that I wouldn't have stayed for him."

"Do you think it would make you feel any better?" asked the consul, upon reflection.

"I believe he ought to know."

"Well, then, I guess I should do it."

The time did not come for her confession till they had nearly reached the end of their voyage. It followed upon something like a confession from the minister himself, which he made the day he struggled on deck with her help, after spending a week in his berth.

"Here is something," he said, "which appears to be for you, Miss Claxon. I found it among some letters for Mrs. Lander which Mr. Bennam gave me after my arrival, and I only observed the address in looking over the papers in my valise this morning." He handed her a telegram. "I trust that it is nothing requiring immediate attention."

Clementina read it at a glance. "No," she answered, and for a while she could not say anything more; it was a cable message which Hinkle's sister must have sent her after writing. No evil had come of its failure to reach her, and she recalled without bitterness the suffering which would have been spared her if she had got it before. It was when she thought of the suffering of her lover from the silence which must have made him doubt her, that she could not speak. As soon as she governed herself against her first resentment she said, with a little sigh, "It is all right, *now*, Mr. Osson," and her stress upon the word seemed to trouble him with no misgiving. "Besides, if you're to blame for not noticing, so is Mr. Bennam, and I don't want to blame any one." She hesitated a moment before she added: "I have got to tell you something, now, because I think you ought to know it. I am going home to be married, Mr. Osson, and this message is from the gentleman I am going to be married to. He has been very sick, and I don't know yet as he'll be able to meet me in New Yo'k; but his fatha will."

Mr. Orson showed no interest in these facts beyond a silent attention to her words, which might have passed for an open indifference. At his time of life all such questions, which are of permanent importance to women, affect men hardly more than the angels who neither marry nor are given in marriage. Besides, as a minister he must have had a surfeit of all possible qualities in the love affairs of people intending matrimony. As a casuist he was more reasonably concerned in the next fact which Clementina laid before him.

"And the otha day, there in Venice when you we'e sick, and you seemed to think that I might put off stahting home till the next steamer, I don't know but I let you believe I would."

"I supposed that the delay of a week or two could make no material difference to you."

"But now you see that it would. And I feel as if I ought to tell you—I spoke to Mr. Bennam about it, and he didn't tell me not to—that I *shouldn't* have staid, no not for anything in the wo'ld. I had to do what I did at the time, but eva since it has seemed as if I had deceived you, and I don't want to have it seem so any longer. It isn't because I don't hate to tell you; I do; but I guess if it was to happen over again I couldn't feel any different. Do you want I should tell the deck-stewahd to bring you some beef-tea?"

"I think I could relish a small portion," said Mr. Orson, cautiously, and he said nothing more.

Clementina left him with her nerves in a flutter, and she did not come back to him until she decided that it was time to help him down to his cabin. He suffered her to do this in silence, but at the door he cleared his throat and began:

"I have reflected upon what you told me, and I have tried to regard the case from all points. I believe that I have done so, without personal feeling, and I think it my duty to say, fully and freely, that I believe you would have done perfectly right not to remain."

"Yes," said Clementina, "I thought you would think so."

They parted emotionlessly to all outward effect, and when they met again it was without a sign of having passed through a crisis of sentiment. Neither referred to the matter again, but from that time the minister treated Clementina with a deference not without some shadows of tenderness such as her helplessness in Venice had apparently never inspired. She had cast out of her mind all lingering hardness toward him in telling him the hard truth, and she met his faint relentings with a grateful gladness which showed itself in her constant care of him.

This helped her a little to forget the strain of the anxiety that increased upon her as the time shortened between the last news of her lover and the next; and there was perhaps no more exaggeration in the import than in the terms of the formal acknowledgment which

Mr. Orson made her as their steamer sighted Fire Island Light, and they both knew that their voyage had ended: "I may not be able to say to you in the hurry of our arrival in New York that I am obliged to you for a good many little attentions, which I should be pleased to reciprocate if opportunity offered. I do not think I am going too far in saying that they are such as a daughter might offer a parent."

"Oh, don't speak of it, Mr. Osson!" she protested. "I haven't done anything that any one wouldn't have done."

"I presume," said the minister, thoughtfully, as if retiring from an extreme position, "that they are such as others similarly circumstanced, might have done, but it will always be a source of satisfaction for you to reflect that you have not neglected them."

XXXVII.

In the crowd which thronged the steamer's dock at Hoboken, Clementina strained her eyes to make out some one who looked enough like her lover to be his father, and she began to be afraid that they might miss each other when she failed. She walked slowly down the gangway, with the people that thronged it, glad to be hidden by them from her failure, but at the last step she was caught aside by a small black-eyed, black-haired woman, who called out "Isn't this Miss Claxon? I'm Georrge's sisterr. Oh, you'rre just like what he said! I knew it! I knew it!" and then hugged her and kissed her, and passed her to the little lean dark old man next her. "This is fatherr. I knew you couldn't tell us, because I take afterr him, and Georrge is exactly like motherr."

George's father took her hand timidly, but found courage to say to his daughter, "Hadn't you betterr let her *own* fatherr have a chance at herr?" and amidst a tempest of apologies and self blame from the sister, Claxon showed himself over the shoulders of the little man.

"Why, there wa'n't no hurry, as long as she's

he'a," he said, in prompt enjoyment of the joke, and he and Clementina sparely kissed each other.

"Why, fatha!" she said. "I didn't expect you to come to New Yo'k to meet me."

"Well, I didn't ha'dly expect it myself; but I'd neva been to Yo'k, and I thought I might as well come. Things ah' ratha slack at home, just now, anyway."

She did not heed his explanation. "We'e you sca'ed when you got my dispatch?"

"No, we kind of expected you'd come any time, the way you wrote afta Mrs. Landa died. We thought something must be up."

"Yes," she said, absently. Then, "Whe'e's motha?" she asked.

"Well, I guess she thought she couldn't get round to it, exactly," said the father. "She's all right. Needn't ask *you!*"

"No, I'm fust-rate," Clementina returned, with a silent joy in her father's face and voice. She went back in it to the girl of a year ago, and the world which had come between them since their parting rolled away as if it had never been there.

Neither of them said anything about that. She named over her brothers and sisters, and he answered, "Yes, yes," in assurance of their well-being, and then he explained, as if that were the only point of real interest, "I see your folks waitin' he'e fo' somebody, and I thought I'd see if it wa'n't the same *one*, and we kind of struck up an acquaintance on your account befo'e you got he'e, Clem."

"Your folks!" she silently repeated to herself. "Yes, they *ah'* mine!" and she stood trying to realize the strange fact, while George's sister poured out a voluminous comment upon Claxon's spare statement, and George's father admired her volubility with the shut smile of toothless age. She spoke with the burr which the Scotch-Irish settlers have imparted to the whole middle West, but it was music to Clementina, who heard now and then a tone of her lover in his sister's voice. In the midst of it all she caught sight of a mute unfriended figure just without their circle, his traveling shawl hanging loose upon his shoulders, and the valise which had formed his sole baggage in the voyage to and from Europe pulling his long hand out of his coat sleeve.

"Oh, yes," she said, "here is Mr. Osson that came ova with me, fatha; he's a relation of Mr. Landa's," and she presented him to them all.

He shifted his valise to the left hand, and shook hands with each, asking, "What name?" and then fell motionless again.

"Well," said her father, "I guess this is the end of this paht of the ceremony, and I'm goin' to see your baggage through the custom-house, Clementina; I've read about it, and I want to know how it's done. I want to see what you ah' tryin' to smuggle in."

"I guess you won't find much," she said. "But you'll want the keys, won't you?" She called to him, as he was stalking away.

"Well, I guess that *would* be a good idea. Want to help, Miss Hinkle?"

"I guess we might as well all help," said Clementina, and Mr. Orson included himself in the invitation. He seemed unable to separate himself from them, though the passage of Clementina's baggage through the customs, and its delivery to an expressman for the hotel where the Hinkles said they were staying might well have severed the last tie between them.

"Ah' you going straight home, Mr. Osson?" she asked, to rescue him from the forgetfulness into which they were all letting him fall.

"I think I will remain over a day," he answered. "I may go on to Boston before starting West."

"Well, that's right," said Clementina's father with the wish to approve everything native to him, and an instinctive sense of Clementina's wish to befriend the minister. "Betta come to oua hotel. We're all goin' to the same one."

"I presume it is a good one?" Mr. Orson assented.

"Well," said Claxon, "you must make Miss Hinkle, he'a, stand it if it ain't. She's got me to go to it."

Mr. Orson apparently could not enter into the joke; but he accompanied the party, which again began to forget him, across the ferry and up the elevated road to the street car that formed the last stage of their progress to the hotel. At this point George's sister fell silent, and Clementina's father burst out, "Look he'a! I guess we betta not keep this up any longa; I don't believe much in supprises, and I guess she betta know it now."

He looked at George's sister as if for authority to

speak further, and Clementina looked at her, too, while George's father nervously moistened his smiling lips with the tip of his tongue, and let his twinkling eyes rest upon Clementina's face.

"Is he at the hotel?" she asked.

"Yes," said his sister, monosyllabic for once.

"I knew it," said Clementina, and she was only half aware of the fullness with which his sister now explained how he wanted to come so much that the doctor thought he had better, but that they had made him promise he would not try to meet her at the steamer, lest it should be too great a trial of his strength.

"Yes," Clementina assented, when the story came to an end and was beginning over again.

She had an inexplicable moment when she stood before her lover in the room where they left her to meet him alone. She faltered and he waited constrained by her constraint.

"Is it all a mistake, Clementina?" he asked, with a piteous smile.

"No, no!"

"Am I so much changed?"

"No; you are looking betta than I expected"—

"And you are not sorry—for anything?"

"No, I am— Perhaps I have thought of you too much! It seems so strange."

"I understand," he answered. "We have been like spirits to each other, and now we find that we are alive and on the earth like other people; and we are not used to it."

"It must be something like that."

"But if it's something else—if you have the least regret,—if you would rather"—He stopped, and they remained looking at each other a moment. Then she turned her head, and glanced out of the window, as if something there had caught her sight.

"It's a very pleasant view, isn't it?" she said; and she lifted her hands to her head, and took off her hat, with an effect of having got home after absence, to stay.

XXXVIII.

It was possibly through some sense finer than any cognition that Clementina felt in meeting her lover that she had taken up a new burden rather than laid down an old one. Afterwards, when they once recurred to that meeting, and she tried to explain for him the hesitation which she had not been able to hide, she could only say, "I presume I didn't want to begin unless I was sure I could carry out. It would have been silly."

Her confession, if it was a confession, was made when one of his returns to health, or rather one of the arrests of his unhealth, flushed them with hope and courage; but before that first meeting was ended she knew that he had overtasked his strength, in coming to New York, and he must not try it further. "Fatha," she said to Claxon, with the authority of a woman doing her duty, "I'm not going to let Geo'ge go up to Middlemount, with all the excitement. It will be as much as he can do to get home. You can tell mother about it; and the rest. I did suppose it would be Mr. Richling that would marry us, and I always wanted him to, but I guess somebody else can do it as well."

"Just as you say, Clem," her father assented. "Why not Brother Osson, he'a?" he suggested with a pleasure in the joke, whatever it was, that the minister's relation to Clementina involved. "I guess he can put off his visit to Boston long enough."

"Well, I was thinking of him," said Clementina. "Will you ask him?"

"Yes. I'll get round to it, in the mohning."

"No—now; right away. I've been talking with Geo'ge about it; and the'e's no sense in putting it off. I ought to begin taking care of him at once."

"Well, I guess when I tell your motha how you're layin' hold, she won't think it's the same pusson," said her father, proudly.

"But it is; I haven't changed a bit."

"You ha'n't changed for the wohse, anyway."

"Didn't I always try to do what I had to?"

"I guess you did, Clem."

"Well, then!"

Mr. Orson, after a decent hesitation, consented to perform the ceremony. It took place in a parlor of the hotel, according to the law of New York, which facilitates marriage so greatly in all respects that it is strange any one in the State should remain single. He had then a luxury of choice between attaching himself to the bridal couple as far as Ohio on his journey home to Michigan, or to Claxon who was going to take the boat for Boston the next day on his way to Middlemount. He decided for Claxon, since he could then see Mrs. Lander's lawyer at once, and arrange with him for getting out of the vice-consul's hands the money which he was holding for an authoritative demand. He accepted without open reproach the handsome fee which the elder Hinkle gave him for his services, and even went so far as to say, "If your son should ever be blest with a return to health, he has got a helpmeet such as there are very few of." He then admonished the young couple, in whatever trials life should have in store for them, to be resigned, and always to be prepared for the worst. When he came later to take leave of them, he was apparently not equal to the task of fitly acknowledging the return which Hinkle made him of all the money remaining to Clementina out of the sum last given her by Mrs. Lander, but he hid any disappointment he might have suffered, and with a brief, "Thank you," put it in his pocket.

Hinkle told Clementina of the apathetic behavior of Mr. Orson; he added with a laugh like his old self, "It's the best that *he* doesn't seem prepared for."

"Yes," she assented. "He wasn't very chee'ful. But I presume that he meant well. It must be a trial for him to find out that Mrs. Landa wasn't rich, after all."

It was apparently never a trial to her. She went to Ohio with her husband and took up her life on the farm, where it was wisely judged that he had the best chance of working out of the wreck of his health and strength. There was often the promise and always the hope of this, and their love knew no doubt of the future. Her sisters-in-law delighted in all her strangeness and difference, while they petted her as something not to be separated from him in their petting of their brother; to his mother she was the darling which her youngest had never ceased to be; Clementina once went so far as to say to him that if she was ever anything she would like to be a Moravian.

The question of religion was always related in their minds to the question of Gregory, to whom they did justice in their trust of each other. It was Hinkle himself who reasoned out that if Gregory was narrow, his narrowness was of his conscience and not of his heart or his mind. She respected the memory of her first lover; but it was as if he were dead, now, as well as her young dream of him, and she read with a curious sense of remoteness, a paragraph which her husband found in the religious intelligence of his Sunday paper, announcing the marriage of the Rev. Frank Gregory to a lady described as having been a frequent and bountiful contributor to the foreign missions. She was apparently a widow, and they conjectured that she was older than he. His departure for his chosen field of missionary labor in China formed part of the news communicated by the rather exulting paragraph.

"Well, that is all right," said Clementina's husband. "He is a good man, and he is where he can do nothing but good. I am glad I needn't feel sorry for him, any more."

Clementina's father must have given such a report of Hinkle and his family, that they felt easy at home in leaving her to the lot she had chosen. When Claxon parted from her, he talked of coming out with her mother to see her that fall; but it was more than a year before they got round to it. They did not come till after the birth of her little girl, and her father then humorously allowed that perhaps they would not have got round to it at all if something of the kind had not happened. The Hinkles and her father and mother liked one another, so much that in the first glow of his enthusiasm Claxon talked of settling down in Ohio, and the older Hinkle drove him about to look at some places that were for sale. But it ended in his saying one day that he missed the hills, and he did not believe that he would know enough to come in when it rained if he did not see old Middlemount with his nightcap on first. His wife and he started home with the impatience of their years, rather earlier than they had meant to go, and they were silent for a little while after they left the flag-station where Hinkle and Clementina had put them aboard their train.

"Well?" said Claxon, at last.

"Well?" echoed his wife, and then she did not speak for a little while longer. At last she asked, "D'he look that way when you fust see him in New Yo'k?"

Claxon gave his honesty time to get the better of his optimism. Even then he answered evasively, "He doos look pootty slim."

"The way I cypher it out," said his wife, "he no business to let her marry him, if he wa'n't goin' to get well. It was throwin' of herself away, as you may say."

"I don't know about that," said Claxon, as if the point had occurred to him, too, and had been already argued in his mind. "I guess they must 'a' had it out, there in New York before they got married—or *she* had. I don't believe but what he expected to get well, right away. It's the kind of a thing that lingas along, and *lingas* along. As fah fo'th as Clem went, I guess there wa'n't any *let* about it. I guess she'd made up her mind from the staht, and she was goin' to have him if she had to hold him on his feet to do it. Look he'a! What would *you* done?"

"Oh, I presume we're *all* fools!" said Mrs. Claxon, impatient of a sex not always so frank with itself. "But that don't excuse *him*."

"I don't say it doos," her husband admitted. "But I presume he was expectin' to get well right away, then. And I don't believe," he added, energetically, "but what he will, *yet*. As I undastand, there ain't anything *ogganic* about him. It's just this he'e nuvvous prostration, resultin' from shock, his docta tells *me*; and he'll wo'k out of that all right."

They said no more, and Mrs. Claxon did not recur to any phase of the situation till she undid the lunch which the Hinkles had put up for them, and laid out on the napkin in her lap the portions of cold ham and cold chicken, the buttered biscuit, and the little pot of apple-butter, with the large bottle of cold coffee. Then she sighed, "They *live* well."

"Yes," said her husband, glad of any concession, "and they ah' good folks. And Clem's as happy as a bud with 'em, you can see that."

"Oh, she was always *happy* enough, if *that's* all you want. I presume she was happy with that hectorin' old thing that fooled her out of her money."

"I ha'n't ever regretted that money, Rebecca," said Claxon, stiffly, almost sternly, "and I guess *you* a'n't, eitha."

"I don't say I have," retorted Mrs. Claxon. "But I don't like to be made a fool of. I presume," she added, remotely, but not so irrelevantly, "Clem could ha' got 'most anybody, ova the'a."

"Well," said Claxon, taking refuge in the joke, "I shouldn't want her to marry a crowned head, myself."

It was Clementina who drove the clay-bank colt away from the station after the train had passed out of sight. Her husband sat beside her, and let her take the reins from his nerveless grasp; and when they got into the shelter of the piece of woods that the road passed through he put up his hands to his face, and broke into sobs. She allowed him to weep on, though she kept saying, "Geo'ge, Geo'ge," softly, and stroking his knee with the hand next him. When his sobbing stopped, she said, "I guess they've had a pleasant visit; but I'm glad we'a together again." He took up her hand and kissed the back of it, and then clutched it hard, but did not speak. "It's strange," she went on, "how I used to be home-sick for father and motha"— she had sometimes lost her Yankee accent in her association with his people, and spoke with their Western burr, but she found it in moments of deeper feeling—"when I was there in Europe, and now I'm glad to have them go. I don't want anybody to be between us; and I want to go back to just the way we we'e befo'e they came. It's been a strain on you, and now you must throw it all off and rest, and get up your strength. One thing, I could see that fatha noticed the gain you had made since he saw you in New Yo'k. He spoke about it to me the fust thing, and he feels just the way I do about it. He don't want you to hurry and get well, but take it slowly, and not excite yourself. He believes in your gleaner, and he knows all about machinery. He says the patent makes it puffectly safe, and you can take your own time about pushing it; it's su'a to go. And motha liked you. She's not one to talk a great deal—she always leaves that to father and me—but she's got deep feelings, and she just worshipped the baby! I neva saw her take a child in her ahms before; but she seemed to want to hold the baby all the time." She stopped, and then added, tenderly, "Now, I know what you ah' thinking about, Geo'ge, and I don't want you to think about it any more. If you do, I shall give up."

They had come to a bad piece of road where a slough of thick mud forced the wagon-way over the stumps of a turnout in the woods. "You had better let me have the reins, Clementina," he said. He drove home over the yellow leaves of the hickories and the crimson leaves of the maples, that heavy with the morning dew, fell slanting through the still air; and on the way he began to sing; his singing made her heart ache. His father came out to put up the colt for him; and Hinkle would not have his help.

He unhitched the colt himself, while his father trembled by with bent knees; he clapped the colt on the haunch and started him through the pasture-bars with a gay shout, and then put his arm round Clementina's waist, and walked her into the kitchen amidst the grins of his mother and sisters, who said he ought to be ashamed.

The winter passed, and in the spring he was not so well as he had been in the fall. It was the out-door life which was best for him, and he picked up again in the summer. When another autumn came, it was thought best for him not to risk the confinement of another winter in the North. The prolongation of the summer in the South would complete his cure, and Clementina took her baby and went with him to Florida. He was very well, there, and courageous letters came to Middlemount and Ohio, boasting of the gains he had made. One day toward spring he came in languid from the damp, unnatural heat, and the next day he had a fever, which the doctor would not, in a resort absolutely free from malaria, pronounce malarial. After it had once declared itself, in compliance with this reluctance, a simple fever, Hinkle was delirious, and he never knew Clementina again for the mother of his child. They were once more at Venice in his ravings, and he was reasoning with her that Belsky was not drowned.

The mystery of his malady deepened into the mystery of his death. With that his look of health and youth came back, and as she gazed upon his gentle face, it wore to her the smile of quaint sweetness that she had seen it wear the first night it won her fancy at Miss Milray's house in Florence.

XXXIX.

Six years after Miss Milray parted with Clementina in Venice she found herself, towards the close of the summer, at Middlemount. She had definitely ceased to live in Florence, where she had meant to die, and had come home to close her eyes. She was in no haste to do this, and in the meantime she was now at Middlemount with her brother, who had expressed a wish to revisit the place in memory of Mrs. Milray. It was the second anniversary of her divorce, which had remained, after a married life of many vicissitudes, almost the only experience untried in that relation, and which had been happily accomplished in the courts of Dacotah, upon grounds that satisfied the facile justice of that State. Milray had dealt handsomely with his widow, as he unresentfully called her, and the money he assigned her was of a destiny perhaps as honored as its origin. She employed it in the negotiation of a second marriage, in which she redressed the balance of her first by taking a husband somewhat younger than herself.

Both Milray and his sister had a wish which was much more than a curiosity to know what had become of Clementina; they had heard that her husband was dead, and that she had come back to Middlemount; and Miss Milray was going to the office, the afternoon following their arrival, to ask the landlord about her, when she was arrested at the door of the ball-room by a sight that she thought very pretty. At the bottom of the room, clearly defined against the long windows behind her, stood the figure of a lady in the middle of the floor. In rows on either side sat little girls and little boys who left their places one after another, and turned at the door to make their manners to her. In response to each obeisance the lady dropped a curtsey, now to this side, now to that, taking her skirt between her finger tips on either hand and spreading it delicately, with a certain elegance of movement, and a grace that was full of poetry, and to Miss Milray, somehow, full of pathos. There remained to the end a small mite of a girl, who was the last to leave her place and bow to the lady. She did not quit the room then, like the others, but advanced toward the lady who came to meet her, and lifted her and clasped her to her breast with a kind of passion. She walked down toward the door where Miss Milray stood, gently drifting over the polished floor, as if still moved by the music that had ceased, and as she drew near, Miss Milray gave a cry of joy, and ran upon her. "Why, Clementina!" she screamed, and caught her and the child both in her arms.

She began to weep, but Clementina smiled instead of weeping, as she always used to do. She returned Miss Milray's affectionate greeting with a tenderness as great as her own, but with a sort of authority, such as sometimes comes to those who have suffered. She quieted the older woman with her own serenity, and met the torrent of her questions with as many answers as their rush permitted, when they were both presently in Miss Milray's room talking in their old way. From time to time Miss Milray broke from the talk to kiss the little girl, whom she declared to be Clementina all over again, and then returned to her better behavior with an effect of shame for her want of self-control, as if Clementina's mood had abashed her. Sometimes this was almost severe in its quiet; that was her mother coming to her share in her; but again she was like her father, full of the sunny gayety of self-forgetfulness, and then Miss Milray said, "Now you are the old Clementina!"

Upon the whole she listened with few interruptions to the story which she exacted. It was mainly what we know. After her husband's death Clementina had gone back to his family for a time, and each year since she had spent part of the winter with them; but it was very lonesome for her, and she began to be home-sick for Middlemount. They saw it and considered it. "They ah' the *best* people, Miss Milray!" she said, and her voice, which was firm when she spoke of her husband, broke in the words of minor feeling. Besides being a little homesick, she ended, she was not willing to live on there, doing nothing for herself, and so she had come back.

"And you are here, doing just what you planned when you talked your life over with me in Venice!"

"Yes, but life isn't eva just what we plan it to be, Miss Milray."

"Ah, don't I know it!"

Clementina surprised Miss Milray by adding, "In a great many things—I don't know but in most—it's better. I don't complain of mine"—

"You poor child! You never *complained* of *anything*—not even of Mrs. Lander!"

"But it's different from what I expected; and it's—strange."

"Yes; life is very strange."

"I don't mean—losing *him.* That had to be. I can see, now, that it had to be almost from the beginning. It seems to me that I knew it had to be from the fust minute I saw him in New Yo'k; but *he* didn't, and I am glad of that. Except when he was getting wohse, he always believed he should get well; and he *was* getting well, when he"—

Miss Milray did not violate the pause she made with any question, though it was apparent that Clementina had something on her mind that she wished to say, and could hardly say of herself.

She began again, "I was glad through everything that I could live with him so long. If there is nothing moa, here or anywhe'a, that was something. But it is strange. Sometimes it doesn't seem as if it had happened."

"I think I can understand, Clementina."

"I feel sometimes as if I hadn't happened myself." She stopped, with a patient little sigh, and passed her hand across the child's forehead, in a mother's fashion, and smoothed her hair from it, bending over to look down into her face. "*We* think she has her fatha's eyes," she said.

"Yes, she has," Miss Milray assented, noting the upward slant of the child's eyes, which gave his quaintness to her beauty. "He had fascinating eyes."

After a moment Clementina asked, "Do you believe that the looks are all that ah' left?"

Miss Milray reflected. "I know what you mean. I should say character was left, and personality—somewhere."

"I used to feel as if it we'e left here, at fust—as if he must come back. But that had to go."

"Yes."

"Everything seems to go. After a while even the loss of him seemed to go."

"Yes, losses go with the rest."

"That's what I mean by its seeming as if it never any of it happened. Some things before it are a great deal more real."

"Little things?"

"Not exactly. But things when I was very young." Miss Milray did not know quite what she intended, but she knew that Clementina was feeling her way to something she wanted to say, and she let her alone. "When it was all over, and I knew that as long as I lived he would be somewhere else, I tried to be paht of the wo'ld I was left in. Do you think that was right?"

"It was wise; and, yes, it was *best*," said Miss Milray, and for relief from the tension which was beginning to tell upon her own nerves, she asked, "I suppose you know about my poor brother? I'd better tell you to keep you from asking for Mrs. Milray, though I don't know that it's so very painful with him. There isn't any Mrs. Milray now," she added, and she explained why.

Neither of them cared for Mrs. Milray, and they did not pretend to be concerned about her, but Clementina said, vaguely, as if in recognition of Mrs. Milray's latest experiment, "Do you believe in second marriages?"

Miss Milray laughed, "Well, not *that* kind exactly."

"No," Clementina assented, and she colored a little.

Miss Milray was moved to add, "But if you mean another kind, I don't see why not. My own mother was married twice."

"Was she?" Clementina looked relieved and encouraged, but she did not say any more at once. Then she asked, "Do you know what ever became of Mr. Belsky?"

"Yes. He's taken his title again, and gone back to live in Russia; he's made peace with the Czar, I believe."

"That's nice," said Clementina; and Miss Milray made bold to ask:

"And what has become of Mr. Gregory?"

Clementina answered, as Miss Milray thought, tentatively and obliquely: "You know his wife died."

"No, I never knew that she lived."

"Yes. They went out to China, and she died the'a."

"And is he there yet? But of course! He could never have given up being a missionary."

"Well," said Clementina, "he isn't in *China*. His health gave out, and he had to come home. He's in—Middlemount Centa."

Miss Milray suppressed the "Oh!" that all but broke from her lips. "Preaching to the heathen, there?" she temporized.

"To the summa folks," Clementina explained, innocent of satire. "They have got a Union Chapel the'a, now, and Mr. Gregory has been preaching all summa." There seemed nothing more that Miss Milray could prompt her to say, but it was not quite with surprise that she heard Clementina continue, as if it were part of the explanation, and followed from the fact she had stated, "He wants me to marry him."

Miss Milray tried to emulate her calm in asking, "And shall you?"

"I don't know. I told him I would see; he only asked me last night. It would be kind of natural. He was the fust. You may think it is strange"—

Miss Milray, in the superstition of her old-maidenhood concerning love, really thought it cold-blooded and shocking; but she said, "Oh, no."

Clementina resumed: "And he says that if it was right for me to stop caring for him when I did, it is right now for me to ca'e for him again, where the'e's no one to be hu't by it. Do you think it is?"

"Yes; why not?" Miss Milray was forced to the admission against what she believed the finer feelings of her nature.

Clementina sighed, "I suppose he's right. I always thought he was good. Women don't seem to belong very much to themselves in this wo'ld, do they?"

"No, they seem to belong to the men, either because they want the men, or the men want them; it comes to the same thing. I suppose you don't wish me to advise you, my dear?"

"No. I presume it's something I've got to think out for myself."

"But I think he's good, too. I ought to say that much, for I didn't always stand his friend with you. If Mr. Gregory has any fault it's being too scrupulous."

"You mean, about that old trouble—our not believing just the same?" Miss Milray meant something much more temperamental than that, but she allowed Clementina to limit her meaning, and Clementina went on. "He's changed all round now. He thinks it's all in the *life*. He says that in China they couldn't understand what he believed, but they could what he lived. And he knows I neva could be very religious."

It was in Miss Milray's heart to protest, "Clementina, I think you are one of the most religious persons I ever knew," but she forebore, because the praise seemed to her an invasion of Clementina's dignity. She merely said, "Well, I am glad he is one of those who grow more liberal as they grow older. That is a good sign for your happiness. But I dare say it's more of *his* happiness you think."

"Oh, I should like to be happy, too. There would be no sense in it if I wasn't."

"No, certainly not."

"Miss Milray," said Clementina, with a kind of abruptness, "do you eva hear anything from Dr. Welwright?"

"No! Why?" Miss Milray fastened her gaze vividly upon her.

"Oh, nothing. *He* wanted me to promise him, there in Venice, too."

"I didn't know it."

"Yes. But—I couldn't, then. And now—he's written to me. He wants me to let him come ova, and see me."

"And—and will you?" asked Miss Milray, rather breathlessly.

"I don't know. I don't know as I'd ought. I should like to see him, so as to be puffectly *su'a*. But if I let him come, and then didn't— It wouldn't be right! I always felt as if I'd ought to have seen *then* that he ca'ed for me, and—stopped him; but I didn't. No, I didn't," she repeated, nervously. "I respected him, and I liked him; but I neva"— She stopped, and then she asked, "What do you think I'd ought to do, Miss Milray?"

Miss Milray hesitated. She was thinking superficially that she had never heard Clementina say had ought, so much, if ever before. Interiorly she was recurring to a sense of something like all this before, and to the feeling which she had then that Clementina was really cold-blooded and self-seeking. But she remembered that in her former decision, Clementina had finally acted from her heart and her conscience, and she rose from her suspicion with a rebound. She dismissed as unworthy of Clementina any theory which did not account for an ideal of scrupulous and unselfish justice in her.

"That is something that nobody can say but yourself, Clementina," she answered, gravely.

"Yes," sighed Clementina, "I presume that is so."

She rose, and took her little girl from Miss Milray's knee. "Say good-bye," she bade, looking tenderly down at her.

Miss Milray expected the child to put up her lips to be kissed. But she let go her mother's hand, took her tiny skirts between her finger-tips, and dropped a curtsey.

"You little witch!" cried Miss Milray. "I want a hug," and she crushed her to her breast, while the child twisted her face round and anxiously questioned her mother's for her approval. "Tell her it's all right, Clementina!" cried Miss Milray. "When she's as old as you were in Florence, I'm going to make you give her to me."

"Ah' you going back to Florence?" asked Clementina, provisionally.

"Oh, no! You can't go back to anything. That's what makes New York so impossible. I think we shall go to Los Angeles."

XL.

On her way home Clementina met a man walking swiftly forward. A sort of impassioned abstraction expressed itself in his gait and bearing. They had both entered the shadow of the deep pine woods that flanked the way on either side, and the fallen needles helped with the velvety summer dust of the roadway to hush their steps from each other. She saw him far off, but he was not aware of her till she was quite near him.

"Oh!" he said, with a start. "You filled my mind so full that I couldn't have believed you were anywhere outside of it. I was coming to get you—I was coming to get my answer."

Gregory had grown distinctly older. Sickness and hardship had left traces in his wasted face, but the full beard he wore helped to give him an undue look of age.

"I don't know," said Clementina, slowly, "as I've got an answa fo' you, Mr. Gregory—yet."

"No answer is better that the one I am afraid of!"

"Oh, I'm not so sure of that," she said, with gentle

perplexity, as she stood, holding the hand of her little girl, who stared shyly at the intense face of the man before her.

"I am," he retorted. "I have been thinking it all over, Clementina. I've tried not to think selfishly about it, but I can't pretend that my wish isn't selfish. It is! I want you for myself, and because I've always wanted you, and not for any other reason. I never cared for any one but you in the way I cared for you, and"—

"Oh!" she grieved. "I never ca'ed at all for you after I saw *him*."

"I know it must be shocking to you; I haven't told you with any wretched hope that it would commend me to you!"

"I don't say it was so very bad," said Clementina, reflectively, "if it was something you couldn't help."

"It was something I couldn't help. Perhaps I didn't try."

"Did—*she* know it?"

"She knew it from the first; I told her before we were married."

Clementina drew back a little, insensibly pulling her child with her. "I don't believe I exactly like it."

"I knew you wouldn't! If I could have thought you would, I hope I shouldn't have wished—and feared—so much to tell you."

"Oh, I know you always wanted to do what you believed was right, Mr. Gregory," she answered. "But I haven't quite thought it out yet. You mustn't hurry me."

"No, no! Heaven forbid." He stood aside to let her pass.

"I was just going home," she added.

"May I go with you?"

"Yes, if you want to. I don't know but you betta; we might as well; I want to talk with you. Don't you think it's something we ought to talk about—sensibly?"

"Why, of course! And I shall try to be guided by you; I should always submit to be ruled by you, if"—

"That's not what I mean, exactly. I don't want to do the ruling. You don't undastand me."

"I'm afraid I don't," he assented, humbly.

"If you did, you wouldn't say that—*so*." He did not venture to make any answer, and they walked on without speaking, till she asked, "Did you know that Miss Milray was at the Middlemount?"

"Miss Milray! Of Florence?"

"With her brother. I didn't see him; Mrs. Milray is not he'a; they ah' divo'ced. Miss Milray used to be very nice to me in Florence. She isn't going back there any moa. She says you can't go back to anything. Do you think *we* can?"

She had left moments between her incoherent sentences where he might interrupt her if he would, but he waited for her question. "I hoped we might; but perhaps"—

"No, no. We couldn't. We couldn't go back to that night when you threw the slippas into the riva, no' to that time in Florence when we gave up, no' to that day in Venice when I had to tell you that I ca'ed moa fo' some one else. Don't you see?"

"Yes, I see," he said, in quick revulsion from the hope he had expressed. "The past is full of the pain and shame of my errors!"

"I don't want to go back to what's past, eitha," she reasoned, without gainsaying him.

She stopped again, as if that were all, and he asked, "Then is that my answer?"

"I don't believe that even in the otha wo'ld we shall want to go back to the past, much, do you?" she pursued, thoughtfully.

Once Gregory would have answered confidently; he even now checked an impulse to do so. "I don't know," he owned, meekly.

"I *do* like you, Mr. Gregory!" she relented, as if touched by his meekness, to the confession. "You know I do—moa than I ever expected to like anybody again. But it's not because I used to like you. or because I think you always acted nicely. I think it was cruel of you, if you ca'ed for me, to let me believe you didn't, afta that fust time. I can't eva think it wasn't, no matta why you did it."

"It was atrocious. I can see that now."

"I say it, because I shouldn't eva wish to say it again. I know that all the time you we'e betta than what you did, and I blame myself a good deal moa fo' not knowing when you came to Florence that I had begun to ca'e fo'—some one else. But I did wait till I could see you again, so as to be su'a which I ca'ed for the most. I tried to be fai'a, before I told you that I wanted to be free. That is all," she said, gently, and Gregory perceived that the word was left definitely to him.

He could not take it till he had disciplined himself to accept unmurmuringly his sentence as he understood it. "At any rate," he began, "I can thank you for rating my motive above my conduct."

"Oh," she said. "I don't think either of us acted very well. I didn't know till aftawa'ds that I was glad to have you give up, the way you did in Florence. I was—bewild'ed. But I ought to have known, and I want you to undastand everything, now. I *don't* ca'e for you because I used to when I was almost a child, and I shouldn't want you to ca'e for me eitha, because you did then. That's why I wish you had neva felt that you had always ca'ed fo' me."

"Yes," said Gregory. He let fall his head in despair.

"That is what I mean," said Clementina. "If we ah' going to begin togetha, now, it's got to be as if we had neva begun before. And you mustn't think, or say, or look as if the'e had been anything in oua lives but ouaselves. Will you? Do you promise?" She stopped, and put her hand on his breast, and pushed against it with a nervous vehemence.

"No!" he said. "I don't promise, for I couldn't keep my promise. What you ask is impossible. The past is part of us; it can't be ignored any more than it can be destroyed. If we take each other, it must be for all that we have been as well as all that we are. If we haven't the courage for that we must part."

"'DO YOU PROMISE?'"

He dropped the little one's hand which he had been holding, and moved a few steps aside. "Don't!" she said. "They'll think I've made you," and he took the child's hand again.

They had emerged from the shadow of the woods, and come in sight of her father's house. Claxon was standing coatless before the door in full enjoyment of the late afternoon air; his wife beside him, at sight of Gregory, quelled a natural impulse to run round the corner of the house from the presence of strangers.

"I wonda what they'a sayin'," she fretted.

"It looks some as if she was sayin' yes," said Claxon, with an impersonal enjoyment of his conjecture. "I guess she saw he was bound not to take no for an answa."

"I don't know as I should like it very much," his wife relucted. "Clem's doin' very well, as it is. She no *need* to marry again."

"Oh, I guess it a'n't that altogetha. He's a good man." Claxon mused a moment upon the figures which had begun to advance again, with the little one between them, and then gave way in a burst of paternal pride, "And I don't know as I should blame him so very much for wantin' Clem. She always *did* want to be of moa *use*— But I guess she *likes* him too."

THE END.

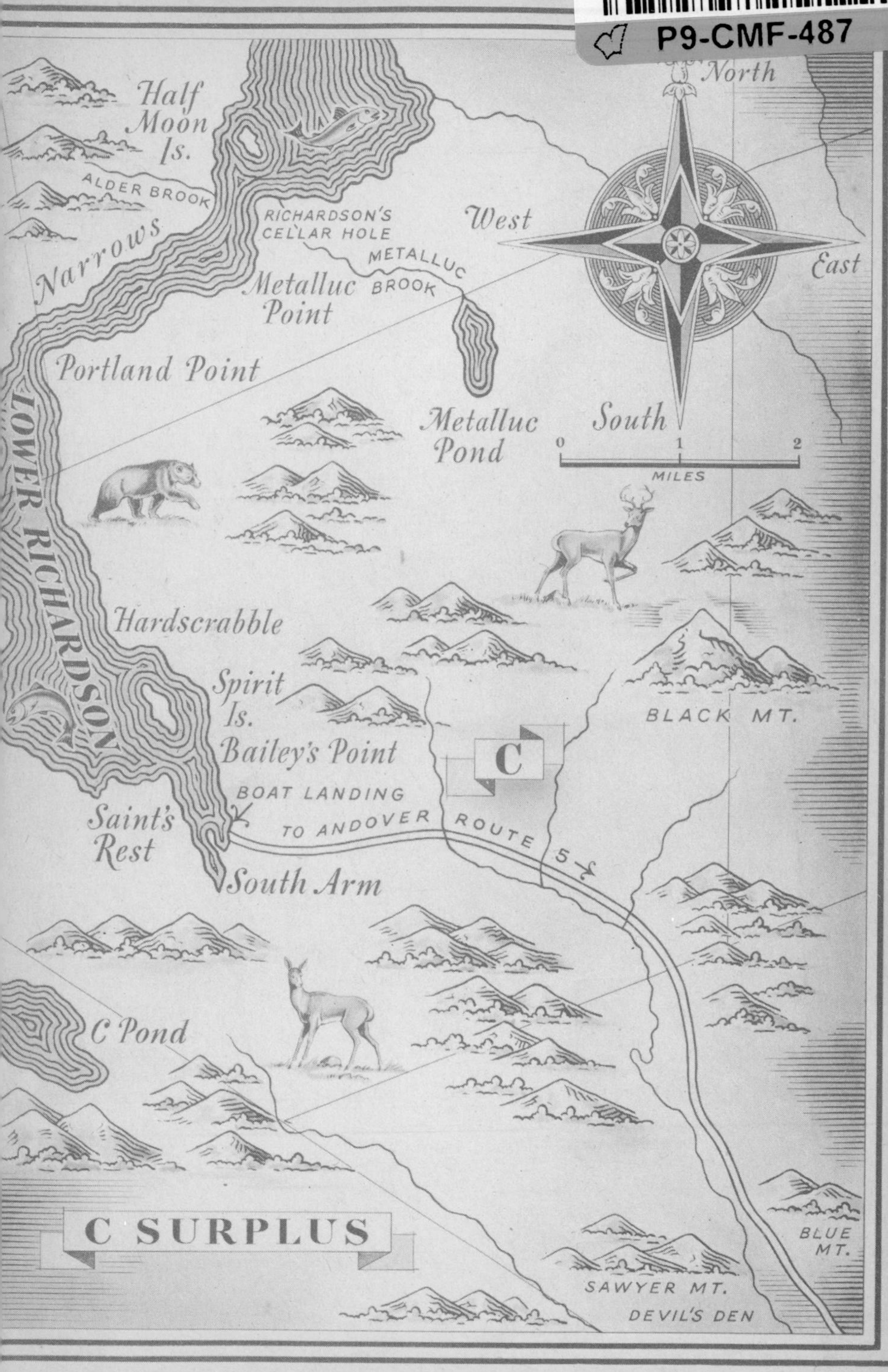
North
West
East
South
0 1 2
MILES
Half Moon Is.
ALDER BROOK
Narrows
RICHARDSON'S CELLAR HOLE
METALLUC BROOK
Metalluc Point
Portland Point
Metalluc Pond
LOWER RICHARDSON
Hardscrabble
Spirit Is.
Bailey's Point
BOAT LANDING
Saint's Rest
TO ANDOVER
ROUTE 5
South Arm
C
BLACK MT.
C Pond
C SURPLUS
BLUE MT.
SAWYER MT.
DEVIL'S DEN

WE TOOK TO THE WOODS

PHOTO BY FRED ADAMS

Pond-in-the-River

We Took To The Woods

Louise Dickinson Rich

twenty-one photographs

1792 1942

J. B. LIPPINCOTT COMPANY
PHILADELPHIA NEW YORK

Printed in the United States of America
by H. Wolff, New York

TO MY BOYS
Ralph
Gerrish
Rufus
Kyak
Tom
This book is dedicated

ACKNOWLEDGMENTS

My thanks to Susan Renwick Driver, of Summit, N. J., for the loan of her old map of the Rangeley district; to Fred Adams, of Brattleboro, Vt., for the photographs he contributed; and to my sister Alice Dickinson, of Newton, Mass., for her help and advice.

L. D. R.

CONTENTS

ILLUSTRATIONS

I

"*Why Don't You Write a Book?*"

DURING MOST OF MY ADOLESCENCE—SPECIFICALLY, BETWEEN the time when I gave up wanting to be a brakeman on a freight train and the time when I definitely decided to become an English teacher—I said, when asked what I was going to do with my life, that I was going to live alone in a cabin in the Maine woods and write. It seemed to me that this was a romantic notion, and I was insufferably smug over my own originality. Of course, I found out later that everybody is at one time or another going to do something of the sort. It's part of being young. The only difference in my case is that, grown to womanhood, I seem to be living in a cabin in the Maine woods, and I seem to be writing.

There is nothing that I so greatly admire as purposefulness. I have an enormous respect for people who know exactly what they are doing and where they are going. Such people are compact and integrated. They have clear edges. They give an impression of invulnerability and balance, and I wish that I were one of them.

I wish that I could say that, from the moment I first

thought about this kind of a life to the moment almost two decades later when I finally began living it, I had been working single-mindedly toward it. But it wouldn't be true. Actually I'd forgotten all about it long before. I did a lot of things—graduated from college, taught school, worked in an institution for the feeble-minded, went to Europe—but none of it was in preparation for an end. At the time it seemed end enough in itself.

I was shocked, therefore, to receive not long ago and within the same week, letters from two old friends saying virtually the same thing, although the writers are strangers to each other. What they said, in effect, was this: "Isn't it wonderful that you're at last doing what you always said you wanted to do! It proves that anything is possible, if one wants it enough to work for it."

My two friends, I thank you for your high opinion of my character, and I hate to have to disabuse you of it. It is wonderful—far more wonderful than you know—that I am doing what I once, without really believing it, said I was going to do. But if it proves anything, it is only that some people are fools for luck. Let me admit that not only is my living in the woods and writing an accident on both counts, but that until I received your letters I had been so busy coping with the situation that I hadn't even realized that I was living my old dream. It's a very queer feeling to wake up and find that the dream has sneaked up on you and become the reality.

There are differences, of course. My idea was a little log cabin in a sort of spacious park. There is nothing park-like about this northwestern-most corner of Maine. Here, between two ranges of mountains, the Boundary Mountains and the Blue Mountains, lies a high, wild valley, the basin that holds the Rangeley Lakes. The country is criss-crossed with ridges, dotted with swamps and logans, and covered with dense forest. There are very few people living here, and no roads down into what we call The Outside. There are a few narrow trails, but travel through the woods is so difficult, with the swamps and blowdowns and underbrush, that the lakes have remained what they were to the Indians, the main thoroughfare.

I like to think of the lakes coming down from the north of us like a gigantic staircase to the sea. Kennebago to Rangeley to Cupsuptic, down they drop, level to level, through short, snarling rivers; Mooselukmeguntic to the Richardsons to Pond-in-the-River, and through Rapid River to Umbagog, whence they empty into the Androscoggin and begin the long south-easterly curve back to the ocean. I like to say their names, and I wish I could make you see them—long, lovely, lonely stretches of water, shut in by dark hills. The trees come down to the shore, the black growth of fir and pine and spruce streaked with the lighter green of maple and birch. There is nothing at all on the hills but forest, and nobody lives there but deer and bear and wildcats. The people keep close to the lakes, building their dwellings in narrow clearings they have made by pushing the trees a little way back from the water.

Our own clearing is on the Rapid River, just below Pond-in-the-River Dam; and because Rapid River is not navigable, being the swiftest river east of the Rockies—it drops a hundred and eighty-five feet in three miles, with no falls, which is some kind of a record—we amazingly live on a road. It doesn't go anywhere. It's really a carry between two lakes, so it is sensibly called the Carry Road.

It starts at Middle Dam, on the Lower Richardson, and roughly follows the course of the river five miles to Sunday Cove, on Umbagog.

Middle Dam is quite a community. There is the dam itself, a part of the system for water control on the Androscoggin, with the dam-keeper and his family, Renny and Alice Miller and their three children, in year-round residence. Then in summer the hotel is open. We only call it a hotel; it's really a fishing camp. In winter it is closed, but there is a caretaker, Larry Parsons, who stays in with his wife, Al, and a hired man or two. So the permanent population of Middle Dam hovers at around nine, and that is comparative congestion. We get our mail and supplies through Middle, and it is the point of departure for The Outside, so its importance is all out of proportion to its population.

Sunday Cove, the other end of the carry, is something else again. The rutted, grass-grown road dips down a last steep hill and ends in the lake. There is an abandoned lumber camp rotting down on the shore, and a pair of loons living in the Cove, and that's all there is to it.

And halfway along, between road and river, is Forest Lodge, the sole address on the Carry Road, and our home.

When I said we lived in a cabin in the woods, I was speaking loosely. Forest Lodge is in the woods all right; there is nothing north or south of us but trees for so many miles that sometimes it scares me to think about it. But actually it consists of one cabin, one shack, one large house in the worst cracker-box style, and an assortment of lean-to's, woodsheds, work-shops, and what are euphemistically known as out-houses. These latter are necessary because we have no plumbing, and therefore no bathroom.

We get our water from the river and from a spring up back in the woods. We do our bathing in wash-tubs in front of the kitchen stove, and for other uses of the bathroom, we resort to the out-houses. This is no great hardship in summer, but in winter, with the snow knee deep, the wind howling like a maniac up the river, and the thermometer crawling down to ten below zero, it is a supreme test of fortitude to leave the warmth of the fire and go plunging out into the cold, no matter how great the necessity. We like to think, however, that it builds character.

The cabin, hereafter to be referred to as the Winter House, was the original Forest Lodge, built for a fishing camp. It is a low building with a porch and an ell, set on a knoll with a view up the river to the Pond-in-the-River. From the outside, it's not a bad little house, but everything that could possibly be wrong with it inside is wrong. The ceilings are too high and the windows are too small, although Ralph, my husband, ripped out the old ones and doubled the window space the first year we were here. The living-room, where we spend much of the time in winter, is on the north side, toward the woods, while the bedrooms, which we use only at night, are on the sunny, open side toward the river. The reason for this irritates me. In the country, the living quarters are always on the road side of a house, so that the inhabitants can keep tabs on the passers-by. In winter there are normally about three passers-by in seven months, here, but still the old rule holds. Apparently it's preferable to sit forever in sunless gloom than to lose one opportunity to speculate about someone's identity, starting point, destination, family connections, and probably discreditable purpose. We can't do anything about the arrangement, because the chimney is in the living-room, and that's where we have to have the stove.

That chimney is another wrong thing. It rises out of a fire-place—which is too shallow to draw properly—and instead of being in the wall, it is set out into the room about four feet. This splits the room into two parts, making the attractive and comfortable arrangement of furniture impossible. In winter the fire-place itself is of no use whatsoever, as anyone who has lived in the country in winter knows. A fire-place is pretty, and on chilly fall evenings, will keep you warm enough; but what you need in winter is a stove. So we have a stove. We boarded up our pretty fire-place, punched a hole in the side of the chimney, and set up an air-circulating wood heater. It isn't very attractive, and it takes up a lot of room, and set cheek by jowl with the fire-place, it looks silly. But it keeps us warm.

The only advantage of that half-witted chimney arrangement that has appeared to date is that the otherwise waste space behind it can be used as a woodbox. Ralph, known in these parts as "an ingenious cuss," cut a hole in the house, fitted it with a beveled door like an ice-chest door, and now we can put the wood in from outdoors. This doesn't sound like much of a triumph, but it is, nevertheless. Nothing will cool a house off quicker than opening and closing the front door forty times, while arm-loads of wood are brought in; and nothing will enrage and discourage the housewife more surely than the pecks of dirt and snow inevitably tracked onto her clean-swept floor. This little wood-box door, therefore, contributes largely to the peace and comfort of the Rich menage.

Why don't we just burn the Winter House down and forget about it? Because it's the only house that can be

The Summer House—Porch Lookout over Rapid River

The Winter House—Note Curious Kyak

heated in really cold weather. Ralph has insulated it properly and finished the inside with really beautiful hand-rubbed pine paneling, and in spite of all I have said against it, it's not half bad, actually. It hasn't any kitchen, either, which is a point in its favor, odd as that may sound. We use the kitchen ell of the Big House all the year round, so the cooking odors that always collect in small country houses in the winter, no matter how often they are aired, never get into the Winter House.

About the last of May, or as soon as it is warm enough, we move down into the Big House, and the Winter House becomes the guest house for the summer. The Big House was built at a later date for a summer camp, and that is all it is good for in its present state. It is big and airy and the walls are too thin for warmth and it sprawls all over the place. I like it because it is on a high bluff over the river, with a view and sun-light and space to spread out in; because it has a huge stone fire-place that will take four-foot logs and really heat the living-room in the wettest, coldest September rain storm; because there is a wide porch over the river; because if I decide to eat some crackers and cheese before going to bed, I don't have to climb into a mackinaw and gum-boots as I do in winter, and cross a clearing in the cold to get them. And most of all I like it because I like to go upstairs to bed, instead of into the next room. For these reasons, we always put off moving out of it in the fall until the last possible moment, and we are rebuilding it so we can live in it all the year. Since Ralph is doing the work himself, for economic reasons, this is a slow process. At the moment the whole structure is balanced precariously on poles over the cellar he has dug beneath it. It looks both dangerous and sloppy, but he says it's perfectly safe, and when you're in a house, its external appearance needn't bother you. In fact, I should think a good way to buy a house would be by the looks of the house across the street, which is the one you see most of.

The house across the street here is the Guide's House, or what would be the servants' quarters, if we had servants. It's called the Guide's House because most people living in a place like this would be summer people, and they would employ a registered guide, who would live in the house across the road. It's a nice little shack, with a living-room and two bedrooms, and Gerrish lives there.

Gerrish works for us, but he is in no sense a servant. He has a guide's license, but that isn't important, because so have Ralph and I. It's a handy thing to own, around here. What Gerrish is, I suppose, is the hired help. We pay him to do certain things, which is the hired part. But since he is practically a member of the family, he does a great many other things for which we don't, and couldn't, pay him. That's the help part. We couldn't ever pay him, for example, for being so good and patient with our four-year-old Rufus, who, not to mince words, is often a pest, unmotherly an observation as that may be. Gerrish has to take his pay for that out of Rufus' adoration of him. We couldn't pay him, either, for being so dependable, and for always giving us a dollar and a quarter's worth of work for every dollar of his wages. We are very lucky to have found him. This is not a place that many people would care to work in. It is remote, not only from movies and stores, but from other people. There is nowhere to go except hunting and fishing, and nothing to see except woods and water. But luckily Gerrish likes it, and I think that he considers the Guide's House, his own undisputed realm, as home. Perhaps that is pay of a kind.

The one building here that looks as though it belonged in the deep woods is Ralph's shop, an old log cabin from long before our day. I can't say much about it, as it comes under the heading of sacred ground. It is full of tools and pieces of board that look like any other boards, but which have something special about them, so that they must never be touched, or even looked at. Hanging from the rafters are old car parts, lengths of rope, chains and boat seats, all of which are going to be used some day for some important project. In the middle is a pile of invaluable junk, and around the edges are kegs of nails and bolts. In my bridal innocence I used, when I needed a nail, to go and take one out of a keg. But it always turned out that I had taken (a) the wrong kind of nail for the job on hand, and (b) a nail that was being conserved for a specific purpose and was practically irreplaceable. So now when I need a nail I find Ralph and ask him to get me one.

He's usually easy to find. I have only to listen for the sound of a motor running. He is completely infatuated with gasoline motors, and collects them from the most improbable places. Once he brought home an old motor that someone had hauled into South Arm for a mooring anchor and then abandoned. It had been under water all summer and frozen into the ice all winter, but he dragged it the seven miles home on a hand sled, brooded over it, took it to pieces and put it together again, and now it runs the saw that saws our firewood.

We have only five miles of road to run a car on, but we are a four-car family. They aren't new models—the newest is a 1930 Model A and the oldest a 1924 Marmon—but they run, and they pay for themselves. All summer long Ralph hauls canoes and duffle across the carry for camping parties, and in the spring and fall the lumber company finds it convenient to hire him to tote their wangans up from Sunday Cove.

This lumber company is our privacy insurance, our guarantee that we won't wake up some morning and find new neighbors building a pink stucco bungalow down the river from us. With the exception of our two acres and a strip owned by a water power company, they own every foot of land for miles around. And they won't sell an inch to anybody. I won't go into reasons and company policy. All that matters is that, come hell or high water, they will not sell.

So here we sit in what amounts to a forest preserve of some hundreds of square miles; and in that "we" the reality differs again from the dream. I was going to live alone, remember. I don't, and that's quite all right with me.

Besides Ralph, Rufus, and Gerrish, there is Sally, Ralph's sixteen-year-old daughter by a previous marriage, and further proof that I am a fool for luck. A step-daughter could be a thorn in the flesh, which Sally certainly isn't. And there are Kyak and Tom, the dog and the cat.

We ourselves wouldn't have named Tom that, but we got him from a lumber camp that was moving out and didn't know what to do with him, so we had to take him as equipped. We compromise by saying that his full name is Thomas Bailey Aldrich, which isn't very suitable. He is the sort of cat that should be called Tom, regardless of banality. He is big and tough and mean, and he'd as soon as not fight the whole family at once. His idea of an average day is to get up at noon, trounce the dog for looking at him, go out and chase a deer away from the clearing, and set out the two miles for Middle Dam, there to visit with his girl, the Millers' cat, after half murdering her other three suitors. Then he comes home, looking so smug you could shoot him on sight, and sleeps until noon the next day.

Kyak, though we love him dearly, we have to admit is strictly an Art Dog. His grandmother was with Admiral Byrd at the South Pole, and his great-grandfather helped carry the serum to Nome. If they could see him, they'd turn in their graves. He is a very good example of the Siberian husky, with a white wolf mask, a rangy big body, and a curling plume of a tail; but he is completely nonfunctional. Try to put a harness on him, and he will lie down with all four feet in the air. Try to teach him to retrieve game, and he will look sorrowful and broken. The only thing he is good for, besides looking beautiful, is a watch dog, and he doesn't even do that well. He barks horribly at nothing, or at members of the family, and then amiably lets strange woodsmen walk right into the house. Then after they are in, and for all he knows, we are lying in a welter of blood, sometimes he remembers his responsibilities and stands outside barking hysterically. There's no use trying to do anything with him, except love him.

Around the blank space on the map where we live are some towns and some things that look like towns, but aren't. South Arm is one of these. We simply call it the Arm, and it's important, because it's at the beginning of the road to The Outside. Once you get off the boat from Middle Dam at the Arm, you have begun to leave the woods behind. There is still a long drive to Andover, the first village, but you can't help knowing that if you follow the road far enough you will land, not at a lonely cove tenanted only by loons, but in Boston or New York, or Butte, Montana. It makes a difference. The Arm itself is not imposing, consisting of a huddle of ramshackle wharfs and a string of tired sheds where people in here keep their Outside cars. But its implications are enormous.

Andover really is a town, with a school, two or three little stores, and a post office, whence comes our mail. Upton is a town, too, and our civic center, where we send Sally to school and where we go to vote. Most of the land around here is wild land, or unorganized territory—just squares on the map labeled C Township, or North C Surplus, or Section 37—but the back line of Upton runs north of us, so technically at least we live in organized territory. Upton has one hundred and eighty-two inhabitants and the loveliest view in Maine.

The only other town that concerns us is Magalloway, which is too small to be on the road map or to have a post office. But it does have the Brown Farm, where our telephone line ends. Let me say at once that the Brown Farm isn't a farm, and our telephone line isn't a telephone line, in the modern sense of the word. It is a fifteen-mile-long piece of wire, frail and uninsulated, strung haphazardly through the woods from tree to tree, and the private property of the lumber company, for communication with their various operations. We are hitched onto it only because once they cut down some of our trees by mistake, and extended this courtesy as reparation and apology. If it hasn't snowed lately, or the wind hasn't blown any trees down across the line, or if the wire hasn't sagged wearily into one of the many brooks it crosses, we can, by cranking three times on the battery-powered telephone which hangs on the kitchen wall, talk to the Millers. Or we can ring four times and talk to Cliff, an old hermit who lives down on Umbagog. Or we can ring twice and get the disembodied voice that is all I know of Joe, at the Brown Farm.

Although not a farm, the Brown Farm is a number of other things, including a hospital and de-lousing station for lumberjacks, a bunkhouse and mess-hall, a rest-cure for work-worn horses, and a store house for the tremendous amounts of food and equipment necessary in the lumber camps. There used to be a clerk in that store house who had a splendid graft. At that time the lumber company was using a brand of canned goods that gave premiums for the labels off the cans:—a pickle dish for ten labels, a baby carriage for five hundred, and, I suppose, a Rolls Royce for a million. The clerk isn't there any more, though. His label-removing activities—they buy canned goods by the car lot—left him no time for his duties; and besides, the cooks in the camps got bored with having to open twenty anonymous cans before they happened on the sliced beets they were looking for. He was about to retire, anyhow. He'd sold the things he didn't fancy himself, and had money in the bank.

Once, seven years ago, I saw the Brown Farm, but I didn't know then what it was going to mean in my life, so I didn't pay much attention. I don't remember what it looks like. I was the school-teacher-on-vacation, and my sister and I and some friends came up through this country on a canoe trip. We went through the Parmachenee section, and then we debated whether we should come back through the Rangeleys and along Rapid River or not. The guide insisted that this was the way to come—that although it involved a lot of work, the country was wild and beautiful and unspoiled enough to be worth a few paddle blisters, pack sores, and lame muscles. So we finally gave in, not too enthusiastically, being travel-frayed already.

And that off-hand decision, in which I didn't even have a major part, was the accident by which I now live in a cabin in the woods. As we walked along the Carry Road, we saw a man splitting wood in the yard of the only house we had seen in days, and we stopped to talk to him. He had just arrived there that morning, and he was about to build his first fire and cook his first meal. He invited us to stay and eat with him, because he felt like celebrating. He'd bought the place for a summer camp during the boom years, but he hadn't been able to come East from Chicago, where he lived, since 1929. Now, however, he'd sold some patent rights and not only was he going to spend the summer there, but if things turned out right, the rest of his life. We were all touched and amused, I remember, by his enthusiasm.

Now that I know Ralph better, I know that there was nothing strange about his inviting us all to spend the rest of the week with him. Since that day, eight years ago, I've known him to invite a week-end guest, whom he liked, to extend his visit from week to week until it lasted more than two years. But at the time I thought, and I guess all the others thought, that he was crazy. We stayed, though.

We stayed, and we had a lovely time. We fished and sunbathed and swam, and in between times I found out why a man so obviously dry behind the ears should want to bury himself in the woods for the rest of his life. Ever since he was twelve years old, he had been spending his summers at Coburn's, and his winters wishing it were summer so he could go back to Coburn's. Middle Dam was the place in all the world where he was happiest, and he'd always told himself that some day he'd live there permanently. It took a long time and a lot of doing, but finally he'd managed. You see, Ralph, unlike me, has a single-track mind.

My mind, however, did fall into a single track before that week was over. I became obsessed with the idea that if I didn't see more—a lot more—of this Ralph Rich, I'd quietly go into a decline and die. It's a common phenomenon, I believe, both in fact and in fiction. It doesn't need any explanation, if indeed it can be explained. It's seldom fatal, I understand, so probably I'd have recovered if I'd had to. I didn't have to. Almost immediately upon my return to Massachusetts, while I was trying to think up a reasonably plausible excuse for happening back to the Rangeley region at the time of year when people just don't go there, I began getting letters, telegrams, and finally telephone calls, almost daily from Ralph. Then he began spending his time and money on the long and painful trek from Maine to Boston. It was, in short, a Courtship, and ended in the usual manner, with our deciding that this was a lot of expensive nonsense, so why didn't we get married?

I know that everybody who was ever in love has speculated along the following lines, but please bear with me while I do it once again. If, on that trip out of Parmachenee, one of us had stopped on the Carry Road two minutes to tie a shoe string, or if Ralph had split wood just a little bit faster, we would never have laid eyes upon him. He'd have been in the house, and we'd have walked right by. But the timing was perfect, and that's how I happen to live in the woods.

How I happened to be a writer was just as sloppy and haphazard. I wrote a little number about Maine guides, at my sister's suggestion, for *Scribner's* Life in the United States Contest. I finished it in May, and the contest didn't close until September, so I thought I'd try it out on a couple of dogs first. I'd get it back in plenty of time to qualify.

Now this is not mock modesty. I was absolutely stupified when the *Saturday Evening Post* bought it. Ralph was, too. But we rallied sufficiently to write another entry for the *Scribner's* contest, since our first had been scratched, as it were, and it won a prize. This double success so went to our heads that we decided that from then on we would be writers.

We weren't, of course, because being a writer involves a lot more than just thinking it would be nice to be one. We sold our first attempt at fiction—which was probably bad for us as it gave us false confidence—and then we settled down to discover that writing is not all beer and skittles. But I think that now, at last, we are nearly writers. We don't wait for inspiration any more, having found that inspiration is mostly the application of the seat of the pants to the seat of a chair. We stall around, trying to put off writing, which I understand is the occupational disease of writers. We earn most of our living by the written word. And we are utterly impatient with people who say, "I've often thought I could write myself."

It's taken me a great many words, I see, to answer the first questions people always ask us when they come out of the woods and find us here, unaccountably installed in a little clearing that is always full of the smell of pine and the sound of the river. That's a question that always crops up early in the conversation—"Doesn't the river get on your nerves?"—because until you get used to it, the dull roar, like heavy surf, seems to shake the air. It is all-pervading and inescapable, and you find yourself raising your voice higher and higher above it. But after a while, unless the tone changes with the rise and fall of the water, you don't even hear it. You learn to pitch your voice, not louder to carry over it, but lower and deeper, so that it's not shattered by the vibration. And finally all the places in the world that are away from the sound of furious white water come to seem empty and dead.

I don't pretend to know all of the answers. I don't know what to answer when people say, "But isn't the way you live Escapism?" I don't even know, really, what escapism is. We haven't tried to escape from anything. We have only exchanged one set of problems for another:—the problem of keeping out from under car wheels for the problem of not getting lost in the woods, for example; or the problem of being bored to death by one's neighbor for the problem of being bored to death by oneself. I don't know what to answer when someone says, "I should think you'd go insane!" It's too cheap and easy and obvious to retort, "And I should think you would."

But some of the answers, the answers to the easy, matter-of-fact questions, like "Why don't you write a book about it?", I do know. The answer to that is, "Well, I guess maybe I will."

And so I am writing a book about it.

II

"But How Do You Make a Living?"

I ALWAYS LIKE TO KNOW WHAT PEOPLE DO FOR A LIVING. This is probably just plain nosiness, but I like to call it a scientific interest. I like to argue that research is simply snooping on a high plane and that the village gossip is a student of applied behaviorism just as much as was Pavlov, shut up in his laboratory with his unfortunate dogs. So when I run across one who seems to be existing as a lily of the field, neither toiling nor spinning, I like to find out how it's done.

Since we would seem to be in that class ourselves, I consider "But how can you make a living up there in the woods?" a perfectly legitimate question. By no stretch of the imagination could our two acres be rated as a farm. There is no place of business within a day's hard journey of us. We don't like to kill things, so our trapping activities are confined to a trap-line for mice and rats run by Gerrish and Rufus in the kitchen and corn patch. How we keep body and soul together is a mystery to the uninitiated. At times it's a mystery to us as well.

We make a living in a variety of ways. For one thing,

there's the taxi and transport service from Middle Dam to Sunday Cove and way-stations. The rates are a little bit flexible, depending on a number of things. Very often, in winter, woodsmen who are leaving the lumber camps call on us to take them and their turkeys—woods for knapsacks—up to Middle Dam. If all goes well, the charge is a dollar. After Thanksgiving the road gets more and more treacherous as the snow gets deeper and deeper, and it becomes easier and easier to slide off into the ditch. The passenger then is obliged to help get the car back onto the road. If this is a matter of a few shoves, the rate goes down to seventy-five cents. If it requires a lot of snow shoveling and strenuous heaving, the fare decreases accordingly. Sometimes it vanishes utterly. You can't charge a man for spending half the morning with his shoulder to the tail board of a 1929 Essex truck, getting his clothes plastered with flying snow. When that happens, Ralph just decides to make a social occasion of it and spends the rest of the morning visiting with Larry Parsons. So far the situation has never seemed to demand that he pay the passenger for riding.

I always feel a little apologetic about our being a four-car family. After all, with only five miles of road available, it seems a little ostentatious, in view of our faded denim pants and patched work shirts, to be discussing which car to take to get the mail. It was worse, though, when the Packard was running.

The Packard was a 1917 Twin Six touring car, built on the general lines of a pre-Revolutionary four poster with canopy, and I always felt like Queen Mary—a nice feeling—when I sat enthroned in it. I regret the passing of the Packard. I don't like these modern cars that you have to crawl into, bumping your head in the process. I don't like to crouch in a cockpit, no matter how luxuriously upholstered, and peer through inadequate slits of glass at the waist-lines of the pedestrians. I like to stalk into a car, sit regally aloft, and view the country o'er.

I won't regret the passing of the Marmon, known locally as Rich's Big Green "Mormon," at all. It is a 1924 sports touring model, at least half a block long. Because of its tremendous power, Ralph uses it for hauling, and I have to ride in back and watch through the rear window that we don't lose our load. I hate the thing. There is no place to brace my feet and the frame of the car is so long that a twig in a rut turns it into a catapault that tosses me helplessly into the air. The Carry Road is nothing but bumps, so it's like riding in a corn-popper. And besides, I have a sneaking notion that Ralph is just a little bit fonder of the "Mormon" than he is of me.

I'd better make it clear at once that we didn't *buy* all of our four present cars. We came by them through a series of deals—all except the Essex which was given to us by a friend who had become too attached to it to be able to bear the thought of selling it down the river for the twenty dollars the dealer would allow him on a trade-in. He wanted to know that it would have a good home with kind people. Men get so emotional about machinery. And the Marmon was a left-over from the days when Ralph lived on The Outside.

The Model T used to belong to Larry Parsons. Larry is very sensible about cars. When they take to swooning in crises he says, "To hell with it," waits until the ice is safe, tows them out into the middle of the lake, and leaves them to go down into a hundred feet of water during the spring break-up. That's what he was doing to this Model T one winter day when Ralph showed up. Gerrish is unhappy driving anything but a Model T—and I might add that anything but a Model T is apt to be unhappy after Gerrish has been driving it. So Ralph ground the valves on the Parsons' snowboat, did something or other about the Parsons' lighting plant, fixed the plug in the Parsons' bath-tub, which had had to be held up with the bather's toe while the water ran out, in return for the Model T. That is what is known as a deal.

The Model A, vintage of 1930, used to belong to Jim Barnett, the local lumber baron. He had it in here one summer when he was getting out hurricane pine for the government. Under the aegis of several non-mechanical-minded straw bosses, clerks, and government scalers, it developed all the ailments that motors are heir to. During its periods of hospitalization, Ralph did Jim's errands for him, and when Jim moved his camp out, he left the Model A in payment. Ralph spent a happy fifty-nine-hour week investigating its innards, with frequent summons for me to come out and view with horror what some damn-fool butcher had perpetrated on the wiring, the pistons or the timing—I was always properly horrified, as a good wife should be, but I never knew quite at what—and now the thing runs.

People always ask how we got all these cars in here, there being no road from The Outside; and we always tell them that we took them apart, packed them in on our backs over the trail, and set them up again. Gratifyingly often we are believed. Of course we really brought them in over the ice, or rafted them in on scows.

The hey-day of the transport business, with this assorted

fleet of animated junk, is summer. That is when the canoe trips go through here. Some guide book of the lakes, which every camper in the world seems to have fallen afoul of, says that one gets from the Lower Richardson to Umbagog by way of the Rapid River. Anyone who can read a contour map can see that that is impossible. It has been accomplished only twice in history, once by mistake—Captain Coburn, when young, got caught in the current and was lucky—and once by design—some guides from up along the border wanted to make a record, but before they got through they wished they'd never started. Cluley's Rips, a mile below us, is the most vicious piece of water I have ever seen. It's frightening just to stand on the bank and look at it. The water pours into a narrow gut, overhung by rocks and dripping spruces, with such force that it has no time to level out. The middle of the river humps up, green and white and snarling, almost to eye-level of the bank-stander. Cluley, whoever he may have been, was drowned there. That's how you get things named after you in this country.

We profit by the guide book's error. Nobody wants to carry a canoe five miles. It would take all day. We can do it in half an hour, if we're lucky. Sometimes we're not lucky.

The most unlucky day we ever had started out all right. Right after breakfast the telephone rang, and it was Cliff, the old guide and trapper who lives down on Umbagog. Sometimes his last name is Wiggin and sometimes it's Wallace, depending on how he's feeling at the time. He was born with one name, but brought up by folks bearing the other. I'm not sure he remembers now himself which was which. He told us that there were two young men at his

Larry and His Snow Boat

Lower Richardson Lake from Middle Dam,
Looking Toward South Arm Where the Supplies Come From

PHOTO BY FRED ADAM

place who wanted themselves and one canoe taken across the carry, and that they'd be at Sunday Cove at ten o'clock. That was fine. That would give us time to go up to Middle Dam and bring down forty-eight cases of canned goods that we were laying in against the winter.

Forty-eight cases of canned goods fill our trailer to the brim and weigh enough to be a strain on the trailer hitch. It was unfortunate that the hitch chose to give way as we were going around a down-hill curve. We kept to the road, but the trailer went flying off into the woods, dodging a dozen trees with uncanny intelligence and coming up whango! against a house-size boulder. Cases flew in all directions, exploding as they landed. Cans of milk, figs in syrup, salmon, string beans, sliced peaches, clam chowder and what have you littered an acre of ground. We got out and looked at the wreck and at each other.

Ralph said a few things, and then he said, "Help me get the trailer back on the road, and I'll go home and fix the hitch while you pick up this mess."

It should be easy to pick up a few hundred cans and put them in piles. It wasn't. It would have been easier to pick up a covey of partridges. They were under leaves, behind rocks, down holes. While I was grubbing in the underbrush a can walloped me on the top of the head. Probably it had been lodged in a bush, but it seemed to have leaped from the ground with malicious intent. I had been hot and mad and disgusted and now I was hurt as well. And I still couldn't find three cans. I haven't found them yet. I went home.

It was half past eleven and Ralph was still working on the trailer hitch, he having had his troubles, too. Our clients were still, presumably, sitting at Sunday Cove, and almost certainly thinking hard thoughts about us. Just as we were debating what to do next, they walked into the yard, having got tired of waiting.

The least we could do was to invite them to lunch, with apologies and promises that everything would shortly be under control, and that as soon as we had eaten we would go after the canoe. I walked back to the scene of the wreck, collected some corned beef, spinach, and pineapple slices, and threw together a meal, while Ralph finished the hitch and the two youths went swimming. Then we all had a drink of rum, which we all needed, and things seemed more rosy.

They looked so much more rosy, in fact, that I decided to leave the lunch dishes and ride down to the Cove, too. We boarded the Packard, then extant, hitched on the trailer, and set out. The ride was without incident, *mirabile dictu.* But in turning around at the Cove Ralph stalled the motor, and then we were sunk again. The Packard's weakness lay in weak coils, and it wouldn't start when the motor was hot. We waited for a while for it to cool off, during which time Cookie, Kyak's mother and our dog of the moment, managed to find a porcupine and get her mouth full of quills which we had no tools to remove. The Packard still wouldn't start, so we walked the three and a half long, hot miles home after the current Ford, a Model T touring, since deceased.

I declined an invitation to ride back again and stayed home to do the dishes, de-quill the dog, and lick my own wounds. Pretty soon the whole works was back again—Ford, Packard, trailer and canoe. Apparently the Packard had cooled off enough to start the minute our backs were turned. The trip to Middle Dam was successfully accomplished, with the customers only about a day behind schedule. I will say they were wonderfully good-natured about it. They still wanted to pay Ralph for throwing their trip completely out of gear; but there are a few things left for which we don't take money.

The worst and final repercussion was delayed two days. Then the money for that ill-starred trip arrived by mail, with no return address. There wasn't a thing we could do but keep it. We felt like a couple of curs.

Ralph has hauled all sorts of things across the carry. He has hauled anything that will float, from a rubber fold-boat to a steel, gasoline-powered work boat. He has hauled woodsmen suffering from third degree burns, all manner of cuts and fractures, pneumonia, and delirium tremens, known hereabouts as "the horrors." He has hauled a litter of pigs, bound for the garbage disposal department of a lumber camp. He has hauled news-reel men and their cameras, covering the National Championship White Water Races, and fire wardens covering a forest fire. But the ones I like best and he hates the most are the girls' camps.

He hates the girls' camps because he claims that, in spite of the fact that the girls are always under the auspices of a guide and two or three counselors, you might as well try to organize a handful of quicksilver. I like them, because I like to see the old boy get his come-uppence. He gets them all packed in nicely around their canoes and duffle, and someone decides she has to have a picture of the outfit, but that Tessie's skinned knee and Vera's camp letter won't show, so will everybody please rearrange themselves? Or Muggsy can't find her sweater, so everything has to be unpacked. Or someone has a notion, and the notion spreads, and in a flash the whole works is streaming off into the bushes. It drives him nuts, being, so he says, me raised to the *n*th degree.

The most recent invasion got even Gerrish down. Ralph went to Middle to get them—fifteen of them from some camp over in Vermont—and stopped here to re-fill his radiator. They swarmed into the yard like a pack of beagles, with an old and completely resigned guide making perfunctory motions of bringing them to heel. While his charges were posing for snap-shots with Kyak, who makes swell local color to show the home folks, he came in to ask permission to build a lunch fire on our land. I asked him how he liked his job. He sighed wearily. "Wal, it ain't no *position,*" he said with feeling.

He could have saved his breath about the fire. Gerrish was tarring the seams of a boat and had the tar pot heating over a little fire between two rocks. According to his rather hysterical story, the first thing he knew he was smearing the boat with tomato soup, and then he realized he had somehow become embroiled in a mass culinary operation. He grabbed the tar pot, fought his way clear, and knocked off for dinner. He believes in co-operating with the inevitable.

I was charmed with that lunch, aimed to fill the hollow brought on by ten miles of paddling since breakfast and to generate enough energy to get the whole shebang to the nearest camp-site, ten miles away, before supper. The menu: Tomato Purée; Cheese Dreams; Lemonade.

Once Ralph got a job with the Geodetic Survey, which was in here for the summer making a contour map of the country. To make a contour map, it seems, you first establish, by some esoteric hocus-pocus with trigonometry, the exact altitude of one point, in this case a stone in Coburn's front yard. (Alt. 1462.27 feet above sea level.) Then, working with surveying instruments, you run in circles from that point, sticking sticks with the new altitudes on them at convenient places along the circumference of the circle. If the reading when you get back to Coburn's stone is 1462.27, you may assume that all points on the circle are correct. You then take any point on the circle and follow the same procedure from there. At the end of the summer the entire country is covered with imaginary circles and actual sticks. Then you start running straight lines across country, re-checking altitude with a barometer at any sticks you may come across—surveyors dignify these sticks by calling them Temporary Bench Marks—and attempting to come out at flags which have been tied according to what system I never did find out, to various inaccessible trees. This is the last step before putting the map on paper, and this is where Ralph came into the picture.

One of the rodmen was taken ill, the appropriation for the survey was almost gone, and the head surveyor was loath to lose time and money waiting for his man to recover. So he appealed to Ralph to help him out, assuring him that all he had to do was stroll through the woods with a string tied to his arm, stop when shouted to, and blaze the nearest tree. He didn't say that they would be working in the B Pond territory.

There is nothing the matter with B Pond. It lies to the south of us, over a beech-covered ridge, and it is lovely and placid and wild. But Ralph loathes B Pond, because the trail over is rough and steep. He'd rather be dead than take a trip over the B Pond trail.

Nevertheless, everyday that he worked for the Survey he

went to B Pond, and he didn't go by trail. That isn't the way the Survey does things. They pick out a point at random, consult their notes and learn that somewhere a mile off to the S.S.W. is a white cloth tied to a yellow birch, take out their compasses, tighten their belts, and start looking for it. The rodman—Ralph—goes ahead, trailing a hundred-yard piece of string. When the end of the string comes abreast of the surveyor, he puts up a shout and the rodman stops and makes his blaze. As soon as the surveyor overtakes him, he sets out again, in theory, at least, letting nothing turn him aside from a perfectly straight line. This would be a cinch on the plains of the West, but this is rough country, and we had a hurricane in 1938.

The results of the hurricane here have to be seen to be believed. Acres of trees are piled up like jackstraws in windrows forty feet high and half a mile long. A rodman doesn't go around these. He goes over and through them. Ralph insists that one whole day he never had his feet on the ground except when he came down for lunch. The despised B Pond trail began to look like a boulevard, especially as he knew it was only a hundred yards off to the west, running parallel to their course. It might as well have been a hundred miles off. It might better have been, because then he could have forgotten it. He tore his clothes to ribbons, and then did the same to his skin. He put a vicious blaze on a little sapling and a porcupine fell out of it, missing him by inches. That's the same as being missed by a twenty-pound ball stuck full of red hot needles. He got three and a half dollars a day and whatever satisfaction went with the chief surveyor's affidavit that (a) Ralph was the best rodman he'd ever had, and that (b) this is the most hellish country he's seen in a career covering every state in the Union.

But I know better than ever again to try to persuade Ralph to take a nice little walk over to B Pond with me.

I have my difficulties, too. I don't much like to cook. I like the results of a morning's hard labor to last more than ten minutes. But once in a while I have to take boarders. This usually happens when I am in the worst possible position to do so. Last spring is a good example.

All three families in Middle Dam had enough food to last, with care, over the break-up and until a load of supplies could be brought in from The Outside. We were feeling pretty good about it, because sometimes we aren't so lucky. Nobody, we fondly thought, could get in to eat up our carefully counted potatoes and beans. We were sitting pretty. I was even entertaining the extravagant idea of making a one-egg chocolate cake instead of a no-egg gingerbread, when the telephone rang. It was Alice Miller, and she was in a dither.

She said, "Louise, how much food have you got? I got a crew of five walked in here along the shore from the Arm to stay over the break-up and do some work on the dam. I ain't got a thing to feed them."

The Millers had helped us out in more pinches than I can remember, and it wasn't often that I had a chance to do much for them. This was a God-given opportunity to lend a hand. I'd peel the larder down to the last bone, and be glad of the chance. If I saved out a dozen eggs and a couple of cans of corned beef, and beans and salt pork and split peas and flour and corn meal, we could eat for the few days until the lake was clear, even if it wasn't a very balanced diet. We had plenty of canned milk and potatoes. I told her what I could let her have.

"Swell! I'll send someone down with a pack-sack!"

She hung up and in due time her emissary arrived. I gave him everything I could spare, and he staggered off up the Carry Road under the load.

Barely was he out of sight when the telephone rang again. A man's voice said pleasantly, "Mis' Rich? This is Ban Barnett. I'm down at Sunday Cove, with a crew of three. We walked in over the old Magalloway trail to fix the Carry Road before the drive comes in, and we'll be right up. We'll stay at your place for two-three days, like always."

"Did you bring any food?" I asked with regrettable lack of hospitality.

"Food? Holy God, Mis' Rich, we had all we could do to get ourselves through that Jees'ly swamp!"

"Ban," I said desperately, "I can't board you. I've hardly got enough food in the house to feed the family. You'll have to—"

He'd have to what? The Millers couldn't feed four more. The Parsons weren't any better off than I was. They couldn't go home, nine miles through the swamp and over a mountain, with nothing under their belts.

"You can feed us," Ban assured me with touching faith. "You got potatoes and salt, ain't you?"

I fed them for three days, and ever since I have had implicit belief in the miracle of the loaves and fishes. We had pea soup, which is very filling. We had baked beans. I sent Gerrish fishing. You can never catch fish when you need them, but he did. We had trout and salmon. We had corn meal mush and molasses. The butter ran out, but we had johnny-cake and the last of the jam I had made the fall before. We had dandelion greens and fiddle-heads, those strange, furry fern fronds that taste something like asparagus and something like swamp water. You boil them and serve them with butter, if you have any butter. My two cans of corned beef made two meals. There are ways of stretching meat enough for three to feed seven, other than Divine multiplication. One can I cut up in cream sauce—a lot of cream sauce—and served on toast. The other I cut up with cold potato—a lot of potato—and browned into hash. The Parsons let me have three cans of tomatoes. One made tomato soup, one went into scalloped tomatoes with bread crumbs—lots of bread crumbs—and the last I strained for Rufus to drink, in lieu of orange juice. You can make one egg take the place of two in scrambled eggs by using too much milk and thickening it with flour. It's not very good, but it's something to eat.

Oh, I fed them. It wasn't according to any known dietetics, but we all survived. And when the ice went out and the first boat came in with supplies, I had left a cup of sugar, five potatoes, three cans of milk, a quart of flour, and one egg.

While I was peeling potatoes paper-thin, diluting canned milk with too much water—we did have plenty of water—and measuring out lard by the quarter teaspoon, Ralph and Gerrish were working with the crew on the road. That's another annual source of income, the reimbursement for which just about covers the taxes. Working out your taxes on the road is routine procedure hereabouts. You spend a week filling in wash-outs, rebuilding caved-in culverts, and leveling out the worst ruts, and the tax sale is forestalled for another twelve months. Oh, you can get along with very little cash money in this country if you know the ropes and are sufficiently adaptable.

I was being very adaptable the day Ted Benson called me up from Pond-in-the-River Dam. Ted is the boss of the dam repair crew that travels about the country from headquarters in Lewiston. They always stay at Miller's when they are in this neck of the woods, and when they are working on Pondy Dam, Alice Miller sends down the makings of dinner, and they prepare it over an open camp-fire. Ted is a Dane, and his name is really Theodore (pronounced Tay-o-dorrr) Bendtsen. He has been in this country ever since, almost half a century ago as an apprentice to the Danish Merchant Marine, he deserted ship at Portland; but when he gets excited he still lapses into Danish on the hard words. He was very much excited on this occasion.

I finally made out that he wanted me to come up to the dam and cook dinner for him and his crew of nine. His long-string-of-Danish cook had been out over the week-end and had too bad a hang-over to be of any use to anyone. It wouldn't be any work at all. Mis' Miller had everything all ready. All I had to do was heat it up. He'd do it himself, only dam repairing had reached a crisis where not a man could be spared. Would I come?

I would be glad to. I like Ted, and I'd like to do him a favor. Ralph had gone to Upton to vote in the state elections, so there was nothing to keep me at home. I locked up the dogs—we had five then; that was when we thought a dog team would be a good idea—put Rufus into a pack-sack—he was too young to walk—loaded him onto my back and went up to the dam.

A fire was already burning under the grate that Ted had

salvaged from an abandoned steamboat and placed on two rocks, and a number of kettles were standing around on the ground. A long-chinned individual named Rush was splitting wood, and Ted was standing by to tell me that the dinner hour was eleven o'clock by the battered Big Ben he had placed conspicuously on a stump. Then he went off down the dam fill, motioning Rush to follow.

Rush put another chunk of wood—only we natives call them "junks"—on his chopping block and reduced it to splinters while Ted moved out of hearing. Then he left his ax in the block and closed in confidentially.

"You want to watch that crazy Dane," he warned me. "I've cooked for him. You know what he does? He gets hungry and comes up and shoves the clock along ten-fifteen minutes. You have to keep an eye on him."

It was half past ten then.

I tied Rufus to a bush and gave him a pannikinful of water and a spoon to play with. Then I looked into the food situation. The big kettle held a boiled dinner—corned beef and cabbage, potatoes, carrots, and turnips. It was all cooked, but it would take at least twenty minutes to heat through again, which left ten minutes in which to make the coffee—at least a gallon in a big, smoke-smudged pot. The grate would hold only one thing at a time. Well, it could be done, with a good hot fire. I set the kettle on and stuffed some dry spruce under it. The flame sprang up with a heartening crackle and I started to unpack the plates and eating tools.

Suddenly I realized that Ted was hovering. He took the cover off the kettle, peered in, put it back, snitched a cookie out of a bag, and wandered back down the dam fill. I looked at the clock. It said ten minutes of eleven. I set it back fifteen minutes and started arranging plates of bread, butter, cookies, apple pie, and cheese in a row on a plank. Alice Miller has a reputation all up the lakes for the abundance and excellence of her fare.

The fire had died down a little, so I put some wood on, saw that the boiled dinner had commenced to steam gently, and took the coffee pot down to the river to fill it with water. When I got back, Ted was again retiring down the dam fill, the clock said five minutes of eleven, Rufus had untied himself and was eating cheese, and there were ants on the pie. I took the cheese away, tied Rufus up, set the clock back fifteen minutes, brushed the ants off, and covered the pies with a clean dish towel. Then I sat down on the stump beside the clock and waited for the boiled dinner to boil. It was quarter of eleven by my time, which by then had nothing to do with any other time on earth.

Pretty soon the big kettle began to rumble quietly, sending out clouds of steam and a delicious odor, and Ted started up from the dam, walking briskly and dangling something in his hand. I took one look and set the clock back five more minutes. It was a two pound salmon, and my prophetic soul informed me, rightly, that he wanted it cooked for his dinner. Boiled, he said, with melted butter on it. I took off the boiled dinner, set the coffee pot on, and went down to the river with an extra pan to get some water for the fish. When I got back the clock again said five minutes of eleven. I set it back to quarter of, edged the coffee pot over to make room for the salmon, and put some butter in a pannikin on the edge of the fire to melt.

Rufus was eating leaves, which might or might not be edible, and although by then I didn't much care which they were, I fished them out of his mouth, getting my finger bitten in the process, and set out the salt, pepper, and vinegar. A loud hissing behind my back indicated that the coffee had boiled over and put out the fire. I took the coffee off, burning my hand, and built up the fire with some birch bark. Ted's fish was boiling, and Ted was coming up from the dam again, so I stuck a fork into it, decided it was near enough done as made no difference, and with no attempt at concealment, shoved the clock along to eleven.

"I guess we're ready," I told Ted, and met his eye. "Right on the dot, too!" I added blandly.

I still take boarders when I have to, but I don't cook out any more. It's too hard on the nerves. I'd rather do something like knitting, which can be confined to the home. I'm a good knitter, and I'm proud of it. I see no point in being modest about things you know you do well. It doesn't indicate humility so much as hypocrisy or lack of perception. So then, I am a very good knitter. I even won first prize at the Andover Fair once for a pair of gloves. Fifty cents, it was, and a blue ribbon. I spent the money, but the ribbon I wouldn't part with for pearls. I can knit while I read, thus staving off boredom and creating an illusion of great efficiency. I can make up my own directions, or I can follow printed directions, which apparently is the harder thing to do, although I don't see why it should be.

I think the difficulty with people who can't follow printed directions for knitting or anything else is that they try to understand them. They read the whole thing through and it doesn't make sense to them, so they start with a defeatist attitude. They try to relate the first few steps to the whole, and there is no obvious relation, so they get discouraged and say, "Oh, I can't learn things out of books. But if you'll just show me—"

You don't have to understand directions. All you have to do is follow them; and you can follow them only one step at a time. What you need is not intelligence, but a blind faith. I never read directions through. I never read beyond the operation I am engaged in, having a simple trust that the person who wrote them knew what he was doing. That trust is usually justified. Oh, there's no trick to following directions, and if I don't teach Sally and Rufus one other thing, I'm going to teach them that. I think it's important.

When I get my own family's sweaters and mittens and socks done for the winter, I knit for whoever will pay me—neighbors, lumberjacks, anyone. Also I sew on buttons and patch clothes for woodsmen, whenever there are lumbering operations in here. I don't like to sew, and I don't sew very well, but I do better than most lumberjacks. Ralph, coming across an article about Father Hubbard, the Glacier Priest, took to calling me Mother Hubbard, the winter I started acting as housemother to the woodsmen. It applied, but not as he meant it to. I'm not a snappy model; I really don't wear Mother Hubbards, but the effect is about the same.

Had Ralph been born a little earlier, he would have been a Yankee horse-trader. As it is, he doesn't do so badly with his car trading, in a country where trading is a religion. Albert Allen, a friend from Upton who has lived all his life in this vicinity, covered the general attitude one day. "Nope," he said, "I'd be ashamed to give it to anybody. 'Tain't good enough. But maybe I can find someone who'll make a trade." No matter what you start with, here, if you stick with it long enough, you'll get what you want. All you need is something to start with. Will Morton, who lives on Rifle Point, off Middle Dam, and who is the oldest working guide in the state, being eighty-two—and one of the best—started out with an electric razor, which one of his sports gave him for Christmas. He ended with a boat, which was what he had in mind all the time. I've forgotten, unfortunately, the intermediate steps.

Ralph's most remarkable operation was the trading of the old Model T touring car. There was a lumber camp over on Sunday Pond three miles north of us then, and one gray November day the clerk of the camp called up and announced that he'd heard Ralph had a lot of cars and would maybe sell one. He wanted it to run up and down Umbagog, now that the ice was safe and the snow hadn't come yet, so he could go out and see his girl.

We'd just acquired the Essex, so Ralph was open to bids on the Model T. The clerk—Mac, his name was—said he'd be over next day to take a look. Ralph spent the intervening time pacing up and down and muttering to himself, trying to decide what price he ought to ask. He concluded finally that he'd ask twenty-five dollars, but would be glad to get fifteen.

The trial run was a huge success. They went everywhere—down to Sunday Cove, across Umbagog to Sturtevant Cove, and up through the woods to the Brown Farm, where they called on Joe Mooney and had a game of ping-pong with the company doctor. Mac was impressed twenty-five dollars' worth, all right, only he didn't have twenty-five dollars to spare. Just as Ralph was about to come big-heartedly down to twenty, Mac advanced a proposition.

"Look, I'll tell you what I'll do. I'll give you fifteen dollars and return the car when the camp moves out."

Every woman occasionally wonders what manner of man she has married. No matter how long she has been living with her husband, once in a while he presents a new face. It's the bunk about women being enigmas and men being just transparent little boys at heart. Or else I'm gullible. I had Ralph down as good old, honest, out-spoken Rich, the guy with the heart of gold; the guy who, offered his price in that frank and open manner, would say, "Oh, hell, fifteen dollars is plenty. She's yours. Drive her away!"

And did he? Oh, my goodness, gracious, no! He hemmed and hawed, while I bit my tongue in an effort not to interfere. Finally he gave in, with the perfectly maddening appearance of granting a favor. "That'll be all right," he said graciously. "When you get through with her, be sure to leave her on this side of the Cove, so I can get her without any trouble." Just like that. And then I swear he went out and measured gas into the tank with a teaspoon, so that Mac could get to the nearest source of supply, but not much further.

That night Mac went to Errol to see his girl. The next day it snowed eighteen inches. The rest of the winter the Ford sat under a drift at Sunday Cove—on this side of the Cove, as requested—and never turned a wheel. In the spring Ralph drove it home. I should think he'd lie awake nights, but he doesn't. He has the horse-trader conscience, I guess.

I haven't. I'm a rotten trader. But I did do one deal that gives me perennial satisfaction. I think I came out all right, but even if I didn't, even if I got gypped out of my

HOTO BY FRED ADAMS

Maine Guide—Will Morton, the Oldest and One of the Best

eye-teeth as Ralph says I did, I'm very happy about the whole thing.

There are three boats and a canoe that go with the place, and of course everybody uses them. But they really were Ralph's boats. I wanted a boat of my own, to use and possibly abuse as I chose. I wanted a boat I could put into a pool downriver and not be asked, "When are you going to bring that boat back to the Pond? I want to use it." So when the Bernier boat—Bernier was a famous builder of the type of boat called the Rangeley boat—began to go to pieces from neglect, Ralph gave it to me. The idea was that I would fix it up myself and it would be mine.

Well, I just didn't get around to it, somehow, and it continued to lie on the shore of the Pond, with the paint flaking off, the wood drying out, and the caulking falling from the seams. And that's where Gerrish enters the picture.

He said to me casually, "Ralph tells me that Bernier boat belongs to you."

I thought I felt a deal coming on, and I'd observed Ralph long enough to have learned some rudiments of the technique. So I just said, "Yeah."

"You ain't going to have no boat if you don't tend to it."

I said, "Yeah," again, and we sat in companionable silence.

Finally he said, "Have a cigarette." Pause while we lighted up. "What'll you take for it?"

"I don't know. What'll you give for it?"

"It ain't worth much. Needs a lot done on it."

"To tell you the truth," I said frankly, "I don't want to get rid of it. I want to cut the stern off square, when I get the price of an outboard motor, and make a kicker-boat out of it. What'll you take for fixing it up for me?" That was in the classic tradition. I'd registered reluctance to part with my property and made a counter offer.

"Half the boat," he said promptly. "I'll do the work and you furnish the materials and we'll own it together. When you get around to buying a kicker—wal, there's places I'd go if I had a kicker-boat."

"Where, for instance?" I asked. I didn't want my half of the boat hauled down to Mount Desert Island along with his.

"Upper Dam. Or the West Arm. I wouldn't take it off the lakes."

So it was a deal. He scraped the boat, caulked the seams, replaced a broken gunwale and put in a new stem and keel. That took a month. Then he gave it two coats of oil and two coats of paint, and it's the best boat on the place. He did a swell job. I don't see why Ralph thinks it was a skin deal. I didn't pay anything for the boat in the first place.

I didn't pay anything for it in the last place, either, and that might be what gripes him. He seems to have a feeling that I should have paid for the paint and oil and steel wool and marine caulking and nails and copper sheathing. But he has a whole shop full of that kind of stuff. I should think he'd be glad—but he doesn't seem to be. It would bother me a lot more if I didn't remember Mac and the Model T.

My sister and I used to play a game called "Husband's Occupation?" It was a simple-minded game that we made up off application blanks of various sorts. One of us would ask suddenly, "Husband's Occupation?" and the other had to think up a possible but not very probable answer. "Flea trainer," for example. Or "Percheron Faulter." Or "Sealer of Weights and Measures." I guess we were easily entertained.

I guess we still are, because I am amused, spasmodically, at being married to a Maine guide. Oh, yes, Ralph's a guide, too, although he doesn't work at it much.

Of course a guide has to be a good woodsman and canoeman and camp cook and emergency doctor, and the State of Maine ascertains that he is, before issuing him a license to guide. But he could never earn a living if he didn't also make the grade with the sports—same as dudes of the West—as "quite a character." He has to be laconic. He has to be picturesque. Maine guides have a legend of quaintness to uphold, and, boy! do they uphold it. They're so quaint that they creak. They ought to be. They work hard enough at it.

Here's the Maine guide. He wears what amounts to a uniform. It consists of a wool shirt, preferably plaid, nicely faded to soft, warm tones; dark pants, either plus-fours, for some unknown reason, or riding breeches; wool socks and the soleless, Indian-type moccasin, or high laced boots. He carries a bandana in his hip pocket and may or may not wear another knotted around his neck. But he must wear a battered felt hat, with a collection of salmon flies stuck in the band, and he must wear it with an air; and he must wear a hunting knife day and night; and he must look tough and efficient. If he has high cheek bones and tans easily, that is his good luck. He can then admit to part-Indian ancestry, accurately or not. Indian blood is an item highly esteemed by sports. Naturally he could do his work as well in mail-order slacks, or in a tuxedo, for that matter; but the sports wouldn't think so. Sports are funny.

"That fellow there," the sport is supposed to say, showing his vacation movies in his Westchester rumpus room, "was my quarter-breed guide. He's quite a character. Never had any education beyond the seventh grade, but I don't know anyone I'd rather spend a week alone with. That's the real test. He's a genuine natural philosopher. For instance, we were talking about the War, and he said —and I never thought of it this way before—." What the guide said he probably lifted from Shirer's book, but translated into Down East, it wouldn't be recognizable.

A few livid scars are a great asset to a guide. It doesn't matter how he got them. Maybe as a barefoot boy he stepped on a rake. The holes make swell bear-trap scars, acquired one night up in the Allagash, when the thermometer was at thirty below and the nearest settlement was fifty miles away. Maybe he cut his hand peeling potatoes. It sounds much better to say a beaver bit him. Maybe he fell downstairs and gashed his forehead. When asked—and he'll be asked all right—he can tell all about his big fight with the lynx. They all make good stories to tell around the evening camp-fire.

Oh, those evening camp-fires! That's when the good guide gets in his dirty work. That's when he sows the seed for a re-engagement next year.

This is the set-up:—Supper—fresh-caught trout with bacon curls, potatoes baked in the coals and slathered with butter, a kind of biscuit cooked in a frying pan and resembling Yorkshire pudding, canned peas and fruit—is over. The sports, pleasantly stuffed and mildly weary from having "helped" paddle for ten or twelve miles, stretch out around the fire. Down on the shingle that natural philosopher, that real character, Bobcat Bill, washes the dishes. The water glows like blood-stained ebony in the leaping light, and the firs stand up behind, black and motionless. Back in the bush a fox barks and a deer crashes away from the scent of wood-smoke. All around lies the wilderness, dark and unknown and sinister. Inside the little pool of light is all that is left of the safe and familiar—the canoes drawn up on the shore, the piled packsacks and blanket rolls, the forms and faces of friends. A loon sends its lost-soul lament over the darkling water, and a shiver runs around the fire. Then Bobcat Bill strolls up from the lake, throws an armful of dry-ki onto the blaze, and begins tossing blankets toward the group. In the flash of a buck's tail the old magic begins to work. The tight little fire-hearted circle of fellowship is formed. We're all brothers here, united by our common cause against the power of the black beyond. We're all valiant, noble renegades from civilization's chafing bonds. We're dangerous and free!

The loon throws its blood-curdling cry against the mountains once more, and laughs its crazy laughter.

"Never hear one of them critters a-hollerin'," Bobcat Bill drifts easily into his act, "but what it 'minds me of one time I was lost up on them big caribou barrens across the lake. That's how I come by this here scar on my shoulder. Reason I was up in there, a feller had met foul play—"

I'm making guides sound like a bunch of frauds, and I don't mean to. They work hard and they're in a difficult position. Like all merchandisers, they're obliged to give the customer what he wants, and it's their tough luck that the customer wants adventure. Adventure, free of actual risk, is hard to produce; and the state frowns on the actual killing off of sports, even by accident. So the guide has to make the customer believe himself Daniel Boone's contemporary equivalent, without actually letting him stick his neck out too far. A little discomfort, yes. That'll make fine telling back in Westchester. Too much discomfort, no. Actual danger, a thousand times no, not even if he insists with tears and pleading that he really wants to rough it, to get off the beaten track into tough country, to pit his own brains and brawn against death by violence or starvation. It's too easy to meet trouble in this country without deliberately looking for it.

So what's the answer? The answer is atmosphere:—tall tales around the camp-fire, a perpetually grim and watchful bearing, a knife and revolver worn always at the ready. The answer is illusion:—jam into bear's blood, bobcat into Canada lynx, vaccination scar into dagger wound.

Ralph's occasional guiding consists chiefly in taking out fishing parties by the day in this immediate vicinity. That's what he's best fitted for, knowing as he does every fish in the river by its first name, and where it'll most likely be hanging out at two-thirty on any given Wednesday. He always comes home exhausted by suppressed mirth. Sports are funny-ha-ha as well as funny-peculiar.

His prize catch was an outfit of politicians from a medium-sized Massachusetts city. At home they were elaborately teetotal; the W.C.T.U. is a force in that city. But they brought fourteen quarts of Scotch and a case of beer—snake-bite precautions—for their three-day stay in the woods. They managed to get rid of it, and I don't think they dumped it in the river. That would argue a little training somewhere along the line, I should think. They'd never been fly-fishing before, but they'd seen pictures of fly-fishermen. So they had the works:—waders, creels, canvas jackets, tapered lines, collapsible landing nets, everything. Everything, that is, except the ability to cast a fly. Ralph spent the day climbing trees to retrieve flies caught in branches and diving into the river to un-snag them from the bottom. Between times he hauled his sports out of the water—they were great fallers-in—and dodged erratic back-casts. He had a very active day. Along about dusk a great outcry went up. Someone had caught a fish. An enormous salmon, so he said. Ralph netted it. It was a small chub. The chub is a poor relation of the carp family, and we natives look down our noses at them. Even the cats won't eat them. The politician wasn't so choosey. He took it home. Probably he has it mounted over his desk now.

Ralph finally got three of his party put to bed. The fourth—he of the chub—refused to go. He'd tasted blood and he wasn't going to waste time sleeping. Ralph left him sitting on the bank of the river with a quart of Scotch conveniently at hand. It was pitch dark, which not only put him in the legal position of being a breaker of the half-hour-after-sunset law, but also in the impractical position of not being able to see his line. The first consideration didn't bother him. The second he got around by using a powerful flashlight trained on his fly. He caught no fish, but he had fun.

The other thing that we do for a living is write. This is the most important, because we spend the most time on it, and because the larger part of our income is derived from it. Probably if we spent the same amount of time and energy working in a factory or selling brushes from door to door, we'd have more money and fewer headaches. But there are other things we wouldn't have.

In theory, at least, one of the advantages of writing is

that you can work anywhere and any time. You aren't tied down. Actually this is true only within limits. I have found that unless I make myself some office hours and stick to them—8.30 to 11 A.M. and 1 to 3 P.M.—I don't do any writing. I pick some wild flowers and arrange them, wash the dog, and make a cake, and then it's too late to start this morning. So I read another chapter of the book I started last night and get dinner. After dinner I think I might as well finish the book and go swimming. Morning is really the time your mind is clearest, I remember being told. There's no sense in trying to start writing in the afternoon. So I'll write to-morrow. I really will.

But I wouldn't if I didn't have my office hours. If I can't think of anything to write about, I just sit in front of the typewriter and brood.

I couldn't write anywhere, either. I couldn't write on a cruise to the West Indies, or in a mining town in Nevada, or in the bayou country, or any other place where the surroundings were new and unexplored. Putting down words on paper is a very dull substitute for seeing new things and people. On my ninety-ninth cruise I could probably write, or after I'd lived two years in Nevada. The real meaning of "You can write anywhere" is that you can choose a place where you're going to like to be and do your writing there after you've exhausted its other possibilities. Your original choice is free.

Another reason I like to be a writer, aside from the fact that I can live in the backwoods instead of off Times Square, is that I like to see my name in print. This is pure exhibitionism, and we'll say no more about it. I don't like exhibitionists, either. And while I'm baring my girlish heart, I might as well admit that I enjoy having people look respectful when I say, "Oh, I write." I get a kick out of it, even if I do feel like a fraud.

Feeling like a fraud is one of the bad things about being a writer. You have to be a little disparaging about your work sometimes. Because of its nature, it is so closely tied up with your own personality that taking it seriously verges perilously close to the pompous. So there's a lot of talk by writers about just doing pot-boilers until one is financially secure enough to embark on a really serious work. Frankly, this is hooey. Writing pot-boilers implies writing down, and condescension is immediately apparent to, and rightly resented by, the editor. I believe that any writer who sells enough to eat off the proceeds is writing the very best he can all the time. When he stops, he stops eating.

I've read a lot of first-rate writing, and I have some critical sense; so I know where I stand. I'll never be first-rate. I'll improve with practice, I trust, but I haven't got what it takes to reach the top. However, I hope I'll never make the excuse that "it's only a pot-boiler, after all." Everything I write, no matter how lousy it turns out to be, is the very best I am capable of at the time. My writing may be third-rate, but at least it's honest. You can't be even a third-rate writer without taking your work seriously.

But if you take it seriously, chances are that others will, too, and I enjoy having a fool-proof excuse for not doing the things I don't want to do. If I said, "Oh, I can't. I have to do my mending," the answer would be, "You can do it this evening." If I say, "Oh, I can't. I'm working on my book," there's no argument about it at all. It's wonderful. I hardly ever do things I don't want to do any more. Except write.

Writing is hard work, and don't let anybody tell you otherwise. It's hard on the eyes, the back, the fanny, the disposition and the nail-polish. It's hard on the nerves. Your income is so uncertain. You never know, when you're sweating blood over a story, whether the editor is going to hold his nose, or cheer and send you a check for—

And that's another thing. People don't mind asking a writer how much he gets paid for a story. There must be some explanation for such a breach of good taste in otherwise well-bred persons. I have been coping with the situation by stalling. I say, "Well, that depends. It would be impossible to say. Some magazines pay higher rates than others, and some writers are better than others—" And blah, blah, blah.

But I'm not going to stall any more. The next time anyone asks me how much I got for a story, I'm going to tell them. I might even tell them the truth. And then I'm going to say, "And what does *your* husband earn in a year?" That ought to settle that.

Upon reflection, I conclude that probably the best short answer to "How do you earn a living?" would be "From hand to mouth."

III

"But You Don't Live Here All the Year 'Round?"

WHAT PEOPLE REALLY MEAN WHEN THEY ASK US IF WE live here the year 'round, is "But good Lord! Certainly you don't stay in here during the winter? You must be crazy!" Well, all right, we're crazy. I would have thought so myself, before I tried it.

I used to hate winter, too. When I was a child it was because winter meant school, and although I got along reasonably well there, school was something to be considered with nausea. Along about February I used to think of the stretch of time until June and freedom with such a hopeless depression as I have never known since. It just didn't seem possible that I could live that long. The only time in my whole scholastic career that I ever liked school was one spell when I was in the eighth grade; and the reason for my change of heart then had nothing to do with my studies. I fell in love with the boy who sat in front of me, and since he lived over on the other side of town, the only time I got to see him was during school hours. It made a difference in my attitude, but it didn't last very long. In spite of all the sentences I diagrammed for him, and the arithmetic answers I slipped under my desk into his eager palm, come Valentine's Day, he spent all his pocket money on a big lace and ribbon heart for a blonde who sat over in the dumb section, and who didn't know a verb from a common denominator. It soured me on the male for a time, but it taught me a lesson that has been valuable ever since: to wit, men may admire and use brains in a woman, but they don't love them. I reverted to my hatred of winter.

After I grew up, I still hated it, and I think that now I know the reason why. In civilization we try to combat winter. We try to modify it so that we can continue to live the same sort of life that we live in summer. We plow the sidewalks so we can wear low shoes, and the roads so we can use cars. We heat every enclosed space and then, inadequately clad, dash quickly from one little pocket of hot air through a bitter no-man's land of cold to another. We fool around with sun lamps, trying to convince our skins that it is really August, and we eat travel-worn spinach in an attempt to sell the same idea to our stomachs. Naturally, it doesn't work very well. You can neither remodel nor ignore a thing as big as winter.

In the woods we don't try to. We just let winter be winter, and any adjustments that have to be made, we make in ourselves and our way of living. We have to. The skin between outdoors and indoors here is so much thinner than it is even in a small town, that it's sometimes hard to tell where one stops and the other begins. We can't dress, for example, for a day in the house. Such a thing doesn't exist. We have to go outdoors continually—to get in wood, to go to the john, to run down to the other house and put wood on the kitchen fire, to get water, to hack a piece of steak off the frozen deer hanging in the woodshed, or for any one of a dozen other reasons. Outdoors is just another, bigger, colder room. When we get up in the morning we dress with the idea that we'll be using this other room all day. When we step into it we make the concession of putting on mittens—if we're really going to be there long enough.

Everyone in here dresses more or less alike, until it comes to foot gear. We all, male and female, wear plaid wool shirts—two of them sometimes—and wool pants, ski or riding. We wear wool caps and home-made mittens, with leather mittens, called choppers, over them. The choppers don't keep the hands warm, but they keep the mittens dry and prevent their wearing out. We all wear wool socks. And there the great woods schism begins. Everyone has his own pet ideas of the proper footwear for below zero weather. No one will listen to any one else's opinion on the subject. Everyone knows he is right, and no one will dabble with experiments. Feet freeze too easily and frozen feet are too painful and serious to be courted deliberately.

Ralph belongs to the great gum-boot school of thought. Gum-boots have high leather tops sewed on rubber feet. They are loose and roomy, and their addicts wear two or three pairs of heavy wool socks inside them. I guess they're all right, if you like them. Larry Parsons swears by laced, all-rubber knee boots and two pairs of socks. He claims that the leather tops of gum-boots get soaked when there is wet snow, and then where are you? The answer to that is that healthy feet perspire a little, and there is no chance for evaporation through rubber. So by night your socks are going to be wet anyhow, and what difference does it make how you get them wet? The Finnish lumberjacks who brought their equipment from the old country—and there are quite a number of them around here—have a good foot gear, consisting of heavy felt boots, knee high and about an inch thick—too thick to wet through, and much too thick to chill through. They look as though they'd be wonderful, but you can't get them in this country. Some of the native lumberjacks try to achieve the same effect by buying old-fashioned black buckled galoshes, about four sizes too big, and wearing four or five pairs of socks in them. They keep the feet warm, but it's like wearing a bucket on each foot. A few people wear high leather boots, but almost everyone else agrees that they are cold damn things. Nobody would be caught dead in a pair of ski boots. They're too stiff and heavy. Let the city folks have them. They don't know any better.

Myself, I wear one pair of wool socks and the lightest, cheapest pair of sneakers I can buy, and nobody can convince me that this isn't the answer. Everyone else is working on the wrong principle, that of getting more and more layers between their feet and the cold. That's wrong. What they gain in insulation they sacrifice in foot flexibility. Their feet are just two petrified lumps wrapped in wool. According to my system, articulation isn't interfered with, and the blood circulates freely, bringing heat from the body to the feet as a hot water heating system brings heat to the radiators. I haven't been able to win any disciples to my belief, but that's all right. Neither have I ever had my feet frost-bitten.

I seem to have devoted a lot of space to what we wear on our feet in winter, but it's quite in proportion to the amount of time spent talking and thinking about it. It's a very vital matter.

Outside, life takes on pace with the approach of winter. It is the gay season, the season of parties and theatres and all the other things that will help people forget that outdoors something that they can't cope with is going on. Here life slows down, just as the world around us slows down. The leaves fall from the hardwood trees. Spruce and fir and pine stop growing and stand, dormant and black and thick, on mountain-side and lake-shore, their slim tips pointing monotonously to the gray sky. Of course they don't move, but they seem to draw silently in around us. We realize suddenly what we have forgotten: that after all, there are only three families of us—only a dozen puny human souls strung out along the lake and river—against all the forces of nature. To the people Outside, "the forces of nature" is a convenient phrase out of a textbook. To us they are a reality. We know we haven't a Chinaman's chance of controlling them. We only hope we can outmaneuver them.

I always feel like a renegade when the first little powder snow comes. It never lasts long, and it isn't serious, but the proper attitude is the long face, the foreboding shake of the head, and the grim comment that it won't be long now. I would like to act as Kyak does, and go tearing around in circles, scooping up mouthfuls of snow as a fast train scoops up water, and leaping crazily and prodigiously over little snow-covered trees. I don't, partly because any tree I could leap over wouldn't be worth bothering with and I'd probably fall flat on my fanny anyhow, but mostly because I'd simply be too unpopular if anyone suspected my antisocial liking of winter. So I try to remember that in February, when the snow is four feet or more deep on the level and I'm flopping inexpertly around on snowshoes, I'll be cursing the day the stuff was invented and offering my hope of Heaven for a good long look at a patch of bare ground. I turn my attention to the first piece of out-maneuvering that we have to attend to.

That is the circumventing of the freeze-up, our official beginning of winter. That's the fall in-between period, when the lake is just frozen and the ice is too thick to put a boat through and too thin to support a man or a horse or a car. We never know when the freeze-up is going to start or how long it's going to last. The only thing we do know is that while it's going on, we are completely bottled up. The nearest A & P is some forty miles away, but it might as well be in Egypt. Whatever we are going to need over a period of two or three weeks, we have to bring in before the Arm starts to freeze over. Tea, coffee, sugar, flour—I go over the list in my sleep. Oatmeal, canned meat and fish, fruit, and vegetables. And canned milk! Good Lord, if I'd forgotten that again! One year we forgot it and the Parsons forgot it, and the Millers didn't buy any because they keep a cow and didn't have to. So the cow chose that time, of all times, to go dry. We all learned, the hard way, to like black coffee and tea. I still like it, but I don't like to remember how oatmeal tastes without milk on it.

The real problem, though, is fresh meat and eggs and butter. If we bring them in too early and the weather warms up, we have the most horrible phonemena known to the thrifty Yankee heart and soul—good food, slowly spoiling. If we cut the margin too fine, we wake up some morning and find a half an inch of ice—a futile and infuriating amount—on the lakes. So we watch the barometer and thermometer and stars and the thickness of Kyak's pelt and listen to the weather broadcasts on the radio and rush out at all hours of the day and night to hold a wet finger to the wind. And sometimes we guess right and sometimes we don't. So far we've managed to survive the consequences of errors in our computations, but it's a pretty harassing period to go through, all the same.

Luckily for our sanity, the deer-hunting season furnishes a distraction around freeze-up time. Of course, everyone in here goes hunting. It isn't sport with us, though. We want and need the deer meat. (Only snobs and city people say venison, I early learned.) Hunting is a business with us. There are plenty of deer. In the summer, when it's against the law to shoot them, they stand around the yard under foot in romantic, negligent poses, fairly screaming to have their pictures taken. They come into the flower garden at night, and with great discrimination eat the blossoms off all the more difficult flowers to raise, turning up their delicate noses at such common fodder as zinnias and nasturtiums. Again in the dead of winter when their natural foods are buried deep under the snow, they drift into the clearing to eat hay or excelsior or cardboard boxes out of the dump, or anything else they can find. We couldn't shoot them then even if the law allowed; they are too gaunt and pathetic—"too poor," as they say up here. Anyhow they wouldn't be fit to eat. They've already been driven to browsing on cedar, with the result that they taste like furniture polish. During the hunting season, when they are fat and sleek and it's legal to kill them, every deer in the country remembers a man he has to see about a horse back in the thick growth on the highest ridges. It's uncanny. Ralph estimates that by the time he has caught up with one and shot it and dragged it out, estimating his time at the current local wage of thirty-five cents an hour and taking into account expenditure of shoe leather, ammunition, and wear and tear on clothes, but with no charge for loss of temper, the meat comes to about ten dollars a pound. He doesn't like deer meat, anyhow, so probably his figures are padded. He says he'd rather eat an old goat and be done with it. So he goes out only when I drive him out, almost at the point of his own gun.

Larry Parsons was in the same frame of mind one year. We were up there one afternoon when he came in from hunting. He'd been out all day, and he was a rig. His shirt was torn, his face was scratched, and frozen mud caked his boots and pants. He told us in no uncertain terms that that was definitely that. He didn't give a damn if he never shot another deer. For all of him, every unspeakable deer in the State of Maine could go climb a tree—an interesting possibility, zoologically speaking, only Larry wasn't speaking zoologically. He was speaking from the heart. He had been over at Black Cat, got into a swamp, crawled through blowdown for two miles or more, and when he went to eat his lunch, found it gone from his back pocket. So he was through. He'd eat potatoes and salt if he had to. He'd eat nothing, if it came to that. But never, never, so help him Hannah, would he step foot out of the house again, after a deer.

At this point Al, who had been listening with the look of sympathy we all learn to assume to cover up the fact that we are inwardly estimating just how soon it will be safe to broach the subject of deer hunting again, squeaked and pointed out the back window. In the middle of the clothes yard stood an eight-point buck. Larry shattered every existing record in oath-breaking. The kitchen floor smoked as he crossed it. He missed the first shot, and the buck obligingly turned broad-side. He couldn't miss the second time. It must have been a feeble-minded buck. From the eugenic viewpoint, it was undoubtedly better for the race that he didn't live to propagate his kind.

The real excitement of the deer-hunting season isn't hunting deer, though. It's hunting deer-hunters. It's always the same, every year. Any night that Ralph comes in at sunset and says, "It's going to turn cold tonight. We'd better get in some extra fire-place wood," I know what's going to happen. We go out into the lovely still dusk for the wood, but I can't really appreciate the black silhouettes the pines on the western ridge make against the orange and apple-green sky, nor the wreaths of steam that begin to rise from the river as the temperature of the air drops below that of the water. I'm too busy wondering how soon the telephone will start ringing.

It usually starts just at full dusk. It may be the Millers calling, or Cliff Wiggin, or the Brown Farm, but it all amounts to the same thing. "Say, you ain't seen anything of a couple of hunters, have you? Yeah, they're stayin' here. Went out this morning and they'd ought to have been back an hour ago. Well, sort of keep your ears open for signals, will you, and call me up if you hear anything—"

We'll hear something, all right. Just after we've decided that, thank God, they're lost in some other neck of the woods and aren't our responsibility, and have changed into slippers for a quiet evening in the home, Kyak will look interestedly out of the window and indulge in a short "woof." We'll go out onto the porch to listen. Sure enough, faint and far away will come the sound of three grouped shots, the universal woods signal of distress. It's a signal that can't be ignored. I don't know what would happen to a person who turned a deaf ear to three shots, but I more than half believe that the nearest tree would fall and crush him to a pulp. It should, anyhow.

Ralph groans, gets his gun, fires the two answering shots that mean, "O.K. I hear you. Now for the love of Mike, stay where you are and keep on signalling," and starts pulling on his gum-boots again. I go to the telephone to report that the missing have been spoken. Ralph collects his compass, a lantern, his gun with lots of cartridges for signalling, and sets forth into the night.

If lost hunters would only stay put, they'd be fairly easy to find. But they rarely do. If they're inexperienced enough to lose themselves in the first place, they're inexperienced enough to get panicky. The thing to do, once you know you are lost, is to find a good, safe place to build a little fire, build it, fire the three shots, light a cigarette, and sit down and wait. If the shots aren't answered wait a while till you are sure it's late enough for searchers to be out looking for you and shoot again. If you've plenty of shells with you, continue to do so every five minutes; if not, space your volleys further apart or until you hear someone shooting for you. But *before* you have used up all your cartridges, resign yourself to a night in the open and make the best of it. They'll be looking for you in the morning—you don't have to worry about that. They'll come shooting, and you'll answer with the cartridges you've carefully saved, and before ten o'clock you'll be back in camp eating bacon and eggs and drinking hot coffee.

This is such a sane and easy program to follow, but no lost hunter that we ever encountered ever followed it.

They all do the same thing. They start travelling as fast as they can, usually in the wrong direction and always in circles. I've been lost, and I know the feeling. It is hard to be sensible—not to be driven by a nameless terror and urgency—but you have to be sensible. You can't go ramming around in the woods in the pitch dark. The least serious thing that will happen to you is that you'll become completely exhausted and demoralized. Much worse things can happen. You can fall in a hole and break a leg. You can trip and shoot yourself. One hunter over on B Pond ridge went running through the woods at top speed, smacked into a tree, and knocked himself cold. It's better, even if harder, just to sit down and wait.

The procedure for finding lost hunters is always the same. First comes a period of swearing at anyone dumb enough not to get himself out of the woods before dark. (This phase runs concurrently with the assembling of paraphernalia.) Because we live so near the river, the next thing that Ralph does when he has to go out hunter-hunting, is walk up the road to where it's quiet so he can hear the shots as plainly as possible and determine their direction by compass. Then he fires two answering shots and starts off in that direction and keeps on walking until he hears some more shots. He re-checks his direction, finds that the lost one has wandered four points to the northeast, say, corrects his course, fires two more shots, hoping that they will toll the quarry in his direction, and keeps on walking. This may continue for an hour or it may continue most of the night. The first time it happened it was fairly exciting, but after years of it it has become a nuisance.

In the meanwhile I have kept the tea kettle boiling so

that when Ralph gets home, complete with hunter, they can have something hot to drink before going to bed. My inclination, after a half a dozen experiences, is to go hastily to bed as soon as I see their lantern up the road, and let them get their own lunch. Six times is enough to hear the same old story, and it always is the same old story.

After the hunting season is over and the lakes have frozen, we can settle down to winter, which consists not of the problem, primarily, of how to keep ourselves amused, but of the much more interesting problem of keeping ourselves warm and fed.

The first thing that has to be dealt with is the wood situation. You don't have to ask anyone what he's doing for busy-work from November until January. He's getting in his year's supply of firewood. What else would he be doing? The wood has to be cut after the leaves have fallen, but before the snow gets too deep and makes it hard to get around in the woods. It has to be sawed into four-foot lengths, split, and piled for hauling when the snow gets deep enough. The hauling is usually done with horses and sleds, although we use a car and have to build a road for the purpose. It's amazing how good a road can be built out of brush and snow over the roughest terrain. Brush is thrown into the holes and wet snow piled on top. Then it is trodden down and smoothed off. You wouldn't think it would hold up a rabbit, let alone a car or a team of horses and a heavy sled loaded with a couple of cords of hardwood. But as soon as the weather settles down to a steady cold, the whole thing freezes as solid as a rock. It seems to have the permanence of the Appian Way. I'm always surprised when I run across an old hauling road in summer to find it nothing but a series of skids, brush piles, boulders and deep holes. It seems impossible that we ever rode on it smoothly where now it's difficult even to walk.

We put up eight or ten cords of wood, all of it since the hurricane being blowdown along the Carry Road. That is not an editorial we. Gerrish and Ralph do most of the work, but the proudest moments of my life are those occasions upon which Gerrish sidles up to me at lunch time and mumbles, for fear of hurting Ralph's feelings, "You got time to come out this afternoon and give me a hand? I got an old son of a bitch of an old yellow birch to saw up." You see, I'm a much better hand on a two-man cross-cut saw than Ralph is. Gerrish says I'm better than a lot of professional woodsmen he's worked with. This sounds like frightful bragging, but I don't care. It's really something to brag about.

Excellence on a two-man cross-cut has nothing to do with size and strength. It's wholly a matter of method. A two-man cross-cut is a saw blade four and a half or five feet long with a removable handle at each end. The sawyers take their stances at either end and pull the saw back and forth between them. That sounds easy, and it is easy if you can just remember to saw lightly, lightly, oh, so lightly. Ralph's trouble is that he hates to saw wood and he wants to get it over with as soon as possible; so he bears down on the saw, instinctively, I suppose, since intellectually he knows better. A lot of people who know better do the same thing. It doesn't make the saw cut any faster, and it makes it run an awful lot harder. It makes all the difference between pulling a four-pound weight back and forth or a forty pound. A very common admonition from one sawyer to another in this country is, "Pick up your feet, will you?" That is probably meaningless to the uninitiate, but a good sawyer resents it very much. It means that his partner is saying that he doesn't mind riding him back and forth with every stroke of the saw, but he does consider it unnecessary to have to drag his feet along the ground, too. It's the obscure local way of telling a man he's bearing down on his end of the saw and it's an implication that he doesn't know his trade.

I don't know how other sawyers manage to retain the fairy touch, but this is how I do it. First I make sure that I'm going to be comfortable, even if this involves shoveling holes in the snow for my feet and lopping off sundry twigs that might switch me in the face. Then I take my end of the saw and pay very close attention to what we're doing for the first inch or so. It's important to start the kerf straight. If it slants or curves appreciably the friction becomes terrible when you get half way through the log. By the time the cut is well started I've got into the swing of the thing and don't have to think about it any more. Particularly do I not think about the fact that we are sawing a log in two.

These are the things I do think about. First, I think with satisfaction how good this particular exercise is for the waistline. I can feel the muscles roll and any accumulated ounces of superfluous padding melt away. Then I look around the woods and think how lovely they are in winter, with the lavender shadows of the bare trees lying like lace on the snow, and the evergreens standing up black and stiff all around. Everything is as still and sharp as an etching in the thin winter sunlight.

About then Gerrish says "Whoa." We have long since agreed that when either of us says "Whoa," we'll finish the stroke we're on and do one more. This gives both our minds a chance to come back from the vacuum they've been wandering in. This whoa of Gerrish's indicates that we're more than half way through the log and it's time to drive a wedge in the kerf to prevent the saw from being pinched. I sit back on my heels while he drives the wedge, and consider taking my top shirt off. Putting up your own wood is certainly the way to get the most heat out of it. It warms you twice—once while you're sawing it and again while you're burning it. I take my shirt off and pick up my end of the saw again.

Now I think of the deer who will be coming in at night and how glad and surprised they'll be to find a new tree down. They can browse all night long in the moonlight on the buds which yesterday were forty feet above their reach. We'll see their tracks in the morning. I look at the sawdust that is coming out in little spurts from our kerf with every stroke of the saw. If it happens to be a white birch with a red heart, the sawdust is lovely on the snow—pale gold and soft warm rose. White birch is the least satisfactory of the hardwoods for firewood, but it makes the prettiest sawdust. Firewood's excellence in order is this: maple, yellow birch, beech, and white birch. White birch is the most expensive to buy, though. People from the city think it's pretty and romantic, and that puts the price up. I'm just thinking about that when the saw drops and we're through the log. Gerrish hasn't had to tell me to pick my feet up, either.

After the wood has been cut, rough split, and hauled into our yard, it has to be resawed into stove length and split into two sizes, a large size for the heater and a small size for the kitchen stove. The sawing is done by power.

We have a circular saw rig, run by a Model T motor that Ralph fished out of the lake and reconditioned. It's certainly a lot more satisfactory than the old-fashioned hand buck saw, but I refuse to have anything at all to do with it. It terrifies me. Just the sight of the saw spinning viciously around, its teeth a bright blur in the sunlight, and the sound of the queer, inhuman rising shriek it gives as it rips through a piece of wood, make the cold shudders run up and down my spine. I'm really and truly afraid of it. It's unreasonable, I know; but some fears lie beyond reason.

I like to help split the wood, though. It's frozen to the core by now, and splits easily. It's fun to stand a chunk—pronounced "junk" here—up on the chopping block, give it a clip with the axe, and watch it explode. Occasionally a knotty piece will give trouble, but the mere fact of reluctance to split puts the whole thing on a personal basis. So! You won't, huh? Well, we'll see about that! All right. I don't have to use an axe. I can use a maul, if you're going to be that way. There! Dammit!

It's invigorating to win a fight, even if it's only against a stick of wood.

We're still fussing around with one or another phase of the wood question when Christmas comes along.

Christmas in the woods is much better than Christmas on the Outside. We do exactly what we want to do about it, not what we have to do because the neighbors will think it's funny if we don't; or because of the kids, who will judge our efforts not by their own standards but by the standards set up by the parents of the other kids. We don't have any synthetic pre-Christmas build-up—no shop window displays, no carol singers in department stores, no competition in the matter of lighting effects over front doors. At the intersections where the deer-runs cross the Carry Road, no Santa Clauses ring bells in the interest of charity. We didn't even have a Santa Claus until last year. We thought it would be nice if Rufus grew up knowing who gave him presents and bestowing his gratitude in the proper places. So we had never even mentioned the name of You-know-who. However, a visitor at Millers let him in on the secret, explaining to him that Santa Claus is the man who brings things for little boys. Rufus knew very well that Larry Parsons brings in everything we get from the Outside. Q.E.D., Larry is Santa Claus. He still persists in this belief, which makes him perfectly happy and we hope it does Larry, too.

We don't even have a Christmas tree. It seems a little silly, with hundreds of square miles of fir and spruce, from knee-high babies to giants of eighty feet on all sides of us, to cut one down and bring it into the house. It seems almost like vandalism to shake the ice and snow from its branches and hang them with pop-corn strings and cheap tinsel. We have our Christmas tree outdoors, for the benefit of the birds, hanging suet and crusts on the branches of one of the trees in the yard.

But we do have Christmas, just the same, and since we are so far from stores and last minute shopping, we have to start planning for it a long time ahead. With no chance to shop for gadgets, we have to make quite a lot of our presents, and the rest we get from what is known here simply as the Mail Order. I give mittens, hand made by me with the initials of the recipient knit into the design across the back. These don't cost much over and above my time, and no one in this country ever had too many pairs of mittens. For people who live Outside I try to think up things that they couldn't buy in stores. After all, it would be simple-minded to send out and buy something, have it mailed in here, wrap it up, and send it out to someone who, doubtless, lives almost next door to the store where it was bought.

I make little mittens about an inch long and sew them onto a bright fourteen-inch length of cord, as children's mittens are sewed onto a cord. These are bookmarks, in case you haven't guessed. To city people who, I know, have fire-places, I send net bags full of the biggest and best pine cones I can find, to be used as kindling. I make balsam pillows. I know these can be bought at any roadside stand north of the Maine border. But mine don't have pictures of Indians stamped in ink on cheap pink cotton cloth, along with the excruciating sentiment, "For You I Pine and Balsam." I collect old-fashioned patchwork quilt patterns from any source I can find them, and use them to make my pillow covers. In the old quilts, each unit is usually from twelve to fifteen inches square, and that makes a very good size for a balsam pillow. I make them, naturally, by hand, and they look very simple and expensive. They don't cost very much either. And I do love the names of the old patterns—Star of Bethlehem, Wedding Ring, Flower Garden, Log Cabin. They have a nice homely sound. You can think of a lot of things to make out of nothing, if you have to.

But making presents isn't half of Christmas in the woods. I'll never forget the year the lake didn't even begin to freeze until well after the tenth of December. We'd ordered our Mail Order, and presumably the Andover Post Office was harboring our stuff until someone could go out to get it. Finally, the day before Christmas, it was decided that an expedition should go on foot, get the stuff, and then, if at all possible considering the thin ice, drive it all in in Larry's old Model T which was down at the Arm.

We had living with us then a friend named Rush Rogers. He and Ralph and Edward Miller and Arch Hutchins, who was working for Larry, joined forces and set off down the ice on foot dragging a couple of sleds behind them to haul the stuff in on if the ice proved unsafe for the car. They got to the Arm all right, and from there into Andover was easy in Miller's Outside car.

Sure enough, all our stuff—we'd sold a story a short while before and were having a fat Christmas that year—was at the Post Office. In fact, since the Post Office was small and space at a premium during the rush season, our packages were all piled in the front window like a display, and the population of Andover was standing outside guessing at their contents. The Middle Dam delegation continued on to Rumford, stocked up with groceries and Christmas Cheer, picked up the mail and packages on the way back, and arrived back at the Arm in the afternoon. The mail and supplies filled the Ford to bulging. Arch wedged himself into the driver's seat, Edward stood on the running board to watch the high-piled packages, and Rush and Ralph tied the two sleds behind in single file and sat on them. I wish I could have seen them. The sleds were hardly big enough to accommodate their rears, and they had to hunch their knees up under their chins and hang on with both hands for dear life. Arch was driving the old Ford as fast as it would go, snow and ice chips from the chains were flying into their faces, so they couldn't keep their eyes open, and the sleds at the ends of their lines were slewing with terrific swoops. As a final touch they held their bare hunting knives in their teeth so they could cut the sleds loose if the car went through the ice ahead of them. Edward told me later that they were the funniest-looking rig he ever saw.

The ice was really too thin to be safe. It bent and bowed under the weight of the car, and rolled up ahead of them in long flexible swells. But Arch followed the rules for driving a car on thin ice—keep the doors open, go like hell, and be ready to jump—and they got home all right, only a little late for supper.

Then started one of the most hectic evenings I have ever spent. First, everything had to be unpacked; and when the Mail Order packs, it packs, what I mean. Corrugated board, excelsior, paper padding—they certainly give it the works. We decided that Ralph would do the unpacking in the back bedroom, with no lamp. He could see enough by the light through the open door. We didn't want any fire on Christmas Eve, and all that packing material around loose was definitely a fire hazard. Rush would assemble all of Rufus' toys that came knocked down—and that year most of them did—but first he had to put the new batteries, which were in the mess somewhere, into the radio so I could hear the Christmas carols.

I would re-wrap packages prettily. I started out with our present to Renny Miller, a five-cell flashlight, which we thought might come in handy for him. A flashlight is an awkward thing to wrap neatly, but I did a fairly good job and went on to the next thing. Rush was back of the chimney doing something to the radio wires, and in a minute he said, "Hey, Louise, where's that flashlight of Renny's? Lemme have it a second, will you?" I unwrapped, let him have it a second, and wrapped it up again.

I'd barely got the bow tied satisfactorily when a yelp came from the back room, "Good-night, there goes a box of blocks! Hey, Louise, lemme have that flashlight of Renny's a second, will you?" I unwrapped it, let Ralph have it a second, and wrapped it up again. The back bedroom, I noted in passing, looked as if a brisk breeze had swept through it. I wrapped up the snow gliders we'd got for the two younger Miller children and looked around for Rush. He had disappeared, so this looked like the opportune time to tie up the mittens I'd made him, and the checked wool shirt that was Ralph's present to him. I got out a suitable piece of Christmas paper and some silver cord.

Then came a rapping on the window, and in the glow of the lamplight I saw Rush's face, framed in icicles and spruce branches. He didn't look like Father Christmas, though. He looked like a man in distress. "Hey, Louise, I can't see a thing out here by this aerial. Bring out that flashlight of Renny's a minute, will you?" I unwrapped it again—carefully, this time, as the paper was getting a little shabby at the creases—and took it out. In passing through the back room I observed that the brisk breeze had risen to gale velocity. I could still see the top of the bureau and of Ralph, but the bed had been drifted under. I held the flashlight while Rush did whatever he had to do. We went back into the house and turned on the radio. A very satisfactory rendition of "Holy Night" rewarded us. I re-wrapped Renny's present, decided it looked pretty moth-eaten, undid it, got fresh paper and ribbon, and did it up again.

"Holy Night" changed to "Oh, Little Town of Bethlehem," and I listened with pleasure, wrapping up presents, while Rush started to put together Rufus' bounce horse. As the music came to an end, I woke up to the fact that Ralph had been shouting for some time from the back room. "Hey, Louise! Bring that flashlight of Renny's—"

Before we went to bed that night I had wrapped that darned flashlight nine times. I had become a much better flashlight wrapper by midnight than I had been at seven o'clock.

At midnight we had some sherry and crackers and cheese. Because this was Christmas, Ralph had a raw egg in his sherry—which I think is barbarous—and Rush brought me a magnificent treat—Camembert cheese, which Ralph considers equally barbarous. We were exhausted and silly and we had a lot of fun. It was the best Christmas Eve I ever had, in spite of the flashlight.

After Christmas, what we call "the long drag" sets in. One day is very like another. The sun rises late over a snow-covered world. It's worth while to get up, even with the thermometer twenty below zero, to see a winter sunrise. The eastern sky flames with red, and the whole world turns rose. The steam, rising from the churning open water of the river, has been freezing all night long on every tiniest twig and spill from the water level to the tops of the tallest trees. Walking down to the kitchen over the squeaking snow is like walking through a fabulous wood where all the trees are wrought silver encrusted with diamonds. It's a marvellous sight, all the more breath-taking because it lasts so short a time. As soon as the sun is up and the wind begins to stir, it is gone and the trees stand again in their winter grays and dark greens.

Getting breakfast in winter is something. The kitchen stove won't hold a fire over night, so in the morning everything in the place is frozen—the wood, the water in the pails, the bread, the butter—everything. Everything you touch is colder than ice—the metal pans, the copper on the drain board, the iron of the stove-cover lifter. You learn very quickly not to take your mittens off until the place has had a chance to thaw out. I can get a whole breakfast wearing my mittens. I think it would be very good training for those occupations, such as surgery, for example, which require unusual manual dexterity.

Dusk draws in early in the winter. We come in for the night about four o'clock, light the lamps, and settle down. I know all about the inconveniences of kerosene lamps. You can't tell me a thing about filling them every morning, about trimming the wicks, about keeping the chimneys bright. But they give such a lovely, soft, golden light that it's worth the bother. I love lamplight.

During the short space between sunrise and sunset, there are a lot of things that have to be tended to. There are the daily chores, chief of which is filling the woodboxes, bringing in the water, and shovelling snow. Snow shovelling sounds like a trivial occupation, but it isn't. It's hard work and it's maddening work. The paths and steps have to be shovelled out, but all the time you're doing it, you know in the back of your mind that (a) it'll probably snow again during the night, and (b) if you could only wait until spring, you wouldn't have to do it at all. I get tired just thinking about shovelling snow. I hate futile activity.

But keeping the paths clear hasn't half the headaches

of keeping the road to Middle open for a car. We can't even choose our time for doing that. We start out in the car as soon as it begins snowing as if it meant business. You can always tell. A really serious snow starts in with fine flakes, which hiss against the windowpane and sting the face. The wind starts moaning up the river, and first the further ridges, then the nearer, then the trees across the river, disappear in a ghostly pall. Probably blizzards start as often at ten o'clock in the morning as at seven o'clock at night, but my impression seems to be that it is always dark when we start out to break out the road. Undoubtedly this is a hangover from my first trip.

It was cold that evening, I remember—too cold, we thought, to snow. We never knew when the sun set; gray afternoon merged slowly into black and starless night. We brought the wood and water in, had supper, fed the dogs, pulled down the shades against the biting cold, and drew up around the lamp with our books. The fire roared softly in the stove; a dog whined in his sleep; outside a tree cracked now and then in the falling temperature. It was a good evening to be inside.

Suddenly Ralph said, "Listen to that wind!" We pulled aside the curtains and peered out into the night. At the bottom of each pane of glass was a little line of white, curving up at the ends. Even as we looked, the lines thickened and something like a handful of smoke momentarily clouded the glass. Ralph dropped his corner of the curtain. "Snow," he said, and reached for his gum-boots. "I'll go get the car started. You'd better put some wood on the kitchen fire. I'll meet you up at the road."

By the time I had put on my sneakers and mended the fire, Ralph was ready to go. He had a cant dog, a couple of shovels, some rope, some empty burlap sacks, and a lantern in the back of the old Model T. I climbed in beside him and we started off. It really didn't seem to me that this was necessary. Only about an inch of snow had fallen so far, and it was crisp and mealy. Why didn't we wait awhile?

I found out. As soon as we got out of the shelter of the buildings, the road vanished. Everything vanished. The headlights showed us only a thick white wall that swayed in the wind, and pretty soon we couldn't even see that. I got out onto the running board and scraped the windshield clean, and we went a few more rods. Then I repeated the performance, and we went on again. It was just like living and trying to work in a heavy, smothering black bag. I hadn't the faintest idea where we were. None of the trees along the side of the road looked familiar. Even our voices sounded odd and muffled. We must be, I thought, about halfway by now. I got out to see if I could find the ruts, and sensed rather than saw something even blacker than the surrounding blackness off to the left. It was the wangan. We'd come only a third of a mile.

Halfway up Wangan Hill we fell off the road. The front left wheel went down with a sickening slump, the rear wheels raced, and there we were. We didn't say anything. We didn't have to. We just lighted the lantern and got out to look. The bottom of the car was resting on the frozen snow shoulder of the road, and neither of the rear wheels had traction. We had to dig the pan and axles free and get her back into the ruts somehow. We did. Don't ask how. I don't know. All I remember is lying for what seemed like hours on my stomach with snow drifting over me, scraping away at that frozen shoulder. Then

I remember shoving for dear life while Ralph gave her the gas. I remember also Ralph's giving me a little lecture on the asininity of anyone my age not being able to drive a car. If I could drive and he might shove, then we might get some place. This annoyed me, as I do feel like a fool to be the only woman east of the Rockies who can't drive a car, and I gave an awful heave. Out she came and I leaped aboard.

The snow had made three inches while we were fooling around, and any last trace of ruts had vanished. Indeed, it had become hard to tell where earth ended and air began. There was only one thing to do. I took the lantern and got out and walked, leading the way. I hadn't thought of it when I decided upon sneakers as the ideal winter foot gear, but this was a place where they were of unparalleled value. No one else could have felt the ruts with the soles of their feet. I walked along one rut, making a track that Ralph could keep a wheel in. That was all he needed to keep him on the road. We made Middle all right—everyone there was in bed—turned around and started home again. The return trip was comparatively easy. Our own tracks were still faintly visible.

We went down to the kitchen, made some coffee, drank it, ate a doughnut apiece, stoked the fire and started out again. It was after eleven o'clock, and snowing harder than ever. We fell off the road three times, and on the return trip the car dragged in the middle all the way. We drank some more coffee, ate some more doughnuts, and set out again. This time we were piling up so much snow with the front of the car that we both got out and stumbled and slid a hundred feet up the middle of the road to break down the crown, came back and rode the distance we had walked, and repeated the performance, until we saw Miller's back pasture gate in front of us. Then we shovelled out a place to turn around in and came home. It was after three o'clock by then, and neither of us could remember a time in our lives when we hadn't breathed snow, and had snow down our necks, up our sleeves, in our faces, and most especially dragging at our feet. And it was still snowing, and we had to keep on making these ghastly expeditions into uncharted space. We set out again.

I can't remember whether this trip, or the next, or the next, was our last. They all blur into one long eon of wallowing and pushing and shovelling, of roaring motors and spinning rear wheels and boiling radiators, of blowing snow and moaning wind, of brief periods in the warmth and light of the kitchen, of scalding coffee, of changing soaked mittens and socks for mittens and socks not quite so wet, and of wishing first that I could go home and go to bed, and, along toward the last, that I could just go to bed under the nearest bush. Somewhere along there, though, we found ourselves standing beside the Ford, tacitly acknowledging that we were licked. We'd shovelled and we'd pushed. We'd practically willed her along the last quarter mile, when she'd been out of the ruts more often than she'd been in. The snow was just too mealy to provide traction, and now it was just too deep to plow through. The last inch had been our undoing, and now we might as well drag ourselves home and go to bed. Ralph drained the radiator. The Ford would keep until spring just where she sat.

I looked around. I could see a little now. The woods were getting, not lighter, but a little less solidly black. I could see a gray smear running away in two directions from where we stood. That would be the road. I could see strange humps and fantastic figures that were trees standing around us in the thinning snow. Yes, thinning. The flakes were falling much slower now. They were big and feathery, and lacked the vicious drive they'd had all night. The storm was definitely letting up. We took one more look at the car, and Ralph shook his head. It was just too late to make any difference. We were on foot now until spring. We might as well accept it.

"Where are we, anyhow?" I asked.

"Top of Birch Hill."

It could have been worse. It was less than a mile home. We could have had to walk all the way from the Parsons' front door. We blew out the lantern and started home through the first beginnings of a beautiful clear dawn.

On foot for the rest of the winter! That's where we always end. Sometimes we're on foot in December, and again we manage to keep the wheels rolling until February, but sooner or later we have to get down the snowshoes from their pegs on the porch and start walking the mail.

When we first came to live here, mail was definitely catch as catch can. The Post Office at Coburn's is a summer office, open only from May 15th until October 1st, and before and after those dates, Middle Dam ceased to exist as far as the Government was concerned. If anyone happened to be going Outside, he took the community letters and brought in whatever postal matter the Andover Post Office had been storing for us. Sometimes we got mail every week. In the dead of winter or when conditions were bad we were lucky if we got it twice a month. Now, however, we have a Star Route to Middle Dam, and we get mail every Tuesday and Friday. It's wonderful for everyone, except possibly Larry, who is the mail carrier. There are times, I imagine, when he'd just as soon stay home as go trekking off down the lake with what he sometimes refers to as "the Christly mail." It's all right while the boat is still running, or after the lake is frozen and he can use his snowboat—an ingenious device that looks like a Black Maria, with skis in place of the front wheels and caterpillar treads behind to furnish the driving power. But in between times he has to carry the sacks around the shore on foot, and that's something else again. The first year he was mail carrier Ralph had two great over-size tires come for the Big Green "Mormon," and, of course, they arrived during the freeze-up. Ralph told Larry he was in no hurry for them and to leave them at the Arm until the ice was safe, but Larry is too conscientious for his own good. He carried and rolled them all the way up from the Arm. That's the kind of a guy Larry is.

On Mondays and Thursdays, then, one of us has to walk to Middle to take up the out-going mail, and again on Tuesdays and Fridays, someone has to go up to bring down the in-coming. I myself don't mind the trip, even on snowshoes, those inventions of the devil. It isn't like breaking a trail through fresh snow. We take pains to tramp down a good, wide, level float up the middle of the road, and in between storms this float is packed so hard that we can sometimes go all the way bare-foot. Bare-foot, I probably don't have to explain, is simply woods for "without skis or snowshoes." It's nice to get away from the house for a while and to visit Al Parsons and Alice Miller, and there's always a lot to think about and look at along the road. There are the woods themselves, which I like better in winter than in summer, because I like the type of design that emphasizes line rather than mass. The bare branches of the hardwood trees look exactly like etchings. There are strange vistas of hill and pond which the foliage blocks out in summer, and which therefore have a rare, new appeal, like glimpses into a far and beautiful country. The view through the bare tree tops from the top of Birch Hill might be a Swiss view, I decide, and the deep black slash between the ranges where the Arm stretches south through its narrowing valley might be a Norwegian fjord. Then I wonder why we all like to pretend that we're somebody else, somewhere else. Why is it more fun to think I'm a Norse woman looking over a fjord than to admit I'm me looking over into South Arm? Probably, because part of being me, looking into South Arm, lies in pretending I'm a Norse woman? This is very involved and gets me nowhere. That's the sort of footling conjecture that I indulge in while walking the mail.

Another great source of entertainment on these mail walks is the tracks in the snow. Sometimes they are just tracks—the clear-cut, chiseled hoof marks of deer, a rabbit's big, spreading pad-marks, with a little dent behind them where its maker squatted in the snow, or the precise line of prints left by a trotting fox. Sometimes they tell of tragedy. You follow the delicate embroidery of a wood-mouse's trail for a quarter of a mile, and then it ends like the snipping off of a thread. Two feathery swept places in the snow, where the wings of an owl brushed as he swooped, tell why. Or you may come to a churned-up, blood-stained spot, with the tracks of a rabbit and a wild cat leading into it, but only the wildcat's tracks leading out. You don't have to have a dictionary to translate that story. Once in a while we see a bear track, but not often. The bears ought to be, and usually are, sleeping somewhere in the winter.

Actually, the only track that has the power to startle us very much is the track of man. We fancy that we know about where everyone belonging to Middle Dam is, at any given hour of the day or night. Moreover, if anyone comes down the Carry Road, it's usually to see us. There isn't any other place to go, in winter. So if nobody has stopped at the house, and yet here's this track on the road—well! It couldn't be any of the Millers. They're all working on their wood. It can't be Larry. He doesn't wear L. L. Bean gum-boots, and only Bean boots have this chain tread. It might be Dorian, who works for Larry. He was talking last week of getting some new boots. But he's supposed to be sawing ice. Maybe it's one of the company timber cruisers, come in from the Outside. Or maybe it's the game warden. Or maybe— It doesn't strike us as odd at all that we have so changed our way of living from that in which we were brought up, that bear and deer and wildcat tracks are all in the day's walk, while a stray human boot-print throws us into a dither.

But that's not all of walking the mail. After we get to Middle there are people to see and talk to. There are all the Millers and both the Parsons, and whoever is working for the Parsons at the time. They may be doing almost anything, but whatever they're doing, it's worth while stopping to watch. Al will probably be sewing or cooking. She's one of the busiest people I ever saw. She's never sewing ordinary things. She runs a gift shop in the summer, for the benefit of Coburn's sports, and she'll be making a very trick apron, or a particularly useful laundry bag. If she's cooking, it won't be just cake and pie and cookies. It will be doughnuts that contain orange juice and grated rind instead of milk and spice—a very tasty dish, by the way—or a spice cake, the basis of which is canned tomato soup, or coconut-chocolate candy, made largely of leftover mashed potato. She gets around among the pages of the women's magazines, all right.

If it's right after New Year's, all the men of Middle Dam will probably be cutting ice. Cutting ice is a man-sized chore. Over two thousand cakes have to be got in for the hotel, so-called, and on top of that there's Larry's own personal ice and Miller's ice. Then they branch out. They go up into the Narrows and fill the ice houses of a couple of summer camps up there, and they fill Mrs. Graves' ice house at the Arm. It's a lot of work, and more involved than would seem at first glance.

First of all, they have to arrange to have the ice the right thickness, a matter that can't be left to Nature alone. This is one of those cases of circumvention. The ice, during the first part of January, is about a foot thick, and that isn't quite thick enough. Before spring it may be three feet thick, but freezing under the insulating blanket of snow that covers the lake after the first of the year is very slow. So in order to speed it up, the snow must be scraped off the cutting area. A couple of below-zero nights after the ice is clear will do the trick. Then the ice field has to be scored for the cutting lines like a pan of fudge, with a tool that looks like an old-fashioned spike harrow with the spikes set sixteen inches apart. Then the cutting begins.

The cutting used to be done with a hand ice-saw, until Larry decided that that was unprogressive. He got hold of a machinist on the Outside who dreamed up an ice-cutting machine for him. This consists of an old Model A motor on steel runners, with a chain-driven circular saw out in front and a handle like a baby carriage handle out behind. The operator walks behind, pushing the rig and raising and lowering the saw as desired. The scored grooves in the ice act as guides for the runners. This ought to have been much easier and faster than hand sawing; and it would have been, if, instead of sawing ahead in a straight line, the thing hadn't inexplicably insisted on sawing backward in a circle. Ice sawing was suspended until the creator could be brought in to take the bugs out of his darling. He came in one week end, toiled long and earnestly, and left Sunday night with assurances that everything was going to be all right, now.

Monday morning ice cutting was resumed. Larry drove his reconditioned labor saver the length of the ice field, parked it for a moment while he organized the hauling and storing brigades, and turned back just in time to see what happened. Ralph was at Middle at the time, and saw it, too. He says it was one of the most impressive sights he ever witnessed.

Larry had unwittingly left the ice cutter on the edge of a triangular floe of free ice, formed by two accidental and invisible cracks and the open water alongside of which he had been sawing. It was a big floe of a thousand square feet or more of ice—too big to be noticeable to a man just walking across it. But it wasn't too big to be affected by the weight of the machine bearing down on its edge. As they looked the point of the triangle rose majestically, and the opposite side dipped. The ice cutter clung for a moment and then started slipping into the lake. It was the slow-motion quality of the thing that made it so impressive. The whole works just hung for a long moment. Then the cutter disappeared into twenty feet of icy water, and the floe settled slowly back. The lake stretched without blemish two miles to the further shore.

They got it out later all right, and sent it out to be overhauled. It's still there, and they're still cutting ice with a hand ice-saw at Middle Dam.

They had some trouble putting the ice in at the Arm one year, too. When a cake of ice has been cut free, naturally it floats and can be hauled up out of the water, loaded on a sled, and taken up to the ice house. The first cake they cut from the ice field at the Arm didn't float, though. It disappeared, leaving a hole. So did the next. Larry stuck his head down the hole to see what went on. He found that he and his men and horses were standing on a sixteen-inch piecrust of solid blue ice, over some three feet of air, with another layer of ice below. The lake had dropped three feet after the top layer had frozen and the lower level had frozen subsequently. Ordinarily the ice would follow the water down, but the ice was so thick it just arched to the shore instead. Larry was relieved to know that the laws of natural science hadn't suddenly been revolutionized. All the same the situation was annoying. One man had to crawl down into the air space and lift up the pieces as they were sawed so they could be hoisted to the top. It was a nasty, cold, cramping job. Nature can think up simply abominable little tricks to pull off unexpectedly.

Some winters we have lumber camps in here. Nobody has to have the general nature of a lumber camp described to him. Literature and the movies have done that quite adequately. They haven't shown, however, what it means to be neighbors to a lumber camp; to have as the boon companions of one's four-year-old son a bunch of the hardest and toughest teamsters, sawyers, border-jumpers and general roustabouts that ever came down a tote road; to find that one is suddenly confronted with a choice of stopping talking or learning an entirely new language—a language consisting of such terms as "bucking up on the landing," "sluiced his team" and "shaking out the road hay." Being what I am, I chose to learn the new language.

I also had to learn to differentiate between a day man, a stump cutter, and a member of a yarding crew. A day man gets paid by the day and does whatever the boss tells him to. He may cut firewood, swamp out roads, pile up brush and tops, anything. A stump cutter is an individualist. He works alone, felling his own trees, limbing them out, sawing them up into four-foot lengths, piling the pieces neatly for the convenience of the scaler, and getting paid by the cord. He's usually pretty good. That's why he works alone. He can make more money that way than he could at day rate or by pooling his ability with that of someone else. Sometimes, however, he's hard to get along with and no one else will work with him. A yarding crew consists of three men and a twitch horse. One of the men cuts down the trees and limbs them, one drives the twitch horse, dragging—or "twitching"—the entire trunk of the tree to a cleared space called a yard, where the third man saws it up with a buck saw and piles it. A good yarding crew can cut and pile an awful lot of wood in a day.

Besides these classifications of woodsmen, who comprise the main population of the camp and who sleep in a long low bunk-house, there are several specialists. There's the boss and the straw boss, who have their own little shack, not because they feel exclusive, but because the men like to sit around their bunk-house in the evening and bellyache about the weather, the food, the administration of the camp, or the way the trees grow, or any one of a thousand other things. The presence of authority would put a definite damper on this favorite of all indoor sports. And while talk is cheap, like other cheap things—air and water, for example—it is invaluable. A man who has cursed the boss all evening to his confreres is almost always a man who goes to bed feeling at peace with the world, and who wakes up ready to put out a good day's work. So the boss lives in his own little hut, dropping over occasionally to join in the poker game that runs continually from supper to bed-time and all day Sunday.

In another little hut, known as the Office, live the clerk and scaler. The scaler, as his name implies, scales the wood for the men. That is, he estimates with the aid of a long marked rule called a scale rule the quantity each man cuts, keeps a record of the scale for the landowners, and reports each man's cut to the clerk, who pays the man accordingly. The clerk keeps the camp books, pays the men, orders supplies, tends the wangan—the little store where tobacco, candy, clothes, saw-blades and axes are sold—and runs the punch board, which is always a part of the camp picture. The clerk and scaler are men of at least some education, and I think they enjoy living alone, because they like to sit up nights and read, and in the bunk-house lights have to be out at nine o'clock.

Behind a partition in the kitchen, which is also the dining-room, and which is by law a separate building, live the cook and his cookees, or helpers. They don't mingle much with the rest of the camp. They're too busy, for one thing. For another they have their discipline to maintain.

If arguments start they're apt to start in the dining-room. That's one reason why no talking is allowed in the dining-room, aside from simple requests to pass the butter, please. And I mean "please." I've eaten a lot of meals in lumber camps, and I've been amazed at the prevalence of "please" and "thank you." I wish my own family were always so punctilious. The other reason for no talking is that the cook doesn't want the men dawdling over their meals. A large percentage of our woodsmen are Canadian Frenchmen, and they can't talk without gesticulating. This means they would have to put down their tools and stop eating, which would slow up the meal considerably. The cook contends that they can do their talking somewhere else. All he wants them to do is eat and get out, so his cookees can get on with their dishes.

Somewhere high on the social scale comes the blacksmith. He sometimes lives with the boss, sometimes with the clerk, and sometimes with the men, depending on his type. He makes the sleds that are used to haul the wood, keeps the horses shod, repairs tools, and is usually an amateur veterinary besides. He and the feeder—woods for stableman—are responsible for the health of the horses, but if anything beyond their ability arises, they take the responsibility of calling a real vet. The feeder waters and feeds the horses, cleans the stable, and keeps an eye on the pigs. Every lumber camp has five or six pigs. They are brought in in the fall, cute little tricks with curly tails, fed all winter on the tons of excellent garbage that are the inevitable by-product of catering to a hundred men or more, and sent out in the spring to be slaughtered. By that time they are simply enormous.

Every lumber camp also has cats. In the fall the cook

brings in a cat to keep the kitchen free of mice and the stable free of rats that come in in the bales of hay. It is always a female cat. If I didn't know our Tom, I'd be inclined to believe the flat statement of an old friend, Beatty Balestier—yes, Kipling's brother-in-law, but he'd kill you if you mentioned it. Beatty told me once when I was trying to locate a tom kitten, "There's no such thing. All cats are female cats, and all kittens are the result of immaculate conception." My observation of lumber camp cats inclines me to believe he had a tenable argument there. But be that as it may, by spring every lumber camp within a radius of ten miles of us has at least a dozen cats—the original and three litters. All the kittens, regardless of their mother's complexion, are black and white. No wonder Tom is such a smuggy.

When a lumber camp first moves in, all the men look alike to me. They're all big and tough-looking and most of them need a shave, which they won't get all winter. They all dress more or less alike, in layers of shabby sweaters and shirts, ragged pants, and wool caps. They all walk along the road with the same swagger, carrying their axes and saws over their shoulders, swearing at their twitch horses, and dropping their eyes upon meeting me. After a while I begin to get them sorted out and those that I meet regularly I start speaking to. The first time I do this the same thing always happens. The man starts obviously, raises his eyes to look at me, looks all around to see if by any chance I mean a couple of other guys, and looks back at me. Then his face lights up in the warmest and friendliest of smiles, and he answers. If he can't speak English, he answers in French or Russian or Finnish. It doesn't make any difference. We both know what we mean:—"Hello, stranger. I'll never get to know you very well. We haven't much in common, but we're both here on this snowy road, with the woods all around us. Stranger, I wish you well." They do wish me well, too. Lumberjacks have a reputation, I know, for being brawlers and roisterers and general trouble-makers, and I guess when they are on the Outside, with their systems full of rot-gut, they often deserve this reputation. But I have never met a lumberjack in the woods who didn't treat me with complete respect and friendliness—and I've met a lot of lumberjacks. What they do Outside, I neither know nor care.

Sometimes, though, we get indications that some individual's conduct before he crossed our ken might not bear the most rigid inspection. This was true, we gathered, of one of Rufus' bosom pals, a big part-Indian named Tony. Tony looked like a ruffian, and was sweet. He rode Rufus on his horse, stopped in the yard to play with him, took him on walks and brought him presents, like partridge feathers or a length of chain carved out of a single piece of wood. I used to worry about these friendships of Rufus' —for Tony was only one of many. After all Rufus was only four and some queer customers do get loose in the woods. I suppose it was the stock maternal stewing. Ralph told me not to worry, and after a while I came to believe him. I'm glad I did. The risk was negligible, I know now, and what Rufus gained in knowledge and poise was considerable.

Then one day the feeder came down to the house at noon simply bursting with excitement. "We got a G-Man, Mis' Rich," he announced, as one would announce the outbreak of a rare and fatal disease. And sure enough, an F.B.I. agent had walked into camp from Upton—a long, hard walk, but you know the F.B.I.—looking for some man. The man had been there, but had left the week before. (I don't know, to keep the record straight, what he was wanted for, or whether they ever caught him.) So the G-Man had some lunch and walked out again. He wasn't in camp more than an hour. But the fact that he came at all was enough.

When the cutting is a mile or more from camp, some of the men carry their lunches with them rather than walk clear in and back again. Tony was one of these. But the man that worked with him preferred to walk back for a hot lunch. He came back to the job that afternoon and told Tony that there was a G-Man in camp. Tony went on with his work but kept deep in the spruce thickets along the back of the cut. When knocking-off time came, he turned his horses loose, with a slap on their rumps to get them started, and let them go into camp, alone—a thing they always did, anyhow. He, himself, didn't go home to supper. He stayed up on the mountain-side, hungry and all alone in the cold and dark until the middle of the night. Then he sneaked into camp and snatched a few hours' sleep. The next morning, bright and early, he was at my kitchen door to say good-bye to Rufus. I didn't recognize him, at first. He'd shaved off the luxuriant beard he'd been nursing along all winter. He didn't know where he was going, he told me cheerfully. He was just going.

These seemed, and still seem to me, to be over-elaborate precautions for complete innocence to take. I still wonder sometimes what Tony had on his conscience.

This visit of the G-Man and Tony's oddly coincidental flight were a source of discussion all the rest of the winter. Nothing is so prized in the woods as a good juicy morsel to hash over. Here is a community of men, practically cut off from the world. Most of them can't read. They have one thing in common—work. They have to talk about something and they'll talk about anything. They'll talk about the number of birds that flew out of a thicket, or the deer they saw eating road-hay—the hay spread on icy places in the hauling roads to prevent loaded sleds from overrunning the horses—or the super-intelligence of their own twitch horse. They'll talk about the snow, which is damned for hindering the cutting, or lack of snow, which is damned for hindering hauling. They'll talk about the food—it was always better at the last camp they were in—or the shelter. That was always better, too. The roof was either higher, permitting better ventilation and air circulation, or lower, conserving heat; or else the floors were warmer, or the lice less numerous. But most of all, they like to talk personalities. In short they like to gossip. They'll take the fact that a man changed his underwear in the middle of the week instead of waiting until Sunday, the conventional underwear-changing day, and make almost an international incident out of it. It's fascinating to observe.

Occasionally there's something worth talking about. Once in a great while someone goes crazy and tries to kill himself or someone else. That's good for a month's talk. Once Rufus got lost, and I, in desperation, called up and asked the clerk if anyone there had seen him. Every man available set out to look. He was finally discovered about five hundred yards from the tar paper shack where the horses are taken to eat their noon-day meals; or as the man who found him said, "About two and a half good twitches." A good twitch is the distance a horse can drag a full-length pulp log without resting. Distances are frequently measured in twitches or fractions thereof by woodsmen. It's a habit I've got into myself.

This search for Rufus furnished talk for a week. Once a big Swede known as Bow (pronounced as in bow-wow, which is what his brother is called, incidentally) decided to relieve the monotony by putting a set-line through the hole in the ice where the horses were watered at lunch time, and catching himself some fish. The fact that if the game warden had caught him, he'd have probably spent the rest of the winter in jail only added spice to the venture. For days he tended his line night and morning and never caught a thing. Then one evening his luck changed. There was something—a considerable something—down in the water at the end of his line. His shouts brought the whole camp onto the ice in time to witness the landing of the fish. It was fish all right—a can of salmon with the label still adhering, in case proof were needed. They're still talking about that, in the woods.

Sunday is the day of leisure in a lumber camp. That's the day the men do their washing, file their saws and sharpen their axes, get their hair cut, and attend to any other odd personal jobs. It's horse-shoeing day, too, except in emergencies. Sometimes the blacksmith lets Rufus "help" by holding the horse's foot for him. This is a great treat for Rufus, but considerably less of a treat for the blacksmith, I would think. What the horses' views are, I have no way of knowing. Sunday afternoon is recreation time. Then the big stud poker game really gets going, and the Russians and Poles start their interminable gloomy hands of *spadowiecz,* a game completely incomprehensible to non-Slav. Then if the ice is good, the athletically inclined join Ralph and Rufus and me in skating on the

Pond in the cove where we keep our boat in summertime. We can't skate for sour apples, but neither can anybody else, so we all have a lot of fun and make a lot of noise falling around on the ice. Then those who can carve, work on their ornamental bottle stoppers and birds in cages, mysteriously cut out of a single block of wood. Then those that are big enough and tough enough to get away with it knit on socks and sweaters.

I never can quite make up my mind whether I like to have the lumber camps move in or not. I really like it best when we're here alone. I've heard enough of the popular Freudian lingo that people in general sling around so carelessly to know that I am no victim of agoraphobia. I like to know that I have miles of unpopulated space around me. The lumber camps don't bother me, but I know they are there. Worse, I know they are cutting down the trees. I feel a great regard for trees; they represent age and beauty and the miracles of life and growth. I don't like to see them destroyed, especially as the cellulose made from them can just as well be made from corn stalks. On the whole, I'd just as soon that the lumber camps went somewhere else.

On the other hand, there are nice things about them. It's nice to have not-too-close neighbors once in a while. But the thing I enjoy most about them is a perfectly silly and inconsequential thing. Our winter bedroom is right next to the road, and I like to hear the men and the horses going to work before we get up. Once in a while a man will whistle or sing, but mostly they go quietly, with only the jingle of a chain, the blowing of the horses, and the squeak of the frozen snow to mark their going. The whole thing doesn't last fifteen minutes, and it really isn't anything to get starry-eyed about. I just like it; that's all.

Winter, to look forward to, is a long, dark, dreary time. To live, it's a time of swirling blizzards and heavenly high blue and white days; of bitter cold and sudden thaws; of hard work outdoors and long, lamp-lit evenings; of frost patterns on the windows and the patterns of deer tracks in the snow. It's the time you expected to drag intolerably, and once in a while you stop and wonder when the drag is going to begin. Next week, you warn yourself, after we've finished doing this job on hand, we'd better be prepared for a siege of boredom. But somehow next week never comes. There's always something to keep it at bay.

Then one day there's a patch of bare ground on a sunny slope, the dog starts going wild with the smell of spring, and someone says that the break-up ought to come early this year. The break-up! But Good Heavens, the lakes only froze up a couple of weeks ago. Well, a little more than that, maybe. Let's see— Why, it's time to tap the maple trees and overhaul the cars and clean house! The next thing you know, the smelts are running and the loons have come back into the growing patch of open water in the Pond-in-the-River. There's an ant hill in the flower garden and a dandelion blossom up by the road. Gerrish has begun talking about a good mess of dandelion greens, cooked with salt pork. It's time to clean up the vegetable garden and paint the boats, and the consensus is that the ice will be out by next Tuesday.

Next Tuesday!

Where has the winter gone?

IV

"Isn't Housekeeping Difficult?"

No. Housekeeping in the woods is—for me—not at all difficult. I'd like to let that statement stand unqualified, testimony to my enormous efficiency and energy. Too many people know the truth about me, though, to make that advisable. The truth is that under the most favorable circumstances—circumstances including linoleum floors, vacuum cleaners, washing machines, and automatic water heating systems—I would still be a rotten housekeeper. My friends would indulgently call me a little bit careless, and my enemies would label me down-right slovenly. My enemies would be the nearer right.

Here I can be a rotten housekeeper, and it doesn't make much difference. After all, this is the woods. People don't expect quite so much in the line of shining silver, polished glass, and spotless woodwork. I can, with a clear conscience —or fairly clear, anyhow—ignore a lot of persnickety details. I can be sensible about these things. I can refuse to allow myself to become the slave of a dustpan and brush. I have learned, because I've had to, to spend money wisely. Now I am learning to spend my time wisely; and I don't think it's very wise to spend two hours waxing the living-room floor on a lovely day when I could be out fishing. If I say this often enough and fast enough, I can convince myself that almost no effort beyond attending to the bare necessities of food, clothing, and shelter is really required of me.

We do have to eat. That I will concede. So I spend a large proportion of my housekeeping time in getting ready to cook, cooking, and recovering from cooking. It makes me tired just to think about it.

This is supposed to be the Independent Life, but as far as getting supplies goes, we're dependent on quite a number of things, ranging from Larry Parsons to the weather. Except during the short summer months, Larry is the one who goes to Rumford and hauls our supplies in by car and boat, and whether or not he goes depends on the weather, the state of the lake, and how much else he has to do. Once Larry goes, whether I have the ingredients to cook what I want to cook, or must, instead, cook what I have the ingredients for, depends on how bright or dull we were while making out the supply list. We try to put in supplies for a week at a time in the summer, and for a month or more, at a time, in the winter. In making out a list of that length, it's very easy to leave off two or three items that are absolutely essential. There is no way of rectifying these errors. Once a thing is forgotten, it's forgotten until next time. Then you find to your surprise that a lot of things you thought were essential aren't essential at all. It's very enlightening.

Try to make a list of all the groceries you're going to be needing for the next four weeks. Go ahead. It won't cost you anything. You aren't in my boots. If you leave off eggs, you won't have to go without, as we do. Remember that fresh fruit, meat, and vegetables won't keep forever, and plan accordingly, listing canned goods for the last part of the month. Remember also all the boxes and bottles in the kitchen that aren't empty, but will be next week. Those are the things I always forget—the vanilla and salt and nutmeg. I used to forget the staples, too, going on the assumption, I guess, that one always has sugar, flour, and tea. It didn't take me very long to learn this little fact of life—one doesn't. Now my lists start with the staples—eggs, butter, milk, oatmeal, cornmeal, molasses, coffee, split peas, beans, salt pork—you go on from there. Next I do the perishables—oranges, bananas, lettuce, whatever vegetables are in stock and good. I leave that to Sam Swett, the manager of the A & P, who, fortunately, is most trustworthy. Rumford is no Babylon, rich in exotic viands. I have to take what I can get. (Once in my ignorance I ordered artichokes, and got back a little note saying, "I heard of these, but I never see one.") Meat next—beef, pork or lamb to start the month with, and then a ham, always, which is only semi-perishable. Then the canned goods—meat, fish, fruit, and vegetables. Then the odds and ends, like cheese and spices and macaroni and rice and cocoa. It sounds easy enough, but I always forget something, like a lemon. So instead of having Eggs Benedict, as I had planned to have as a special treat, I end by having plain ham and eggs which are no treat at all.

I've just been over the foregoing list, and there is a very serious omission, which I'll bet a button no one spots. Of necessity, everyone in the woods makes his own bread. I've left off yeast, which means that we eat corn bread or baking-powder biscuit until Larry goes out again. Almost everyone thinks he likes hot breads, and they are all right once in a while. But they get terribly, terribly tiresome, both to make and to eat, after a week.

The usual supply difficulties are intensified twice a year by the fall freeze-up and the spring break-up, those periods when, as I've explained before, you can't get out of here because the ice isn't safe to cross but is too thick to put a boat through. Cold weather, though, isn't an unmixed curse. When it really gets cold, with a cold you can depend on not to waver, then you can stop vilifying the temperature and begin to use it. You can make ice-cream, for example, following any good recipe and putting it outdoors in a pan to freeze. This involves running out every half hour or so, to stir the custard and scrape what has frozen away from the sides, but it's worth the bother to me. I've loved ice-cream from my childhood, when a cone was an event. I still love it enough not to be too bitter about the fact that here in the woods we almost never can have it in summer, when the weather is hot, but must wait until the time of year when scalding soup and hot buttered rum would be the reasonable man's choice.

The important use of cold, though, is to keep food. Early in December we buy a case of butter—thirty-two pounds—and freeze it. This will last us until spring and the final pound is exactly as sweet and fresh as the first was. We buy meat in quantities and freeze that, too, It's wonderful to know that in the Arctic regions of the summer house living-room, fifty pounds of pork loin dangle from the ceiling, out of reach of dogs and cats, awaiting our pleasure. Frozen meat is all right to eat if care is taken to thaw it slowly. Otherwise it will be tough. And, of course, it can't be thawed and frozen again and thawed and eaten. You're apt to die horribly if you're not careful about that,

I understand—although so far my knowledge of that is hear-say.

Like everyone else in this country, we freeze up a deer whole, if we're lucky enough to get one, and if we get it late enough in the season. We let it hang long enough to be tender—about two weeks—in an above-freezing place, and then we hang it out in the woodshed. There are two advantages to using the woodshed for a cold storage room. One is that it is cold. The other is that we're no butchers, and we need a lot of room and a lot of tools to get a steak off a frozen deer. I found a chart in Fanny Farmer for the guidance of housewives in buying beef, and while a deer doesn't seem to be constructed exactly like a cow, still we can get the general hang of the thing from the chart. So we always take Fanny to the woodshed with us when we're going to butcher. Then we lower the corpse from where we've hoisted it to the peak of the roof, and lay it across the chopping block. By using an axe, the buck saw and once in a while the two-man cross-cut, we manage to worry off what will pass as a roast or a steak or a collection of chops.

If we get the deer early in the season before it's cold enough to freeze it, the problem of keeping it is complicated considerably. The liver and heart are eaten first, by me. Ralph won't eat what he inelegantly calls "guts." Then we save out two or three of the choice cuts to be eaten fresh, and I have to can the rest. The steaks I fry for about a minute, first on one side and then the other, in a good hot spider, so they'll brown. Then I roll each slice in a tight little roll, pack the rolls into jars, semi-seal, and boil the jars in a washboiler full of water for two hours and a half. After the jars are removed from the boiler, I complete the sealing, stand them upside down to cool, scrutinizing them at intervals for tell-tale air bubbles which mean leaks and consequent spoilage, and finally put them away. Later these can be unrolled and broiled or fried as ordinary steaks; but unless they are lightly fried before canning, they'll be nothing more than plain boiled meat.

The tougher cuts, such as the forequarters, I hack up and boil in large kettles. Next day I cut the lean meat from the bones, pack it tightly into pint jars—pints are better for our size family—fill the jars with gravy, partially seal, and go on from there with the same routine as above. This meat can be used in the winter for meat pies, pot roasts, hash, or just plain meat and gravy.

That takes care of the bulk of the deer, but there are still the neck, horns and hoofs to be accounted for, and we're the Thrifty Riches. A live deer, grazing by the riverside, is a beautifully proportioned thing; but the minute that it's dead something happens to its neck. It doubles in length apparently. There's a lot of meat on it, but the meat's no good. It's tough and stringy and can be used for only one thing—mince meat. It makes the best mince meat in the world.

This leaves only the horns and hoofs. No, we don't make our own gelatin. Ralph uses sections of horn for decorating hunting knife handles, and makes gun racks and coat hooks out of the hoofs and thin lower legs. They are bent at the ankle, dried and cured, and driven into holes bored in the walls. We have a dozen or more of them over the house, and they look very nice indeed and are very handy.

And that's that, as far as a deer is concerned.

I always think I'm going to can some partridges, too, but

I never have yet. We don't get very many, and they're so small that it takes several to even make a decent meal. So we never have any left over to can. I've never tried salting fish, either, although it can be done, I guess. We eat them fresh, in season—fried, if they're pan trout, or baked if they are big salmon. Those, and smelts in the spring of the year, are the only kind of fish we get here, except chubs and suckers, which aren't fit to eat. We've never tried eating porcupine, either. We've never had to. We don't kill them, though, even when we find them chewing our houses down. They are edible, and they're the only animal that an unarmed man can kill for food. They're so slow and stupid that they can be clubbed to death if necessary. No woodsman will kill them wantonly. Someday he may be in a spot where a porcupine will save him from starvation. Some states—Montana, for example—have game laws to protect the porcupine, for this very reason.

In Maine, as in all other parts of the world, there's a lot of talk goes around about the excellence of the native country cooking. In Maine, as in all other parts of the world with which I am familiar—not so many, I'll grant you, but enough—this is largely eye-wash. There are a few fine country cooks around here, but most of the food is very undistinguished in character. Most local cooks have two ideas about what to do with food. They either fry it—and I think the steady diet of fried food in Maine accounts largely for the high incidence of chronic indigestion and stomach ulcers—or else they make a chowder out of it. We have a by-word in our family. When confronted with the disposal of almost anything from a dead fish to a pair of worn-out pants, someone is bound to say, "It'd make a nice chowder!" That really isn't stretching the point much, either.

I'm indebted to the local cooks for another expression. That is "smitches and dabs." We have a meal of smitches and dabs about once a week, usually on wash day. This consists of a smitch of this and a dab of that. In other words, that's the meal that cleans up the ice box. It's a family institution by now, and a very useful one. Sometimes these left-overs are just warmed up separately and sometimes they are combined into one dish. You dump some odds and ends of meat, any stray vegetables, a can of beef broth—to make gravy—into a baking dish, top the whole with biscuit dough, bake, and you have a shepherd's pie. Or you put left-over salmon, peas, ham, and a can of mushroom soup into a dish, cover with buttered crumbs, and again bake. I suppose this is some kind of a casserole, but it doesn't really make much difference what it is. It comes under smitches and dabs in our family.

We have Desperation Dishes, too. These are things we eat when we run out of food, for one reason or other. A stand-by, of course, is baked beans, which we have every Saturday night anyhow. In a minute I'm going into the proper baking of beans in detail. It's a subject that deserves attention. Baked beans can be terrible, or they can be swell. In our family Gerrish is the judge. He's a baked bean expert from away-back. If he says after the first forkful, "Your hand slipped a mite this week, didn't it, Louise?", I feel like crawling under the table. But if he says, "You hit it about right this time," my chest swells to the button-bursting point.

Even good baked beans can become tedious. I remember one year when the lake didn't finish freezing and we couldn't get in any supplies, we had them twice a day for ten days. One of these days was Thanksgiving, too. In honor of that day I invented another Desperation Dish. Besides beans, we had in the house a very small can of Vienna sausages and a half a bottle of ketchup. I put a layer of cold baked beans in a baking dish, sprinkled lavishly with ketchup, and arranged half the sausages on it. Then I repeated, ending with a layer of beans, and heated the whole until it bubbled gently. It was really pretty good. We have it now every once in a while, even when we aren't desperate. Desperation Dishes often turn out much better than you'd expect.

Now about the baking of the beans. Baked beans have to be baked. That sounds like a gratuitous restatement of the obvious, but it isn't. Some misguided souls boil beans all day and call the lily-livered result baked beans. I refrain from comment.

We use either New York State or Michigan white beans, because we like them best, although yellow-eyes are very popular, too. I take two generous cups of dry beans, soak over night and put them on to boil early in the morning. When the skins curl off when you blow on them, they've boiled long enough. Then I put in the bottom of the bean pot, or iron kettle with a tight-fitting cover, a six-by-eight-inch square of salt pork, with the rind slashed every quarter of an inch, a quarter of a cup of sugar, half a cup of molasses, a large onion chopped fairly fine, and a heaping teaspoonful of dry mustard. This amount of sugar and molasses may be increased or cut, depending on whether you like your beans sweeter or not so sweet. This is a matter every man has to decide for himself. The beans are dumped in on top of this conglomerate, and enough hot water is added to cover, but only cover. The baking pot should be large enough so there's at least an inch of freeboard above the water. Otherwise they'll boil over and smell to high heaven. Cover tightly and put into a medium oven—about 350° is right. They should be in the oven by half past nine in the morning at the latest, and they should stay there until supper time, which in our family is at six.

So far there is no trick in making good baked beans. The trick, if it can be dignified by such a term, lies in the baking, and like a great many trade tricks, it consists only of patience and conscientious care. You have to tend the beans faithfully, adding water whenever the level gets down below the top of the beans, and you have to keep the oven temperature even. If you're lazy, you can put in a lot of water and not have to watch them so closely. But to get the best results, you should add only enough water each time to barely cover the beans. This means that you'll give up all social engagements for the day, as you can't leave the baby for more than half an hour at a time. I think the results are worth it—but then, I haven't anywhere special to go, anyhow. My beans are brown and mealy, and they swim in a thick brown juice. They're good. I always serve them with corn bread, ketchup and pickles.

Another Desperation Dish is Mock Tripe. It is an old home recipe of that almost legendary Norwegian guide, Travis Hoke, and is very useful in disposing of otherwise unusable odds and ends. If you have a fresh salmon you can put its skin in a light brine until you are ready to use it, or the skin of a baked fish, carefully removed, will serve as well. Save the daily leavings of the oatmeal pot and spread them out about a half inch thick to dry. When you have amassed a sufficient quantity and it is covered with a heavy brown crust, season well and wrap in the fish skin. Dredge this with flour and put it in your roasting pan with a small amount of water or milk, cover, and bake at least an hour in a medium oven. The result is truly amazing.

Every cook is supposed to have some short cuts or labor savers that experience has taught her. I ought to have a million, for Lord knows I have learned to cook in a hard school. But I have only a measly little list of discoveries. The first is that an egg beater can be used for a lot of other things than the beating of eggs. I'd almost rather throw my stove away than my egg beater. I use it to take the lumps out of gravy or chocolate cornstarch pudding or cream sauce. When the cereal sinks in a leaden mass to the bottom of the pan, because I didn't have the water boiling briskly, or didn't stir it enough, I beat it up with the egg beater, and it comes out smooth and creamy. I beat mashed potato with it, and squash. I beat anything and everything with an egg beater, and I always put it immediately into a deep pan of cold water to soak. Otherwise all the time it saves will be spent in washing the thing. It's devilish to get clean if it is allowed to dry.

My second little device is a pane of window glass which I put over my open cook book. I'm a messy cook, splashing flour and milk and batter and egg yolk all over the table. If they splash on the book, the pages will stick together and you can't use that recipe again, as I have found to my sorrow. If they splash on the glass, that's all right. Glass washes.

My third and last contribution to the culinary world is a way to crumb fish or croquettes or cutlets or what-have-you easily and quickly. I put my crumbs or flour in a paper bag, drop in the object to be crumbed, close the bag and shake violently. This doesn't sound like much of an invention but it saves an awful lot of mess. When you're through you have nothing to clean up. You just shove the paper bag into the stove and burn up the scanty leavings.

Now I'm probably going to discover that all these things are common practice among cooks everywhere, and that I'm just tagging tardily along behind my brighter sisters.

There are two factors which complicate the cooking situation for me. One is that I never know how many people I am going to have to feed. I always have to allow for at least one more than the family, in case anyone drops in. In the woods the first question you ask anybody, no matter what time of day he arrives, is, "Have you eaten?" This is absolutely obligatory, and the reason is easy to see. A man can't drop into a dog cart for a hamburger or a cup of coffee, if he's hungry. He expects the population to feed him, and in return he expects to feed whoever drops in at his place. It's an understood thing, just as it is understood that in winter, no matter whose house you go into, if they are not at home you immediately look at the fires and add wood if necessary. You do this even if you are a stranger to the householder. It may be serious to let a fire go out. So we feed game wardens and fire wardens and timber cruisers and lost hunters and stray woodsmen and anyone else who happens along, and they tend our fires as required. Once we even fed the census taker, a gentleman whom, by the way, we were very much surprised to see come staggering out of the snowy woods. We'd figured that we would be among the submerged and forgotten one percent, when it came to census taking.

The other difficulty I have to surmount is the kitchen itself. In the country, and even more in the woods, a kitchen is much more than a place to cook. It's the place where people sit, for warmth or sociability, or to do odd jobs. We have the usual kitchen furnishings—straight-backed chairs, table, work bench, sink, ice box, stove and woodbox. We also have a comfortable rocking chair and a pile of books and magazines. Half the time, when I'm cooking, I'm also hurdling over someone's legs, or a dog or cat, or a pile of guns and coats. Or I may have to walk around a landing net that has been left by the stove, or an inner tube that Ralph is patching in the middle of the floor. In all seasons except summer, I have to dodge a lineful of wool socks, hung up to dry, and skirt two pails of water left by the end of the stove to keep warm for car-starting purposes. Often my pots and pans have to find what space they can around a soldering iron thrust into the firebox and my pot roast is shoved back in the oven to accommodate a pair of newly oiled boots that must be dried.

I used to try to keep the kitchen sacred to legitimate kitchen activities, but I finally gave it up. No matter how often I chased Gerrish and his tackle-mending or Ralph and his car-repairing or Rufus and his fleet of trucks into the living-room, they always insidiously filtered back. Actually there's an advantage to having them right there. If they're in the room they can't very well pretend not to hear me when I start hollering to have my water pails filled or some wood brought in from the woodshed. And I might as well break down at last and admit that I like having them underfoot. The few times that they stayed in the living-room when I sent them there, I felt like a social pariah out in the kitchen all alone with my efficiency.

To augment our larder, we have a vegetable garden, and believe me, please, that's quite a feat when you start, as we did, with a little plot of land which has excellent sun and drainage, but which also has a growth of brush and evergreens all over it, and under that nothing but thin, acid woods soil studded thickly with rocks and boulders and solidly interlaced with a mat of roots. Our garden is splendid now, but it's taken us eight years to get it that way.

The first year was spent in cutting the brush and trees and removing the roots and the worst of the rocks. This was honest-to-God hard labor, particularly as we didn't have the right equipment for it. Ralph and Gerrish and I have spent a whole day getting out a boulder that weighed more than the three of us put together. The first step, always, was to trench around the thing so we could get at it, and Ralph and Gerrish did this. Then they collected an assortment of chains, levers, and cant dogs, and summoned me. My part consisted solely of lending my weight on the end of a twenty-foot beam that served as a pry, or dodging around the edges of the operation with an armful of blocks of assorted sizes. "Over here! Over here!" Ralph and Gerrish would shout in chorus, their faces red and strained with lifting. "For God's sake, stick a block under her before—" I'd thrust a block in to hold what they'd gained and they'd relax, panting and perspiring, to get their breaths and plan the next step. The general modus operandi was to lift the boulder up with levers to ground level, building a scaffolding of blocks under her as she came—I'm catching this "she" habit, too—and then roll her across an extremely precarious bridge of planks to solid earth. Then we worried her onto a stone-drag and dragged her away behind our then current work car, the old twelve-cylinder Packard. Frequently, with only six inches to go before we could roll her out, the entire scaffolding would collapse and drop the boulder back to the bottom of the pit—a perfectly maddening thing to have happen. I do believe in the malevolence of the inanimate, and of all inanimate objects, stones are the most malevolent. In the first place the stones in our section lack symmetry, so if you apply pressure where you think it will do the most good, they are just as apt to roll to the left onto your foot, as to the right where you plan to have them roll. In the second place, they are ponderous, and once they start rolling, you can't stop them. All you can do is jump clear and start swearing. In the third place—and this to my mind is the worst of all—after they have flopped the wrong way and have ruined an entire morning's work, they just lie there. There's something about the bland face of a stone, lying in the middle of a pile of wrecked scaffolding at the bottom of a hole, that makes you want to throw yourself face down on the ground and kick and scream.

We got enough rocks and roots out of the ground that first year so that we could plant a few things in the cleared spaces. But we didn't get them all out, by any means, and haven't even yet, in spite of a yearly session with them. We put in peas and string beans and carrots and beets and corn. Ralph and I were no gardeners but Gerrish had had a garden in one place or another ever since he wore diapers, so in most things we bowed to his superior wisdom. But when it came to corn, he and Ralph disagreed. Ralph contended that the growing season as far north and as high as we are is too short to allow corn to reach maturity, and that it should be started in the house and transplanted into the garden as soon as the weather was warm enough. Gerrish announced categorically that one did not transplant corn. It wouldn't grow, and even if it did, there was no point to it. The season was plenty long enough.

They argued two or three days about this, and then they decided that they'd divide the corn patch, and each would take half to cultivate as he saw fit. Ralph made himself some nice little starting flats, filled them with dirt, and started his corn in the house. Gerrish put his corn away in a drawer and forgot about it until the ground warmed up.

Ralph's corn came up very nicely and he tended it as if it were black orchids. On the same day that Gerrish put his seed into the ground, Ralph transplanted his thriving little shoots. They looked very green and tender and brave out there in the cold world, and he covered them carefully every night, to guard them against a spring frost. They didn't grow very much at first. I suppose they were getting themselves acclimated. After about a week, Gerrish's corn started to come up, and that's where the double-dealing entered the picture.

Gerrish came home from fishing one evening with a whole string of chub. Nobody eats them, so I couldn't imagine why he had saved them, or why he was hiding them so carefully under the back steps. He didn't mind telling me, after swearing me to secrecy. He'd remembered that the Indians used to plant their corn over dead fish, for fertilizer, and he was going to tunnel into his corn hills and put dead chub where they'd do the most good. He'd show Ralph how to raise corn.

Well, a promise is a promise, I know, and I usually try to keep mine. But this was supposed to be a controlled experiment, and I've been brought up to respect the scientific attitude. I couldn't let that go. I told Ralph—swearing him to secrecy, of course—and that night he went chub fishing, with some success. Thereafter the two of them spent a lot of time sneaking fish corpses into the garden and burying them under their respective corn hills. I used to help them both, which was probably traitorous of me, but it afforded me a lot of fun.

We had corn off both sides of the patch on the very same day, and there was nothing to distinguish the one from the other. Now we plant our corn by the Gerrish system. It's a lot easier.

Oh, the troubles we had that first year! No sooner had our vegetables broken ground than the deer started coming in at night and eating the plants. We decided at once that we had to fence the garden, but it was going to take a little time to get the fencing material in from the Outside. In the meantime something had to be done. For a while we worked days cutting and setting fence posts, and sat up nights with a shot gun. But you can't keep that up forever. Then the game warden told us to spread some blood meal around. This is a packing house product that is used primarily for fertilizer. The smell of blood is supposed to frighten the deer away. It didn't, though. On the contrary, I think it attracted them. Then someone told us that if we made a little tent in the garden and kept a lighted lantern in it all night, the deer would keep their distance. The tent material had to be thin, so the light would glow through, and the color had to be changed often, so the deer wouldn't acquire the contempt bred by familiarity. We tried that—we'd have tried anything—and rather surprisingly it worked. At least, it worked for a week. Then one morning we went into the garden and found the tracks of a dozen deer, all converging on our little tent. Apparently they'd held a meeting and decided on a mass investigation. They hadn't touched any of the vegetables, though. I guess they were too intrigued with the light to bother about anything else.

That very afternoon the wire for the fence came, and next morning we put it onto the posts we'd set so fast that it smoked. And that was that.

That wasn't the woodchucks, though, that crawled through the mesh of the wire. We had to set traps for them. *That* wasn't the heavy rain, either, that gullied out the slope of the garden and washed out half the crop. We had to terrace the whole slope, the next year, to prevent a recurrence. But neither fence nor traps nor terracing was any answer to our basic problem, the problem of the soil. It's taken us all these years to lick its thinness and acidity and infertility. We've spaded in tons of manure which we've hauled from Miller's and various lumber camp stables, to add humus and give body to the soil. We've bought hundreds of pounds of lime and raked it in, to counteract the acidity which is always a characteristic of forest mold. We've scattered hundreds of pounds of commercial balanced fertilizers, too. What we've accomplished, really, is to make arable earth out of the rubble heaps of sand and clay and gravel that the great glaciers dumped here ages and ages ago. It may not be a becoming attitude, but all the same, we do point with pride to our vegetable garden. I consider that my skill with a spading fork is just as much a part of my housekeeping ability as is my urban sister's nose for a bargain in canned goods. They both result in putting better, cheaper vegetables on the family table.

The clothing problem causes me very little concern. One of the reasons I like to live here is that I don't have to bother to try to be a snappy number. I couldn't, anyway, no matter where I lived; but in civilization I'd at least have to make the effort, in fairness to Ralph and Rufus. I couldn't humiliate them by putting them in the position of having to answer, when someone asked, "Who's that funny-looking woman?"—"Oh, that's my wife" or "my mother," as the case might be. And, boy! would I be miserable! I can't stand having things tight around my waist or neck or wrists, and you can't be stylish unless you have your clothes anchored in a few places, at least. My idea of an ideal costume is slacks worn low on the hip bones, and a cotton shirt with the sleeves rolled up and the neck band unbuttoned. I can wear that here. I look thoroughly sloppy, but here it doesn't matter. Ralph and Rufus love me—I hope—for my good nature. There wouldn't be even that about me to love if I had to try to be chic.

This is what my entire wardrobe consists of at the moment.

1 pair of blue denim pants
1 pair of canvas pants (my garden, fishing, and berrying pants)
1 pair wool whipcord jodhpurs (Ralph hates them)
1 pair wool ski pants
3 cotton shirts (the 59¢ variety)
3 wool shirts
4 pairs of cotton ankle socks (17¢ a pair)
3 pairs of wool ski socks (I made them myself—39¢ each, but worth a lot more)
2 sweaters

1 wool jacket
1 denim jacket
1 bathing suit and cap
3 changes of underwear and nightclothes
1 very old bathrobe
1 wool bonnet and mittens to match
3 pairs of 79¢ sneakers
1 pair of leather moccasins
1 large kerchief, to use as hat, scarf, berry pail, dog leash, depending on the circumstances.

I did have a belt, but I never wore it, so I gave it to Gerrish. And I have a .22 revolver, but I don't suppose that comes under wardrobe, really, even here. I've also got a tweed suit and a pair of silk stockings and some shoes in case I have to go Outside in a hurry; but it's been a long time since I've even looked at them. They've probably perished of dry rot by now. The last time I had to go out in a hurry was when Kyak became suddenly and terrifyingly ill and needed to be taken at once to the veterinary. It was at night and raining pitchforks, and I had no time or inclination to dress up. I wore my fishing pants and Gerrish's raincoat, which was just as well. The only people besides Ralph that I saw were Larry Parsons and the vet. I didn't really see Larry. He was running the boat, but it was so dark and foggy that he had to make the trip down the lake by compass, and all I could distinguish of him was a dark shadow up in the bow and a faint blur of features when he inhaled on his cigarette or turned the flashlight onto the compass. And later in the car it was almost as dark. The vet was too much interested in Kyak's symptoms to bother about what I had on. I'm sure the next time an emergency arises, the conditions will be duplicated. So I don't have to worry about my Going Out Clothes.

Ralph's wardrobe is about like mine, except he has gumboots for winter and work shoes for summer and a canvas parka and a mackinaw. He prefers canvas pants the whole year through and refuses to have riding or ski pants. Rufus wears overalls and cotton shirts, or sun suits, for summer, and ski pants and sweaters in the winter. Once when he was very little I did buy him a little wash suit, with shorts and frilled shirt. He looked perfectly adorable in it the one time he had it on. But he and his father and Gerrish all pronounced it sissy, and I could never get him to wear it again. Sally is the best-dressed member of the family. She goes Out to school, so she has to have the usual quota of dresses, presentable shoes, and street coats. At her age, too, these things would matter, I suppose, even if she never went Outside.

There are a few general aspects of the clothes situation that interest me very much. One of them is the growth of ski pants as a national institution. When I was a child, ski pants were absolutely unknown in this country. I realize that they were introduced along with the vogue for winter sports, and that is not surprising. What surprises me is their acceptance by non-skiers of all ages. It has apparently reached the point where everyone owns a pair of ski pants, just as everyone owns a skirt or a pair of trousers. This really is a tribute to the practicability of the garment. People in general don't own baseball caps or football pants. The most non-athletic types own ski pants.

Another thing that interests me is the false notion held by almost all city people that you can get wonderful bargains in the country. Ralph, for example, owns a very handsome red-and-black-checked shirt, made of wool material so thin it tailors marvellously. He calls it his sporting shirt, and wears it only on special occasions. Occasions special enough for the sporting shirt usually involve people from the city, and before long someone will get up the courage to ask, "*Where* did you get that shirt and how much did you pay for it? I want one like it."

The answer is, "My sister-in-law gave it to me for my birthday and she got it at Jordan Marsh's in Boston and I've no idea what she paid for it."

The let-down is always tremendous. "Oh, I hoped you were going to say that you got it at some cross-roads country store for two dollars. You always hear about the wonderful things that people pick up back in the sticks for practically nothing—"

Yes, you do. But there aren't any wonderful things in country stores, for any amount of money. The stock in a country store consists of cheap clothes, cheap food, cheap everything. Usually they cost more than the same article in the city. Cheap things are all that country people can ordinarily afford. If you want marvellous things, you have to go to the luxury trade stores in cities, and pay accordingly. You can't get something for nothing, even in the country. I buy homespun yarn from various farmers' wives around on the Outside, and I pay very little for it. It's all wool, from sheep reared on the place. That sounds like one of those marvellous bargains; but it isn't. It's worth exactly what I pay for it. It's harsh, and it's unevenly spun, and there are only two colors—gray and a tan mixture. For my purpose—work socks and mittens—it's quite all right. But when I want to make a sweater, or a nice pair of socks for

Ralph, I send away to the Mail Order for some decent yarn.

The truth of the matter is that in spite of the literary convention of bursting barns, overflowing larders, and cellars crammed with luscious preserves and delicious smoked hams, in spite of the accepted version of the countryman as being clad in the warmest and best of wools, the thickest and softest of leathers, and the deepest and darkest of furs, country people are clothed much more shoddily and poorly than city people, class for class. In short, the country standard of living is very much lower than the city standard. This is actually not as hard on country people as it would seem to be. You don't mind cheap clothes if everyone else is wearing clothes just as cheap. There are other things that contribute to health besides a balanced diet. There are fresh air and sunlight and lack of nervous tension. I think, probably, whether you're better off in the country or in the city depends, in the final analysis, on where you'd rather be. You're best off where you're the happiest.

As I have said before, we do all our purchasing from the Mail Order—more formally, from Sears, Roebuck and Montgomery Ward. Having been brought up in a medium-sized town within easy reach of Boston, I never had a chance to become familiar with the great American institution of the Mail Order until I came to live in the woods. Now, I couldn't get along without it. It's wonderful as a source of supply, and their catalogs are a fascinating source of entertainment. We sit by the hour looking at the illustrations and reading the descriptions of the thousands of items in the enormous twice-yearly catalogs, and we buy anything from motor parts to ankle socks from

Sears' or Ward's. If, for my sins, I ever have to live at the corner of 42nd and Broadway, I shall still trade with the Mail Order. I'm completely wedded to the idea.

Everybody in this country is thoroughly familiar with the Mail Order. I show up at Middle in a new pair of slacks, and Alice Miller says, "Oh, those are those Ward's slacks. A dollar ninety-eight. I was thinking about getting me some, only in brown." Or somebody comes in from Upton sporting a new hunting shirt, and I can put the price tag and percentage of wool on it with the accuracy of a purchasing agent. Fifty percent wool, and two seventy-five in the big catalog; but he paid only two forty-nine for it. They had them on sale in the latest flyer. There are no secrets between Mail Order devotees.

I never realized how revealing a filled-in order blank can be until one day I happened on the sample order blank in the back of the Sears catalog. This is a facsimile of an order, made out in full, for the guidance of the customer in making out his own order. Very likely the name and address at the top of the blank are fictitious, but the order itself looks genuine. I read it through carefully, and I felt at once that I knew the woman who made it out as well as I know myself.

The goods were to be sent to John T. Jones, R.F.D. No. 1, Tipton, Iowa, but Johnny Jones didn't make out the order. Mrs. Jones did that. She hadn't been married very long, I think, and she didn't have very much money to spend. But she had ideas. She wanted her house to be nice. She lived in the country in Iowa, but she didn't want to let herself go. She wanted to look smart like the town girls. I know just how she conned the catalog night after night, between finishing the supper dishes and going to bed, to be sure she was getting the best possible value for her money. She made a lot of selections and jotted them down —the names of the articles and the prices—on an old envelope, before she made her final choices. I know, because I have done the same thing. She had only thirty dollars to spend. I know that, because the order came to $29.42. That's just about as close as you can come to a specified sum.

I know that this order was important to her, because it is written so carefully and neatly in ink. The penmanship is obviously not her note-to-the-milkman hand. It's her very best penmanship, stiff and careful, with the t's crossed accurately. That's the way I write when I make out an order to Sears' or Ward's. That's the only time I do write that way.

This is what she bought. Four yards of rose-printed chintz, a dusty rose chenille bedspread, and a pair of dusty rose curtains. You see? She was fixing up a bedroom, with spread, curtains, and dressing table to match. Probably it was for the spare room; she'd at last saved enough to redecorate it as a real guest room. None of the articles is the best grade—that I remembered from my own perusals of the catalog. But they're the best she could afford. She wanted her house to be nice.

Then she bought three pairs of flag-red ankle socks—that's how I know she must be young, and therefore newly married—and a green suit, Cat. No. 55H7186, which cost $15.50. I remembered Cat. No. 55H7186. It's a nice suit, very young and dashing. She hesitated a long time before she spent that much money on a suit, I know, but in the end she remembered how proud of her Johnny always acted when he took her to the movies Saturday night before they were married. In the end she sacrificed I don't know what—a two-quart double boiler, perhaps, or an extra pair of sheets—to keep him acting that way.

The last item was a Craftsman hammer, for ninety-eight cents. That was for Johnny. She had a little over a dollar left, and he'd been fussing about that old hammer with the loose head out in the shed— Oh, I know Mrs. John T. Jones of Tipton, Iowa. Perhaps she is just someone dreamed up in the advertising department of Sears' Chicago office! But she's me, too, and a million other women like me, scattered from here to the Rio Grande, who do their shopping through the magic of the Mail Order.

All my life I've had a very clear idea of the kind of living-room I'd like to have. It's the living-room so often described in English novels or novels of country life among the gentlefolk in Virginia or the Berkshires. Everybody knows the room well, with its wide windows, its books and flowers and faded chintz, its open fire and comfortable shabby chairs and sleeping dogs. It sounds attractive and comfortable. It's comfortable, all right, but not necessarily as attractive as it's made out to be. I know. That's the kind of a living-room we have in the summer house.

The trouble with faded chintz, let me tell you, is that instead of looking soft and old and precious, it looks like chintz that should have been replaced two years ago. The trouble with the dogs is that instead of lying in front of the fire and lending atmosphere, they lie in the middle of the floor where you fall over them. Or else they lie in the shabby chairs and look so hurt when you try to oust them that you can't bear it, and you'd almost sit on the floor yourself rather than cause them pain. The trouble with the open fire is that it throws embers onto the rug—a

Rufus, Kyak and Ralp

Gerrish and His Sap-Gathering Equipment

screen holds in the embers, but holds in the heat, too—so that eventually you decide to take up the rug altogether and have a bare floor—unless you've already taken it up because it's too hard to keep clean, what with the men-folks of your family, and the dogs and cats, tracking in mud, sawdust and snow. There's nothing the matter with the flowers and the books and there's nothing the matter with the shabby chairs, if you can accept them as shabby chairs and don't try to make something interesting out of them. BUT —and this is never taken into consideration in the novels—if you're the kind of weak-minded person who will put up with faded chintz and dogs in shabby chairs in the first place, you're too weak-minded to put your foot down there. You allow the corners of this interesting room to become jammed with fishing tackle and guns; the table and mantle are soon buried under a mound of fly-tying material, magazines, odd pieces of rock, and work gloves; the floor is littered with toys and tools; and several pairs of boots for all types of weather are parked at the end of the couch. In short, the place is a mess. The only thing that can be said for it is that there is nothing in it that can be hurt by the roughest usage. It's a room you can let yourself go in, for what that's worth. It's a room where you can put your feet up and relax.

That's the kind of a home Ralph and I have made for ourselves in the backwoods, and that's the kind of marriage we've managed, together, to make, too. There are drawbacks to living off the beaten track, but there is one thing that more than offsets any number of drawbacks: if you can stand this life at all, your marriage has a much greater chance of success than it would have anywhere else. I believe that a great many marriages fail because there is no true dependence between the partners thereof. Somehow, when a well-dressed, well-fed, sleek and contented male says to me—and there have been such occasions in my palmy youth, believe it or not—"I need you!", I just can't quite believe it, much as I'd like to. It's nice to hear, but it's silly. When, however, Ralph comes into the house with the sleeve of his shirt torn and blood dripping from a gash on his arm, and shouts at the top of his lungs, "Damn it, where are you? I need you!", he's obviously telling the truth. He may be interrupting me in the middle of something that I don't want to leave, but that doesn't make any difference. He does need me, and he needs me right then. There isn't any doctor he can go to to tie him up. There isn't any restaurant where he can get his meals, or any laundry to wash his shirts. I'm necessary to him; and by the same token, he's necessary to me. It's a terribly trite thing to say, I know, but most of us have to be needed to be happy.

Is it, then, necessary to live the hard way, just so you can feel you are needed? For me, yes, it is. I know myself too well to be able to delude myself that my wit or my beauty or my wisdom or my intelligence could ever become indispensable to anyone. I have to have things demonstrated in material terms that I can understand. And I have found this to be true: that the material makes a very good and solid foundation for a dependence that cannot be defined, an inter-dependence of mind and spirit which we might never have known had we not first had to depend on each other for the tangible, demonstrable things.

We've managed to make a good marriage. This I say with all humility. It's a marriage in which there is nothing that can be hurt by the roughest usage. It's a marriage that you can let yourself go in, a marriage in which you can put up your feet and relax.

V

"*Aren't the Children a Problem?*"

THE TRUE YANKEE ANSWER TO THE QUESTION, "AREN'T THE children a problem?" is, of course, another question: "Aren't children always a problem, no matter where you live?" If they aren't, I've wasted a lot of time in my civilized past listening to the bridge table chat of the young mothers of my acquaintanceship. Unless my memory plays me false, parenthood anywhere from the heart of Texas to the middle of Manhattan is one long coping with maladjusted personalities, crooked teeth, allergies to goose feathers, and lamentable traits inherited from the other side of the family. In short, certainly children are a problem, only in the woods the details of the problem aren't quite the same as they are on the Outside.

The problem starts with getting them born. Of course, with Sally, I skipped this. She's my step-child, and sprang into my life, full-panoplied, as it were, at the age of twelve. I skipped not only the actual giving birth, but also the house-breaking and habit-forming. This advantage is offset to an extent by the fact that I'm responsible for her not only to her father and my own conscience, as I am with

Rufus, but also to her mother as well—no mean responsibility. It would be bad enough to have something happen to your own child. It would be almost impossible to have to go to another woman and say, "So sorry, but I let your daughter get drowned." That's the chief reason that the first thing I did about Sally when I took her over was to insist that she learn to swim. All in all, though, I would say that I came by Sally in the easy way.

Rufus I got the hard way, on the 18th of December at 2.55 A.M., with the thermometer down to 10° above zero. That's a night I won't forget in a hurry. Neither will Ralph, I imagine. Ralph has always been the type that, if he heard it rumored that the wife of one of his friends was going to have a baby eight months from date, took to crossing the street and raising his hat politely from the opposite sidewalk, when he met her. He was taking no chances of having to ride in a taxi with her to the hospital. The mere thought caused him to break out in a cold sweat. Well, the night Rufus was born he didn't have any time to worry about what might happen in a taxi. He was much too busy coping, single handed, with what was happening right then and there. In spite of the temperature, though, he was doing his quota of sweating. I can see him now, with a wool cap pulled down over his ears, his mackinaw collar turned up to meet it, and his mittens on, reading by lantern light a little book called, "If Baby Comes Ahead of the Doctor." Perspiration was running down his face. You see, he knew the doctor couldn't possibly get there for ten hours or more.

Nothing is more tiresome than the details of some other woman's pregnancy, but just bear with me for a minute. I've been wanting to say this for a long time. I don't believe most women need be miserable at all. There are two simple preventive measures to take. First, they can stop regarding themselves as being for the period, interesting and unique and fragile, and treating themselves like rare porcelain. It's very bad for them. No wonder they feel rotten. A coal heaver would feel rotten too, if he kept telling himself that he ought to on general principles. And second, they can just not listen to their married friends' and maiden aunts' tales of the terrible things that may happen to them. Some of the things that otherwise sensible women tell prospective mothers are enough to frighten the wits out of anyone. They won't let you remember that these ghoulish tales are the exceptions and that most babies are born with some discomfort, it's true, but not much else. Personally, I'd almost rather have a baby any day than go to the dentist. My friends tell me that this is just because I was lucky. I think I made my own luck. I felt swell, so why should I alter my normal behavior and curtail my normal activities? And—this I will admit was just plain luck —I was so situated that there were no married friends and maiden aunts to scare the pants off me. Result: I had a very pleasant pregnancy, thank you.

End of Lecture on Prenatal Care, by Mrs. Rich. Thanks for listening.

I was supposed to go out to Rumford to have Rufus; but then he wasn't supposed to be born until the first of the year. The idea was that I would stay in over Christmas, and then in a leisurely way, betake myself to the hospital to wait the necessary week or ten days. Consequently we hadn't moved out of the summer house which is without heat upstairs. Ralph was going to move the things in my absence. In the meantime I pursued my program of

"Business as Usual," and the usual business of a lovely day such as the 17th of December turned out to be, was sliding on the Pond. I never saw such a beautiful winter day. It was warm and sunny, and the ground was covered with a light fluff of snow, which was blue in the shadows, and gold in the sun, and faint rose and purple on the distant hills. On the Pond it had blown into tightly packed patches which were white, as snow is supposed to be, against the sky-reflecting deep blue of the glare ice. We'd started to go to Middle Dam, but when we saw the Pond, we went there instead. The sliding was perfect. We could run on the snow islands and slide across the intervening spaces of ice to more snow. Cookie went with us—she was alive at the time, Kyak's mother—and she had a lovely time, too, racing and barking and falling down and scrambling to her feet. We all fell down dozens of times before we completed the mile circuit of the Lamonts' island, which may have had something to do with Rufus' premature arrival. I don't know. I felt quite all right.

All I know is that I woke up in the middle of the night, out of a sound sleep, with a stomach-ache. Only it wasn't a stomach-ache. It was an emergency, and there were no lights on the Ford, and I didn't have a bag packed. I woke Ralph up, and he went down to telephone the Millers and, of course, woke them up, while I wandered around with an old pair of slippers in one hand and a cake of soap in the other. I couldn't seem to think where I'd put my suitcase or what I should put into it. Pretty soon it became obvious that it didn't matter. I got back into bed just as Ralph came up with the information that the Millers' Ford had no lights either, and since it was pitch black outdoors we wouldn't be going anywhere. This didn't upset me as much as it would have fifteen minutes before. I'd already come to the same conclusion but for an entirely different reason.

I don't want to give the impression that I was calm and unruffled through this whole proceeding. I wasn't. But I took one look at Ralph's face and saw that he was ten times as alarmed as I was. I'd never seen him really alarmed before, and it was the best thing in the world that could have happened to me. I suddenly felt very brave and confident. I remembered that lots of babies are born without benefit of the medical profession, and that the best thing in a crisis is to keep busy. I was busy enough myself. All I had to do was to give Ralph something to occupy his mind.

"You'd better heat up a lot of water," I said. I didn't know quite what for, but I remembered that in books people always heat water under similar circumstances.

He went away and I could hear him rattling away down in the kitchen. By and by he came back and said that he wanted a nice wool blanket to warm over the stove before he put it in the laundry basket. "Got to have some place to park the kid," he explained, and I stopped worrying about him. He was functioning again, that was plain. I told him where to find the blanket, in between pains, and he went away again. When he came back, five minutes later, he was a father.

Usually a father has no immediate responsibilities toward his new off-spring aside from running up to the hospital once a day for a viewing—and of course paying the hospital bill. Ralph's responsibilities, on the contrary, were immediate and pressing. There was the little matter of the umbilical cord to be cut and tied, first of all.

"And don't you wash new babies?" I asked.

"Nope. You grease them." I don't know to this day how he came by this piece of knowledge, but he was right. Perhaps he read it in the *Reader's Digest*. That's where much of our information originates. He folded his new son in a bath towel and went away with him, while I lay in bed and worried. What did he know about greasing babies and tying cords? The new baby was crying, too, a little but furious bellow. I could hear him from away upstairs. What was his father doing to him? Or wait a minute—you were supposed only to worry, weren't you, if they didn't cry. So probably it was all right. It was criminal, I decided, for a grown woman to arrive at motherhood knowing as little about the whole thing as I did. By and by Ralph came back.

"Did you get him greased all right?" I asked anxiously.

He looked offended. "Certainly I did. I should hope, after all the pistons I've oiled in my lifetime—" Pistons, mind you!

"What did you use?" I asked, horrified, "Motor oil?"

"Olive oil, naturally."

"Where did you get it? We haven't any olive oil."

"I've got a can. I use it to make fly-dope out of."

Well, why not, after all? If early experience molds a child's life, I could see from where I lay that I was going to be the mother of another mechanic and fly-fisherman.

"He's all right and he's all there," Ralph went on. "Fingernails, toenails, hair, everything. I went over him carefully. And, my God! is he homely!" He threw out his chest. "I never did like pretty men, anyway," he added complacently. "He's got a grip like a wrestler, and Cookie likes him, so I guess he'll get along all right. And say. What am I supposed to do with all that hot water?"

Oh, yes. The hot water. Well— "Why don't you make some coffee?" Suddenly I was starved. "Make me a sandwich, too—a ham sandwich with a lot of mustard."

Alice Miller came down in the morning, as soon as it was light. Lying in bed, I could hear her laughing down in the kitchen. She laughed all the way upstairs. "What do you suppose Ralph used to tie his cord with?" she demanded before she was halfway into the room. "A piece of rope! That poor little kid! The knot's bigger than he is. I guess I'll call the doctor in Rumford when I get home and tell him there's no need of his coming way in here. No sense in spending twenty dollars for nothing—"

And so Rufus missed his chance of having a doctor look him over. I guess it didn't do any harm. He's never seen a doctor from that day to this, except in a purely social capacity.

I frequently read in magazines articles which begin:—

DO YOU REALIZE—

That blank percent of the homes in America have no running water?

That blank percent have no bathrooms?

That blank percent of our children are born with no doctor in attendance?

These appalling figures show that the huge army of the underprivileged—

I cluck my tongue, suitably appalled for a moment until true realization hits me between the eyes. "My God," I think, and then I am truly appalled. "That's *us* they're talking about! Why—*we're* the underprivileged! Why—Why—"

But are we? I'm not stupid enough to recommend that all, or even any, children be born with only their fathers in attendance. But because it happened to Rufus doesn't make him underprivileged. In fact, I would say he was especially privileged—not in that he was held up by the heels and oiled with piston-oiling technique, but because from that moment on, his father has had a very special feeling for him. All normal fathers love their children, we will assume. They all feel a responsibility toward them. But—and I think I am not being merely sentimental when I say this—that early, primitive responsibility that devolved upon Ralph toward Rufus left its mark. Fatherhood is necessarily a less intimate relationship—physically at least—than motherhood; but Ralph can't think of himself only as the guy who buys Rufus' food and clothes and administers spankings. Fundamentally he is always the guy who tied his cord and greased him, when there was no one else to do it. That is something I wouldn't want Rufus deprived of, for all the hospital treatment in the world.

Nor can I bring myself to believe that our children are hopelessly handicapped because they take baths in washtubs in front of the kitchen range, read by the light of kerosene lamps, and sleep in unheated bedrooms. We'll give them a bathroom and steam heat and electric lights when we get the house rebuilt; but perhaps we'll be making a mistake. Soft living isn't important to them now, because it never has been. They're never going to be miserable because of physical inconveniences. Perhaps the best thing we can give them in a world where the possession of material things becomes more and more precarious, in a world of marching armies and destruction-dealing skies, is a tough-fibered indifference to heat and cold and comfort and discomfort.

What can we give our children then, that won't be outmoded, that won't, under some eventuality that we can't foresee, prove to be a handicap to them? I don't know the answer to that one. Once I would have said "Ideas and Ideals." But I grew up in the years after the first World War, when perpetual peace was supposed to be the easily attainable ideal. I was trained in that ideal, and I believed in it with all the sincerity of which I was capable. Perhaps it is still attainable—but if it is, it will be by some different means than those I was taught to trust in. I don't want my child ever to feel as lost in the world as I do right now; nor do I want to inculcate in him the doctrine of force and aggression at no matter what sacrifice of the rights of others.

We can give him a happy childhood to remember, a way of life that he will be willing to die to protect, if the need arises. That sounds like a grim and Spartan gift to a little boy, but it's not as dangerous a gift as the belief in pacifism and universal well-wishing to which my generation was exposed. I don't want to raise my son to be a soldier—but if he has to be one, I want him to be a good and capable one. I want him to know what he's fighting for—and Freedom and Democracy won't mean a thing to him, unless they are all tied up with memories of things that he has loved ever since he can remember—things like the sound of the river, and the way Kyak lies and dreams in front of the open fire on a crisp autumn evening, and the picnics we've held at Smooth Ledge. The name of his country won't be worth fighting for, unless he can remember from experience that his country is the place, not of equal opportunity, not of universal suffrage, not of any of those lofty conceptions so far above a little boy's ability to comprehend, but the place where he walked with his father down a woods road one evening and saw a doe and twin fawns; or the place where he came in from playing in the snow and found the kitchen warm and fragrant and his mother making pop-corn balls.

That's all that I can give him; that's all that I dare to try to give him—something that he will love enough to want to preserve it for himself and others against whatever danger may threaten from whatever quarter, and the toughness and courage with which to fight for it. To bring him up untouched by war, insofar as is possible in a world where no one is completely unaffected by war today, is about the only contribution that I know how to make for the future.

Even here I am working in the dark. He won't remember the things I expect him to remember. I don't remember from my own childhood the important things that happened; but I can recall a hole in the ground among the roots of a maple tree that grew in front of our house. It was a small hole, about as big as a pint measure, but there was something about it. It was moist and smelled of earth and water when I lay on my stomach and thrust my four-year-old face into it. It was everything that was mysterious and marvellous to me then, and somehow it still is. I couldn't have explained to anyone then what that little hole in the ground meant to me, and I still can't. But the memory of it makes me wonder what Rufus is carrying around in his head that he can't share, and never will be able to share, but which will affect him. Sometimes I get a clue. Sometimes I see him lay his hand on a rock with a special gesture, or I find a piece of broken china that he has carefully hidden away, or I hear him talking to himself about a rabbit. But since I, myself, loath nothing quite so much as having someone prying into my thoughts and feelings, there is nothing I can do but wonder.

I wonder, too, if all the houses he ever reads about in books will be this house, just as all the houses I read about are in the end the house in which I grew up. It was a low, white, old-fashioned house, and some of the houses in books are huge mansions. But no matter how carefully the author explains the arrangement of the rooms, no matter if he goes to the trouble of drawing a floor plan, when his characters go from the drawing-room down long corridors into the dining hall, in my mind's eye they pass from our little living-room through a door to the left directly into the low square room where we ate. I only hope that Rufus won't spend his life picturing lords and ladies taking baths in the middle of the kitchen.

Of course the biggest problem we encounter in bringing up our children in the woods is their formal education. They do have to go to school. Even if there weren't laws requiring their attendance, even if we were quite capable—which we aren't—of giving them a solid foundation in the three R's, we would still have to send them. One of the most important parts of education is learning to get along with other people, and we just can't supply a society of their peers for them to rub up against. Rufus has seen so few children of his own age that he has no idea how to act with them. He lets them walk all over him, he's so happy to be with them. So we'll shortly have to ship him out to his grandmother's where he will learn among other things, I hope, to stand up for his rights. It's going to be rather a painful experience, so the sooner he gets it over with the better.

I certainly hope the school authorities don't start out by giving him an Intelligence Test before he's learned the ropes. If they do, his I.Q. will be about 50. (I don't believe in I.Q's. anyhow. My own is up in the near-genius group, and nobody knows better than I the abysmal depths of dumbness I can plumb. I just happen to have a very good memory for the sort of things they ask on Intelligence Tests.) But poor Rufus! All the questions dealing with such common things as running water, electric lights, hens, and railroad trains will leave him completely in the dark, and they don't ask how to tell a fox track from a dog track—a difficult thing that he can do easily—or how to use a birch hook, or how to employ a cant dog to its utmost efficiency. I suppose that is what the textbooks dismiss blandly as Feeble-mindedness by Deprivation.

Sally's education has been somewhat peculiar. The first twelve years of her life she lived in Southern Illinois and attended school regularly. Then she came with us for a while. Just as she was getting used to our peculiar mode of life, her mother sent for her to come to Liechtenstein—a small country between Switzerland and Austria, in case you didn't know—and she spent two years there and in the West Indies. She didn't go to school at all, but she was being educated, nonetheless. She learned, among other things, not to giggle when a Count kissed her hand, no matter how much it tickled, how to get through the customs with the least trouble, how to wear clothes, and how to order a meal in German. Then came the War, and Sally came back to us. She goes to school in Upton now, boarding with the Allens, who are among Ralph's oldest friends. She certainly ought to be adaptable. She's had a varied enough experience. I think that she is. When she was fifteen, her birthday party was held in the bar of a hotel in Haiti, closed to the public for the occasion. When she was sixteen, her birthday party was held in Allens' kitchen —open to the public for the occasion, I judge. Apparently everyone in town attended. As far as I can tell, she enjoyed both parties equally.

The school in Upton is a two-room school, and I'd forgotten that such a thing existed. If I'd remembered it, I would have delivered a speech beginning, "Well, in this day and age, with all the fine schools available, no child of mine—"; I would have been wrong. Sally learns as much, if not more, in what is known as the Upstairs Room, where Grades 7 to 10 inclusive sit under one teacher, as she could possibly learn in the biggest and best-equipped school in the country. Her Mr. Flanders is a very good teacher. The excellence of a teacher has nothing at all to do with his background, or the amount of salary he is paid, or anything else except his own personality and inherent bent. A good teacher is born, I am convinced, and his presence would make a good school out of a woodshed.

But Sally gets more than book learning out of going to school in Upton. She gets, for the first time in her life, the sense of being a member in a community. This is a thing more easily acquired in a small town than in a large one, and it's very important to feel, I believe, that you are a member of a whole. There's time enough, later, to be an individual. Later, when she gets out into the world, she will be "different" because she went to a rural school. It will make a good story. It will set her apart. We all want something to set us apart from the rest, to make us interest-

Rufus' First Picture.
Jonesy, the Crew's Cook,
Holding Him

Rollo, the Skunk, in the
Background with Rufus
and Two of the Pups

ing. It doesn't have to be very much. I, myself, derive a great deal of satisfaction from the fact that I'm the only person I ever encountered who grew up in a family where they had family prayers every morning after breakfast. My sister and I are probably the only people in the world who grew up in a household where the immutable winter Sunday morning breakfast was oyster stew. Ralph says now that he wishes that on the night of Rufus' birth he'd thought to move me out into his work shop. It couldn't have been any colder than the bedroom was, and Rufus might then have had the distinction of being the last American child to be born in a log cabin. Not that it would have made any difference—unless he wants to run for the Presidency of the United States some time, which God forbid—but it would have been something to talk about. That's what I mean.

So Sally, some night in the future when she's sitting in the Stork Club all done up in gold lamé—also God forbid—can smile reminiscently and say, "You know, I got my education in a rural school in the backwoods of Maine." I think the effect will be very piquant.

Right now, though, she's having too much fun to worry about being different. She belongs to the 4H Club, and goes to church and teaches a Sunday School class of infants, and has a boy-friend. In fact, she has a different one every time we see her, practically, which makes it nice. If she stuck to one I'd probably think I had to worry about its being serious. In short, she's living the usual life of a small town American girl, only she's getting a lot more out of it than most small town girls do. She's been around enough to value it at its true worth.

Probably I ought to be able to draw some valuable deductions and conclusions from my special set of circumstances in regard to the problem of child-raising. I'm sorry to say that I can't. The only conclusion that I've come to is pretty general and pretty trite. All any parent can do is to stagger along as best he is able, and trust to luck.

VI

"What Do You Do With All Your Spare Time?"

THIS IS WHAT I CAN'T DECIDE:—WHETHER I DON'T HAVE ANY spare time at all, or whether most of my time is spare time. Spare time, as I used to understand it, was the time left over from doing the necessary, unpleasant things, like correcting Sophomore English themes or washing out silk stockings in the bathroom. It was the time I frittered away on useless, entertaining pursuits, like the movies or contract bridge. Now almost everything I do—except cooking—is fun, and it is also useful. There is no line of demarcation between work and play. It makes it hard to explain what I do with my spare time.

Take the matter of smelting, for example. I happen to be among those who consider going smelting a form of sport. Gerrish agrees with me, but Ralph thinks it's hard work. Therefore, since someone has to stay home and mind the fires, he's the one to do it, while Gerrish and I sally forth into the night.

Smelts are not, unfortunately, the most co-operative of

fish. In this country they're about the size of average sardines—the Norwegian kind—and normally they live deep in the lakes, where you never see them. In the spring, however, after the ice is out of the brooks but before the lakes break up, they run up into the brook mouths to spawn. We stand on the bank with dip nets, dip them out into pails, take them home, and eat them. The hitch—and never let anyone tell you that Nature hands over anything without a string attached—is that they don't start running until after dark, and they're extremely coy about the whole thing. You can never tell what night or what time of night they'll pick to run, so you have to be there every night.

We do our smelting at the Head of the Pond, where the upper river empties into it. That's almost two miles from the house, and of course the road is deep in soggy snow at that time of year, so we have to walk. Right after supper Gerrish and I start out, leaving the dishes for Ralph to do, because if we are going to get there before dark, so that we can collect fuel for a fire to keep warm by, we've got no time to waste. It wouldn't be so bad if we had only ourselves to consider, but we have to take lanterns and buckets and nets—fine-meshed dip nets attached to long handles. The walking is terrible, the kind of walking where you can go along fine for a few steps on an old snowshoe float, and then you sink in suddenly to your knees. It's much harder and more nerve-racking than just plain wallowing to your waist at every step, but if you leave the road and start wading in the soft snow at the side, you find there is a foot of running ice water underlying it, and that your boots aren't quite a foot high. It's a most disconcerting discovery to make.

After a while, though, we get there, coming out of the

gloom of the path through the pines onto the shore of the Pond. The snow has shrunk back from the water, here where the sun can reach, and the ice has receded beneath the insistent attack of the current from the river. We stand on bare gray rocks and look out over an open stretch of fretted gray water to the dirty white line of the ice pack. All the delicate and subtle coloring that is a part of the winter landscape—the faded gold of dead grass heads, the fine red lines of the stems of low bushes, the orange of a fungus on a stump, the lavender of distance—has been drained away by the dusk that lies on the surface of the Pond and the darkness that lurks in the enfolding hills. There is nothing at all to be seen but gray—a hundred different tones of gray, from not-quite-white to almost-black. It's dreary and desolate and lonely, and I love it.

In the middle of the river is a little, low, rocky, scrub-covered island, and that is the best place to establish our base, because from it we can cover both channels. We take our impedimenta across, leaping precariously from rock to rock, and then start collecting a pile of firewood. The fire started, we sit down close to it, shivering a little in the penetrating wind that blows across the ice, and talk for an hour or so, while we wait for full dark. The flames leap up, staining the black water crimson. The river gurgles over a reef of gravel with a soft, incessant chattering sound. Off in the open water toward the ice pack a loon, the first of the year, raises its dismal, wailing hoot. A fox barks back in the woods. Finally we light our lanterns and go down to peer into the water.

If luck is against us we see just the clear water, deceptively shallow in the lantern light, running swiftly over the clean stones. We blow out the lanterns and go back to the fire to wait a while, not really expecting that things will be different in half an hour, but because, since we're there, we might as well make sure that tonight is not the night. Our initial opinion that there's no sense in hanging around usually proves to have been correct, so we leave our paraphernalia under a bush and go home. That's one nice thing about living in the woods. You can leave anything anywhere, for any length of time, and be sure of finding it when you come back to it.

But if luck is with us we see the smelts running up against the current, millions and millions of them, like a long black snake, and the fun begins. We scoop frantically, and the fish that were black in the water turn to living silver as we lift them out, struggling in the nets. Water streams from them like silver fire in the unsteady light of the lanterns, and we call back and forth to each other, "Come over here! There's millions of them—" or "How're you doing over there?" We get excited and careless, and misjudge the depth of the water, so that our boots are soon full. But it doesn't make any difference. The pails are filling, too, and the smelts are running thicker than ever. Gerrish freezes suddenly, like a dog going into a point. "Gosh, I think I heard a salmon jump! Let's come over here early tomorrow night and bring our rods." I agree. Suddenly I don't see how I can wait until even tomorrow to feel a three-pound salmon fighting on the other end of a line.

The pails are full. We put out the fire, leave the nets and one of the lanterns, and start home. It is inky black in the woods, and sooner or later, usually sooner, whichever is carrying the remaining lantern falls down and breaks the chimney. Then we flounder around an interminable time, running into trees, falling down and spilling the smelts, gathering them up by the light of matches—until the matches give out—and listening to the loons laugh with a laughter that suddenly has an extremely personal note to it. Eventually, we see the lights of home, and stagger in, exhausted.

Why is this so much fun? I don't know. It just is, if you happen to like it. Even if you don't, it's worth while to go smelting. After the winter's diet, the first fresh fish of the year taste wonderful. Gerrish and Ralph clean them for me, cutting the heads off and slitting the bellies, and I dip them in a thin batter and fry them in deep fat until they're brown and crisp. They look like French-fried potatoes, and served with lemon juice or tartar sauce, taste like manna. We have them every day during the brief fortnight they are running.

The very last time that we go, Gerrish and I always bring home twenty or thirty live ones in a pail of water. These we dump into the wangan spring hole as we go by, to save as bait when we go trolling at B Pond. They'll live there indefinitely, I guess. I've never had a chance to find out. Most of them escape down the brook before very long.

Along about smelting time is usually sugaring-off time, too, and this I don't particularly relish. I like the new maple syrup all right, and I don't have to do any of the work. Ralph and Gerrish tap the trees, going back into the woods across the road on snowshoes, and carrying the pails and spiles by the armload. It takes them about all one morning to get the tapping done. Then one or the other of them goes out morning and evening with two buckets on a shoulder yoke, and brings in the sap. In good years we make enough syrup to last us through the whole twelve months. It's good syrup, too—heavy in weight and delicate in flavor.

Good sap weather is clear weather in which the temperature during the day rises to above fifty and drops well below freezing at night. The sap is supposed to be drawn by the warmth and sun up into the branches daily, and driven by the cold back into the roots at dark. I say *supposed,* because this is the old country-man's explanation of it, and I've gone through life discovering that, no matter how reasonable these homely bits of scientific data sound, often they are completely wrong, and the real explanation is something involved and improbable. That may not be the case here. I don't know anything about it. I'm just protecting myself.

Our equipment is mostly homemade. Some of the spiles are just wooden spouts that Gerrish and Ralph have whittled out by hand. They are driven into the holes bored into the south side of the tree trunks, and the sap drips through them into the pails which are hung beneath. These are simply No. 10 tin cans in which we have bought fruit or vegetables, with covers roughly fitted to them to keep out rain and snow. The rain and snow doesn't do any harm, but it makes that much more water to evaporate before we have syrup. Our evaporating pans are a series of large shallow cookie pans, which we put on the kitchen stove top. They're the reason why I don't like the sugaring-off season. Every time I want to put a stick of wood in the stove, or toast a slice of bread, or heat a flat iron, or fry an egg, I have to move one of those damn syrup pans. If I hang up a pair of mittens over the stove to dry, the chances are that sooner or later they'll fall into a syrup pan.

Briefly, the whole thing is a nuisance, and before we're through, I wish to Heaven I'd never heard of maple syrup.

It's nice to eat, though, on griddle cakes, for supper. Sometimes we boil it down a little more, beyond the aproning consistency which is the standard weight for syrup—syrup is said to apron when it runs off the side of a spoon in a solid sheet, or apron, instead of in rivulets—and pour it hot onto dishes of snow. It congeals as it cools to a thick gumminess, and is wonderful to chew on. It's fun to give it to Kyak for he loves its sweetness so, but at the same time gets his jaws all stuck up, to our great amusement. This over-cooked syrup makes a marvellous sauce for vanilla ice-cream, too. A common country dessert that we sometimes have is fresh raised doughnuts and hot, new syrup. Each member of the family has a cereal dish of syrup, and dips the doughnut into it as he eats. This is not very elegant, but it's very good. Lots of people have hot baking-powder biscuit with butter and new syrup for breakfast, during the syrup season, instead of the more conventional griddle cakes and syrup. Probably this is good, too. I wouldn't know. I have trouble enough getting breakfast on the table without going into hot baking-powder biscuits.

I know one man who drinks a full cup of new syrup every night before he goes to bed, for its medicinal properties. He says it accomplishes the same thing as sulphur and molasses, but a lot more pleasantly. That may be so. I know that all over the countryside here, woodsmen and farmers and trappers drink maple sap out of the pails at the trees. They seem to have a craving for it, which isn't accounted for by its taste. It hasn't much more taste than spring water; it has only what I can best describe as a green feeling in the mouth. I believe, therefore, that it is a natural spring tonic which supplies minerals or vitamins or some other elements that have been lacking in ordinary country winter diet. I can't see, otherwise, why men who usually drink no more than four or five glasses of water a day suddenly take to drinking two or three quarts of maple sap.

To complicate matters in the spring, our semi-annual moving day rolls around. My mother always says that two movings are as good as a fire, when it comes to eliminating unnecessary possessions, and she's about right. All the things that have been collecting in the winter house against a sudden unforeseen need—the leaky gum-boots, the nests of cardboard boxes, the crop ends of boards, the links of chain, and the broken toys—I suddenly see in their true colors, and take them down to the dump. Of course Ralph and Gerrish and Rufus trail me like a pack of hounds and salvage most of the trash, uttering outraged cries of horror at my vandalism, but I manage to accomplish a little thinning out. To take care of the remaining worthless treasures—and of what use is a felt hat with four holes in the crown and no brim to speak of, or a piece of rubber belting six inches square?—I have instituted in the kitchen what is known as the culch corner. This is a sort of exterritorial ground for junk. Anything that's been put in the culch corner—a wide corner shelf with a box on it—I can't touch, much as my fingers may itch to pitch it out. There's everything there—old bolts, old wrought-iron cut nails, bits of unrelated metal, old wool, wiping rags, coffee cans, broken hack saw blades, a divorced work glove or two, parts of a dog team harness, lengths of fish line, a coil or two of synthetic gut leaders (known woodswise as "sympathetic gut"), and some odd wooden wedges. It's a mess, but it's better to have this one big mess in the corner of the kitchen than a patina of messiness spread all over the house. I didn't, by the way, name the culch corner. Culch is the New England word for that clutter of partly worn out or obsolete objects that always gathers, like moss, on a non-rolling household. I don't know who first used the term culch corner, but it stuck. Now we all call it that.

It's nice to be down in the summer house again. There's more space to move around in, and the river is nearer and louder. We wake up in the night and hear it, and for a night or two mistake it for the sound of wind and rain. But real rain is different. It starts slowly, with individual drops striking the roof only three feet over our heads, in an almost ceremonial roulade. Then it comes faster and faster, with the full symphonic orchestration of rising wind in the trees and the river's roar. The walls of the summer house are not ceiled like those of the winter house, and the storm seems much nearer to us when we're living down there. Paradoxically, this makes us feel that much warmer, and safer, and more protected.

There's always one thing I forget on moving day. We manage to shift all the favorite chairs, and the lamps, and the radio, and the typewriters, and footstools, and personal belongings, and ash trays. But come bed-time, Ralph always says, "Where's my sleeping hat?" He thinks his head gets cold at night without it, although he goes around bareheaded all day. It's always in the same place—hanging on the head of the bed in the winter house bedroom. Sometime I'm going to establish a record and remember it—unless he establishes the same record first.

As spring moves into summer, the berries start getting

ripe. All through the woods, wherever there is enough of a clearing to let the sun in, acres and acres of raspberries and blueberries come into fruit. I never can quite believe that this dour and grudging country has suddenly suffered such a complete reversal of form. This princely generosity seems just too good to be true. I feel we must go berrying right now, right this minute, before all the berries vanish again.

Ralph loathes picking berries. I used to try to sell him on the idea that since for once we were getting something for free, it was his *duty*— But my wifely pep-talks never raised his enthusiasm above a Laodicean luke-warmness, which started cooling the first time he tripped and stretched his six-feet-two in a bramble patch, and from then on declined rapidly to absolute zero. So I gave up. He just isn't the type. Fortunately, Gerrish is the type.

Gerrish always refers to me as She, just as he always refers to Ralph as The Boss. He'll say to Ralph, "She claims She wants to go ras'berryin' t'morrer mornin', so if you ain't got nothin' special in mind—"

Ralph never has. He's only too thankful that I don't try to enlist him.

To get to the best raspberry patch, we have to take a boat and row about a mile across the Pond to where the dead stub of an old "punkin" pine stands on a ridge, dwarfing with its towering height the by no means insignificant growth along the shore. From the boat, the shore line is an unbroken wall of forest, but we know that if we land near a maple a little to the left of the stub, and scrambled up a steep, spruce-covered slope to the foot of the pumpkin pine, we'll come out into an old, overgrown birch cutting. Here the raspberries grow on tall rank canes among the rocks and fallen trees and rotten birch tops and around clumps of young spruce and fir. It is a quiet place, sheltered from the wind, and when we arrive there early in the morning, it is wet with dew and laced with long shadows from the surrounding forest. It is cool and full of the stir of birds and the scoldings of red squirrels and little striped chipmunks. That's why we always go there early. Later, when the sun is high, the place is like a furnace, breathless and so hot that even the birds and squirrels retire to the shade of the woods. It is silent then, and dead, except for the hum of insects; but the heat and stillness account for the size and quality of the berries. If you stand still and listen, you can almost hear them grow, swelling and stretching as the rich red juice fills them.

The minute we get into the clearing, I find that I am alone. Gerrish has vanished. I hear a dry stick snap somewhere, but the bushes are so high I can't see him. It would be useless to call. He wouldn't answer. Like me, when he goes berrying, he wants to berry, not stand around doing what he calls "jawrin'." When his pail is full, he'll whistle and I'll go down and meet him at the boat. My pail will lack a half an inch of being full. Gerrish takes a proper pride in being the best and fastest picker he ever saw, and there's nothing I can do about it, try as I will.

The raspberries hang on the underside of the canes, glowing like jewels against the green of the leaves. They are dead ripe, and will drop off at the lightest touch. Raspberries are the most care-demanding of all berries to pick. They mash easily, so they must be handled lightly. Even setting the pail down too often and too hard will result in a shapeless mush in the bottom. That's why Gerrish and

I suspend our pails from our belts; thus we'll have both hands free to pick and avoid constant jarring of the berries. The canes have to be lifted delicately. It's infuriating to raise one and have all the fruit tumble off to be lost among the rocks and debris on the ground.

I don't know where Gerrish goes after he shakes me. I keep away from the south side of the cutting. That is, by tacit consent, his stamping ground. I don't even know what's over there. I have my own beat to patrol, working slowly up a vague remnant of hauling road near the middle of the clearing to the top of the ridge, and coming back down along the edge of the woods on the north side. At the top of the loop the earth is thin and shallow and the bushes aren't very big or productive, but I always go there just the same. There is an outcropping of ledge there, gray and weathered and warm with sun under the hand. I love stone. I won't try to explain why, because I don't know. But everybody loves the feel and quality and essence of some material. It may be leather, or wood, or fine porcelain. It may be satin or bronze or tweed. Whatever it is, there is almost a spiritual kinship between that substance and that person. That's the way I feel about stone, and that's why I always go up to the top of the raspberry patch.

We're not the only ones that pick berries. The birds eat them, of course, and the foxes. Bears love them. One day I followed in the path of a bear down my north side of the cut. I could see by the bent bushes where he'd been ambling happily along, stripping the canes as he went, minding his own business and thinking his own thoughts, even as I was doing. Suddenly I came to a place that looked as though a tornado had hit it. The undergrowth was all flattened out, the ground was torn up, and a couple of saplings were broken off. Right smack in the middle of the devastation, dangling from a low branch, was what was left of a big hornets' nest, gutted and destroyed by one furious sweep of a huge paw. The poor old cuss had evidently been attacked by a squadron of dive bombers before he knew what it was all about. I could see where he had started for the Pond. He certainly hadn't stood on the order of his going either. Every jump must have been ten feet long. I'd like to have seen him, clearing rocks and bushes and fallen trees like a bird on the wing. There, but for the Grace of God, might have gone Louise Rich. Well, better him than me. I have only two legs, and it would have broken my heart to have had to jettison a pail half full of raspberries.

On the way back across the Pond, I always think about the delicious jam and preserves I'm going to make out of our twelve or fifteen quarts of berries. This is purely mental exercise, but it makes me feel smug and thrifty, and I might as well enjoy the feeling while I can. In our family everybody, even the dog, will eat raspberries until their eyes pop, so there aren't ever enough left after twenty-four hours to do anything fancy with. I do, though, usually manage to squeeze out a couple of pies, making a special effort to have the crust flaky and sprinkling flour over the berries lightly before baking to prevent the juices all stewing out. Too much flour is bad. It takes all the juice up. With the remnants of crust I make turn-overs for between-meal snacks. If the weather is sultry and the berries start to mold, I stew them up with sugar for supper-sauce, to be eaten with cake or cookies. Then if there are still some left, I make jam, to be put away against the winter.

There is really only one dessert to be made out of raspberries, when there aren't enough to go around. This is a sort of cooked up-side-down shortcake. In the bottom of a cake pan I melt a little butter, add about a half a cup of sugar, and a cup or two of raspberries—whatever I have left after saving out a cupful. Then I mix up a good short biscuit dough, using two cups of flour, four teaspoons of baking powder, a generous third of a cup of shortening and a half a cup of milk. This I roll out about a half an inch thick, cover with the raspberries I've held out and some more sugar, roll up into a jelly roll, and slice into inch slices, which I put cut-side-down in the pan. I bake in a hot oven and serve hot with milk or cream and the hot cooked berries from the bottom of the pan. It's nothing, really, to write home about, but it accomplishes its purpose, which is to keep the family from hollering too loudly and long about the inferior desserts that are being handed out to them recently.

Blueberries are more common and therefore much less highly esteemed than raspberries. We don't have to go on any boat trips to get plenty of blueberries. They grow all along the Carry Road, and in a half an hour I can pick enough for a couple of pies, some blueberry muffins, and a little spiced blueberry jam. The only trick about pies is to add a little salt and lemon juice to the berries to give them zip. Blueberries are apt to be flat. The only trick about blueberry muffins is to roll the berries in flour so they won't sink in a sodden mass to the bottom of the batter. Blueberry jam is easy to make. Add sugar to the blueberries, pound for pound, and boil until the mixture starts to thicken. Then add cinnamon, nutmeg, and allspice—a pinch of each to the pound—and pour into glasses.

It jellies readily—I think there must be a lot of natural pectin in blueberries—and is good with hot or cold roasts and fowl.

There are plenty of other things to do, too, to fill in spare time. Before the ice goes out all the boats and the canoe have to be overhauled and painted. Usually one or more of the boats has sprung a leak somewhere and we have to find out just where and repair it. Usually, too, someone during the preceding season—probably I—has left a boat improperly secured on a windward shore, and it has chafed badly on the rocks. This rough spot has to be sandpapered smooth and oiled before the painting can begin. Any broken thwarts and gunwales have to be mended, and missing irons replaced and oarlocks repaired. Anchor ropes have to be examined for frayed places, and Ralph's trick anchor control gadgets have to be gone over to see that they are in working order. These rigs, which he invented and made himself, are very clever. The rope feeds over a pulley wheel in a bracket bolted on the bow and back through a special casting attached to the rower's seat, which allows the rope to be locked anywhere by a cam lever. If you're handling a boat alone in a current, jockeying for the right fly-casting position, it's a great advantage to be able to drop your anchor without leaving the seat or missing a stroke. It's also a great advantage, when you have somehow become involved with a six-pound salmon who is either going to break your rod or run your line all out unless you do something and do it fast, to be able to up-anchor without putting your rod down.

I like to paint boats. Ours are all painted the same, like our houses, which are a soft Nile green with buff doors and window sashes. Our boats are green outside and buff inside. The basic principle—to put on several thin coats instead of one thick coat—applies to boats as well as to any other paint job, and you have to be careful not to let drops form along the edges of the strakes. But after a while you can paint automatically and let your mind wander where it will. It's sunny and sheltered down on the boat float, and it's a nice place to be in the early spring. The birches along the shore of the Pond are beginning to show the faint and tender green that is so different from the black-green of the conifers, and the maples are blossoming red. The water, in the patches where the ice has gone out, is a deep indigo blue, and the ice pack in the distance is a line of snowy white. The wind smells of spring.

Ralph spends the before-break-up period, which is also the period when the road is hub deep in mud and therefore impassable for anything but foot traffic, in overhauling the cars. This I won't attempt to go into. I don't know anything about it, except that it involves lying in mud and dirt under the cars, and coming into the house with simply filthy hands, and moving my potatoes to the back of the stove, where they stop boiling, so that some motor part or can of oil can have the place of honor. It also involves dozens of trial runs around the loop of the driveway, and a great deal of breathless listening to what sounds, to my untutored ear, like a perfect performance, and then a flood of language and another taking down of the motor to locate the seat of a murmur that may some day develop into a bad chest cough. It's a very trying period for everyone except Rufus, who crawls under the cars right along with his father, and sticks his nose into gudgeon grease, and gets his clothes plastered with mud and oil, and has a wonderful time.

About two years ago Gerrish and I took up fly tying. There were several reasons for this. We thought it would be nice to have a hobby for our evenings, for one thing. For another, flies are expensive to buy if you fish as much as we do. We're always losing flies, or having them ruined by a big fish, and it's always the fifty-cent types that meet with grief. It runs into money in the course of a season. Besides that, it was getting embarrassing for us to have to look respectful when city sports said, "Oh, of course I tie all my own flies!" as though that were a feat beyond such inept souls as we. So we took up fly tying.

I, myself, didn't intend to become a slave to the habit. I thought I'd just dabble in it, but it didn't work out that way. We were too proud to ask anyone how to go about tying flies, so we got ourselves a book of instructions and a batch of feathers and set out to teach ourselves. Gerrish gave me fair warning before we started that he couldn't learn things from books. He had to be shown; but if he could just see someone actually *do* a thing once, then he could do it all right the next time. I can follow printed directions fairly well, so the idea was that I would follow the book and Gerrish would follow me, and in that way we'd both learn. We both did, but what started out as a hobby became almost an obsession, especially with Gerrish. He's a rabid fly tyer now, and I might add, a very good one. He makes a much better fly than I do, for all that his hands are bigger and look clumsier than mine. The heads of his flies are small and smooth, while mine sometimes get beyond me and turn out large and rough. That's where the amateur betrays himself.

We thought at first that we'd be satisfied if we could make a few streamers and some of the simpler stock patterns of wet flies. We weren't going into anything complicated. We weren't even going to consider tying dry flies. We knew our own limitations. Neither of us was going to invest a lot of money in equipment. Ralph had a small vise he'd lend us, and I had nail scissors and some odds and ends of embroidery silk and yarn for bodies. There was plenty of black thread around the house, and some silver and gold string left over from Christmas wrappings, and Ralph had some beeswax in his sailmaker's outfit. He also had shellac, and we could probably find plenty of feathers and fur around the woods. All we'd have to buy was two or three dozen hooks and maybe a few feathers not indigenous to this soil, such as jungle cocks for eyes. We wouldn't have to spend more than fifty cents, all told. That's what we thought, at first.

That state of mind lasted about a month. During that month we saw everything in the light of possible fly-tying material. We brought home dead birds, and the tails of deceased flying squirrels we found, and quills out of other people's feather dusters. We clipped stiff fur from Kyak to make buck tails, and went hunting with my .22 revolver for red squirrels. (We never managed to get one.) We hounded chance acquaintances from Upton to bring us in hen feathers and hackle feathers from roosters the next time they came. And we tied up enough Plymouth Rock streamers to last us a lifetime. We had plenty of Plymouth Rock feathers, you see. Then we faced the truth. The bug had got us. We'd have to buy some more equipment—not very much, of course; just a few necessary things. After all, this was partly an economy measure. We'd just spend a dollar or two.

Last spring our feather bill was over fifteen dollars. We'd already spent five or six dollars on special scissors, a pair of hackle pliers, a bottle of head varnish, a special wax preparation, and a box of assorted hooks. Heaven knows what our bill would have been if some friends hadn't presented us with a fly-tying vise. That's what fly tying can do to you. It can make you lose all sense of proportion. We even lost our pride. When a professional fly tyer, Frank Walker, of Oxford, Maine, came to stay at Millers' that summer and offered to show us a few tricks of the trade, we forgot all about our lofty ideas of independence, and spent all one Sunday afternoon with him. He's an old man, and he's tied thousands of flies, over the course of years. He's found short cuts and practical methods that the books never dreamed of, and that it would have taken us twenty years to dope out for ourselves. And even if I never intended to tie a fly in my life, I would have enjoyed watching him work. It was really something to see him tie a Black Gnat on a No. 14 hook, with his big hands, a little stiff from rheumatism, moving slowly and delicately and surely around the almost invisible little object in the vise. Great skill and competence in any line is always impressive.

It's hard to tell exactly where the great fascination of tying flies lies. Of course, there is the satisfaction in creative work. It's fun to take a pile of raw materials and make something out of them. The more demanding the work, the greater is the satisfaction. It's fun to finish shellacking the head of a fly, hold it up, and be able to think,

"There! I'll bet nobody could tell that from a bought fly!" You feel so pleased with yourself.

But that's only the beginning. People are easy to fool. The real test comes when you try the fly out on a fish. If you can catch a fish on a fly you tied yourself, then you can commence to regard yourself as a fly tyer. Still, there are always a few fool fish about that will rise to anything, so it's better to get several strikes on the fly before you indulge in too much own-back patting. But that isn't the end, either. Pretty soon you start regarding the copying of the proven, standard patterns as mere tyro's work. Anybody can copy a fly, you think. Most people know the Yellow May is good at this time of year in these waters. So there's nothing remarkable about catching a good fish on a Yellow May, no matter who tied it. Now if YOU could think up a new pattern that would catch fish, that would really be something.

So you start watching the fish. Tonight they're rising to some silvery gray little bugs that are flying up the river. If you could tie a fly that looked something like that, with perhaps a touch of yellow in the body— You reel in and go home. By working fast, you can get it done in time to try it out before dark. Perhaps it won't catch fish. All right; maybe if you used a little tinsel in the tail— There's no end to it, as you can see. And there's no feeling quite like the lift you get when eventually you hit on the right combination, and a walloping big trout comes surging up out of the shadows and grabs your very own fly, the fly you conceived and executed all by yourself.

One of the things that always surprises people who visit us, anticipating, prepared for, or resigned to—according to their various natures—a period of total quiet, is the number of excursions and alarums which preclude any chance of monotony. Something is always cropping up, and you never know when you get up in the morning what will have happened before you go to bed at night. It may be nothing more momentous than a visit from the game or the fire warden, but they always have something of interest to offer.

Our fire warden lives with his wife and dog on Pine Island at the upper end of the Narrows between the two Richardson Lakes, and he and Ralph are kindred souls. They both collect junk. Fortunately, where Ralph collects car motors, Amby Hines collects motor boat parts, so they don't chisel in on each other's rackets. I haven't been up at Pine Island lately, but I gather that Amby is running into the same trouble that Ralph is—not enough space to store his loot and a wife that objects to having to clamber over a pile of cold metal when she gets out of bed in the morning. She won't let him make a junk pile out of her boudoir. (I won't let Ralph, either, but he does, just the same.) Amby is really in a worse position than Ralph. The Island isn't very big, and he's used up about all the available space. He's loath to start a boat motor dump on the mainland. "They'll rob 'em off me," he explains matter-of-factly.

The last time he was down, he was having trouble with his dog, a young terrier, who had not yet encountered a porcupine. Amby thought, quite rightly, that the sooner the pup got that over with and learned better, the happier they'd all be; but there weren't any porcupines on the Island. However, while patrolling his beat down the Lower Richardson, he stopped in at Spirit Island, where a group of boys were camping, and found that they'd caught a porcupine and had it in a box. It is against the law to confine a wild animal without official permission, although ordinarily Amby wouldn't have bothered about a porcupine, because he knows that whenever it got ready a porcupine could gnaw its way in half an hour out of any box ever made. This time, however, he needed it himself, so he confiscated it and took it home in a water pail.

When he got to the Island he turned it loose and called his dog. Porcupines are slow and clumsy, but nevertheless it managed to scramble up a tall pine before the dog caught up with it, which is probably just as well for the dog. This was about four o'clock in the afternoon, and the dog sat at the foot of the tree and howled until half past three the next morning, ignoring all commands to come into the house and forget it, and completely shattering any ideas of sleep that the Hineses might have been entertaining. At half past three the dog called it a day and retired under the porch to rest. As soon as the coast was clear, the porcupine came down, swam to the mainland, and vanished. Amby was discouraged when he stopped at our house. He had to start his porcupine hunt all over again, and this time he wasn't going to be lucky enough to find one all crated for him.

A fire warden has to work hard. He has an area to patrol, and he has to see that no one builds a fire within that area, except at State-designated camp grounds. You just can't go into the woods and camp anywhere, for obvious reasons of safety. Then if there is a lumbering operation going on, he has to manage to show up in the slashes, unheralded and ghost-like, often enough to deter the men from smoking in the woods. This involves a lot of walking in the course of a week, and lots of patrolling around the lakes in a kicker boat. If a forest fire starts in his territory, he has to organize the fighters, and if it's in someone else's territory, he has to go over there and help. He has to co-operate with the game warden in seeing that the game laws are observed, although naturally this is a reciprocal arrangement, and he can call on the game warden for help whenever he needs it. If someone gets lost, they both have to join the search, along with whatever talent they can scrape up around the countryside. But the really rush period in a fire warden's life comes when the State does what is colloquially known as "slap a band on the woods."

The band is slapped on whenever there is a protracted drought, and the woods are consequently tinder-dry. Actually the Governor proclaims that the woods are closed to hunters, fishermen, campers, and any other unauthorized persons; in other words, it *bans* use of the forest areas, and forbids building of fires or smoking by anyone whatsoever. The fire warden is like a cat on a hot griddle when a "band" is on. He has to be everywhere at once, telling people to leave the woods immediately, and riding herd on legitimate occupants like us, who belong there, and on himself. Neither he nor we want a forest fire—he, because it's his business not to have one, and we because we naturally don't want to burn up. But you'd be surprised how easy it is, if you are an habitual smoker, suddenly to find yourself in the middle of a dangerous area with a half-smoked cigarette in your hand and no recollection at all of having lighted it. We just stop carrying smoking materials when a "band" is on, and so does the warden. If you haven't got them, you can't smoke them. The result is that every now and then he appears at our door with the announcement, "My tongue's hanging out for a smoke. Mind if I bum a cigarette and come inside and smoke it?" It's all right to smoke in the house during a "band."

Our game warden, in spite of the fact that he is a respectable married man with four children—including a pair of twins—looks like the scenario writer's dream of the perfect Northwestern Mountie. He wears his uniform with style—he's got the right build for a uniform, with wide shoulders and slim hips—and he walks with a sort of cat-footed swagger. His face is lean and handsome and dark, and he has a tough and reckless air about him. I guess he is tough, if he wants to be. Fortunately, we keep on excellent terms with him, simply by observing the game laws. I don't want to sound holy and smug about this, but we do make a point of not breaking them, because we believe in them. In fact we believe some of them are not rigid enough. They are necessary laws and if we weren't convinced that this is so, we'd probably be the worst poachers in the county.

We always ask the game warden how business is, and often he has an unusual arrest to tell us about. He tells a story well. A recent adventure happened over on the other side of his territory. He was up on a mountain patrolling a closed brook when he came on a boy fishing with his pockets crammed with short trout, about twenty of them. Naturally, he took the offender into custody and led him down the mountain to where his car was parked by the road. But he saw no reason why he should carry the four or five pounds of illegal fish over the rough trail. Let the guilty party do it. The guilty party had other ideas, however, and managed to put them into effect. By the time they had reached the road, he had surreptitiously got rid of the evidence, dropping the little fish quietly at intervals along the trail. So there was our Mr. Leon Wilson with a prisoner, but with no evidence and no case. He was pretty mad about the whole thing.

But not for long. Presently the boy's father came out of the woods, having apparently been just behind them all the way down, all ignorant of his son's arrest. He didn't notice the bad company his son was keeping. (By most people around here, a game warden is generally considered about the worst company to be found in.) "Hey, Bud," he hailed. "You must have a hole in your pocket. I been picking up your fish along the trail for the last couple of miles!" He had the missing illegal fish in his creel.

Ho-hum! Possession is all that needs to be proved against you, according to the law. It didn't make any difference to Leon whom he pinched. Both of them knew better.

We used to set our guests to work helping pull porcupine quills out of the dogs. This was when we had five dogs, and ideas about a dog team. They didn't work out. In the first place, it cost more to feed five huskies than to feed the whole Rich tribe. In the second place, we were always in hot water with those darn dogs. Either they'd get loose and chase game, or else they'd scare people going along the road—the dogs were perfectly harmless, but some people are timid—or they'd tear the wash off the line and chew it up. And one or the other of them was always coming in full of porcupine quills. They always chose the most inconvenient times for these forays into the sporting life, and you can't postpone a de-quilling operation. The longer you wait, the deeper the quills work in, until you can't get them out at all. This won't necessarily prove fatal, as often they fester and eventually come out by themselves, after a week or so. But if you love your dog—and we loved each and every one of that wolf pack of ours—you can't stand seeing him suffer. So we've delayed dinner three hours on occasion, to pull quills. We've even arisen at one o'clock in the morning and worked until daylight, with me sitting on a dog's head in my nightgown, while Ralph wielded the plyers.

We don't have that trouble any more. Thor we had to shoot, because he tried to swallow a porcupine. Cookie, the dearest and smartest dog that ever lived, was struck by lightning. Metak and Mukluk we finally had to give away. It doesn't take long to write those four lines, but every word of them represents heartbreak. We loved the big bums, even if they did keep us in a continuous turmoil. Now we only have Kyak, the art dog, left. Kyak's stupidity doesn't extend to sticking his own neck out. He ran afoul of a porcupine just once, when he was very young. A great many dogs never learn to leave them alone, but will go through the agonizing experience of quills weekly until the day of their death. Not so Kyak. He'll look, but he's never touched one since that long ago disaster.

I have referred to the dogs and a dog team and I suppose I'd better clear up the matter once and for all. We thought at one time it would be a good idea to have a dog team. In this country the cars go out of use after the deep snows come, there being no possible way of keeping the road open, and that means that every pound of mail and food and material must either be carried on someone's back, or dragged on a hand sled, the two long, hilly miles from Middle Dam to here. And that's no fun. It's really mysterious how a reasonable load of groceries can multiply its weight so enormously in the time it takes to walk it two miles.

The second winter that we lived here, in the middle of February—a very well chosen time, since we were just about fed to the teeth with lugging things on our backs—Stumpy Crocker and Norman Vaughn came in to see us, and they came from below South Arm by dog team. Norman had been a dog driver on Admiral Byrd's first Antarctic Expedition, and he was full of enthusiasm for this particular mode of travel. His team consisted of nine dogs. I had always been led to suppose that huskies were vicious brutes, but these nine weren't. They were sweet. Of course, they periodically fought terribly among themselves, but as far as humans were concerned, they were a bunch of softies. Ralph and I fell in love with every last one of them. Our infatuation blinded us to the fact that for three days' stay, Norman brought in over a hundred pounds of food just for the dogs, and we fell easy victims to the notion that a dog team was just what we needed and wanted most of anything in the world. This notion was clinched after Norman had ridden us up to Middle a couple of times. It was marvellous just to sit and be whisked up Wangan Hill. Besides, we didn't really need nine dogs, Norman assured us. Five would be plenty.

So when, the next spring, Stumpy offered us a husky pup, offspring of one of Norman's team, we accepted with alacrity. That was Cookie. From the same source the Millers acquired another husky, Karlok—he was an albino, and one of the most beautiful dogs I have ever seen—so what could be more natural than a match between them when they grew up? The final result was a litter of four pups, of which Kyak was one. And there was our dog team in embryo. Nothing could have been simpler.

The pups grew. Norman had told us that when they were about half grown was the time to start training them; so when they were five or six months old, we put them in harness. He had said nothing, though, about the desirability of having an experienced dog with them to show them the ropes. So we just hitched them up and told them to mush. Cookie looked at us in amazement. This was a new game, and one she wasn't sure she liked. Kyak lay down on his back and went limp, his legs like boiled macaroni. Nothing we could do would get him onto his feet. Every time we stood him up he just collapsed. Metak and Richard just stood and shivered. Only Mukluk got the idea, and he very soon became bored with pulling not only the light sled we had, but all his relations as well. He finally sat down and looked disgusted, and I didn't blame him.

We might have given up the idea then if Stumpy hadn't made a fevered telephone call from Fitchburg, where he lives. Would we give one of his dogs a home? (He was a victim of the dog team obsession at the time, too.) We wanted to know, naturally, what was the matter with the dog. People don't give valuable dogs away without any reason. It seemed that nothing was the matter with the dog except boyish high spirits. He was a wonderful dog—gentle, obedient, well-trained to harness. The only trouble was that he was a little too powerful. He'd run away with Stumpy's young son Weyman, and had frightened some saddle horses on a back road. Unfortunately the saddle horses were complete with riders, and, even more unfortunate, one of the riders was Stumpy's boss, who didn't appreciate the situation at all. Hell was about to pop unless something was done about Thor. Now we had no saddle horses up our way, so— We'd really stopped listening at the "well-trained to harness" clause. Here was the answer. Thor could be a sort of tutor to the other dogs. We said, "Yes." It seemed evident that Providence wanted us to have a dog team. No sooner did a problem arise than the solution appeared right behind it.

Thor arrived and we immediately renamed him the Hound of the Baskervilles. He was almost as big as a Shetland pony, and had a head like a basket ball. He didn't have teeth. He had fangs. He looked horrible, and he was the biggest bowl of mush I ever saw. He thought he was a lap dog, and tried to sit in my lap whenever I sat down. I just haven't got enough lap for that, so he finally compromised by sitting beside me by the hour with that huge head on my knees, gazing adoringly into my face. My legs would grow numb under the weight, and consciousness of all my shortcomings would rise to the surface under that worshipful regard. Nobody could be that wonderful, me least of all. It was very embarrassing for me. I could have stood it, though, if Thor had been a good teacher. He wasn't. He was perfectly willing to work, and the others were willing to let him. Our dog team, obviously, was going to consist of Thor and Mukluk. Kyak, instead of being shamed by this example of usefulness, just grew limper and limper. It got so that whenever he saw one of us with a harness in hand, he fainted. The dog team, as such, was getting no place fast.

On top of this, it was costing more to feed the dogs than to feed us, and we were continually deluged with complaints by a lot of damn fools about keeping dangerous animals—definitely untrue. My Monday laundry was periodically ripped from the line and torn up, and the only way to insure keeping a whole pair of shoes in the house was to hang them by the laces from the ceiling beams, where the dogs couldn't reach them. In short, we had nothing but trouble and expense in connection with those darn dogs. We were told by experts that we'd never have a dog team unless we stopped making pets of the dogs. It was all wrong to feed them twice a day and let them have the run of the house. Dogs won't work unless they are half starved and kept tied up outside, away from human association. Working dogs aren't pets; they are slaves and should be treated as such. Well! That doesn't go for us. Neither Ralph nor I could ever treat any dog like that—certainly not our own dear dogs that we loved. So we gave up the dog team idea. But we still had the dogs.

Then one by one, things began to happen to them, and, viewed cosmically, it was probably just as well, much as it hurt at the time. After every disaster I said my little say—"Here we had six dogs, and five of them were swell. We're going to end by being left with the only lemon in the bunch, just you wait and see." And so we were. Oh, well, Kyak isn't much of a dog; but he suits us. He's nice with Rufus, and we love him dearly. And that's all we want.

Lots of things crop up to entertain us and our guests. There was the time for instance that we enlivened my sister Alice's visit with a fox hunt. Don't be thinking of red coats and Irish hunters, because it wasn't like that at all. We wore our night clothes and raincoats and rode in a Model T, our sole weapon was a landing net, and while Alice and I strove to establish the right note by shouting "View halloo" and "Yoicks" at intervals, Ralph rather

PHOTO BY FRED ADAMS

The Author and Two of Her Boys

ruined the effect with his insistence upon bellowing in moments of stress, "There goes the little son of a bitch!"

You see, he'd gone up to Middle Dam late to mail an important letter, and he'd got talking. By the time he arrived back home, Alice and I had gone to bed. He came busting into the house with the news that at the foot of Birch Hill he'd seen, gamboling in the glow of his headlights, a whole litter of fox pups, apparently strayed from their den while their mother was away, and quite evidently having a time for themselves. In fact, he'd had to stop the car to keep from running over them, and when he got out to look, they'd just sat down in the road and looked right back.

"They're so tame," he concluded, "that I could have picked them right up, only I remembered in time that they bite like the devil."

This inspired Alice. "Look, why couldn't we take a landing net and a big box to put them in—" She didn't have to finish. We got the idea. Before we quite realized what we were about, we were headed up the road, complete with net, box, and flashlight. Ralph was driving, Alice was standing on one running board with the light, and I was on the other with the net. The plot was that as soon as a fox was sighted—or is "viewed" the right term? —the viewer would shout, the car would stop, and we'd all three pile off for the kill—or capture, in this case.

We saw the foxes all right. They were the cutest little articles that ever ran the woods—round and fluffy, with little pointed masked faces, up-standing ears, and wide grins. But they weren't to be caught. The moment we tried to clap the net over one, he just eased off into the darkness where the beam from our flashlight, which wasn't very good anyhow, couldn't pick him up. We spent hours riding up and down the road, shouting and laughing and jumping on and off the car, until we were exhausted. I've always doubted the English theory that the fox enjoys the hunt as much as the hunters, but I do believe these foxes did. They knew perfectly well that they were in no jeopardy whatsoever, which isn't true of a fox with a pack of hounds after him. They kept coming back into the road for more. When we finally decided that if we didn't go home we'd all get pneumonia, they were still dodging back and forth in front of the car, daring us to try to catch them. But we knew when we were licked. We went home, built up a fire, and spent the rest of the night drinking coffee and Barbados rum. (Courtesy of Alice.)

Ralph and Gerrish are forever needing a third person to lend a hand in furtherance of one of their projects, and I'm invariably elected. A plank has to be held while they saw it, or the combined weight of the two of them is just too little to push a crippled car out of the driveway, and will I please come and lean on it, too? Or they want me to hold a rock drill for them. I don't know whether they don't trust each other, or whether they figure that if someone has to get hit on the head with a sledge hammer, I can best be spared. Whatever it is, I have sat for more hours than I care to count, with a sledge whistling down past my nose as I concentrated on holding the top of the drill steady, while giving it a quarter turn between blows. I have got so I can tell by instinct just when to shout "Mud!"—when the water that has been poured into the hole has just exactly been taken up by the rock dust, and the whole works can be lifted out on the drill, leaving the hole dry and clean. Or they want me to be handy with a cant dog in case a motor they are shifting from one cradle to another starts to tip; or to block up a rock as they raise it; or take down the figures while they scale a pile of pine logs; or read a spirit level while they do the leveling. If it isn't one thing, it's another.

And, after all, I'm supposed to be a writer, so I do have to spend a little time writing. Some of the work of writing can, of course, be done concurrently with other things. You can figure out, while washing the dishes, just how to get around the difficulty of having Her discourage His suit without having Her appear to the reader just silly, and also without forcing Her to reverse Her attitude, along toward the end of the story, so completely as to seem actually feeble-minded. You see, there are certain ill-defined but nonetheless definite rules that have to be followed in the writing of magazine stories. There are some things you simply can't do, and some subjects you simply can't touch upon. Within the frame-work of these rules, you have to try to produce the illusion of some originality. It's not as hard as it sounds, but it does require a little figuring, just as it requires a little figuring to get a grand piano up a stair case with two turns in it. I might add that these rules apply to poor, medium, and good stories. If you have a simply swell story in mind, you can forget the rules. A swell story takes care of itself.

VII

"Don't You Ever Get Bored?"

We are often asked if we never get terribly bored here and I'm a little diffident about telling the truth. There is something so smug about people who say, with horror and umbrage at the very suggestion, "Oh, no! I'm never bored!" It sounds a little like, "Who, me? With my rich mine of inner resources? ME? With all my rare memories and rich philosophy?" I hate people like that. They're infuriating, and I think they are liars as well. Everyone is bored sometimes. It's a very painful illness, and completely undeserving of moral censure.

But be that as it may, the answer still is no. We're almost never bored. In winter we work too hard. In the summer we still work hard, and there are always distractions to fill in the chinks between jobs—things like guests, and fishing, and swimming. Nobody could be bored in autumn, when the air is like wine, and the hills are hazy tapestries with the red and gold thread of the frost-touched maple and birch embroidering a breath-taking design on the permanent dark fabric of the evergreens. The lakes then are unbelievably blue. All the things you've meant to do all summer but didn't get around to suddenly start crying to get done, and the days aren't long enough to crowd them all in before the first snow.

The only time left to be bored in is spring, when winter is over but it's still too early to plant the garden or move to the big house, and there's nothing very much to do but wait. Spring, as far as I'm concerned, is a vastly over-rated season, and I'd be bored to death with it, for all its burgeoning buds and returning birds and coy extremes of temperature, were it not for the spring log drive. The log drive was not designed solely for my entertainment; that's what is so remarkable and providential about its falling, as it does, in the slump of the year.

The idea of the drive is simple. All up the lakes, from Umbagog to the Little Kennebago, that tiny lost pond in the mountains fifty miles to the north, the winter's cut of four-foot pulp-wood lies boomed on the thick ice, waiting for the spring break-up. Before the first step of the metamorphosis from so many sticks of wood to so many Sunday Supplements, or high explosives, or evening gowns can begin, it must be got to the mills in Berlin, N. H., on the Androscoggin. The obvious method is to float the wood down. So even before the ice is out, the driving crews start filtering into the woods, to the company wangans along the chain of lakes. There is a lot to be done before the wood can start south.

I should explain "wangan." It is an Indian word, and can mean almost anything, like the Latin *res*. It can mean a camp or building. Pond-in-the-River wangan—or Pondy wangan, as the drivers call it—is a long, low shack a third of a mile above us, where the Rapid River crew lives during the drive. There is a sign in the bunk-house that reads,

"Wangan open an hour after supper." That refers to the store where the cook sells candy, tobacco, snuff, and clothing. (It really is a big box in the kitchen, and the reason it isn't open all the time is that the cook doesn't want to be bothered in the middle of his baking to hand out and charge against wages a nickel's worth of makings.) The cook may say, "I lost my wangan when the work boat swamped," and that means that his dishes are at the bottom of the lake. Or he may complain, "The wangan's runnin' low," meaning this time that he's short of food. Or a man may take his wangan and fly—leave the job with his little bundle of personal belongings. You can tell only by the context what the word means, and it's a very convenient word to know. I use it myself a lot, in non-driving connections.

The first year I was here, I couldn't wait for the drive to begin. I knew all about log drives, having subsisted at one time on a literary diet consisting exclusively of Stewart Edward White and Holman Day. I knew all about the thrill and perils of white-water driving—the big jam, the narrow escapes, the cat-footed agility of the drivers on the huge, plunging logs. I knew just what a river driver would look like. He should be big and bold and dark, with plaid shirt, well-cut riding breeches, caulked boots, and a mouthful of picturesque curses and ribald songs.

There is a stir that goes through the woods just before the drive moves in that is difficult to explain. Actually it consists only of suddenly increased activity on the telephone. The telephone man, Fred Bennett, who has long, blowing white hair, the delicate and transparent fragility of great age, and the toughness and staying-powers of a cross between a Shetland pony and a camel, comes slogging in through the woods and swamps and wet snow between here and the Brown Farm, and adds a half-dozen phones to our line. There is one at Middle Dam wangan, one at Pondy wangan, above us, and one at Hedgehog wangan, below, at the mouth of the river. The rest are hung in tar-paper cubicles on trees, in places where crises demanding immediate aid may arise.

Almost as soon as the phones are in, they begin to ring, strange numbers that have nothing to do with our simple, year-round, one, two, three, and four. They ring all the time, and I, neglecting my housework and throwing overboard all ethical scruples that first year, listened in. (That's all right to do, here. Often when I ask someone where they got a piece of news, they say quite frankly and shamelessly, "Oh, rubbering on the telephone.") Just by standing in the kitchen with the receiver to my ear, I could see the drive get under way all up the length of the lakes.

At first all the calls were to Joe Mooney at the Brown Farm, who acts as a sort of liaison officer. First of all came the reports as to the condition of the ice in the various lakes. "She's pretty rotten here on Umbagog this morning. If a west wind comes up she'll be clear by night. The river's all open and we've got the steamer *Diamond* in."—"She's blackin' up fast toward the Narrows. Give her two or three days of hot sun and she'll be out of the Richardsons." (Why are things like ice that won't melt, or inclement weather, or balky motors always "she" to the men who deal with them?) "They brought a horse 'n' sled down the big lake this morning. She won't go out for a week-ten days."

Then—"She's out of Pondy River, and we're puttin' in the *Alligator* tomorrow."—"The *Rowell's* in at Upper

Dam."—"The *Frost's* just goin' off the ways at Cupsuptic."

Then it speeds up. "This is Henry Mullen at Pondy. The cook claims he wants a barrel of flour, couple of crates of eggs, an' a half dozen hams. We got about thirty to feed tonight."—"Middle Dam talkin'. I got to have some inch an' a quarter line and a bunch of pick poles."—"I need ten more men. Thurston's boom's broke loose in the Arm, 'n' it's scattered all over Hell."—"I gotta have some pitch. This bateau at Middle leaks like a sieve."—"Where's that cookee? The cook's raving."—"I gotta close Pondy dam. I can't string no sluice boom with all this water runnin'." And finally, "When's that first boom comin' down? We're ready any time."

The ice is out; the winch boats are in; the crews have come; the ground work is done. The drive is ready to start.

That first year, when the news came over the telephone that they were going to launch the *Alligator,* we thought we'd go up and watch. We had seen her sitting patiently on her ways on the shore of the Pond all winter long, a big, twin-screw, square-ended craft, with a flat deck and a tall wheel-house perched on top. She was ugly and clumsy, but we felt a sympathy for her. We had watched the red leaves of autumn sift down on her deck and lie in fading, flattening windrows. We had seen the snow drift higher and higher about her, the wind-sculptured curves lending her a false and fleeting beauty. We had seen it shrink in the March sun, leaving her exposed and ugly again. We wanted to see her come to life.

Alligator is both the name of this winch boat in the Pond and the name of her type of amphibian boat. Alligators are built like barges, flat and rectangular, but they have a huge steel cable running from a winch in the bow.

The anchor is dropped, the winch unwinds as the *Alligator* runs backward to the boom, and hooks on; then the winch winds up the *Alligator* to the anchor, trailing behind her the boomful of pulp-wood which it is her business to move from the Head of the Pond to Pondy dam, at the foot. When the cable is wound up the anchor is run ahead again and the process repeated. At the foot of the Pond the boom is opened and the wood turned loose and sluiced into Rapid River, to be corralled three miles below in a catch boom, which the *Diamond* will winch to Errol Dam on the Androscoggin. Meanwhile the *Alligator* has gone back to the Head of the Pond for the boom that the *Rowell* has winched down the Richardsons from Upper Dam to Middle Dam and which has been sluiced down the upper section of Rapid River into the Pond. It sounds complicated, but it's just the old bucket brigade principle.

In Canada, where they hail from, an alligator doesn't stick necessarily to one lake, but goes right down the chain. Between lakes they pull themselves across bare ground by fastening their cable ahead to a stump and winding the boat up to it with its own winch. Many of the old pines along the Carry Road have deep girdling scars from the cable on their trunks, left from when they brought the *Alligator* in here.

As we were walking up the road to my first *Alligator* launching, we heard sounds of activity on the Pond-in-the-River Dam, so we swung off down the side trail that leads to it. I'll admit I was in a dither. The men in my life to date had been distinguished more for their intelligence, good citizenship, and consideration for their mothers than for dashing and romantic attributes. The most athletic played good tennis. The most daring crossed streets between traffic lights and talked back to cops. I'd never known any men in the business of danger.

We came out of the woods onto the dam. A tall, sad, thin man with a long upper lip was drooping on the rail, staring morosely across to where the sluice-booms were being strung—two long, floating log walkways from the dam up into the Pond, to guide the pulp-wood down to the open gate of the dam after the *Alligator* let it go. Presumably the stringers were river drivers, those daring heroes of song and legend. They looked like—

They looked like any gang of men going about a routine job, except they were a little shabbier, a little more nondescript, a little less arresting than any bunch of road menders I ever saw. There wasn't a plaid shirt in the crew. Some of them had on faded cotton shirts, but most of them were covered from the waist up with what my grandmother used to call "nice, sensible, woolen underwear," of the long-sleeved, knitted variety. Nothing is less glamorous, especially when south of them is worn a pair of ordinary, store-bought suit pants, which have seen better days, and which have been cut off, with a hack saw, apparently, just below the knee. (I later learned to say "stagged" below the knee. One stags one's pants, one's shirt sleeves, anything that needs to be abbreviated quickly, even one's hair.) The head-gear, too, was strange without managing to be piquant. First, tied like a baby's bonnet under the chin and tucked into the shirt at the back of the neck, was a bandanna handkerchief or, failing that, just an old piece of cloth, such as a shirt tail or a square of flour sacking. On top of that was the hat proper, which might be a cheap felt, a visored cap, or a battered derby.

They didn't even do the job with a dash. They just walked apathetically up and down the logs, boring holes, driving pegs and fastening ropes.

Of course I should have remembered that people who do things well almost always do them without flourish. That's the trouble with expert performances; they look too easy to be exciting, unless you can do them a little yourself. I can't skate much, so to me Sonja Henie's stuff looks pretty simple to have so much fuss made about it. But I can shoot and swim and cast a fly fairly well, so a champion in those fields has me standing on my chair. I'd never tried to walk a floating spruce log, so I would have been a little more impressed had there been some arm-waving and catching of balance. I've tried it since, and I know enough now to be plenty impressed, especially since I now know that very few river-hogs can swim.

(Blow No. 2 to my romantic notions:—river-drivers live in books; in life the term is river-hog. And I might as well deliver Blow No. 3 right now:—in a pulp drive there are no log jams; the wood is too short.)

To get back to the log-walking—I can imagine nothing worse than being out on the sluice boom in the middle of the night, as is sometimes necessary, with the black water snarling three inches from my feet. The current goes by with express train speed when the gates are open, and the wood hurtles past in the dark. The boom, although two or three logs wide lashed together, is wet and slippery and anything but steady. Even if a man could swim, he would have little chance. No one would see him go, except by great luck. No one would hear him call, if he had time to call before being knocked senseless. The first time he would be missed would be when the men came back off the boom. And the water is like ice. It would be a cold and lonely way to die.

I also found later that the peculiarities of costume are not merely a misguided attempt at quaintness. Riding breeches bind the knees, and long pants catch on brush and trip the wearer and get wet around the bottoms. The simple solution is long pants stagged. Black flies and gnats can make life Hell in springtime in the woods, and the best protection against them is to keep covered. Hence the woolen underwear and the bandannas. The hats are added, not as a sop to convention, but to keep the neck covering up and the glare out of the eyes.

The sad man spat dourly into the water and looked at us, so Ralph said, "Nice day."

The man said, "Yeah," as though he were cursing it.

So Ralph said, "I'm Rich. I live down below here."

"Yeah, I know," the man said. "I'm Mullen." He didn't have to add that he was the Pondy boss. We knew that from our illicit listening on the telephone. I'd pictured him as being what they call here a "bull of the woods"—a big swaggering bravo who could lick his weight in wildcats. He didn't look to me as though he could lick Rufus, who was six months old at the time.

Ralph rallied first. "Drop in sometime if you're cold or wet and have a drink. I've got some pretty good liquor."

Mullen shook his head and winced. "Not me. Thanking you all the same." He squinted at his crew out on the booms. "I'm off the stuff," he stated violently, and spat again. "I was down to Berlin last week an' I bought me a quart. Then me an' another joker split another quart. Then a feller give me a pint. It was all good stuff too," he explained defensively. "Cost ninety cents a bottle. Then

I went into a lunch room an' got me a can of beer." His face twisted. "You know that God-damned Jees'ly beer pizened me," he concluded simply. "So I'm just through with all that stuff."

We left him alone with his hangover and continued up to the *Alligator*.

There was a great deal of commotion there. Steam was up, and the winch cable was hitched to a dead-man across the cove. The *Alligator* was creaking and groaning and rumbling and not budging an inch. A head appeared through the afterhatch. The sulphurous blue haze of profanity thinned a little when the owner saw me, out of respect to my sex. It simmered down to a few heart-felt "Comical Christs," "God-damned blue-bottomed old tubs," "Desprit Jesuses," and "Christless onery bitches," which in the woods is practically parlor conversation. What he needed, it seemed, was some grease for the ways.

"You ain't got no grease?" he asked Ralph hopefully. "If I had a little grease—"

This didn't seem to be my department, but it wouldn't hurt to ask. "I've got some old doughnut fat, if that would do you any good—"

"How much you got?"

"A kettleful. Ten pounds, about."

He climbed down onto the ground. "Lady, you saved my life. I'll have the cook return it to you, soon's he gets his in."

So the *Alligator*, that first year we were here, slid down cinnamon-scented ways into the Pond, and a few days later the cookee delivered at our door an equal quantity of lard and an invitation from the cook to come to lunch.

"Either first or second lunch. Ten o'clock or two. Don't

matter." On the drive there are four meals a day, breakfast at six, first and second lunch, supper at five, and then, if the men have to sluice after dark, another lunch before they go to bed, which may be anywhere from ten P.M. until two the next morning.

We decided we'd go to second lunch, because Rufus would be asleep and we could leave him. Before we started up to the wangan, Ralph said, "Now look. There's a guy up there named Casey that has My Ideal of a hat. It's a swell hat and I want to make a deal with him if I can for it. So I'll point him out to you, and if you could sort of be nice to him—you know, soften him up—"

I knew, and I knew too without asking, what the Ideal Hat of Casey would look like. It would be a battered felt, of no recognizable style, with the crown squashed out of shape and the brim drooping dejectedly. Ralph had been working on one of his old city hats for years, trying to achieve that special abandoned and disreputable look; but it takes a long time to get it. "All right," I said resignedly. "What is he, an Irishman?"

Every married woman knows the look he gave me—the very special look husbands save for their wives when they say something more than usually stupid; the look combining in equal proportions disgust, resignation and nausea, with a dash of dismay at the prospect of living to be a grandfather with such a half-wit.

"With a name like Casey?" he asked. "What do you suppose he is, a Frenchman?"

The meals on the drive are buffet affairs, unlike the sitting-down meals in a logging camp. All the food is laid out on a long trestle table in the kitchen, with the knives and forks and tin plates and pannikins stacked at the end.

You get your tools first, and then go down the table, filling up your plate with whatever looks good to you. The trouble is everything looks good. There are always two kinds of meat—a hot beef pot-roast, for example, and cold sliced ham—and potatoes and three other vegetables. Then there are always baked beans, and fresh bread, and pickles, and applesauce, and, to top off with, three kinds of pie, cake, cookies, and doughnuts. When you can't get any more onto your plate, you look for a place to sit down and eat it. The cook wanted us, as company, to sit at the table, but I saw a hat that could belong to no one but Casey. So I said I'd rather do as the river-hogs did, if he didn't mind, and went outdoors and sat down beside the man with the hat, under a pine tree.

He looked a little terrified, but he couldn't get away, as there was a man on the other side of him.

"Lovely day," I said cordially, and he grunted. "Good cook you've got," I went on, and he showed the whites of his eyes like a nervous horse. "Been working in the woods long?" I asked with neighborly interest, and he definitely shied.

The man on the other side took pity on us both. "He don't understand no English, lady," he explained kindly. "He's a Frenchman."

I gaped at him. This was absolutely too marvellous to be true. After that look Ralph had given me— "With a name like Casey?" I asked.

"Oh, they just call him Casey. He's got some frog name nobody can pronounce. So when he went to work for the company, they put him down as Casey. Sounds as near like his real name as they could get."

I beamed on Casey, not minding that he didn't beam

back. He was unshaven, and ragged and dirty, but he looked wonderful to me. He'd given me a weapon I could use in domestic crises for years to come. I loved him like a brother.

Apparently he misunderstood my intentions, because he got up in a panic and fled. Incidentally, Ralph never did make the hat deal, because next day Casey asked to be transferred to the Middle Dam wangan. I don't know whether it was I who scared him, or whether it was the predatory way Ralph kept looking at his hat.

The remaining driver said to me comfortingly, "Don't mind him, lady. He's bashful. All us fellers is bashful. Lots of folks think we're tough, but we ain't. Any time you want to come up here or to the dam, you come right ahead. Nobody'll hurt you. An' any time you want some chores done down to your place, like splittin' wood, say, you just call me. Just call the cook on the phone and say you want to get hold of Venus."

Would I not! Not every woman has a chance to confound her husband by saying, "Oh, don't bother, if you're busy. I'll get Venus to do it."

We thanked the cook kindly for his hospitality, and said we had to get home, because the baby would be waking up.

"You got a baby?" His eyes lighted. "Bring him up here. There's nothing I like so much as a baby. Any time you want to go any place, you leave the baby here with me an' the cookee."

He meant it too, and I took him up on it a dozen times. I'd come back from an afternoon off, to find Rufus propped up on the cook's bunk, chewing a piece of dried apple, with a circle of men around him, trying to make him laugh. They were wonderful with him—much better

The Alligator

Pulpwood Waiting to be Sluiced Above Pondy Dam

than I was. Most of them were homeless and familyless, and a baby was a treat. As a matter of fact the first picture ever taken of Rufus was taken in front of the wangan in the arms of Jonesy, the drive cook.

That cook, Jonesy, and his cookee, Frank, were the first of a long line of woods cooks that I now know, and I hold them in especial esteem. Jonesy and I used to hold long conclaves on the culinary art, and he taught me how to make a tough pot-roast tender by smothering it with raw onions and adding a cup of canned tomatoes, salt, pepper, and a little water. Then you cover it tightly and leave in a slow oven for hours. The acid in the tomatoes, so Jonesy claimed, eats the tough fibre in the meat. Anyhow, it works. Another valuable thing he taught me was how to cut fresh bread into thin slices—a neat trick if you can do it, as everyone who has hacked jagged chunks off a warm loaf can testify. The knife must be reasonably sharp, of course, but the trick is to have it hot. Lay it on top of the stove for a minute, every four or five slices. This also works.

In return I bootlegged vanilla extract for him. Extracts aren't allowed in woods camps, and "you know yourself, Mis' Rich—you're a cook—you know a cake tastes like sawdust without no extract."

I thought this was a senseless regulation, and said so.

Jonesy sighed. "They have to have it that way. Fellers'll drink it up as fast as they can tote it in, an' there's nothing meaner'n a vanilla drunk, 'less it's a canned heat drunk."

"But imitation vanilla has no alcohol. That I just gave—"

"Sure. But lots of the woodsmen can't read. It smells like vanilla and tastes like vanilla, so they drink it and get drunk anyhow."

I was glad to hear this, as it confirmed an opinion of mine that getting drunk is fifty percent wishful thinking.

As a cookee, Frank wasn't too good, but he was entertaining in an unintentional way. He spent most of the time when he should have been peeling potatoes and washing dishes—a cookee's lot in life—strumming on a guitar and singing cowboy songs. His ambition was to get onto the Radio, on a hill-billy program. I've heard worse than he, though that isn't saying much. So he'd drone "When the Work's All Done This Fall" happily through his nose while Jonesy and Ralph and I peeled his potatoes.

We were all thus engaged one day when he discovered that by calling the Brown Farm and asking Joe to switch him onto a Magalloway line he could talk to the Camerons. The Camerons have some very pretty daughters, one of whom Frank had met at a dance. He put his guitar away under the bunk and began to bustle around.

"You got a flat-iron, Mrs. Rich?" he asked. "Can I borrow it? I got to press my pants."

I said, "Yes," and Ralph said, "Aren't you a little ambitious, young feller? It's fourteen miles from here to Camerons', and most of it's uphill. You can't walk that distance and back after supper."

Frank was surprised. "Oh, I wasn't planning on it. I'm just going to call her up. An' I ain't going to talk to no girl on the telephone with my pants looking like I'd slept in 'em."

That remains to this day the yard-stick by which I measure all chivalry.

Frank's, I'm sure, was the only singing I ever heard in a driving camp, in spite of the fictional convention that rivermen and loggers top off a hard, twelve or more hour day by sitting around a camp-fire singing French-Canadian chansons and talking about Paul Bunyan. Our river-hogs come in from work, eat their suppers, and go to bed. On the days that there is no boom to sluice or other work to be done, they wash their clothes and mend them, and play stud poker, and sleep. A few that have licenses go fishing and some pitch horse-shoes in the wangan yard, and a very few, since so many are illiterate, read old magazines that we give the cook. But none sing.

The only stories that are told are woods gossip. Nobody ever heard of Paul Bunyan. The nearest thing to him is Sock Saunders, who is more of a poltergeist than a hero. If a man drops a picaroon into the river he says, "Well, take it, Sock Saunders!" If he slips on a log, but catches himself in time, he says, "Foxed you that time, Sock Saunders." If he cuts his foot, he explains, "Sock Saunders got me." There are no stories about Sock Saunders. He's just the guy who hangs around and makes life complicated.

But nobody sings as they walk the boom in at Middle Dam, an event that should call for a chanty, with the boss lining out the verse and the walkers roaring the chorus. At Middle the *Rowell* can't get in close enough to the dam for the current to take the boom in, so on either side of the inlet above the dam is a headworks—a big log raft with a capstan on it. Hawsers are hitched to the boom, and four or more men man the capstan and walk the boom in. It comes reluctantly, inch by inch, as they walk doggedly round and round. It's hard, monotonous, drugging work. But nobody sings.

Around the camp the cook is the boss, no matter who the boss of the rest of the job is. What he says, goes. One year we had a cook named Scotty Maxwell, a veteran of the Boer War, who was at the relief of Ladysmith. How he landed in the Maine woods I don't know, but he is a good cook and he brought British Army discipline right along with him. He's a holy terror in the kitchen. He always has a meat cleaver handy, but he never has to do more than glance at it. He liked sit-down meals, where he could get people lined up in orderly rows instead of having them sprawled every which way, all over the yard. But nobody could sit down if his face and hands and fingernails couldn't pass Scotty's inspection. Whoever fell below his impossibly high standards went back and washed, ten times, if necessary. I went into the kitchen one day at first lunch and found five terrified Frenchmen sitting in a row on the floor with their plates between their knees. They'd worn their hats to the table, and were being taught gentlemanly conduct the hard way.

The third functionary around the drive is the bull-cook. This title puzzled me, as I never saw the bull-cook, a wizened little man answering to Bones, cooking. Jonesy cleared the matter up. "He's called the bull-cook, but he's really the barroom man."

"*Barroom?* But if you can't even have vanilla—"

"Oh, not that kind of a barroom. It's where the men sleep."

"Bunk-house?"

"Well, city folks might call it that." City folks also call a place to eat a mess-hall. In the woods it's the kitchen.

The barroom man is a combined chore-boy and chambermaid, and his job is no sinecure. He has to keep the barroom clean, keep a fire going in cold weather and a smudge going on nights when the bugs are bad. He also has to keep an outside fire going under an oil drum of water, so the men can bathe and launder. The cook won't have people using his hot water. Then he has to saw wood for his own and sometimes the cook's fires and row the lunches out to the *Alligator* crew when meal-time overtakes them in the middle of a haul.

This last was Bones' cross, because he couldn't row a boat. We used to make book on how long it would take him to get near enough to the *Alligator* to catch a line thrown him by the crew. But his sea-faring career ended one day when the wind came up while he was waiting on the *Alligator* for the crew to finish eating, so he could bring back the dishes. He was afraid to come ashore in the rowboat and spent the rest of the day on the Pond. The barroom fires went out and the boss was raging as was the cook. The *Alligator* crew missed two meals as he sat there and were not pleased. After that Frank rowed the meals out, and Bones helped with the potato peeling.

As May wore on toward June, we became used to waking up in the morning to the hollow *thunk* of the wood as it bumped down the rapids in front of the house. It is a pleasant sound, like distant, slow-beaten drums. We learned to watch the dam from our porch, and to grab our fly-rods and run when a boom came in. In the short interval between the arrival of a boom and the opening of the gates to sluice it, there is often a quarter hour's glorious fishing. The big trout and salmon follow the wood down out of the Pond, feeding on the grubs and insects that drop from the rotting bark. They come up from the green shade below with that powerful and accurate surge that so delights the heart to behold. Standing on the sluice-booms, one sometimes forgets to fish, so lost in awe and admiration does one become for their vicious grace.

After a little the water at our feet begins to stir almost imperceptibly, tugging gently at the wood that is held back by the "trip"—a single long log swung like a gate across the channel. That means the boss has had the gate raised a few inches to warn any fishermen who may be on the river below that they'd better high-tail it for the bank.

We had a boss once named Phil Haley who would not observe this convention. Fishermen got in his hair. They were always underfoot, walking out on the sluice-boom, snagging his men with their backcasts, and asking foolish questions. They disrupted work, because everyone always stopped everything in the hopes of seeing a hundred dollars' worth of Abercrombie & Fitch fall into the river and maybe drown. So when it came time to hoist, Phil hoisted. Let the jokers scramble. Phil it was who once gave Ralph ten dollars to hold for him as safeguard against losing it in a stud game. He said he might need it when he got Outside. He observed that "a ten dollar bill is an awful handy rig to have 'round," which seems to me to cover that both simply and adequately.

Most bosses, though, will warn the fishermen, so when we begin to see the boom stir and the drivers start climbing down onto the sluice-booms with their pick-poles, ready to pole the wood along toward the gate, we reel in our lines and climb up onto the dam to watch them hoist (pronounced heist) the gates.

Pond-in-the-River Dam is an old-fashioned wooden dam with a long, unpainted shed over the center section sheltering the gate-works. The gates are raised by man power, teams of several men each manning the big wheels at the ends of the heavy timber gates. They start turning the wheels over slowly, and the gates creak as they move against the enormous pressure against them. Then, as the tempo increases, the gates come up slowly, dark and dripping, groaning and protesting, and the water begins to flow under them, impatient to be free. The first white spate deepens and greens, and the low whispering rustle changes to a roar. The whole dam vibrates as the gates clear the water, and the boss shouts, "Let go your trip!" The men who have been on the gates come out on the dam, their chests heaving, their faces glistening with sweat, and watch the first wood go through. "She's runnin' good," they will say; and "Ain't that handsome pulp, though? Comes from up back of Metalluc. I was cuttin' on the stump up there last winter."

It's lovely on the dam on a bright spring morning, with the wind blowing down across the boom and filling the air with the sharp smell of resin, so strong and fresh that you can taste it. The planks tremble under your feet, and the roar of the river and the thumping of the wood fills the ears. The river is deep blue and crisping white, and the cut ends of the pulp are like raw gold in the sun. All the senses come alive, even that strange rare sense that tells you, half a dozen times between birth and death—if you are lucky—that right now, right in this spot, you have fallen into the pattern of the universe.

We would like to spit on the last log of the last boom of the drive as it goes through the dam, but we're not sure that this brings luck to any but those who have worked on the drive. So we give the good spitting spots to the river-hogs, who put a lot of store by the ceremony. They spit copiously and accurately, and I hope the charm works. I thought I'd discovered a new folk-way when I saw a driver last year throw an almost new pair of work gloves into the sluice after the last log.

"Is that good luck, too?" I asked.

"Nope. I ain't needin' 'em any more, that's all. I'm through."

"Aren't you going on the rear?"

"Nope. I got a date over at the college in West Stewartstown."

That is the euphemism for the county jail, and so I started to cluck the sympathetic tongue.

But my man threw out his chest. "They can't get along without me over there, when it comes time to plant the gardens," he said with modest pride. "I bossed the plantin' there now five years runnin'. Just happened I got picked up in Berlin every year there for a spell in the middle of May, for drunk an' disorderly. Last year I missed. We didn't get off the Diamond till late, an', Hairy Jesus, what a mess they made of them gardens! So when I got pinched last Christmas they turned me loose—deferred my sentence, the judge called it—till planting time. They weren't takin' no chances this year. Tomorrow mornin' there'll be a boat at Cedar Stump for me, an' I gotta be there."

After the last log has gone through the dam, there are still two or three days of "rearin' " before the drive moves out. Rearing is going down the river and cleaning up all the wood that has been left in the rear, caught on rocks or washed up on the banks. It is pitched back into the river again and finally gathered in the catch boom below. It's the hardest part of the drive. By that time it is hot, and the bugs are bad, the water is still like ice, and the men are wet from morning to night. But it marks the point at which you can begin to think definitely about getting drunk in Berlin, so the crew works with great speed and good humor. Before we know it the flash boards are off the dam, the river is clean as a whistle again, the roar of the rapids is back to normal, instead of rising thunderously one hour and startling us by sinking to a whisper in the next. (Here silence is an uncanny noise.) The men start trekking to Sunday Cove, where the work boat will pick them up and take them out. They call to us as they go by, "My regards to the little feller!" and "See you next year."

The cook does not walk to the Cove. He has his position to think of. He comes in, strange and formal without his white clothes and apron and in a store hat, and asks Ralph to drive him down. "I'll pay you," he says.

That's a pathetic thing about woodsmen. If they ask you a favor, they make it clear at once that they can and will pay for it. It's a telling comment on the treatment they receive on the Outside, where they are considered bums, and are always asked to pay as they enter, as it were. "I'll pay you," they say, protesting their self-respect. They are always so pleased and puzzled when we won't take money, pointing to all the favors they have done us. "Oh, that! That wa'n't nothin'."

So Ralph says to the cook, "Naw, you can't pay me. I'm going down that way anyhow."

The cook climbs into the car, and at the last minute leans out and says to me, "I left a few odds an' ends for you up at the wangan. No sense of throwing good food to the squirrels." I'm used to woods computations now, but the first year I was flabbergasted at the loot. There were a half a dozen pies, a flour barrel almost full of cookies and doughnuts, and ten huge loaves of bread—the cook's idea of a few odds and ends.

The first two or three days after the drive goes out we always feel a little lonely and lost. The wangan looks so forlorn as we go past, with no smoke coming out of the chimneys, no sound of Bones' axe ringing crisply from out back by the wood-pile, no men sitting on the long bench in front, or rinsing their clothes in the brook where it flows under the Carry Road. The windows are shuttered once more, and the benches have been taken inside. By the brook a forgotten pair of socks droops from an alder bush where they were hung up to dry. The trampled grass in the yard is beginning to spring upright again. Down by the Pond, the *Alligator* is high and dry again on her ways.

The drive is over. It wasn't what I had expected it to be. The men weren't romantic, or daring, or glamorous. But they were something much better. They were good neighbors. We're going to miss them.

But not for a week or so. Not until Fred Bennett comes in again and takes the phones out. While they stay we'll be too busy to miss anyone. The fishermen have begun to swarm into the woods. "Sports" the natives call them here; it is a term like the cowboy's "dudes" or the stage farmer's "city slickers." Fishing up and down the river, deep, so they think, in the wilds of Maine, they are amazed and baffled to find telephones hanging on trees.

I know just what they say. They say, "Well, for crying out loud! Look at the telephone! Gee, let's ring it and see if anyone answers."

So they ring it. Naturally they ring one, which is our number, and by the time Fred Bennett gets in we are half insane with trying to explain in a million well-chosen words the whys and wherefores of the situation.

But now, I think we have at last evolved a system. We've got now so we can tell a "sport's" ring from a native's. It has a feeble, wavering quality, quite unlike that of the firm hand accustomed to cranking a battery phone. So when that kind of a ring comes over the line, we take down the receiver, say briskly, "Grand Central Station, Information Booth," and hang up. It almost always stops them.

To be fair to the writers of the romantic school of logging fiction, what they invariably dealt with is the long-log drive, which is quite different from the pulp drive of today. They used to drive long logs—and by that I mean whole trees, sometimes as long as sixty feet—here. But those days were a decade or more ago. We would never see their like again, the old river-hogs mourned. And we never would have, if it hadn't been for the hurricane that hit New England in 1938.

The hurricane blew down millions of feet of pine. Pine isn't used for pulp, so there was no chance of its being cleaned up on the next pulp operation. Nobody would gamble on taking it out as the market would be glutted with pine after the hurricane. The prospects were that it would just lie where it had fallen in crazy jack-pots. Inside of a year the worms would be in it, unless a forest fire got there first; and what the worms and fire missed would burn in the slower, surer fire of decay. It's a truly sad thing to see a big tree lying on the ground, even if you know that the bringing low of so much beauty and majesty will serve some useful end. It's heart-breaking when nothing but waste will result.

And then the Government had a good idea—"for the

Gov'ment," as they say up here. They set up a Timber Salvage Administration for the saving of the pine. The lumbering was let out to local contractors who would get the blowdown out of the woods and into Government storage booms in specified ponds and lakes, whence its release onto the market could be controlled. Worms will not attack wood that is in the water, and water won't injure it for years. The Government paid a fixed price, depending on grade, and Government scalers and graders oversaw the work, and presumably prevented the woodsmen, who were paid on a piece-work basis, from cutting any standing pine. It's a lot easier to cut a standing tree than one that is not only down, but also tangled up in a half a dozen others. It's a lot safer, too. You can never tell what a blowdown will do when you get a saw almost through it. It may drop as you plan it's going to. On the other hand the stresses may be such that it will jump with the force of a forty-mule-kick and knock you galley-west. You never can tell, and maybe you won't get a chance to make a second guess.

The nearest Government storage booms were below us in Umbagog, and Jim Barnett contracted to get out the pine lying on the slopes along Rapid River and into the booms before winter set in. He moved his men and wangan into the Pond-in-the-River driving camp in early summer, and by the first of October he was ready to drive the logs, which he had temporarily boomed up in the Pond, down the river to the Government booms. I, personally, was looking forward to this drive with a great deal of interest, because I had long since given up hope of ever seeing a long-log drive. I wasn't glad the trees had blown down, you understand, but since they had, I was glad to be on the spot to see them driven.

And then the Government had another idea. We should have been warned when we read in a two-week-old Boston Sunday paper a feature article on the Romance of Hurricane Timber—that was what they were calling our blowdown Outside—and the Revival of the Old Long-Log Days. We should have been warned, but we were only entertained. We had no inkling of what was in store for us until Jim came in from Outside one day and began telling about meeting the Timber Salvage agent, who, it seemed, had discovered a publicity angle to the pine drive. This long-log drive on Rapid River would probably be the very last of the old time drives ever to be held, and he thought it should be perpetuated for posterity. He was going to bring in a bunch of newspaper reporters and newsreel cameramen to make a living record of this rapidly dying bit of the American scene—his verbiage, not Jim's or mine—and Jim's share in the project was to give them something to take pictures of and write about. It would be interesting to people, he said, and it would be good publicity—for whom he carefully didn't specify. The tax payers were footing the bill for the salvage, after all.

All this seemed fair enough to Jim, and he was perfectly willing to co-operate. The only trouble was that the agent seemed to take for granted deeds of derring-do, heart-stopping crises, and a plethora of almost legendary figures whose prowess had been told in song and story all up and down the rivers of Maine. In the fall of the year there isn't enough water in the lakes to put much of a head on the river, so it was going to be impossible to open the festivities with the expected forty-foot wall of water racing down the channel, the long logs turning end over end along its face like match sticks. And as for legendary figures, Jim was fresh out of them. The men he had had working for him all summer were just natives who knew how to use an axe and a two-man cross-cut, and he'd planned to use the same men on the drive. They were strong and willing, and they could get the pine down the river all right, if allowed to go about it in their own way. But they weren't old-time river-hogs. Most of those boys were either dead or retired to parts unknown. The only legendary figure Jim knew anything about was reposing at the moment at the county jail. However, he was willing to make a stab at putting on a show for the Fourth Estate.

The first requirement seemed to be more water, so Jim had a couple of courses of flash-boards added to those already on Pondy Dam, and stopped driving altogether for two days to give the Pond a chance to fill up. The second requirement seemed to be a prima donna for the occasion. The man over in the jail—whose name I have forgotten but whom I'll call Black John—seemed to be the logical choice. He was presumably available through the simple expedient of paying off his fine; and he had plenty of legends clustered around his name. He was said to have crossed the Androscoggin on floating logs, once when young and drunk, just to give one example. So Roy Bragg, who was bossing the drive and had a drag at the jail, went over to get him.

He came back with Black John all right, but announced that they'd have to return him in good condition as soon as the emergency was over. Black John had been arrested during the preceding month and it was now the last of

September and the court records were closed and couldn't be opened again. They were terribly sorry, over at the jail, and they wanted to oblige; but they didn't make the laws. However, if Roy wanted to *borrow* Black for a couple of days, they'd be glad to lend him, if Roy would be sure to return him in good order. Roy was sure. Why wouldn't he be? There would be no liquor and he had plenty of strong-arm boys to keep their eyes on Black.

Early the next day the work boat brought in the camera-men and reporters. None of the woodsmen had ever been exposed to the gentlemen of the press before, and they were fascinated. So was I. They were exactly what I hoped they'd be, from reading and movie-going. They got every-body in a dither by running around poking their noses into everything and asking questions. The woodsmen were all ready to go out and start driving the logs, and I think they were a little baffled when it developed that first they were to take off their coats and sit around the camp and barroom occupying themselves with their usual Sunday diversions—stud poker, clothes mending, saw filing, reading, and sleeping—while they had their pictures taken.

Then the newsmen got a look at Black John, the star of the show. He wasn't much to look at, I'll admit—just a wizened up little old man with a grizzly stubble of beard, a bleary eye, and a slept-in suit of clothes. So the press went to work on him. They combed the camp for a suitable outfit for him, snatching riding pants—known in the woods as puff-panties—off someone, making someone else kick in with his hat, and assembling every plaid shirt in the outfit until they found one that would not only fit reasonably well, but that would also photograph well. By the time they were through, Black John did look a little legendary, and he'd begun to act legendary, too. I don't think he'd ever in his life had such a fuss made over him. But he rated it. We all realized that, as soon as the gates were hoisted and the river began to roar.

There is a lot of difference between a river full of pulpwood and a river full of long-logs. Pulp is just thousands of chunks—pronounced "junks" in our country—of wood. There is nothing particularly impressive about it, and it can be a nuisance, collecting in our swimming pool, clogging up the little basin between two rocks where I rinse my Monday washing, and spoiling the fishing. But long-logs—well, they come surging down the current like express trains, shedding green water from their backs, and leaping over boulders. There's something vicious about their bulk and speed—something alive and dangerous. Of pulp you say, "There's a lot of wood." Of a long-log you find yourself thinking, "There was a tree."

Black John climbed down through the dam and clung to the pier, waiting, his feet in their caulked boots a few inches above the racing water. Pretty soon he saw what he wanted plunging down upon him—a big high-riding pine butt. He leaped, and when he landed, light as a cat, his feet were going in a little dance step. The log spun and twisted and water boiled up to his knees, but he kept right side up. He didn't even seem to be paying much attention to what he was doing, and, to give him credit, he wasn't paying attention to the cameras, either. He was just standing there motionless except for his dancing feet. But when his log crashed onto a reef and half its length reared out of water, Black John was in the air a split second before the crash, and as the two wings of water flung out by the settling log collapsed, he was ten feet away on another log, still poker faced, still keeping his feet moving. He was good, all right.

After the cameramen had taken what they considered enough feet of that, they announced to Jim that now they wanted a log jam. So the boss went downriver to find one. With the amount of water running, that should be easy, but just to play it safe, Jim told him to take a crew, and if they couldn't find one ready-made, to make one. In the meantime he suggested that maybe the newsmen would like to see Black John go through the sluice of the dam on a log. Black John balked, however. He'd go for ten dollars, but he wouldn't go for nothing. In the first place this was supposed to be a vacation from jail, and he wasn't going to exert himself too much. He could work back at the clink. In the second place, if he fell into the river, as he was likely to do, it would cost him money. He'd have to reimburse the owners of his borrowed finery, and he'd have to buy himself a bottle of pneumonia preventative. However, he did finally compromise to the extent of agreeing to go down the sluice in a bateau if Jim would get him a crew. By the time the crew was found and had been taken out of their overalls and put into something more suitable, and the sluice had been successfully negotiated, the boss was back with the news that he hadn't been able to find a jam, but he'd managed to start a honey on the rips just above Long Pool. So we all adjourned the half mile down the river.

It was a pretty good jam. The logs were coming around the bend and hurling themselves onto the key log that the men had managed to lodge across the current, hitting with a hollow booming and jumping clear out of water when they struck. The newsreel men set up their cameras and the reporters got out their pencils, and the entire personnel of the camp swarmed out onto the jam to break it up. Half of the men had never seen a log jam before (pulpwood doesn't jam), but by this time they were all infected with the desire to get into the movies, so it wasn't very surprising that almost immediately some real action began. Somebody heaved too hard, and somebody else who was watching the cameras instead of what he was doing fell down into the crack between two logs. It was no joke. He went down to his armpits in the icy water, and all that prevented him from going further was the fact that he flung his arms around the logs. And the logs kept piling up from above, and nothing was giving an inch below. It's not very pleasant to stand on a river bank and watch a man being crushed within twenty feet of you, especially when there's not a thing you can do about it except yell. We all yelled, except the cameramen. They just kept on turning their cranks. That was their job, and I decided then that it wasn't a job I'd care for. It requires too much nerve.

And then Black John ran out onto the jam. He looked frail and ineffectual beside some of the woodsmen already there, but he was a river-hog from 'way back. He knew what to do. It was a very telling demonstration of the superiority of brains and experience over brawn. One heave with a cant dog, and the jaws of the nutcracker opened six inches. Six inches was enough. Out came the nut, so to speak, and high-tailed it for shore, leaving his cant dog behind him. Another heave or two, and the whole jam started downriver.

This I will say for Black John. He didn't let the situation die like that, with a bunch of logs floating off into the unknown. He threw back his head and howled, "Never mind the man! Grab his cant dog! That cost the company money!" That was the old river-hogs' battle cry. It put the finishing touch on the episode. Black John had a true feeling for style.

That about ended the famous long-log drive—except, of course, for the actual driving of the logs down to Umbagog. Its like will never be seen again. As a matter of fact, I doubt if its like was ever seen before in the annals of lumbering; it was unique. But everybody was satisfied. The newshawks—to quote *Time*—got their stories; the cameramen got their pictures; the salvage agent got his publicity; the woodsmen got their faces in the "moom-pitchers"; and the rest of us got a field day. I'm not sure what Jim Barnett got, except a lot of trouble and expense. If it's any comfort to him, we Riches think he managed the whole affair with graciousness and tact.

P.S. Black John was returned safely and in good condition.

VIII

"*Aren't You Ever Frightened?*"

THERE'S NOTHING TO BE AFRAID OF IN THE WOODS—EXCEPT yourself. Nothing is going to hurt you—except yourself. This, like all sweeping statements, is subject to a few amendments; but the basic idea still holds. There is nothing at all to be afraid of in the woods—excepting always yourself.

When I investigate what lies back of the statement, "I'd be simply terrified most of the time, living the way you do," I usually find bears. For some reason the non-woods-wise expect to be eaten by a bear the minute they get out of calling distance of a main highway. If it isn't a bear that's going to attack them, it's a wildcat, and if it isn't a wildcat, it's probably a rabbit. There may be a little more danger from a bear than from a rabbit; after all, a bear is larger. Animals in the woods aren't out looking for trouble. They don't have to look for it. Their lives are nothing but one trouble after another. The sentimental view is that wild animals live an idyll, doing what they want, browsing on herbs and flowers, wandering happily along woodland glades, and sleeping where night overtakes them. Actually the poor devils must live in a constant state of terror. So many things can, and do, happen to them. They can starve or freeze in winter. They are fly-ridden in the summer. Men and larger animals constantly harass them. Their young may be taken from them by any number of means, all violent. They know trouble too well to be interested in making any more. I pity all animals, but especially wild animals, from the bottom of my heart; and it's very hard to be afraid of anything that arouses pity.

I don't want to pose as an expert in animal life. In other words, I want to hedge a little. I don't know anything about lions or rogue elephants or hippopotamuses. People who know about them claim they're something to steer clear of, and I'll take their word for it. I've never happened to get in between a she-bear and her cubs, but I understand that that's not a good thing to do. I'm just talking about the Maine woods and the animals you ordinarily encounter there.

The way to see wild animals to the best advantage is to see without being seen. As a matter of fact, that's about the only possible way to see them. They don't stand around, if they see you first. I always wonder as I walk down the road, how many pairs of eyes have me under surveillance, how many hearts beat with suffocating rapidity until it is certain that I am going straight along the Carry on my own harmless business. I can feel that constant mute and questioning regard from hillside and thicket and roadside tangle of grasses and weeds; deer and bear and coon, and fox, mink and partridge and little white-footed, bat-eared mouse—they all stand and watch.

My favorite animals to watch are the deer and foxes. They are both so quick and pretty and well co-ordinated, and they're both such a lovely red color in the summer. We don't see foxes very often. They do their sleeping by day and their prowling by night. Once I saw one, though, eating blueberries off a bush. Usually we see them trotting their precise and dainty trot along the road. This one looked so informal, with his feet braced and his head outthrust, pulling the clusters of ripe berries off the bushes, and ducking as the branch snapped back.

We see deer all the time, but we never get tired of them—or almost never. The exception was a deer we named Joe. He started coming into the yard when he was just a young spike-horn, and we took such pains not to frighten him that he soon became very tame. He'd stand around and watch us work. Deer are very curious, and it almost got to the point where before Ralph could drive a nail into a board, he had to shove Joe's nose out of the way. That was all right; what finally fed us up with Joe was his destructive attitude toward our flower gardens.

We'd worked hard on those gardens. One was an old ant hill, which we'd chosen as the site for a bed because it had good exposure and didn't need clearing. All it needed was to have the ants exterminated. Before we got through with that little chore, we wished we'd never been born. Two or three of the beds just had to have the underbrush and roots and rocks cleared away—and, of course, the soil changed over from acid woods mold to good garden earth. But the last of them we made on the vestigial remains of an ancient bridge pier. No one has ever been able to account for that pier. It is just above the house on the river bank and apparently once there was a very sizable bridge there. The pier is made of huge boulders, much too large to have been moved by anything less than an ox team, so the bridge was more than a temporary structure. There must have been a road through there once, but there is no record of there ever having been such a road. Where would it have come from and where would it have gone to? Nobody knows. There is no trace of it now. Someone once advanced the theory that Arnold might have built it on his way to Quebec, but I think his route is pretty well established as having been well to the east and north of here. Whatever the reason for the bridge, it was built a long, long time ago. We had to cut trees with six-inch butts when we cleared off the pier for our flower garden.

But that was only the beginning. When we got the trees cut and the roots and sod cleared away, there was nothing left but bare rock. We had to haul dirt in, from any place we could scrape it up, to fill the pockets in the rocks, and we had to haul in about an even amount of stable dressing to make the earth arable. We'd been all through this with the vegetable garden, but this was worse, because there was no hauling the trailer with the Packard to the scene of the operation and pitching the load off. It all had to be transshipped from the road by wheelbarrow, down narrow planks laid on a steep bank. It was a lot of work, and when we got it done and planted we didn't appreciate having Joe go in there to stamp down all our seedlings and later eat all the blossoms off any plants that survived his first treatment.

It may well be asked why we bother with a flower garden, considering all the sweat involved, especially when we have a whole forest full of wild flowers for the picking. The answer may sound a little silly, especially to those people to whom we have so carefully explained that no, we don't miss seeing other people. We don't miss them at all.

It may sound a little pixyish and whimsical to say that what we do sometimes get lonesome for are civilized flowers, and stretches of lawn and ordered gardens. Our tangles of zinnias and larkspur and violas, slopping over into rather shaggy grass paths, may be a pretty far cry from shell walks and clipped hedges and roses around a sun dial; but we love them and I can have tame flowers to put on my dinner table and around the living-room part of the year.

I hope the foregoing explains why we got bored with Joe. Unfortunately, he didn't get bored with us. He'd go back onto the ridges every fall, and we'd hope for the best. But every spring he'd show up again, bigger and lustier than ever. It didn't make us much happier to learn that a full grown buck makes a dangerous pet. After he has reached maturity, he may, without a moment's warning, turn definitely nasty, lashing out with horns and hoofs for no reason at all. The Durkees in Upton had a tame buck that, after living off their bounty for several years, suddenly chased someone into the lake—it was fall, too, and the water was cold—and wouldn't let him out until someone put a bullet through his head. We didn't want that to happen to us. The situation was solved when we developed that dog team idea. The smell and sound of a pack of huskies was enough to scare Joe into the next county. So some good did come out of that impractical dog-dream after all.

Probably the cutest, sweetest animals in the woods are new born fawns. They aren't red like their mothers, but spotted tan and white, so that when they stand still—as they do, instinctively, in the presence of danger—they look like just another patch of sun-dappled shadow. There is nothing quite so defenseless as a new little fawn, so Nature takes over its protection until it can at least outrun the more deadly of its enemies. Not only does a fawn become practically invisible when it stands still, but it has no scent whatever to betray its presence. A dog that can smell a deer a half a mile away will pass a fawn almost within touching distance, and never turn its head. Oddly enough, the fathers of most of the wilderness young are hell bent on their destruction, so Nature attends to that, too. During the spring and early summer, when the does are dropping their fawns, the bucks are in the velvet. They have shed their antlers during the previous winter, and on their heads are the beginnings of the new horns—two swollen, velvet-covered knobs, which are not only soft, but are also extremely sensitive. The mildest-mannered doe, inspired by mother love, has no trouble at all during the velvet season in bull-dozing the toughest buck that ever breathed. Nobody ever told us that this is the reason for the apparently extravagant antler-dropping, but to us it seems obvious, and I mention it because so many people have remarked to us that they didn't see any point in a buck's growing a fine set of horns only to lose them before the next spring.

Some people who should know better—like some guides and woodsmen—believe that a doe will desert her fawn if she detects the man scent on it, and they warn you not to touch a spotted fawn. I'm happy to be in a position to state authoritatively that this isn't so. This is how I happen to know.

One day in the early summer, Ralph was coming down from Middle Dam in our old Model T, and, as usual, he wasn't sparing the horses. He broke over the crest of

Wangan Hill and around the bend in the road, and there in front of him right in the middle of the road was a doe and a fawn that couldn't have been more than a few hours old. Its spots were bright and it wavered on its slender, impossibly delicate little legs. Ralph slammed on everything and skidded to a halt just as the doe, who stuck until the radiator was almost touching her, jumped clear. She had courage, poor thing. The fawn couldn't jump. It was too little and weak and confused. It went down in the road. Ralph swarmed over the door, heart-broken. He's often hardboiled in his attitude toward his own kind, but when it comes to animals, he's just a bowl of custard. Then he saw that he'd stopped well short of the fawn. It hadn't been touched. It had simply obeyed a command from something that had been born within it—a command to play possum. It lay flat on its belly with its hind legs under its body in a crouch and its front legs stretched straight out, its head between them. The grass between the ruts arched over it, and it lay perfectly supine, even when Ralph bent over it. Only its eyes moved, rolling back to follow his movements. Even when he ran his hand along its spine, to make sure it was all right, the only sign of life it gave was an uncontrollable shrugging of the loose skin on its back. It didn't know what this was all about; after all, it had had only since about dawn to get used to this world; it had nothing to go by except that inner voice; but it was doing its poor little best to follow instructions.

It was obvious that it would go on lying there until snow flew, unless something was done, and Ralph had to get home to dinner. So he picked it up in his arms and started to carry it to the side of the road. Then it came to life. Legs flew in all directions. It was like trying to cuddle an indignant centipede, Ralph informed me later. He put it down off the road in a hollow by a large rock, and leaped into the Ford.

The first thing I knew about the affair was when I heard the car come into the yard, and Ralph's voice shouting for me to come quick and ask no questions. Fortunately, I have long been accustomed to following orders first and finding out afterwards, so I set the pudding I was making back off the fire and ran. On the way back to Wangan Hill, Ralph explained what had happened, so I was all prepared when we left the car at the foot of the hill and walked the last hundred yards to where he had left the fawn. The hollow by the rock was empty.

Then we looked up. There, not twenty feet from us, were the doe and fawn, standing in a little patch of sunlight. It was one of the prettiest sights I ever saw. The little fellow was standing perfectly still while its mother lapped it over from head to tail, to get the obnoxious human smell off it. They both stared at us gravely for a long moment, and then the doe wheeled and trotted away—not frightened, not even nervous—with her child galloping obediently at her heels. If I'd been a mother then—which I wasn't—I'd have known that this was all that would have happened. There have been times since when Rufus didn't smell exactly like a lily, but I've never considered abandoning him for that reason.

The animals we see most, next to deer, are porcupines. I can't seem to find it in my heart to love a porcupine. They're perfectly harmless—they *don't* throw quills, by the way—but they're stupid and ugly, and besides, they do a lot of damage. They fill the dogs full of quills, which is the dogs' fault, I'm willing to grant—and they try to gnaw our houses down around our ears, and they climb trees and sometimes girdle the tops, thereby killing them. The quills stick up all over their backs in an untidy mess, and they have blunt rodent faces with dull, slow eyes. They don't make any noise, except a rattling sound, which I've read is made by clacking their quills, but which I think, myself, they make with their teeth. I can't vouch for this. I don't have much traffic with them. I did catch one once and put it under a water pail in the middle of the garage, so that when Ralph went to back the car in, he'd have to get out and move the pail. I knew what his frame of mind would be toward the blankety blank so-and-so that would leave a pail there, and I thought it would be fun to have him kick it viciously aside, only to unveil a furious porcupine. It didn't work. The porcupine escaped by a sapping operation, and Ralph didn't get home until after dark and never saw the pail. We did have an albino porcupine that lived for a while out back of Gerrish's house, and that, being rather rare, was interesting enough. But porcupines as a tribe are very, very dull. We had a weasel living in the chimney base once, too, but we never could get very matey with him, either. He was too quick for us. We'd see him, brown in summer and white in winter, flowing like quicksilver in and out of the rocks and bristling his whiskers at us. He always gave me the shivers. He was so deadly purposeful, and he had such a vicious eye. I was glad when he moved away.

We've never seen a wildcat, though there are plenty of them around. We see their tracks often enough, and sometimes hear them yowling on the ridges. They aren't dangerous, unless cornered, but they like to make you think they are. One of their tricks is to follow you along the road, just about dusk. They don't stay out in the open, where you can turn around and heave a rock at them. They keep in the bushes at the side. When you stop, they stop. When you hurry, they hurry. After a while it gets on your nerves.

Once in the late fall I was sitting in the living-room of an evening with Ralph and our friend Rush Rogers, knitting. It was a very peaceful scene. For once the room was reasonably tidy, and for once the dogs—we had two then, Kyak and Mukluk—were sensible of their responsibilities, and were lying in picturesque postures in front of the fire, instead of trying to crowd us out of our best chairs. The firelight glanced off the backs of the books on their shelves in a satisfactorily colorful manner, and a little light snow brushed the window panes gently from time to time. The radio was coming in well, and the room was full of music. I should have been purring like a cat, with contentment, but I was uncomfortable, for some reason. I couldn't settle down.

Rush said, "Good Lord, Louise, what ails you? I never saw you twitchy before."

I said, "I don't know. I just feel someone looking at me."

Ralph hooted. "I suppose so. Who, for instance?"

I said stubbornly, "I don't know. I only know someone's looking at me. I can feel it."

I didn't get any sympathy. I just got told that neither of them could stand notional females, and if I was planning to develop a temperament, I'd better go somewhere else and develop it. They both knew a lot of sure-fire cures for temperament.

But I still felt someone looking at me.

Finally I couldn't stand it any longer. I got up, lighted a lantern, and went out on the porch. The dogs raised their heads somnolently, and Ralph and Rush exchanged looks of bored amusement. It was snowing lightly outside and the porch floor on the open end was sugared thinly over—all except for a little spot where a furry rump had been planked, and two smaller ones that were clearly paw marks, directly outside the window at which I was sitting. A scramble in the snow told of a hasty departure when I had opened the door. The evidence was easy to read. A wildcat had been sitting within three feet of me all evening, watching me knit. I learned later that this is not at all uncommon. They love to look in at lighted windows. I can't imagine why. I can't imagine, either, what ailed the dogs that they didn't put up a howl—except that they have a real talent for always doing the wrong thing, even when the wrong thing is nothing.

We see bears only once in a while, although there are plenty of them around here. They are shy animals, not easily caught unaware. We usually come on them in various berry patches, when their attention is concentrated on picking berries and they are off guard. These encounters are carried off with a minimum of excitement. We say, "Oh," and start south, and the bear says, "Oh," and starts north. Not that anybody is afraid of anybody, you understand. We just don't like to intrude on each other's privacy.

We don't believe in confining wild animals. Nothing makes me madder than to see a lion in a cage or some luckless racoon chained up at a gas station. I'm not a reformer by nature, but that's one thing I will crusade about. I think it's all right to kill animals if you have to, or even if you want to, but it's not all right to imprison them. I always feel like declaring a holiday, and Ralph does declare one, when we hear about a service station's confined bear running amok and maiming a few attendants and customers. It serves them darn well right. So, feeling as we do, we never try to make pets of the wild life around us. Just once did we make an exception, and that was none of our seeking. It was more or less wished on us by circumstances.

This is the way it happened. I had asked Coburn's driver to bring me in three lemons, so when Ralph came home with the mail and handed me a little paper bag, I thought I knew what was in it. I tipped it up and dumped the contents out on the kitchen work bench. Then I did a typical female, clutching my pant legs and shrieking, "Eeeee! Take that thing away from here." My lemons had suffered a sea-change into a two- or three-day-old skunk.

When I recovered my composure enough to look the thing over, I had to admit it was cute. It was about three inches long, with an equally long tail and about half inch legs, and it was striped black and white like any other skunk. Ralph had seen it in the road when he went up to get the mail, and when he came back over an hour later, it was still there. By then it had fallen into a deep rut and was unable to get out. He stopped the car to help it, and found that it was almost too weak to stand. We discovered later that, the day before, a mother skunk, accompanied by her new and numerous offspring, had had a skirmish there with one of Coburn's guest's dogs. (The dog lost, incidentally.) In the fracas, this little fellow, whom we named Rollo, got lost.

You can't go off and leave a young thing to die of starvation, naturally, so Ralph picked it up and brought it home. He put it in the lemon bag so he could hold it without hurting it while he drove with one hand. He thought he could probably figure out some way to feed it after he got it home.

Cookie, Kyak's mother and the best dog we ever had, was our dog of the moment. Not to put too strong a point on it, she was the best dog anybody ever had, bar none. Kyak and the other pups were a couple of weeks old, and we were still keeping them in a pen in the corner of the kitchen, where they'd be warm and where Cookie could reach them easily. While we were debating the skunk commissary question, she came in to dispense the evening meal to her family. That seemed to be the answer. We found an unoccupied nipple, told Cookie everything was under control, and added Rollo to the roster. She looked a little startled, but, being the dog she was, took our word for it that the situation was entirely *comme il faut*. That's the kind of a good dog she was.

Cookie was willing, and Rollo had the right idea, but a husky is built on a somewhat grander scale than a skunk, so it wouldn't work. Then we thought of a medicine dropper, and that did work. Poor little Rollo went at it, clutching the dropper frenziedly with both front paws, and never stopped drinking the warmed canned milk and water until his little stomach was as round and hard—and about as large—as a golf ball. By this time Cookie's four pups were gorged and asleep, so we dumped Rollo in with them. Cookie looked at us, smelled of him, and looked at us again, trying to understand what was expected of her. Cookie definitely was a lady, and she always tried to live up to her station in life. She understood that we meant that she was to take care of this odd-looking addition to her family. So she rolled him over with her nose and, despite his struggles, lapped Rollo thoroughly from stem to stern, just as she washed her own children. After that Rollo belonged. Nobody was going to accuse Cookie of favoritism; and from that day on, Rollo was just another husky puppy, as far as she was concerned.

I think he, himself, thought he was a dog. Certainly the other pups treated him like one of themselves. The whole lot of them played together as puppies do, roughhousing and mock-fighting, chewing each other's tails and ears, and attempting mayhem in any form. At first we used to try to rescue Rollo. The pups were almost ten times as big as he was, and I was afraid he'd get killed. But he didn't thank me at all for my solicitude. When I put him down again at a safe distance from the fray, he'd stamp his hind legs in a towering rage—the skunk method of expressing extreme irritation, and the last step before the gas attack—and rush back to fling himself into the battle. I still don't understand why he didn't get completely ruined. I've often seen one dog grab him by the scruff of the neck while another grabbed his tail, pulling him in opposite directions with all their might, growling and shaking him as puppies will do with a piece of rope. It made my stomach ache to watch, but he apparently loved it for when they released him, he'd always rush in for more. It's my opinion that that twenty-four hours of being lost in the wilderness so early in life left a bad scar on his subconscious, so that he valued any attention as preferable to no attention. He'd never let himself be left alone for a moment, if he could help it, and when the pups slept, he was never content to sleep on the edge of the heap. He'd always burrow down into the center, completely out of sight.

He used to follow me around like a shadow as I did my housework. He'd be at full gallop never more than six inches behind my heels, and if I reversed my field, he'd side-step and fall right in again. It was lucky he was so fast on his feet. Half the time I'd never know he was there and, if I'd ever stepped on him, there wouldn't have been even a grease spot left. He was so tiny he could easily curl up in one of my shoes and have plenty of room left. It made him simply furious to have me go upstairs. The risers of the steps were much too high for him to negotiate, and I'd come back down again to find him stamping back and forth in a dudgeon below the first step. That stamping never failed to amuse me. He'd not only be mad—he'd be just damn good and mad! And yet, though he obviously wanted to make a noise like thunder and stamp the house down, the best he could make was a little pattering sound on the floor. If you're ever gone out of a room in a fury and slammed the door behind you with what was supposed to be a shattering crash, only to find it was equipped with a pneumatic check and so eased soundlessly into place, you can appreciate how he probably felt. Still despite his rages, he never in all the time he was with us made the slightest smell in the house. We thought some of having him operated on, but the vet in Rumford said frankly he had never done such an operation, so we let it go. We are glad now that we didn't find someone who could do it. He was cleaner around the house than any cat we ever had and he never, even in his infancy, made a single error.

Only once that we know of did he ever make a smell and we couldn't blame him for that; in fact, Ralph applauded him. We had at that time a cat named Jane, and she and Rollo had always hated each other, for no good reason that we could ever see, for they always left each other strictly alone. One evening I had made a chocolate malted milk for Rollo—that was his favorite food—and set it out. Rollo was just starting in on it when Jane appeared around the corner. Rollo stamped violently but Jane continued to approach and sniffed at the saucer. She wasn't going to touch the contents, I'm sure; she was just curious. But he had warned her and she had paid no attention. Faster than the eye could follow, he turned end for end, arched his tail over his back, and—whisht! smack into Jane's face at a range of less than a foot. She rolled right over backward, scrambled to her feet, and went off like a bullet. She never came back. Presently she took up her abode at the nearest lumber camp.

We had been afraid that after the pups and the skunk reached the age where they could eat solid food, Rollo would starve unless we fed him separately. He could never hold his own, we thought, against that gang of ruffians. We might as well have spared ourselves the worry. He was quite capable of looking out for himself. When the crush around the communal pan of puppy biscuit and milk became too great, he would wade right into the middle of the dish, forcing the pups to eat along the edges while he stuffed himself practically into a coma.

Rollo became a terribly spoiled brat before the summer had advanced very far. We gave him too much attention, and so did the dogs, and so did the sports who kept coming in in increasing numbers as the news of our pet skunk spread. I never thought to have my social career sponsored by a skunk, but that is what it amounted to. I met more new people during that summer than I ever have before or since in the same length of time. Perfect strangers, they'd come drifting into the yard from God knows where, say "Good morning" and then come to the point:—"We heard you've got a pet skunk." The upshot was always the same:—would it be all right for them to have their pictures taken holding Rollo? The folks back home— Rollo became as camera conscious as a child movie star, and as objectionable. He'd look bored and sulky—but he'd never miss the chance to have his picture taken. His complete composure served as an excellent foil, I might add, to the nervous apprehension on the faces of his picture-companions. Nobody ever seemed to quite take our word for it that he was perfectly safe.

Skunks are a horribly maligned animal. Everyone shuns them. Everyone accuses them, and without ascertaining the facts, of various crimes, such as hen-killing and egg sucking. They do no such things. Actually they do no damage at all; on the contrary, they are the natural enemies of vermin of all sorts and among man's best friends in the country. They are naturally gentle and easily tamed. A skunk will never attack until he is sure his person is in danger, or unless he is suddenly startled. I wish more people would bother to be nice to skunks. We were, and it paid. Rollo, in spite of being spoiled, made a perfect house pet while he was with us.

We never made any effort to confine him so it couldn't last forever. He was always free to come and go as he pleased. We even untacked a corner of the screen in the kitchen door so he could get in and out at will. As he grew older, he began to revert to nature, and the skunk nature is nocturnal. He slept more days, and roamed about nights. When we went out to the woodshed in the early, dewy morning to get kindling to start the breakfast fire, we would more and more often meet him, just coming home from a night's ramble. Then for a while he wouldn't come home for two or three days at a time, and finally he didn't come home at all. We'd meet him sometimes a mile or more down the Carry Road, and he'd run up to us and we'd pick him up. He never forgot us, and we never forgot him. We just grew apart, as those whose interests diverge always grow apart. Finally we stopped seeing him altogether. I don't know what eventually did happen to him—whether he wandered away, or whether he met with an accident. Very few wild animals die of old age. One thing we were glad of then—that if he did meet with death in any of the common swift wilderness forms, at least he was able to go down fighting. We hadn't rendered him defenseless.

Actually I've only been frightened once by animals since I came here to live. That was up at Miller's, and was a completely silly performance. It happened a long time ago, when Cookie was only a puppy. She had an enemy—Miller's older cow—who never overlooked an opportunity to chase her. I don't know how the feud started, and I don't know whether the cow would have hurt Cookie if she had caught her. It may have been just her bovine idea of a game. However, that may be, she certainly looked like business as she thundered after that terrified little ball of fur, with her head down, her nostrils flaring, and her tail out stiff behind. I don't blame Cookie for putting her tail between her legs and scuttling.

It was in June, and Alice Miller had a houseful. There were her sister Amy and two small girls, a half dozen men who were working repairing the dam, a woman named Polly Gould who was doing the cooking for them, and her little girl, besides Alice's own family. We went up there one evening to visit with the assembled multitude, and in the course of events, Alice, Amy, Polly and I took the collection of five small children and my small dog up into the back pasture to see if the blueberries were ripe. The two cows and Betty, the horse, were grazing off toward the edge of the woods, but we didn't pay any attention to them. Betty is as cross-grained a piece of horse-flesh as ever drew breath, but usually she minds her own affairs.

Cookie saw her old enemy in the distance, too, and I suppose she thought that now her inning had come. She'd been the chasee all too often. Now she was with me, the all-powerful; it was her turn to be the chaser. I don't suppose it ever entered her addled little head that the creature lived and breathed that would have the temerity even to think of attacking me or Ralph. We were God, as far as she was concerned. If you're walking with God, there's nothing you don't dare. You even dare to run yapping after a dragon and nip at its heels.

Unfortunately, neither the cows nor that limb of Satan, Betty, were True Believers. As one, they threw back their heads in affronted amazement, snorted, and took off after Cookie, who knew only one thing to do. She turned in her tracks and sought sanctuary under the shadow of my wing.

The first I knew about the whole business was when Amy shrieked, seized her youngest by the arm, and started running for the gate. The rest of us looked up. I don't know how two cows and a horse could create the illusion of being a whole herd of Texas longhorns gone loco, but they did. We each grabbed a child, and the whole bunch of us streamed off across the field, women shouting for help, children screaming with terror, and poor little ki-yi-ing Cookie bringing up the rear. None of us up to that time had been famous for her track work, but that evening, in spite of the rough ground, the boulders, and the bushes, we shattered all records for a two-hundred-yard dash. I swear that as we fell over the rail fence, hot breath was fanning the backs of our necks and horns were grazing our posteriors.

That's the only time I've been frightened in a country where bear and wildcats are common, and cows and horses extremely rare; and because I was so scared, and the whole thing so ridiculous, my immediate reaction, once we were safe, was unbounded rage. I was mad at Miller's livestock, at Cookie for bringing them down on us like a wolf on the fold, and at myself for running. But I was maddest of all at Ralph and Renny Miller and the crew of workmen off the dam. When we had got our breaths, and the spots had stopped dancing around in front of our eyes, did we see them running anxiously to our aid? We did not! We saw them all lying helpless on Miller's back stoop, weak with laughter.

Classed with animals as an A Number One Menace, by females from the city, are what they always refer to as "drunken lumberjacks." I am not a psychiatrist, but as a writer whose stock in trade is human nature, I am interested in all its various manifestations. One of the least explicable to me is the phenomenon of the woman who would not allow such a crude and lusty word as "rape" to pass her well-bred lips, but whose every inflection indicates that that is what she is hoping to be told about when she asks obliquely and with bated breath if I am not afraid of drunken lumberjacks. Well, I'm not. In the first place, very few of the lumberjacks I see are drunken. They may have been when they left civilization, but by the time they get in here, they're only sick and sorry, and in no state to menace anything larger than a day-old chick. In the second place, drunk or sober, they're twice as scared of me as I am of them. I hope that settles that question once and for all. I'm just a little bored with women who claim to be afraid of men, or who feel either inferior or superior to men, or who consider men as being anything other than so many more people.

There are, of course, a few things in the woods that anyone with sense is afraid of. So are there in the city, or on a farm, or at the seashore, or anywhere else, except possibly in the grave. A reasonable amount of danger is part of the price of living.

The hurricane of September 21st, 1938, was something to be afraid of—only none of us except Ralph had ever been in a hurricane before, so we didn't know enough to be afraid until it was all over. Then there was so much else to do that there didn't seem to be any time for fear. I'm not going to go into any great detail about the hurricane. Everybody who lives in New England has his own version of that cataclysm; and everybody in the world knows somebody in New England, and has therefore heard all about it, probably *ad nauseam*. Let me just say that after three days of pouring rain, along about dusk of the fourth day the wind started to blow very, very hard. Ralph was at Middle with Fred Tibbott, who was visiting us, and Edith Tibbott and I were at home with Rufus. After we'd waited supper half an hour, they called up from Miller's to say they couldn't get the car started, so they'd have to walk home, and for us not to worry. Up to then we hadn't considered worrying. We'd heard quite a lot of noise outside, but the woods are always noisy when the wind blows.

I decided that this was as good a time as any for me to go to the john, so I threw open the kitchen door, and almost walked into the top of a tree that was lying where the porch had been. The porch was at the bottom of the cellar hole, twelve feet below. That was the big birch at the corner of the house, I made mental note, and Ralph was going to be good and mad when he saw it down. In the meanwhile I still had my errand to perform, and there was still the front door. I turned the knob, the door crashed back against the wall, and I stepped out into the top of a pine that lay across that porch. This was no night, I concluded, to go ramming around in the dark. I shut the door and tried to call up Miller's, to tell Ralph and Fred not to start home. The line was dead. With rare perspicacity I diagnosed it as trees down across the wire. There was nothing to do, so Edith and I ate our supper, brought Rufus downstairs to sleep—a tree had fallen across the roof right over his crib, waking him up and starting a leak that dripped onto his pillow—and sat down to read. This sounds like courage and composure, but it was only ignorance.

After a while Fred and Ralph came in, soaking wet and full of tales about dodging falling trees all the way from Middle Dam. There must be, they said, at least two dozen blowdowns across the road. Ralph was, as I had foreseen, sick about the trees in the yard blowing down, but since there was nothing to be done about it, the two of them ate their supper, we all had a game of Mah-jongg, and went to bed.

In the morning we woke to a ruined world. We couldn't even get across the yard; trees lay criss-crossed in a giant tangle from the back steps to the road. The sky line all around us was unrecognizable. Where had towered tops that I regarded as personal friends and eternal landmarks, now gaped ugly holes. It was heart-breaking. A house you can rebuild; a bridge you can restring; a washed-out road you can fill in. But there is nothing you can do about a tree but mourn, and we had lost twenty-eight of our largest trees right in our front yard. Somehow it made it worse that the sun shone brightly, and that the still, washed air was as soft and warm as down. The day was like a bland and lovely child under whose beauty lay the horror of idiocy.

Fred and Ralph worked all day with axes and a two-man cross-cut, cutting a way through the mess to the road, the woodshed, and other frequently used points. Late in the afternoon, one of the dam crew staying at Miller's managed to get through from above with the news that instead of two dozen trees across the road, there were over two hundred. We needn't let it worry us, he concluded comfortingly. There was no reason for us to go up to Middle anyhow. The Lake Road to the Arm from Andover was plugged, too, and the mail wouldn't be coming through until God knew when. By that time they'd have the Carry Road open, for they had to be able to use it to get back and forth to Pondy Dam which they were repairing.

I thought then, and I still think, that it was a terrible waste that no one was murdered on the night of the hurricane. The writers of the whodunits work dreadfully hard thinking up and presenting plausibly the very strict frameworks of their stories. Here we had it all handed to us on a silver platter. We were a very limited group; we were cut off from the police and from all outside help; there was no way of escape for the murderer; the night and storm served not only as suitable atmosphere for crime, but created the confusion necessary for the successful perpetration of that crime. And nobody even got hit by a flying branch.

We don't have hurricanes more than once in a century in New England, so they rate rather as an exciting novelty than a true source of apprehension. We've had our allotment of hurricane. What we have to worry about now are the consequences of it.

The consequences are not all bad, we discover, in spite of our initial myopia to silver linings. The birds, deer, and small animals have increased greatly in numbers around here since the Blow; the condition of the woods has made it difficult for hunters to get around, and the great windrows of blowdown afford marvellous cover. I'm all for anything that will conserve wild life, even if it incidentally jeopardizes my own roof-tree. And actually my own roof-tree will profit, too. Old opportunist Rich immediately saw the possibilities.

After the hurricane, as I have explained before, the Government organized a pine-salvaging project. However the pines that had blown down across the Carry Road couldn't be salvaged by them because they had been butchered into every imaginable odd length when the road was cleared out. The idea then was to open a thoroughfare, so every tree lying across the road was cut twice—where the gutters would be, if we had gutters—and the piece in the middle was rolled off to one side. The result was several hundred good pine logs of no commercial value because they were in crazy, hit-or-miss, non-saleable lengths. We had long been planning extensive remodelling of the summer house, building a new shed for the rolling stock, and what not. We didn't object to unorthodox lengths for the jobs we had in mind. So Ralph made a deal with the landowners whereby he acquired them to the benefit of all concerned. All the next summer he and Gerrish worked like dogs getting these logs into a boom they strung in our boat cove in the Pond, where they would be safe from worms, fire, and rot.

That's easy to write, but it wasn't easy for two men to do. What they lacked in numbers, they had to make up in ingenuity. They finally worked out a rig that was the marvel of all beholders to take the place of the rest of a four-man crew. They took the front axle of the deceased Packard, complete with wheels and tires, and equipped it with a drawbar that could be fastened to the rear of the Big Green "Mormon." The butt ends of the logs rode on this, while the top ends dragged. But two men can't lift a three-foot green butt eighteen inches off the ground and roll a pair of wheels under it. So they built a portable ramp which they carried along in the car, studded with spikes to prevent slipping, and rolled the ends of the logs up onto this, using a combination of cant dog leverage and roll hitches. Once the log end lay on top of the ramp, projecting sufficiently ahead, the axle was rolled under, the log was dropped on it and secured with ordinary logging chains, and off they went, as merry as could be. At the Pond they had built a log rollway, and it was comparatively easy to unchain the log, haul the axle out from under it with a quick jerk of the car, roll it over to the top of the rollway with cant dogs, and let her go. I used to go up and watch them unload and roll in for the simple and elemental pleasure of seeing the big splash. I felt a little sheepish about this at first, and advanced the excuse that I really went because Rufus liked to watch the water fly. Very soon, however, I noticed that many of the crew that worked on the pine drive managed to be around kibitzing when unloading time came, and that, while they were interested in the mechanics of the operation, they always cheered when the great fan of water rose twenty feet into the air. After that I didn't apologize for my simple tastes. After all, where would Niagara's popularity be if people didn't like to see water splash?

This landing the logs in the Pond, however, wasn't even the beginning, since we aren't planning to build a deluxe log cabin. We're planning to rebuild a house, with pine paneling throughout the common rooms. So the logs in the Pond have to be transmuted into boards and timbers, and since that is impractical to do by hand with a broadaxe, we have to build a small sawmill. You see how one thing leads to another, when you can't just call up a dealer. At present the foundation of the mill is partially built, and sooner or later it will be running, powered by the old Packard Twin Six motor. I can already foresee the end. The logs in the Pond will be hauled out and sawed up, and the paneling will be made and put up, and the house will be finished. Then we'll have a sawmill with nothing to saw. This will be a challenge to Ralph, and he'll start thinking up other things to build, so he can use the mill. Then after every available inch of our property is covered with buildings of one sort or another, we'll probably end with an eighty-foot schooner, or something.

The most immediate result of the hurricane is really a legitimate worry—or rather, an increasing of one of our few standard dangers—the danger of forest fire. That's a thing that is never out of our minds, and a thing we have a right to fear, because we have so little control over the starting of a fire. We, ourselves, are almost fanatically careful about matches, and cigarette butts, and lunch fires. Everyone who lives in the woods is. I've known men to get to worrying over whether every ember of a fire they'd made at noon was out, and to back-track eight miles, after dark, just to make sure. But these were woodsmen. People from the Outside aren't conditioned to the fire hazard as we are. They don't mean to be careless, probably. They just don't know any better. If you're used to throwing a cigarette butt down wherever you happen to finish it, it doesn't register whether it lands on an asphalt pavement or in a brush pile. (Just thinking about the latter makes my palms sweat.) And fires aren't always started by humans. There are plenty of instances where they have been started by lightning, or even by a bit of broken bottle, acting as a burning glass. This chance element is what brings our heads up and sends us running for the field glasses to scan the horizon at the suspicion of a whiff of wood smoke.

It was bad enough before the hurricane, but now it is a hundred times worse. Now the woods are full of dried, dead tops that will burn like tinder. If a fire should start over back of a mountain somewhere, it might take a half a day or more for the fire fighters to get in to it through the blowdown, instead of two hours as formerly. With a brisk breeze behind it, and bone-dry brush to feed on, a fire can travel ten or twelve miles an hour, or even faster. You see, it doesn't burn evenly. It may jump a half a mile over the heads of the fighters, leaving them in an extremely unenviable position. That's why, when a pillar of smoke arises somewhere off in the bush, the telephone begins to ring, and we get out a compass and a map to determine, by comparing the sightings of Joe Mooney and Upper Dam, say, just exactly where it is. If no ponds or barrens lie between it and us, and the wind is in our direction, we get ready to start to collect the things we're going to evacuate.

We don't have to discuss what we'll take with us when we leave. That was all decided long ago. We don't have to discuss where we'll go. If the fire is below us we'll go to Middle, where there are boats to get us out onto the lake. If the fire should be above us or cut us off from the lake, we'll go to the Pond-in-the-River and take to our own rowboats and canoe. If it's a big fire it will get pretty hot and smoky out on the Pond, but we can always submerge ourselves. We won't be very comfortable, but the odds will be in favor of our surviving. For just such an emergency Ralph always aims to have at least one car in good running condition, regardless. The first load out of here will consist of all of us, Kyak, Tom (if we can catch him), the typewriters (which are our living), an envelope containing birth certificates, will, deeds, and other documents, and Ralph's cedar box of Scotch flies (which he sets great store by and which are practically irreplaceable). If there is time to come back for more loads, we can get clothes, guns, and fishing tackle. It's very illuminating to have to make a list, which you will very possibly have occasion to use, of the things you'd save in an extremity. It reduces one's material possessions to their proper place.

Since the hurricane, we have had two or three fires within danger-distance of Forest Lodge. One was over by Magalloway, and the fire-fighters got it under control before it burned over very much woodland. These fire-fighters may be volunteers, but they are as likely as not conscripts. The wardens have a right to draft any able-bodied male they may run across and oblige him to fight a forest fire for thirty cents an hour and meals—if the meals can be got to him at his post of duty. Often they can't. Fire wardens are only human, and it's my opinion that nothing delights them more than to force some stray sport, all done up in the expensive outfit that goes with a fifty-thousand-dollar income, to dirty his hands and burn his clothes for a measly thirty cents an hour. I'm a meany, too; I, too, think it's funny.

The other fires were across the river from us between C Pond and Upton. They were started through the carelessness of the river drivers on the Dead Cambridge. We could see the smoke, travelling fast and low on the wind, about four miles away, and at night the skyline pulsed with light. When you can see that variation of glow caused by a whole tree suddenly exploding into flame, then you know the fire is too close for comfort. If the wind had shifted and come drawing up the river valley, as up a gigantic flue, nothing could have saved Forest Lodge. We sat up late nights, during that time.

Then the wind died down and a slow and drizzling rain started, the sort of rain that people living as we do actually pray for, forgetting the fashionable scepticism with which education has veneered us. It was a steady, quiet, increasing rain, with the promise of a long wet night in it and, come morning, the surety of sodden woods through which no fire could travel. We tipped the porch rockers against the wall to keep the seats dry, and brought the deck chairs up out of the garden. We closed the windows on the

The Carry Road after the Hurricane

The "Mormon" Hauling Hurricane Pine

southeast side of the house, and placed a pan on the floor under the annoying gable that always leaks a little after a long drought has shrunk the shingles. We dashed out after forgotten clothes on the line, and brought in logs and kindling for the fire-place. It would be safe to have a fire this evening; the roof would be well soaked and inhospitable to sparks. And everything we did, we did with a sense of reprieve, with the realization that doing these homely things was a privilege of which we might have been deprived. We knew then that it is true that the only way to know how much you love a thing is to see it in peril of being lost.

Another legitimate worry in the woods is sickness and unavoidable accidents. Fortunately, woods life is very healthful. We are never sick, literally. Aside from the period directly following Rufus' birth—and I count that as a natural phenomenon, not an illness—I haven't spent a day in bed since I've lived here. Ralph has spent only two, with a bad cold. He doesn't count that against himself, as he didn't cook up his own cold, but caught it from some Outsider who came in here teeming with germs. If ever medical science wants data on the nature of the common cold, we're the persons who can supply it. We do all the things that are supposed to cause colds—things like walking half a day through wet snow with our clothes sopping wet, or not changing our shoes after coming in after a day in the rain, or sitting on cold stones, or lying full length on damp grass—and the only time we have colds is when someone brings them in from the Outside to us. We don't have things like mumps or measles, because people with ailments like that aren't fit to travel in here. What it amounts to is that we are living in a sort of reverse quarantine, with the germs locked out instead of in. It's wonderful—although I can't help feeling that the minute we get Outside among the coccuses and viruses that are rampant there, we'll be bowled over like nine-pins. Any immunity we may have built up in previous years has probably long since atrophied.

Almost every accident that can happen to you in the woods is avoidable, and soon you learn to avoid them. You have to, with a doctor usually no nearer than twenty miles—and twenty pretty tough miles, at that. You learn to hold wood that you are splitting by the edge and not by the top, so you won't take off a thumb. I don't have to remember here to look both ways before crossing the road —but I do have to remember always to keep an axe on the off side of the log when I'm limbing out, to carry it over my shoulder with the blade away from my head, and never, never, to take a full swing with it unless I've made sure first that I've got plenty of room behind and above me. These things I no longer have to remind myself to do; I do them quite automatically; and if this seems like odd habitual behavior for one who was brought up more or less as a lady, I can only say that there's no comfort in being a lady with a few inches of cold blue steel inbedded in your skull.

If you get cut by an axe in the woods, all you can do about it is to try to stop the bleeding, disinfect the wound —with salt, probably, as that is most easily available—and tie it up to get well by itself. If you can't stop the bleeding, you can send for the doctor, if it will make you feel any better in your mind. Almost certainly, however, the bleeding will have stopped by itself, or the patient will have bled to death, before the doctor can get in, unless the accident occurs in the summertime and there happens to be a doctor staying at Coburn's. The three weapons to use against axe cuts then are: (a) sense enough not to get cut, (b) a good working knowledge of how to apply a tourniquet, if the worst occurs, and (c) a philosophical attitude.

Burns are fairly common in the woods, and they're almost always the result of carelessness, too. You can easily get burned pouring kerosene into a stove to boost up a slow fire, or by tripping over the cat while carrying a kettle of scalding raspberry jam, or by unscrewing the cap of a boiling car or tractor radiator, or in any one of a dozen other damn fool ways. The only time I ever heard of anyone getting burned in complete innocence was last winter when a lumberjack was walking by the stove in the barroom, minding his own business, and for no reason at all the stove tipped over at that moment and dumped its blazing contents onto his feet. That was just tough luck, but it didn't make it any the less painful. As usual in an emergency of that sort, we were summoned, and we applied our sole remedy for burns—compresses of strong, cold, freshly made tea. This may sound like witch doctoring, but of course it's really the standard tannic acid treatment. He got well. Our burn patients always get well if they stick with the tea treatment faithfully.

Tea, therefore, besides being a beverage in our house, is a permanent item in our medicine cabinet. So is iodine, for small cuts and bruises. So is a five-pound package of Epsom salts, which we wouldn't dream of administering to our worst enemy internally. We use it solely in hot saturate solution for soaking infections. Because our lives are far from sedentary, and our diet is correct, we never need what are euphemistically known as "little pink pills," but we do keep on hand a bottle of Castoria, in case Rufus needs it, and one other laxative, for the use of visitors. We also have a bottle of fruit salts for alkalizing the system after we have been exposed to someone else's cold. I keep aspirin on hand, and take perhaps three tablets a year. Ralph takes none. Gerrish sometimes suffers from neuritis, and he takes the rest. Add a jar of some soothing salve, some gauze bandage, some adhesive tape and absorbent cotton, and baking soda for insect stings, and you have our complete medical equipment. Ralph also keeps a couple of pound cans of anaesthetic ether on hand in case the doctor if called for broken bones should forget to bring any. Our equipment isn't elaborate, but it's quite adequate.

You can break bones in the woods, by not paying attention to what you are doing or where you are going. You can drown, by the same method, or freeze to death, or smash yourself up in the rapids, or lose yourself in the woods. It always boils down to the same thing, though—you weren't using decent judgment. So I still insist that, aside from forest fire, there's nothing to be afraid of in the woods, except yourself. If you've got sense, you can keep out of trouble. If you haven't got sense, you'll get into trouble, here or anywhere else.

I lost myself just once, and I'm glad I did. It was an experience worth having, since it turned out all right. It was, of course, my own fault, from the very beginning. The reason I made up my mind to go to B Pond three days after the hurricane was because the day before one of Coburn's old guides started out for there, got lost, never even saw B Pond, and after hours and hours of wandering, finally came out on the Dead Cambridge, some four miles beyond his goal. From there he eventually got out to Upton. I decided to show the world that I was a better guide than he was; and that, I submit, is the world's least worthy excuse for taking a chance. I would even have gone without a compass, if Ralph hadn't made me take one. Me get lost just stepping over the ridge to B Pond? Don't be silly. I don't need a compass. But I took it to save argument, pinning it into my shirt pocket with a safety pin, because Ralph said he'd scalp me if I lost it.

Well, I got to B Pond all right. It took a lot of doing. The trees were down across the trail in windrows, some of them twenty feet high. I could see how Coburn's guide got lost. He did what I did—went around the piles instead of over them. I did what he didn't do—always worked back to the trail again before trying to go forward. Therefore I never piled up any considerable drift away from the correct line, as he did. His error eventually added up to several miles. Mine was never over a hundred yards, a fact for which I take no credit. I was only profiting by his mistakes. I got to B Pond. There was a watchman, Fred Davis, staying in the lumber camp over there, so I have his affidavit to prove it.

It was on the way back that I got lost. Fred Davis fed me doughnuts and coffee and advice before I left for home. I think he was a little doubtful of my sanity, because he talked to me as if I were a child. "You've got a compass? All right. If you have to use it, remember it's *right.* A compass is always right. Remember that. You've got matches? All right. If you find yourself hurrying, sit down and smoke a cigarette. Smoke it slowly, right down to the end. Don't get scared, no matter what happens." I listened politely. He meant well, even if I didn't need his advice.

I'd already been over the ridge once, hadn't I? Well, then—

It was that cocky attitude that lost me. I didn't think it was necessary to follow the trail quite as closely as I had coming over. That was primer stuff. I knew roughly where the trail was. I could get back to it any time I wanted to.

Only I couldn't, I found. Suddenly nothing was familiar. I was in the middle of a black-growth swamp that I hadn't even known existed. I had no idea whether I was east or west of the trail. I thought I was on the west side, but I could have crossed the trail unwittingly while crawling through or over one of the tangles of blowdown. There was just one thing to do—get out the compass and go by it. If I went slightly east of north, I'd come out somewhere on the river, and from there I could find my way home.

My first look at the compass shocked me. I was going directly southeast, according to it, and that was obviously crazy. The compass was wrong. I must have broken it coming over. Or else there were mineral deposits around here that no one knew about. Whatever the reason, the compass was obviously wrong. I *knew* I was going in the right direction. Then I remembered what Fred Davis had said. "The compass is always right." Ralph had told me the same thing many times. "*Always* believe the compass." All right, then, I'd give it a try, in spite of my better judgment. I lined up a topless maple about a hundred feet away, pinned the compass back into my pocket, and started across the tangle of spruce and fir blowdown.

That was the most hellish trip I ever took. I was almost never on the ground. Sometimes I was twenty feet in the air, with nothing to step on, with twigs scraping my face, and with the knowledge in my mind that if I slipped here, I could easily break my back and die slowly and horribly, with not a chance in the world of being found. But worse than that was something that wasn't mind or heart or anything else that I've ever felt before, pulling me irresistibly around to the southeast. To go against it, to follow the compass, was almost physical agony. It was something that can't be conveyed to anyone who hasn't experienced it. I would climb laboriously over a tangled jack-pot, and stop and get my breath. All around me, hemming me in, were more towering piles of blown down trees. I would start over a pile of them, and then remember that I was supposed to be following the compass. I would unpin my pocket, take the damn thing out, and look at it. If it was right, my proper route lay almost at right angles to the way I was going. But it *couldn't* be that way! However—I'd pick a landmark by it, put the compass back in my pocket, pin it in and start climbing; and all the time that thing inside me was twisting and turning and pulling me over to the right. Fighting it was harder than fighting the blowdown. I've talked with other people who have been lost, and they all agree with me that the feeling is something that can't be conveyed. It's like being under a spell.

Then at long last I heard the river. It wasn't where it should be at all. It was where the compass said it would be, which was something quite different. I came over one last gigantic windrow, and could see it shining through the branches. I heard an axe. There, only a few rods above me on the other side was home. I could see Ralph chopping away at a tree in the yard, and Edith Tibbott sitting with Rufus on the porch. They looked like people in a mirage, small and clear and unconcerned. I felt as if, should they glance in my direction, they wouldn't see me at all. If I shouted, they wouldn't hear me. They couldn't really be there. I took a long drink of river water, washed my face, wiped it on my shirt tail, and started up the shore toward the dam.

I'm glad I got lost; it was an experience. I hope I never, never get lost again, and I don't think I ever shall. You see, there's nothing in the woods that can hurt you, except yourself. I know better now than to hurt myself that way again.

IX

"Don't You Get Awfully Out of Touch?"

SOME TURNS OF SPEECH ARE USED SO FREQUENTLY THAT THE meaning has worn off them, just as a hero's head wears off an old, much-used coin. They still pass as legal tender between one mind and another, but they are really only blank and worthless tokens for what once were ideas. We use them just as we use a thin dime; we accept them for what they represent, not for what they are; but if we stop to weigh and examine them on the scales of sense and in the light of reason, we see by how much time and rough usage have reduced them.

I know perfectly well what people mean when they say, "I should think you'd get frightfully out of touch!", but it's a silly expression all the same. Out of touch, indeed! I don't see how anybody, actually, can be "out of touch." The demented are in touch with some world of their own. The castaway is in touch with his physical surroundings, his material needs, his thoughts and his memories. The sleeper has his dreams; and the dead—who can say surely what or where the dead touch?

So I ask sourly, "Out of touch with what?"

The answer is always the same, and always delivered a little vaguely, it seems to me, in my annoyed and hypercritical mood. "Oh, the new books, and plays, and music. You know. Culture and world affairs. Your own sort of people."

There's no answer to that, except, "Oh, nuts!", and ordinarily I don't go around saying "Oh, nuts" to anybody outside the family.

The reasons I feel like saying "Oh, nuts" are manifold. Just as a starter, I have often read more new and old books during the preceding year than my interlocutor, and I might add, read them with considerably more attention and appreciation. I don't have to do my reading, you see, for any other reason than my own enjoyment. We happen to have a great many new books, because we are lucky enough to have a rather tenuous connection, through my librarian sister, with a book shop in Boston, and one of the owners—feeling sorry, no doubt, for "Miss Dickinson's poor sister, stuck way off up there in the woods"—sends us, at intervals, boxes of advance copies which are given her by the publishers. These are occasionally bound galley proofs and sometimes regular copies as they will appear on the book stands, except that they have paper covers. Now this, I know, is childish, but I get an awful kick out of reading books in galley proof, in spite of the fact that they are tough on the eyes. It makes me feel tremendously in the know and *au courant* of literary matters. If I happen to find in the book, as we often do, a little slip of paper announcing the first day of sale to the public, and if that date happens to be, as it sometimes is, some time week after next, then my cup of bliss is full. Not only am I reading a new book, but I'm reading it before my friends in the city, so enviably "in touch," can possibly get it. All right; I admitted it was childish, didn't I?

Then, too, I actually do have time to read those books that I always planned to read, but never got around to, or that I have read once hastily—in the days when I lived in civilization and had to read the books "everybody" was reading, or else suffer looks down the nose because of my ignorance—and always planned to go back to for more intelligent perusal. I have read all of Proust, for example, under this scheme (I didn't think very much of it, either), and "The Education of Henry Adams" (which I think very highly of indeed), and I've reread "The Case of Sergeant Grischa," which I remembered rightly over the years as containing some passages of extremely beautiful and moving prose—notably the description of the march to face the firing squad. I memorize a lot of poetry, too, so I'll have something to be saying to myself on long walks. A poem to repeat, either aloud or silently, will help you over a hill or on a long mile as surely as a neighbor who stops his team and gives you a lift.

I never can get over the power of some combinations of words to stir the heart. They are, after all, just words, and taken separately they don't quicken the pulse at all. But there's something about certain alliances—. Take for example "Fills the shadows and windy places with the lisp of leaves and ripple of rain." Take almost all of "The Garden of Proserpine," which doesn't even make sense, but is so musical and beautiful that it doesn't have to mean anything. It is full of such lines as "Blind buds that snows have shaken" and "Red strays of ruined springs." Bertrand Russell can make my scalp crawl any old day with such examples of his own particular brand of cold and chiseled prose as the last paragraph of "A Free Man's Worship," which begins "Brief and powerless is man's life; on him and all his race the slow, sure doom falls pitiless and dark," and ends "—to sustain alone, a weary but unyielding Atlas, the world that his own ideals have fashioned despite the trampling march of unconscious power."

What wouldn't I give to be able to write like that!

I'm very sorry to say—and I mean this; I am truly sorry, because I know I miss a lot—that I don't appreciate good music. I don't understand it and it doesn't speak to me at all. I wish it did, but about the most complicated compositions I can enjoy are Sibelius' "Finlandia" and something called "Kammenoi-Ostrow" by Rubinstein, and these I can hear on the radio often enough to satisfy me. If I did comprehend and love classical music, I could still hear it on the radio, for I could listen to the Philharmonic, and it would cost me neither money nor effort. I could sit in my pet rocker with my ski-panted legs folded under me and smoke a cigarette and have a fine binge for myself; but that just isn't my kind of binge.

The same applies to plays. I never was a theater fan. When I lived in cities, I missed a great deal of possible pleasure because of this blind spot of mine; but since I have lived here, it has proved to be a blessing. I'd be miserable if I read of the opening of something new and enormously good, and knew that there was no possible way I could get to see it. As it is, my appetite for the dramatic has to be satisfied with the situations that arise in my own life, or the lives of my friends, or in the general world condition. These bits of theater are less artistic and well-shaped than the scenes that appear on the stage, but since

I don't know enough about good theater to be critical, they keep me happy.

If the foregoing is a confession of self-centeredness, lack of imagination, of taste, and of background, I can't help it. It's the truth.

I don't see how people living in cities, instead of off in the woods as we are, can really know so very much more about world affairs than we do. If living in civilization meant that they were in the confidence of Winston Churchill or had daily tête-a-têtes with even a second under-secretary of an under-secretary of the Secretary of the Navy—maybe yes. But as a matter of fact, they know only what they read or hear, and that's exactly what we know. The only difference is that in the city you can get ten conflicting reports a day on any given situation, while we have to wait until *Time* comes in the Friday mail to find out what the whole thing really boils down to. We get our news a little late, but I wouldn't be surprised if in the long run we have a clearer and more sensible idea of what is going on than those who read every special edition and listen to the special spot-news broadcasts on the radio all day long. Frankly, I don't see how they can possibly know where they're at from one moment to the next, and I should think they'd all go raving mad.

We have a radio, too, of course, so if we wanted to, we could hear news broadcasts every half hour or so. But we don't want to. We have too much else to do; and, since ours is, perforce, a battery set, we have to consider before turning the radio on whether what we are about to hear is worth running the battery down that much. It's amazing how much you decide can be eliminated under those circumstances. If it would help humanity or the course of the War by so much as one iota, I would gladly sit all day long and listen to eye-witness accounts of air raids and hour by hour reports on the progress made or not made along the numerous fronts. But it wouldn't help anything, and it would keep me in a constant state of turmoil and indigestion. So we have our fifteen minute dose of everything's-going-to-hell each evening, and the rest of the day we try to forget about it. There's not very much tranquillity left in the world today. It may be that in striving to preserve a little of it we are making the best contributions within our powers. Or it may be that this is pure rationalizing, and we are guilty of the most abysmal selfishness.

In our house, when you turn the radio on, it's because someone wants to listen to something specific. As the batteries get low, we listen to fewer and fewer things, saving the power, until the batteries we have ordered arrive, for what we want most to hear. Elmer Davis, Ezra Stone in "The Aldrich Family," and "Information Please" are the very last things to go. No matter where they stand nationally, they're at the top of the Rich Poll. If we have a little more leeway, we listen to Jack Benny's program, partly because we think it's extremely funny, and partly because we're always in hopes of being able to put our finger on the reason why it's so funny. Then there's a program called "I Love a Mystery," which probably hasn't anything to recommend it at all from an artistic point of view—except the sound-effects—but which we adore. It's full of creeps and horrors and hair-breadth escapes, and the actors are splendid. If there's a prize fight of importance, we listen to that. Ralph and I could once take or leave prize fights, but they are Gerrish's meat, and he's finally managed to get us into the same frame of mind. The idea is that we try to keep our radio in its place. It is our servant, and we try not to let ourselves become its slaves.

I'm not decrying the radio at all. I think it's marvellous —so marvellous that I won't let anyone try to explain to me how it works. We explain too much, in this day and age. Even if I could understand all about wave lengths, which is doubtful, I'd much rather not. I like to feel myself in the presence of a miracle when I turn a switch and the voice of a man in California comes all the way across a continent of snow-covered farms and frozen rivers and mountain ranges and empty plains to fill our living-room with song. Perhaps the miracle would be even greater to me, if I knew just how it's done, but that's a chance I don't dare to take.

In the summer we have a daily paper from Boston, and all the rest of the family read it religiously. I have to admit, though, that aside from reading the headlines and the Household Page, I use it mainly for a game that I play with myself. Like all the rest of my solitary games, it is simple-minded; but, like the rest of them, it entertains me. It consists of scanning the pages carefully and deciding which of the events reported I am gladest I didn't have to attend. Usually there's a wide choice of material, and I'm hard put to it to choose between the Girl Scout Jamboree at Old Orchard Beach (five thousand Scouts between the ages of twelve and sixteen were there, and mustn't that have been a headache for someone!) or the Forty-and-Eight Costume Parade in East Fairview Centre (where three women fainted, and if I know my costume parades, feuds for a generation to come were started over the charges and counter-charges that the judges had been suborned). If this game served no other purpose, it would serve to make me—if such were necessary—satisfied with my lot well off the beaten track.

Another thing that I am happily aware of being "out of touch" with is the world of fashion. I was never very clothes conscious, so my best efforts at chic were never very satisfactory, when I was in circulation. If I looked smart, I felt most uncomfortable and self-conscious; and if I felt at my ease, my appearance was such that my friends would feel called upon to explain to their friends, "You mustn't expect her to look too snappy; but she's awfully good-hearted. When you get to know her, you'll like her."

It's wonderful to sit up here in the woods and look at the pictures in the advertisements of the hats I don't have to wear. (It's my belief that a hat should help your face, not do its best to increase a Simple Simon effect.) My sole attempt at glamor so far has been the purchase and use of a ten cent bottle of red nail enamel, and this was somewhat less than successful in its purpose. I put it on twice, and both times was rewarded by shudders and averted eyes on the parts of Ralph and Gerrish, and wails from Rufus because "Mummy hurt self!" I finally abandoned it and Rufus appropriated it. He painted Kyak's toenails red and slopped some on his fur. The game warden came in, gave the dog one look and said, "I thought you told me your dog wasn't a deer killer." It took some demonstrating to prove to him that Kyak wasn't reeking with the blood of innocent victims, and when that was over I pitched what was left of the enamel into the river.

There has been just one time in my life that I regretted bitterly not being beautiful and glamorous and marvellously apparelled; and that happened, as of course

The Big, Green "Mormon" at Work

Bateau Crew

PHOTO BY FRED ADAMS

it would happen, just before the spring break-up. At that moment my wardrobe was at its very lowest ebb as the transition from winter to summer clothes had not yet taken place. It consisted of a pair of worn flannel slacks, a pair of really impossible ski pants, and some faded wool shirts. Moreover, I was about twenty pounds overweight, my hair was as straight as a string, and I couldn't get Outside to have a permanent—not that a permanent would have helped much, but I think it would have given me moral courage in a situation that I think any woman would have found difficult.

This is the way it happened, and I'll have to go back a little to fill in the background. Ralph has a great many qualities which I love and admire, but tact is not among them. He is just about as intuitive and sensitive to nuances of feeling as an iron hitching post. This works as much for me as against me. If he sometimes seems insensitive to my feelings, I by the same token don't have to worry about his being wounded by a chance word or look of mine. The result is a sort of rough-and-ready understanding of each other that I wouldn't exchange for all the romantic twaddle in the world. But it was not always thus. When we were first married, Ralph used to tell me occasionally what a good cook and sempstress and conversationalist and what-not Sally's mother was. I did have sense enough not to burst into tears, in the bride tradition, and accuse him of not loving me. But all the same, I felt inferior.

Then Sally came to live with us, and she sang her mother's praises, too. There was no reason in the world why she shouldn't and every reason why she should. She naturally loves her mother dearly, and moreover, it is greatly to her mother's credit that Sally never showed the slightest resentment of me as her father's second wife. Intellectually I could see that; but emotionally I developed a simply horrible case of jealousy. I'll never underestimate the power of jealousy to drive its victim to any length. It's a dreadful thing to be jealous. It distorts your whole mental outlook. I, who know, say so. Ralph, the insensitive cluck, of course never sensed that I felt that way, for which I now give thanks.

Then Sally went to Europe to join her mother, and I managed to forget about the whole thing, most of the time. I had Ralph, and then Rufus, too, and a life of my own that was proving more and more absorbing. In short I began to get sense. And then—

Then one fine early April day, Alice Miller called me up on the telephone and said with an air that chilled my blood even before I heard the message, "Well, I've got some news for you that you're not going to like! At least, *I* wouldn't like it, if I were in your boots."

My heart sank. "Now what?" I asked.

"Well, we just had a call from Baltimore on our Outside phone. It was really for you, but of course we took the message as they can't get you on that phone." She was deliberately keeping me in suspense. Before break-up is a slow time in the woods. Then she threw her bomb. "It was from Ralph's first wife. She and Sally are coming in to visit you."

I had thought Sally and her mother were in Haiti. I don't remember what I said to Alice. I do remember, to my shame, walking around the kitchen telling Ralph, "I won't have it. You've got to do something. I simply won't have it!" It really wasn't so much that I *wouldn't* have it, as that I *couldn't* have it. I just couldn't cope with the situation. Here I was, plain, everyday Louise, with a shiny, wind-burned nose and chapped hands, expected on practically no notice to compete with a beautiful cosmopolitan, fresh from the salons of Europe. I didn't have any clothes. I didn't have any conversation. I hadn't been anywhere or done anything interesting. She'd been everywhere. She'd have lots of interesting experiences to talk about. She'd have trunks full of gorgeous clothes. She'd be witty and fascinating.

"I won't have it," I repeated. "You've got to do something."

I know Ralph was stunned by this sudden metamorphosis of house cat into tigress. He just looked at me as though he didn't know me. "But what can I—"

The upshot of it was that poor old Ralph walked up to Middle and called practically every hotel in Baltimore until he found the one at which Sally and her mother had been registered. They'd left half an hour before for Boston. And that, as it turned out, was one of the best breaks I ever had.

Even I in my half-maddened condition—and I can see now that I was being impossible, although I think that almost every woman can understand how I felt—couldn't refuse hospitality to a guest who had come all the way from the West Indies. It was really a compliment to me, I suppose, that Terp felt she could come. Whatever Sally had told her mother about me must have been at least reassuring. Now, after it is all over, I can feel pleased about that.

At the time, though, I simply felt defeated and hopeless when Ralph made his report. "What'll I do now?" he asked.

"Nothing," I said. "There's nothing you can do. Don't worry about it. I'll be nice." I gritted my mental teeth. "If it kills me," I added silently.

It didn't come anywhere near killing me, because as soon as I met Terp, I liked her. I'd better make that absolutely clear at once. Naturally, everybody within a radius of about fifty miles knew about the whole situation before forty-eight hours had gone by. The local grape vine smoked, and the taxi driver who brought Terp and Sally up to the Arm from Rumford must have stopped at every village and farm on his way back, as near as I can figure it, to make his report. I could actually feel a wall of suspense and anticipation tightening up all around us.

Everybody knew who had gone in to Rich's, and they were just sitting waiting to see who would come out. Some probably thought it would be Terp, with a black eye and most of her hair pulled out. Some thought it would be me, with my chin elevated righteously above the folds of a cloak of outraged virtue. But none thought it would be possible for us to live two minutes under the same roof. That it was possible is owing chiefly to Terp's tact and absolute honesty of purpose. She was the perfect house guest, and she had no ideas whatsoever of breaking up my home. She wanted to leave Sally with us again, and she wanted, before she did it, to ascertain what manner of woman she was handing her child over to for a longer or shorter period. This is a motive that anyone can respect.

I'm afraid, however, that locally I got most of the credit for preserving the status quo. I know exactly what everyone was saying and thinking all around us. I know all about the interminable analyses of the situation, and the speculation that was rife, and the inevitable final conclusion—"Well, all I can say is that Louise is better natured than I'd ever be. *I* wouldn't put up with it!" I began to feel like a character in a Russian novel. There was the snow and the deep woods and the surrounding waste spaces, and in the middle of it we sat, a man and his two wives and assorted children. Terp even has red hair, and in Russian novels someone is always a beautiful redhead. All that was needed to complete the picture was a troika and a wolf pack.

It's always nice to have made a new friend, but this visit gave me more than that. It gave me freedom. It made me realize that the things we fear are almost always things which needn't be feared at all. They are creatures of our imagination. There was never anybody like the Terp of whom I was so jealous, but I would still believe in her and make myself miserable on her account, but for the fortunate chance that Ralph got that hotel in Baltimore on the telephone half an hour too late.

Not long ago, a friend who was about to marry a widower said to me, "Tell me honestly, weren't you ever insanely jealous of Ralph's first wife?"

The idea was amusing. I started to say, "No, of course not."

Then I remembered, dimly at first and then with increasing vividness. Yes, I had been exactly that—insanely jealous. I hope I never forget it. As long as I can remember that particular needless hell, there isn't much chance of allowing myself to repeat the experience for any fancied provocation.

We're supposed also to be objects of commiseration because we are out of touch with what are referred to as "your sort of people." There are two major weaknesses in this premise. The first is that I haven't been able to find out in thirty-odd years of living exactly what sort of a person I am. I think that this is a fairly common difficulty. It's hard to evaluate oneself, and self-evaluation is usually tiresomely self-conscious and absolutely inaccurate. When I hear someone say, in all honesty, "Now I'm the sort of person who'd give the shirt off my back," I decide immediately never to ask him for the loan of a common pin. If the analysis runs, "I never forget an injury," I know that I can count on immediate and generous forgiveness and forgetfulness for any injuries I may have inflicted. The only clue I have to my own character is a family saying which runs something like this—"That old loafer! Sure, he's a bosom pal of Louise's. The bigger the bum, the surer he is to be one of Louise's friends."

As a matter of fact, I don't know exactly what is meant by "your sort of people." There are plenty of people around here that we would be highly complimented to be classed with. Perhaps they didn't come from Boston, and perhaps they aren't college graduates. So what? They have the qualities—generosity and honesty and humor—that we would be happy to feel we shared.

The other weakness is that we aren't out of touch with anybody that we want to stay in touch with. After all, the U. S. Mail still operates. Because we have more leisure to write letters than we had in civilization, we are actually closer to a great many people than we ever were before. I know all about the great efficiency of the telephone and telegraph, but I still think it's too bad that the old-fashioned habit of long letters has fallen into desuetude. Brevity and speed are all right in business matters, but friendships can't be put on a business basis, even in the matter of communication. I like to know what my friends are thinking and feeling. If too long a time elapses without my checking up on these things, I find that where once was a friend there is now a pleasant stranger. When I lived in the city, I had lunch and went to the theater with these strangers at fairly frequent intervals. Since I took to the woods, I haven't seen them at all, but some of them have become my friends again. We've had to fall back on letter writing, you see.

There is this to be said for writing a letter instead of having lunch downtown: when you are writing a letter, you are thinking only of the person who is going to receive it. Nothing else is bidding for a share of your attention—neither the funny hat on the woman at the next table, nor the quality of the service, nor the nagging worry as to whether that odd sensation around the calf of your leg a moment ago was or was not a run starting in your new stockings. In short, there is no static. In addition to this, I find it very difficult to discuss intimate matters with anyone. It is embarrassing for me. I start talking about the weather as soon as the conversation shows a tendency to get personal. On paper though there's nothing I wouldn't hash over. Any of my correspondents will probably be glad to corroborate this.

Since I have to depend on letters for many of my contacts, especially in the winter, when, perforce, we have very few visitors, I have developed a few loose rules for being a good correspondent. I don't have to point out, I'm sure, that letters received should be answered within a reasonable time—say a month; but there is such a thing as answering too promptly and writing too long a letter. It makes answering a burden to your correspondent, who will feel obliged to do at least as well as you have done, and will soon be heartily sick of the whole thing. I always try, at least, to answer any questions that have been asked me in a letter I am replying to. Nothing makes me madder, myself, than to have people ignore my questions. I wouldn't have bothered to write them if I didn't want to know the answers. I try also, in order to avoid my frequent difficulty of sitting down to write a letter in which I had thought I had plenty to say and suddenly finding that I've forgotten all the gems I was going to pass along, to make notes from time to time on the back of the envelope of the latest letter received from my correspondent. These make odd reading—"Spare ribs, O. K."; "C. V. arrested for stealing bear out of trap"; "Al's report on Jake"—but I know what they mean. This is a little trouble, but not so much trouble as trying to make the brick of a letter without the straw of subject matter. And finally, I don't expect to get any answer to a letter. Then I'm never disappointed or annoyed when nothing comes of it, and I'm delightfully surprised when something does. This same attitude can be adopted with profit toward almost any aspect of life, I have found.

Not only do the mails run, but the boat still runs, and when in winter it has been hauled out, Larry's snowboat runs. So we can and actually do see some of our Outside friends in the flesh, from time to time. Naturally, we feel drawn to anybody who cares enough about seeing us to make the long, hard trip in here, and most of all to our very favorite flock of loons from Massachusetts whom we refer to as "The Crocks." This isn't a reference to their physical condition, but to the fact that a couple of them are named Crocker. Actually they're a rugged crew. They come in here, singly or collectively, at any time of the year, and by every conceivable method, snowboat, snowshoe, dog team (Stumpy once owned a dog team, but like us decided it wasn't worth the trouble), boat, canoe (Stumpy has some aluminum canoes with outboard motors, that are the marvel of all beholders), and, if necessary, on foot through the woods. They haven't arrived by airplane yet, but that will come as Ralph Smart was a pilot in the last war. It doesn't make any difference how or when they come, we're always enchanted to see Stump and Big and Bill and Ralph. It makes it nice that one of them is named Ralph, too, since that is also Gerrish's first name. When the Crocks are here, all I have to do is request, "Ralph, get me a pail of water, will you?" and I get three. I accomplish this by carefully not looking directly at any one of the three Ralphs.

The Crocks presumably come in here for a rest, but they have the strangest notions of resting that I ever heard of. They must endorse the theory that a change is a rest. The minute they get here, they start splitting wood, or going on jaunts to B Pond, or helping with whatever is the current project around the place. Stumpy and I always plan to go to Sunday Pond across country by compass, just to show it can be done, but so far the world has still to be shown, by us, at least. Meanwhile, my Ralph and the others sneer audibly. Bill is the most normal in his choice of amusements. If it's summer, he goes fishing, which is all right. It's even all right to fish as he does, about ten hours a day. Gerrish adores Bill because he's always crazy to fish, and goes too. Big spent all one Sunday morning, when Ralph was cleaning up the hurricane pine along the Carry, understudying the driver of a tractor that Jim Barnett had very kindly let Ralph have the use of that day. I can see how anybody who has never driven a tractor might want to try it once, but Big started at nine o'clock in the morning and, with Ralph, was two hours late for lunch, while Bill and I waited. That's quite a stretch for a man who ordinarily spends his day behind a desk. And it wasn't as if this was his one chance of a lifetime to horse a tractor around. Big's company in Fitchburg, Mass., owns a dozen tractors, and he could go out and run one any old time he chose. But I suppose that would be work.

Besides themselves, which would be amply sufficient, The Crocks always bring us all the new stories that are going the rounds Outside—and they hear them all and tell them well—and a collection of swell food, always including exotic viands, such as caviar, shad roe, artichokes or palm hearts. I know these things aren't really necessary to the sustaining of life, but it certainly does something for you in the middle of winter, when you have been living on pot roast and carrots, to drink a Cuba Libre and then sit down to a really sophisticated meal—the sort of meal that you have always before eaten off snowy linen, under soft lights, and to the accompaniment of muted music. It doesn't, surprisingly perhaps, taste any the worse for being eaten by kerosene lamp light, off a linoleum table top, to the sound of sleet against the window. If anything, it tastes better for this seasoning of incongruity.

The general impression which seems to be shared by most of our city friends is that we live in the middle of a desert and never see anybody. This obviously isn't true, as I think I have made apparent. We see lots of people, ranging in rectitude from the game warden to border jumpers and notorious poachers. (One thing I have noticed that all poachers have in common is a manner that can best be described as piety put through a collander, a sort of purée of noble thoughts and too-good-to-be-true motives.) Our friends and acquaintances range in geographical origin from Alice Miller, who was born in Andover, Maine, to a lumber camp cook named Roland Thibault, who was born in Saskatchewan and arrived here via Alaska and the West Coast.

In addition to the people we see, we also have friends whom I, at least, have never seen. Joe Mooney at the Brown Farm is one of these. I've talked with Joe countless times on the telephone; we have some very spirited encounters, yet I've never laid eyes on him. Joe is quick on the trigger. He can and does come back instantly with a pertinent comment upon any situation; but unfortunately for purposes of illustration it is usually unprintable. Joe is a swell guy. Johnny West was another. I never spoke to him in my life; I wouldn't have known who he was if I'd met him face to face on the Carry Road; I don't imagine he knew any more about me than my name and where I lived, if he knew that. But I always felt comfortable in my mind when I heard Johnny West go over.

Johnny West was a flyer who ran an air service out of Berlin, N. H., up through the lake country, and anywhere else for that matter. It wasn't a very big business and it didn't run on any regular schedules, but if you had to go somewhere in a hurry, either into or out of the woods, you could call up the Brown Farm, who would call Berlin, and get Johnny to come and get you. His plane had pontoons in the summer and skiis in the winter—he could always find a lake to set his crate down on in our country where landing fields don't exist—and it was always painted red. We'd hear an airplane motor and go out and look. There high up through the tree tops we'd see a flash of scarlet.

"There goes Johnny West," we'd say to each other. "Wonder where he's going."

We might well wonder. He did the oddest business, I should imagine, of any pilot in New England. He flew lumberjacks into camps, when they'd missed the tote team on account of too much conviviality. He came into camps in the winter and flew out cases of the horrors or compound fracture. Once he went into Upper Dam, in the middle of the spring break-up when Upper Dam was inaccessible, to get an old man who was very, very ill. This was to be the old man's first time in the air, after almost eighty years of living. He died before Johnny West got there, but he still got his ride. The body had to be taken out somehow.

Johnny West flew fishermen, and he also flew fish. When the State put about eight thousand stock trout into B Pond, he flew them in in milk cans lashed to the pontoons. That was the only practical way they could be brought in alive. The alternative was to pack the cans in on the backs of guides, which would have been too expensive, and trout die if too many are confined in too little water, unless the water is aerated. Even the sloshing around in the cans that the water would get on the B Pond trail, probably wouldn't be enough to keep the air supply replenished. But they could be flown in in five minutes from South Arm, where they arrived in special tanks with aerating blower attachments. It worked out very well.

I'm not awfully sure, though, that I approve of the

whole thing, on general principles. If you fly fish into B Pond, the next step is flying fishermen in to catch them, and that puts B Pond in the class with any little mud hole on the State Highway. I think a few places ought to be left in a hard-to-get-to condition. There should be some reward for willingness to make an effort. I wouldn't climb a mountain for anything I could think of, off-hand. I loathe mountain climbing. But still I don't think motor roads should be built to the tops of the best peaks. I'd be awfully annoyed if, after a ten-hour scramble up the side of a mountain, I arrived breathless and exhausted at my goal just in time to see a fat dowager in printed chiffon drive up in a limousine to park between me and the view. I'm going to be awfully annoyed if some day I stagger out of the woods onto the shore of B Pond, after negotiating that rough trail, just in time to see a plane full of playboys and girls make a landing.

Johnny West was a beautiful flyer. When he set his plane down on a lake, it was like seeing a red maple leaf flutter to the water. He was company for us, and he made us feel secure. We knew that if something perfectly dreadful happened—something beyond our ability to handle, like double pneumonia or a broken back—we could always get Johnny West to fly a doctor in, or fly us out. He saved a woman's life up in Parmachenee by flying a doctor in in the middle of a bitter winter night, about a year before his death.

Johnny West is dead. He died when his plane struck a high tension wire in the course of a forced landing, just as the early winter night was drawing in. I hope it was the way he would have chosen to die, but I don't know. I didn't know Johnny West. He was nothing to me but a flash of red across a lonely sky, and a thin, steady throbbing over the noise of the river. He was nothing to me but a name—and our margin of safety.

Aunt Hat is even further removed from my orbit than Johnny West was; she must have died years before I ever dreamed of coming into Maine. She didn't even live here. Her place of business was in Bangor, when that was still a lumber town. But Aunt Hat nonetheless is a very real person to me. You see, instead of going to the theater, we who have taken to the woods while away some of our long winter evenings sitting around each other's kitchens, drinking coffee, eating doughnuts, and talking. Talk is the backbone of our social life. It was during one of these evenings in the Millers' kitchen, when the wind was swooping down across the back pasture and the loose snow was driving across the lake like an army of gigantic ghosts, that Renny Miller brought Aunt Hat to life for us. We've loved her ever since.

Renny has his own way of telling a story. He starts slowly with no emphasis, filling in all the details as he goes along. That night he was telling us about his boyhood on a farm near Bangor, and how his first job was in a livery stable in town. "That's how I met Aunt Hat," he threw in casually. "Aunt Hat? Why, in them days Aunt Hat was the toniest Madam in the State of Maine. She ran a house up on the Orono car line. There wasn't a more respected businessman in Penobscot County than Aunt Hat, for all she wore skirts. She ran her place right, too. You didn't find no drunken lumberjacks in her house, like you did down the other side of Bangor. She kept the place clean and quiet, and it was furnished elegant—all gold furniture with red plush upholstery. And her girls were ladies, every one of 'em.

"Just to show you how smart she was— One Hallowe'en night a bunch of boys moved one of them little waiting stations the trolley car company had strung all along the line for the customers to take shelter in during bad weather. They lugged it down from a couple of miles up the track and set it up on the edge of Aunt Hat's front lawn. Now a lot of women in Aunt Hat's business would have been sore, figuring they was being guyed. But not Aunt Hat. She was real pleased. She seen right off what a good idea it was, and she made the company leave it there. They had to build themselves a new one, up where that one was robbed from. She was a smart woman."

"Were you one of her customers?" Ralph asked.

Renny grinned. "Aunt Hat and me was just like that." He crossed two fingers. "We set an awful lot of store by each other. Like I told you, I was working for a feller that ran a livery stable in Bangor. I was a pretty good hand with horses, and after he'd sort of tried me out with the old hacks he had in there for two-three weeks, he figured he could trust me, and he put me in charge of his show rig."

Renny sighed and his blue eyes grew dreamy. "Now there was something you don't see no more," he said nostalgically. "That rig was the prettiest sight I ever laid eyes on. Four coal black horses, he had—not a white hair nor a blemish on any one of 'em. Just like peas in a pod, they were. Them horses was curried twice a day till they shone, and the boss kept 'em so full of oats they danced, instead of walking. Them horses was so proud of themselves, by God, they made a man proud to be seen with 'em. He had a set of white harness with silver buckles made special, and it was as much as my job was worth to let a speck of dust get on that rigging. Every time it was used, I had to clean it and do it up in fresh tissue paper. White plumes it had, too, kind of sprouting off them four black foreheads, and he had a big white carry-all, with black cushions and silver trimmings. On either side of the driver's seat was a big silver lamp, and the whip set in a silver whip-socket. The driver had a uniform, sort of, that he had to wear, in keeping with the rest of it—tight, white britches, and a black cut-away coat and white gloves, and a silk hat with a bunch of white ribbons on the side of it. You'd thought I'd have felt like a fool in that outfit, me being about seventeen at the time, and fresh off the farm. But after I got to know them horses, I wouldn't have any more disgraced them by making them appear in a public place with me in my work clothes than I'd have let them go hungry. The boss hired this rig out for swell picnics and such, and I guess the biggest times of my life then was to go spanking down the main street of Bangor on that high seat, with the silver shining and the plumes tossing and them four big horses arching their necks and stepping high, wide, and handsome. Swell cars is all right—but there was a turn-out!"

That was before my time, but I could see it, too, prancing across the kitchen floor.

"Then," Renny continued, "then come September and Fair time and the Boss busted his arm. He called me into the office one day and said, 'Renny, I don't see no way out of it but that you got to drive Aunt Hat and her girls over to the Fair. I always do it myself, but no one-armed man can hold that team of hell-raisers, and there's no one else I'd trust them with. So it looks like you're elected.'

"Well, for all I was young and green, I knowed all about Aunt Hat. Every year she took her girls over to the Fair in this rig. She'd lease space and set up a swell striped tent she had, and she did a rushing business, besides giving the girls an outing.

" 'I won't do it,' I says to him. 'I won't drive them hussies clear out there in broad daylight and on a public road. I won't be made no laughing-stock.' He pled with me, but I wouldn't listen, so finally he says he'd appeal to Father. My father was a God-fearing man, so I thought that'd settle that.

"But Father took me to one side and says to me, 'Renny, your mother and I ain't going to like this any better than you do. It's going to cause a lot of talk. But it would hurt us a sight worse if we thought we had a son that backed out of a job he'd undertook. Jim's hurt and he's depending on you to take his place. He's been good to you, and don't you go back on him.'

"Aunt Hat wanted to get out to the Fair Grounds the day before the Fair opened, so's to get settled and ready for business. I was out to her place at daylight, planning on getting an early start, before there was too many people on the streets. But she thought different.

" 'What?' she says. 'Go sneaking through town like that at this ungodly hour and throw away all that free advertising? Like Hell, young man! You come back here at ten o'clock; and you can put in the time till then on that silver-work. It may shine bright enough for the Methodist Sunday School picnic, but it ain't bright enough for Aunt Hat!'

"We got going about half past ten. There was four seats besides the driver's, and Aunt Hat piled three girls in each seat. They was all dressed alike in black satin, and they had white feather boas around their necks and big black hats with white willow plumes. Sounds kind of plain, but believe me, it wasn't. Must have been the way they wore them outfits, but they looked a sight flashier than any red dress I ever see. Aunt Hat was dressed the same, only she had a big gold chain around her neck and a watch pinned on her bosom. I was wondering where she was going to sit, she not being spare, exactly, when she hollered to me, 'Where's your manners? Get that rump of yours off that seat and give a lady a hand. I'm sitting up in front with you.'

"I'd counted on skirting around the center of town, but I see there was no use even thinking about that. So I hunched my head down into my collar and tried to look inconspicuous, while I let the horses out a little, so's to get it over with quick. Next I knew, Aunt Hat had her elbow in my ribs; and for a woman as well larded as she was, she had a right sharp elbow.

" 'You hold in them horses, or I'll skin you. Hold up your chin and throw out your chest. There ain't a man on this street that wouldn't swap places with you right now, and don't you think different. You'll drive this rig and be proud of it, or, by God, I'll pitch you off this seat and drive it myself.' "

Renny smiled reminiscently. "She'd 'a' done it, too," he assured us. "So I see there was no use. I threw back my shoulders and set up straight and cocked my silk hat a mite to one side, and Aunt Hat threw out her chest until the seams of her dress strained. I had the checks and the martingales both on; the horses bent their necks pretty nigh into bows, and they trotted as though the street was paved with eggs. When we went by the Bangor House, I see our reflection in them big front windows, and we was something to look at. Them twelve girls looked just as proud and well curried as the horses. They looked the passers-by over, not brash, you understand, like you might expect, nor giggling like some of the girls I'd drove on picnics, but sort of dignified like. I tell you folks that before I got out of town, I'm damned if I wasn't proud to be driving them."

We could all understand that, I think. Renny made us feel just as he must have felt on that long ago September day.

"After we left town Aunt Hat turned to me. 'You done fine, Renny,' she says, and after a minute we was chatting together like old friends. She was a real nice woman, once you got to know her. When we got out to the Fair Grounds, the gates was closed as the Fair wasn't officially open yet. I made to hand the reins to Aunt Hat, so's I could get down and open them, but she put her hand in its black kid glove on my arm.

" 'You set still, Renny. I'll tend to this.' And she stood right up and shouted, so's you could hear her all over the grounds, 'Open up these gates, you sons of bitches! Here comes Aunt Hat and all her whores!' "

Renny laughed aloud at the memory. "I like to died," he said. "I tell you, I never hear that there hymn, 'Unfold, Ye Portals Everlasting,' but what it brings to mind them gates. Unfold—that's just what they did do, and we drove through with a flourish. The Grounds was full of folks getting their exhibits ready, and Aunt Hat says, 'Drive around the race track, and drive like you did back in Bangor.' She shoved my hat over one ear, and off we started. The crowd all come running to the rail to see us, and somebody started to cheer. Round we went, and the cheer growing louder all the time, till when we come around again and drove off, it was bedlam let loose. Aunt Hat never batted an eyelash. When we pulled up in front of her tent she ordered the girls down, kind of crisp like, but pleased, too. Then she says to me, 'Thank you, Renny. You come back and get us Saturday night,' as genteel as you could ask.

"She was a great Aunt Hat. After that I took her and the girls out on plenty of airings and picnics. She'd always ask for me when she ordered the rig. The Boss didn't have a look-in, no more."

Ralph said, just to keep the record straight, "Then you weren't a customer of Aunt Hat's, at all?"

Renny looked at him. "Customer, hell. Anybody could be a customer. I was a friend!"

No, poor Riches, we don't have plays and music and contact with sophisticated minds, and a round of social engagements. All we have are sun and wind and rain, and space in which to move and breathe. All we have are the forests, and the calm expanses of the lakes, and time to call our own. All we have are the hunting and fishing and the swimming, and each other.

We don't see pictures in famous galleries. But the other day, after a sleet storm that had coated the world with a sheath of ice, I saw a pine grosbeak in a little poplar tree. The setting sun slanted through a gap in the black wall of the forest, and held bird and tree in a celestial spot-light.

Every twig turned to diamond encrusted-gold, and the red of the bird's breast glowed like a huge ruby as he fluffed his feathers in the wind. I could hardly believe it. I could only stand still and stare.

And then I repeated to myself again something that I once learned in the hope that it would safeguard me from ever becoming hardened to beauty and wonder. I found it long ago, when I had to study Emerson.

"If the stars should appear one night in a thousand years, how men would believe and adore; and preserve for many generations the remembrance of the City of God which has been shown!"

X

"Do You Get Out Very Often?"

THE FIRST WINTER THAT I LIVED HERE, CLIFF WIGGIN-Wallace used to call me up. He still does, for that matter, whenever he gets bored with his own society and that of his several cats. I'd only seen him once, but we'd have a good gossip every now and then, and about once a month he'd ask me what day of the week it was. I'd tell him, shaking my head and clucking my tongue to myself. You see, Cliff hadn't been Outside for three years, and I thought I recognized the first sign of his going woods queer. Woods queerness is a real and serious and fairly common thing here, brought on by solitude and a growing awareness of the emptiness all around. It starts in little ways, and gets worse and worse, until finally it may end in raving insanity. Every now and then, someone along the lakes is taken out to an asylum. I thought Cliff ought to go out on a spree. Three years is too long a time to stay in the woods.

Or so I thought then. I didn't know that it would be over four years before I myself saw the Outside; and if I had known it, I wouldn't have believed that the time could pass so quickly and lightly, that season could roll so smoothly into season, and year into year.

I didn't spend the whole four years sitting in my own back yard, of course, unless you interpret back yard loosely as stretching from here to the border. I covered the territory hereabouts fairly thoroughly.

For example, Gerrish and I make at least one annual trip to B Pond. It's supposed to be a fishing trip, but we've never yet caught any fish. There are some enormous old trout in there, and once in a while someone brings one out. They're pretty cagey—that's why they've lived to be enormous—but we always hope. This hope is one of the reasons why we continue to go. The other is that we like B Pond.

B Pond deserves a better name. It should be called Benediction Pond, or Sanctuary Lake. It might even be called the Pool of Proserpine:

> "Here, where the world is quiet,
> Here, where all trouble seems
> Dead winds' and spent waves' riot
> In doubtful dreams of dreams . . ."

There is that feeling of remoteness and calm and timelessness about it that makes the scramble of ordinary life seem like a half-forgotten and completely pointless dream. It just lies there in a fold in the hills, open to the sky and wind and weather. Ducks and loons breed in its coves, the gulls fly over it in great white arcs, and the great fish go their secret ways in its dim depths. Once in a while human beings, like Gerrish and me, invade its privacy, but we don't make any impression on B Pond. I always have the feeling that the whole valley in which it lies—the hillsides and the deer on the hills, the trees that grow down to the water and the birds that build in them, the pond itself with all its myriad life—simply waits for us to go. I always want to turn back, after we have entered the woods on our homeward trek, to see what enchanting things take place the minute our backs are turned. It's that kind of pond. There must be many like it in Maine, that the map-makers could so callously label it B Pond, simply because it lies in what was once B Township, and pass along to other matters. There must be, but I can't believe it.

I hope that when I'm sixty and Gerrish is eighty, we'll still be going to B Pond every spring. We'll still politely invite Ralph to go too, of course; and he, of course, will still refuse to have any part of the expedition. That's one of the things I can't fathom about the spouse of my bosom—why he won't go to B Pond. He says it's because of the walk over the steep, rough trail, and because you never catch any fish there, and because he doesn't like trolling anyhow, being a fly-fishing addict, and because he just doesn't like B Pond. The last is probably the real reason. Somewhere he has acquired a deep-seated aversion to the place, so there's no point in arguing with him about it, or trying to understand it. He just doesn't like B Pond.

Let me tell you about the best trip we ever made to B Pond. Some days are enchanted, as everybody knows. Every detail of the day, even the most trivial, falls into exquisite juxtaposition with the next. Commonplace things take on significance and beauty. Perhaps it's a matter of timing. Perhaps for once one walks in sympathetic vibration with the earth, disturbing nothing as one treads. However that may be, this was one of those days.

We got up before dawn and ate breakfast by lamplight. The stove didn't sulk or smoke, and neither the oatmeal nor the bacon burned. The coffee was good—hot, strong, and clear. When I put up our lunch, the bread sliced without crumbling, and the ham curled pink and thin from under the knife. The butter was just right to spread, firm but not hard. I found a box at once that was just the correct size for our sandwiches and bananas, and I didn't forget sugar and canned milk for the coffee we would make at noon over a camp-fire. Gerrish came in from the garden with a canful of the liveliest, juiciest worms a fish could hope to see. The shiners that we had been keeping in a minnow trap down in the river had neither escaped nor died, and we found a tobacco box that was ideal for carrying them. None of our tackle had been mislaid or broken, and Ralph didn't wake up and come down and sneer at us for going to B Pond.

We went up the road and across Pond-in-the-River Dam just as the sunlight struck the tops of the trees on the ridge. The valley was still in shadow, with steam rising white from the churning water and turning to a lovely pearly pink as it reached the sun-shot air above. I knew how fish feel as they swim about in the depths and look up to see the light of day above them. We went into the woods and climbed the ridge, with the sound of the river fading behind and below us. I never can tell exactly when I stop hearing the river. It fades and fades, but still is there. Then suddenly it is there no longer, and the silence is much louder than the roar ever was.

For once I could keep up with Gerrish with no effort. Usually he has to dawdle, which is terrible for him; or I trot, which is terrible for me; or we strike a working compromise whereby each goes his own pace and we have a reunion at our destination. This morning we moved along together swiftly and silently, watching our footing on what passes for a trail, admiring the woods in the early gray light, and not talking. That's one of the good things about Gerrish. I can talk to him or not, and silence is as comfortable for both of us as speech. When we got to the top of the ridge we met the sun. The woods were suddenly pierced with long, green-gold lances of light, and instantly a thousand birds began to sing. They sang us right down to the shore of B Pond. I'm not a bird lover by trade, but that morning I felt like St. Francis. I felt like an angel coming down a heavenly stair, with the air alive and alight around me with music and the rustle of wings.

The boat slid smoothly out of the lean-to where we keep it and into the water, without the usual knuckle-barking struggle. We sat down on the shore to assemble our tackle, and a shelldrake came flying in from the east, not seeing us at all. The sun was behind it, and as it spread its wings and tail to brake for a three point landing almost in our laps, the delicate rib of every feather was silhouetted black and single, and the down along the ribs was gold and translucent. We could see how wonderfully and intricately it was made. Spray flew up like a fountain of jewels as it plowed the water. It was a bird of fire, coming to rest among diamonds and emeralds.

We got into the boat and pulled slowly away from the shore, paying our lines out behind. The rods vibrated as the spoons began to turn beneath the glass-smooth surface. No breath disturbed the water. Each pine and spruce and budding maple on the shore stood upright on its perfect, unbroken reflection. We went around the pond once—about two miles—and then it was my turn to row. The boat seemed to have no weight at all. The slow and steady pull and recovery were like an opiate, and time stopped.

Two loons appeared from somewhere and swam out to look us over.

Loons are my very favorite birds in all the world. This pair circled around us, curious and unafraid, turning their big hammer-heads pertly and halloo-ing back and forth about us. They showed off, diving and staying under water for incredible periods, and bobbing back to the surface in unexpected places. They stood on their tails and stretched their huge wings, and rolled from side to side, smoothing and preening their broad white bosoms. Then they looked at us again. We were really just as funny as they had thought in the first place. They exchanged glances and their weird laughter echoed from the hills. My eye caught Gerrish's, and in a flash there were four of us laughing crazily instead of two.

Nothing could go wrong that day. A breeze came up, but it only crisped the surface of the water, without making rowing a chore. Big, fleece-topped clouds rolled up from the horizon, breaking the smooth blue of the sky into lovely patterns and sending their shadows chasing over the far hillsides; but they never came near the sun. We went by a little point, and I said, "Isn't that a pretty place!" It was. It was covered with grass and a low growth of scarlet-stemmed bushes. A gray ledge cropped out along the water's edge, and a little clump of white birches, budding misty green, leaned over its own image. Just as Gerrish turned his head to look, a red doe stepped out of the black spruce copse behind and stood with her head high, looking at us. That would never happen again in a hundred years, and I'm glad I have a witness that it happened then.

Finally Gerrish said, " 'Bout time we were leaving, ain't

it?" He rowed a few strokes. "Noticed anything missing?"

"The gulls!" I exclaimed. "They haven't come yet."

We turned toward the rock that serves as a landing. And then we heard a faint and faraway crying. Through a high gap in the mountains the gulls came winging from the east, a dozen of them, screaming with excitement. They flew around the pond three times, white against the dark hills. They swooped to the water and soared to dizzy heights, riding the currents of air up and up without moving a wing, their plaintive mewing filling the air. Then they settled down on the rocks which have been their breeding grounds for centuries.

I'm glad that we didn't catch any fish. I'm not sentimental about fish. I'd just as soon kill them as not. But that day we had enough to bring home with us without adding any corpses.

Trips to B Pond aren't always so idyllic. Fairness demands that I should report on the most horrible one we ever took.

We didn't get started until after lunch. It had been threatening rain all morning, so we should have known enough to stay at home. But the ice had been out two or three days, and we had a theory that now was the time when the fish would be rising. After lunch the clouds looked thinner, so we hastily scratched together our tackle and set out.

I don't know how we did it—we'd each been to B Pond a hundred times—but we got lost. There were some new woods-roads criss-crossing the ridge from the winter before's cut, but we knew the country. We shouldn't have become confused. However, we were. We wandered all over the ridge for an hour, trying to find something that led somewhere. We always brought up in a pulp-yard. Finally we went back to the dam and started all over again, and this time we made it.

We came out at the lean-to, hot and disgusted and tired, and Gerrish held out his hand for the key. Of course—oh, so utterly and completely of course! I didn't have the key. It was too good a padlock to break, although by then only its strength, and no ethical consideration, deterred us from breaking it. We were mad. We'd come to B Pond to fish, and we were going to fish, if we had to build a raft and paddle it with our hands.

It didn't quite come to that. We found an abandoned and water-logged old boat drawn up in the bushes, along with a pair of home-made oars. It leaked quite a lot, but by bailing with our bait can—we dumped the worms out into the boat, where they squirmed around our feet—we thought we could keep afloat.

"We ain't got much time," Gerrish said. "You start rowing while I set the tackle up."

There was a nasty, biting little wind blowing, and the water was gray and choppy. The boat handled very badly, and pretty soon a fine, chilling rain set in. I didn't chill much. I was working too hard keeping up steerage-way. Every time I seemed to be getting somewhere, the water started coming in over the tops of my boots and I had to bail, while the wind drifted us back the way we had come. I could feel a blister developing.

Gerrish in the meantime had his gear laid out on the stern seat and was assembling it. He had a gang-hook full of worms on the end, and along the leader a couple of drop hooks, Archer spinners, spoons, and various gadgets. It was a very imposing and lethal array.

"There!" he said finally, with a craftsman's satisfaction, and threw it grandly over the side.

He hadn't tied it to the line. Paralyzed, we watched it sink irrevocably out of sight. Then we looked dumbly at each other.

Gerrish found words first. He had a very sound suggestion to make. "What say we tie some stones around our necks and jump overboard, Louise?"

And that's the other side of the B Pond story.

There are lots of places to go, all in the woods, it's true, but all different. There's Prospect, a logged-off, burned-over point, eight miles up the lakes, near Upper Dam. You go by boat, past unfamiliar coves and promontories. At one place is a walled cellar hole, now under water, which is all that remains to show where Richardson, for whom the lake is named, tried to establish his ill-fated colony. The fields that the score of families who went with him cleared so laboriously have all gone back to the forest. Nobody knows anything about Richardson—what vision inspired his undertaking, or what lay at the root of its failure. All that remains of him is a piece of excellent dry-masonry and a name curving down a map. A man could have worse memorials. "He was strong and patient and honest," the painstakingly laid stones bear silent witness. "He had courage and imagination," say the letters of his name, so strange and incongruous on the map between Mooselookmeguntic and Umbagog.

From the entrance to the Narrows you can look back across the hills and see Mount Washington, a whole state away, and so faint and lofty as to seem more like an idea than a mountain. From nowhere else on the lakes can you see it. And nowhere else are there blueberries like the blueberries of Prospect, which are what you go there for in the first place. They grow as large as your thumb nail, and have a peculiar dull black lustre under the bright surface bloom, as though soot from the old fire still stains and sweetens them. There are acres and acres of them, and no matter how long and fast you pick, working in the ceaseless wind that blows across the barren from the lake, loud with the lovely sound of water lapping on stones, you can no more than scratch the surface of the plenitude. We come home, wind-burned and juice-stained, with forty or fifty quarts; but no one could tell we had ever been there.

At night, after being at Prospect, I lie in bed and see great clusters of berries slide by endlessly against my closed lids. They haunt me. There are so many of them yet unpicked, so many that never will be picked. The birds and bears and foxes will eat a few, but most of them will drop off at the first frost, to return to the sparse soil of Prospect whatever of value they borrowed from it. Nature is strictly moral. There is no attempt to cheat the earth by means of steel vault or bronze coffin. I hope that when I die I too may be permitted to pay at once my oldest outstanding debt, to restore promptly the minerals and salts that have been lent to me for the little while that I have use for blood and bone and flesh.

Then there is Sunday Pond, small and remote, with a cliff on the north shore. You can see right across the Carry from that cliff, from Richardson to Umbagog. There is the Sandbank across the lake, where the best swimming is; and Smooth Ledge, with the river raging around a great out-cropping of rock. The loveliest pool on the river is at the Foot of the Island, and at Long Pool the deer come to drink and a disreputable old bank-beaver lives. There is the Pocket of the Pond, running up through a hellish black cedar swamp to a tiny icy spring. And there is rumored to be a nameless little pond somewhere up on the hog-back between the Carry Road and Sunday Brook. No one knows exactly where it is. No one knows, really, if it exists at all. But some day soon I'm going to find out. If I get lost, perhaps they'll name the pond after me—if there is a pond. That's the surest way to achieve immortality in this country. Who would have heard of Cluley if he hadn't been drowned in the rips?

I spent four years ramming around the woods, and I could have gone on for the rest of my life in the same way, if it hadn't been for Alice Miller.

She called me up one day in April to tell me that she was going out over the break-up to visit her sister in Lewiston. I said, for something to say, "Well, see a couple of movies for me. I haven't seen one for myself for over four years." I was just talking. I can take movies, but I can just as well leave them alone.

"You'd ought to go out, Louise," she said. "First thing you know, you'll be going woods queer."

I laughed, but she didn't.

"I'm not fooling," she said. "You can laugh, but how do you know you ain't queer already? For all you know, come to get you in crowds and traffic, you'll act like one of these farm dogs in a town, running into doorways and shivering and howling. You'd ought to go out."

I continued to think that was pretty funny for about five minutes after she'd hung up, and then I wasn't quite so sure it was so very funny. After all, she'd spoken with conviction. She'd really snatched at an opportunity to make the suggestion. Maybe she'd noticed something about me— Or maybe Renny had. Renny'd been around the woods most of his life. He knew the symptoms. Maybe he'd said

The Front Yard

TWO REASONS WHY WE DON'T GET BORED

View from Our Porch

PHOTO BY FRED ADAM

to her, "If you get a chance, drop a hint to Ralph about Louise. It's time she went Outside. Or if it comes right, say something to her—" How did I know? The clerk at Barnett's Number One camp the winter before had thought he was all right long after even I could see that he wasn't. So had that big Russian up in the Narrows, and it had taken four men to tie him and get him aboard Larry's boat. So had the lumberjack who had tried to hang himself in the horse hovel down by the *Alligator*, and the woman up on Mooselookmeguntic. And so did I.

It's ghastly to wonder seriously about your own sanity. First you start remembering things. I remembered breaking my pet needle the week before, and all the talking I had done about it.

"Haven't you got another one?" Ralph asked.

"Certainly. I've got dozens. But this one was different. It was balanced just right."

"Well, for God's sake! Whoever heard of a balanced needle? You're nuts."

Of course, he often says "You're nuts" to me. But hadn't he looked at me queerly this time? *Was* it odd to think that a needle could have correct balance? I didn't think so—but how could I tell?

I thought of my Columbiana Pump pencil. It was painted cream-color with gold lettering on it, and it was round. I don't like hexagonal pencils. They hurt my fingers. Most round ones, especially free, advertising pencils, have specks of grit in the graphite. Not my Columbiana Pump pencil, though. The lead was soft and smooth. It was the best pencil I had ever taken in hand, so I said it was mine. I hid it in my mending basket, and nobody was supposed even to think about it. And then one day it was gone.

I flew into a froth. You know:—"Considering the very few things I'm fussy about around here, I should certainly think that when I ask to have a measly little pencil left alone, it could be left alone. I'll find out who took my Columbiana Pump pencil, and when I do—" You can imagine.

It didn't seem to me to be an unreasonable attitude, but how could I be sure? Do sane people go into rages about pencils? Do they make horrible threats? I didn't know, and whom could I depend on to tell me honestly? I remembered the clerk from Number One saying pitifully, "I think I'm going crazy. Do you think I am?" I remembered my answer. "Of course not. Crazy people don't wonder if they're crazy. You're all right." I remembered wondering what I'd do if he suddenly went into a violent phase.

There was only one answer. I had to go Outside. If I weren't on the way to woods queerness already, I soon would be if I began to question and scrutinize my every act and thought. I'd begin to see hidden meanings in what people said to me and in the way they looked at me, or in the things they didn't say or look. Merna and Albert Allen, with whom Sally was boarding while going to school in Upton, had invited me repeatedly to come out with Rufus and stay over night. I'd have to see if I couldn't manage somehow to get out there.

The ease with which my going was arranged, once I let it be known that I wanted to go, did nothing to re-establish my peace of mind. Actually, of course, people were just being nice. In spite of all that is said, and more especially written, about the crabbed New Englander, New Englanders, like all ordinary people, are nice. Their manner of proffering a favor is sometimes on the crusty side, but that is much more often diffidence than surliness. I shouldn't have been surprised and suspicious at all at the co-operation I received after Ralph asked one of Barnett's tractor drivers to ask Merna the next time he was out in Upton if it would be convenient to have me some time during the next week. Ordinarily I wouldn't have been. But I couldn't help remembering how hard we'd all worked, the winter before, to get that clerk out on a legitimate pretext before a strait-jacket was necessary.

The tractor driver, Edgar Worster, said that he knew it would be all right. He lives next door to the Allens and he'd seen Merna two days before. She'd told him to bring me out on the tractor the next time he came, and as it happened, he was going the next day. The camps were breaking up, and he had to take out the beds, stoves, some lumber, and the pigs, and there was no reason in the world why he couldn't add Rufus and me to the load. If I'd just be ready to start around noon—

Ordinarily to get to Upton from here is a problem. You can walk seven terrible miles, or you can go down Umbagog in a boat—if you can get a boat and the ice is out—or you can go to the Arm and then drive thirty-odd miles around over East B Hill. To be able to ride out on the tractor was a break. You can't do it just any old time. There is no road at all. It's possible only when there is enough snow to pack into a reasonably smooth surface. There are limits to what even a tractor will do. So I accepted the invitation with alacrity.

Then the question of what to wear reared its ugly head. Rufus was all right. He had a fairly new snow suit. But as for me—

"Don't give me any of that 'I haven't got a thing that's fit to be seen' business," Ralph begged. "That's what women always say."

Maybe it is, but for once it was absolutely and literally true. I *didn't* have a thing that was fit to be seen, even in far from dressy Upton. I almost didn't have a thing, period. I hadn't bought anything but woods clothes for five years. Woods clothes would have been all right, but even Upton has prejudices in favor of reasonable neatness and cleanliness. My old ski pants had holes in the knees and seat, and my newer ones were filthy and I didn't have time to wash them. I thought briefly of the days gone by when I had worried over such esoteric details as the exact shade of my stockings. Now I had one pair of silk stockings, five years old, and when I put them on, they went to pieces, rotten from lying in the drawer. Mice had eaten the shoestrings out of my one pair of Outside shoes.

Well, that was all right. I didn't have any overshoes, anyhow, so I could wear what was left of the silk stockings, for something to fasten my garters to and hold my unaccustomed girdle down, some wool knee socks, for decency and warmth, and my gum-boots. So far, so good. Then I had a twelve-year-old Harris tweed top-coat. God bless a good tweed! It's passable as long as two threads hold together. I didn't have a hat, of course, or gloves, but nobody wears them in Upton anyhow, except to church. I had no notion of going to church. And I had a suit. It was seven years old, completely out of style, and slightly on the snug side. But if I moved the buttons of the jacket over so it would close, took up the hem, and eked out the waist-band of the skirt with a piece of twine, and then was careful not to ever unbutton the jacket, it would do. It would have to do.

It did do, although when I was ready to go, I understood fully for the first time the term "a haywire rig." Since haywire is a fairly common commodity in the woods, it is used universally for emergency repairs. Therefore anything that is held together with haywire is a haywire rig. Broadening the scope of the term, so is any makeshift expedient whatsoever. If you run out of cornstarch and have to thicken a chocolate pudding with flour, that's a haywire rig. As I walked through the snow down to where the tractors were waiting, I was the haywirest rig north of Boston.

Two tractors were going instead of one, and the driver of the second tractor I had never seen before. Now, I'm shy. I know that's old stuff. I know I'm awfully tired, too, of having just plain snooty people excused to me by their friends on the grounds of a fundamental shyness. But I stick to my story. I am shy. So I said to Ralph, "You'd better introduce that man to me, if we're going to ride out together." If Ralph knows a person, he is apt to assume that by a sort of social osmosis I know him too.

He said now, "Why, that's Paul Fuller. You know him."

I didn't. I knew he had a wife named Linda, who was one of Jim Barnett's daughters, and that he had four children, one of whom was Rufus' age almost to the day. I knew these things as I know who isn't speaking to whom in Upton, and why, without ever having seen any of the characters in the drama. But I didn't know Paul Fuller.

It didn't make any difference. "Hi, Louise," he said before Ralph could go into his introduction. "Four years since you been out, isn't it; and Rufus hasn't ever been out at all. Well, he's going to get an eyeful. You can ride on the big sled, next to the pig crates. Keep an eye on them, will you? Don't want to lose the pigs off. Let's see, the last time you was out must have been when you and Ralph—"

I don't know where I ever got the impression that the

grapevine only works one way—that I sit up in the woods, invisible and inaudible, collecting my data. It came as a distinct shock that, while I knew that the youngest Fuller child is allergic to tomatoes, the Fuller family undoubtedly knew all about the loose filling in my second left upper molar.

We crossed the river on a corduroy bridge that bowed and quivered under the weight of the tractors. I sat on a pile of lumber, beds, and horse-blankets, twelve feet above the ground. There was no road and the sled had no springs. Very shortly I felt as if my spine were coming through the top of my head. I looked forward to where Edgar was hunched in the saddle of the tractor, fighting his machine. It would crawl slowly and powerfully up an outcropping of ledge, balance, and come down *zoonk!* on the other side. Every time that happened—and it happened about every sixty seconds—I saw six inches of daylight between Edgar and the seat. I shuddered for him and took a look at the pig crates, which were inching toward the rear of the load. The pigs weren't happy, either. The only one who was happy, as far as I could see, was Rufus. Tractors are his passion and tractor drivers his gods. He was in seventh heaven.

We crossed a high, beech-covered ridge and came down to B Pond, and from then on it was new territory to me. We left the shore of the pond at the outlet and struck out through a long narrow swamp, between dark, crouching ridges. I had never been there, and yet it was familiar. After a while I realized that it was exactly like that terrible and desolate country of "Childe Roland to the Dark Tower Came," which has always been for me one of the most diabolically inspired pieces of horror writing in English.

It was a level, somber place, with stunted cedars growing out of the swamp, and the snow wasting away from about black bog holes. As for the grass, Browning covered that:

> ". . . it grew as scant as hair
> In leprosy; thin dry blades pricked the mud
> Which underneath looked kneaded up with blood."

There was even the sudden little river, which crossed our path as unexpected and as vicious as an adder. Then came a place where a forest fire had passed. Nothing grew there any more. Black, limbless stubs pointed to the gray sky. It was neither swamp nor forest—"mere earth, desperate and done with." The tractors, lumbering along like prehistoric monsters, were not incongruous. They were like the incarnation of mindless brutality in this mindless, brutal place. The whole thing got me down, which probably proves that too much education doesn't pay. Rufus and Edgar and Paul hadn't read Browning, and were all innocent of literary connotations. They seemed perfectly happy and unimpressed.

It was odd to be Outside. It was odd to see modern cars, looking like a bunch of water-bugs scooting up and down the road, after our collection of angular antiques. It was odd to go into a house that had electric lights, and to have Merna say, "Sally, run up to the store and get two pounds of sugar." I had forgotten that people lived near enough stores to be able to run up to them at a moment's notice. I ran, too, for the novelty of it, and we took Rufus along. He'd never been in a store before, and he couldn't believe his eyes. I bought him his first candy bar, and he didn't quite know what to do with it. It didn't take him long to find out, though. Probably buying it was an example of misguided motherly indulgence.

There were several people in the store, and they all said, "Hi, Louise. How does it seem to be out?" Sally told me their names, which were familiar to me, and now I sorted them out to go with the right faces. They didn't seem like strangers and they didn't treat me like a stranger. I had a fine time. Albert Allen gave me a bag of carrots to take home, and Jim Barnett tried to give Rufus a pair of white rats, but there I drew the line. White rats give me the creeps. Rufus forgot his disappointment in the excitement of viewing the Allens' hens. Horses, cows and pigs he had seen before, but never a hen. He was fascinated. We kept losing him and finding him leaning transfixed against the hen-yard fence. He watched the cows being milked, too, with amazement. Milk heretofore had been something that came out of a can. He saw a new little calf and a lot of things that turned out to be dogs. I suppose it is news to one whose entire dog experience has been Kyak that a Cocker spaniel is a dog, and, surprisingly, so are such divergent types as setters and toy bulls. It must be baffling. But he loved best of all the other children. It was a discovery that he and Junior Miller weren't carrying the whole burden of perpetuating the race.

The things I loved best, next to watching Rufus react, were eating someone else's cooking and meeting so many friendly people. It wasn't until we were half-way home the next morning that I remembered to be relieved that in a traffic jam in front of the store—three cars and an ox-team all at once—I felt no compulsion to scuttle into the doorway and shiver and howl.

Our one legitimate reason for going to Upton is to attend Town Meeting, which all over New England comes on the first Monday in March. Town Meeting is supposed to be a political phenomenon, the purest form of self-government, or something. That sounds a little overwhelming. It sounds as though the citizens ought to put on their best clothes and pace solemnly to the Town Hall on Town Meeting Day, in full consciousness that they are about to share in the freeman's most priceless privilege and most sacred responsibility, that of determining their own destiny. It sounds, in short, a little stuffy and dull.

It's nothing of the sort, in Upton. Town Meeting Day there combines all the better features of Old Home Week, a session of the Lower House, a barbecue, and an encounter between the Montagues and the Capulets.

When we arrived a half an hour before the meeting was called to order, everyone in the township who could stand on his feet was present at the big, bare town hall, perched on top of Upton Hill. The village half-wit and the town drunkard stood on the steps, shaking hands with all comers, a self-constituted welcoming committee. A wave of noise, as solid as water, met us at the door. School was out for the day, and the children chased around the room. Around the red-hot, air-tight stove at one end the women sat, exchanging gossip, recipes, and symptoms. At the other end, around the speaker's table, stood the white-collar class, the minister, the school-teacher, the hotel proprietor, and the storekeeper–postmaster-telephone-operator. They were white-collar in name only, as, like the rest of us, they wore flannel shirts, sheep-skins, and corduroys. Half-way between, a group of farmers exchanged views on politics, crops, and the price of grain, while over in a corner the ribald lumberjack element swapped dirty stories and lent color to the scene with their bright mackinaws and high boots. The game warden, tough and trim in his blue uniform, came in and sat down beside our leading poacher. The one had had the other thrown into jail the preceding fall, over a little matter of an untagged deer, but that didn't seem to shadow their social relations. The town's oldest citizen, Silas Peasley, from whom Rufus gets his middle name and in whom every one of us took an affectionate pride, held court down one side of the room. We all went up and spoke to him, and we all got together later and sadly agreed that he had failed considerable. Last year, on his eighty-second birthday, he had been able to leap into the air and click his heels three times. It would be a wonder if he could manage twice this year.

When the meeting was called to order, things simmered down. The children went out-doors, the men tip-toed to seats, and the women lowered their voices. In theory, they have a hand in the town government, but unless a really bitter issue is at stake they sacrifice the franchise for speculation as to whether the town's latest marriage was a shotgun affair or not. The first business on the Warrant was the electing of a moderator, and someone nominated Cedric Judkin, who runs the store, the post-office, and the telephone exchange. (They are all under one roof, along with his living quarters, so this doesn't require the ubiquitousness that would seem to be implied.) This nomination was routine. Cedric has been moderator since the memory of man runeth not to the contrary. This year he dealt precedent a mortal blow.

"Nope, I can't do it," he announced from the stove that he was stoking. "I'd like to, but my mother-in-law is sick, and my wife has to stay with her, so there's no one to tend store and sort the mail. I got to be back and forth 'twixt here and there all day. You'll be obliged to get someone else."

"But, gosh-a'mighty, no one else knows this here parliamentary procedure!"

"Well, I'll be in and out. If you get sluiced, I'll help out," Cedric promised.

There was a flurry of nominations, all declined. Nobody wanted to stick his neck out. Finally the hotel proprietor allowed himself to be persuaded, because if somebody didn't, the meeting would never get going. He made it clear that nothing that happened was to be held against him, and climbed onto the platform with the well-mixed metaphor, "Don't know how this is going to pan out, but I guess we'll get through somehow."

We got through the electing of the town officers very nicely, since this is largely a matter of re-electing the present incumbents, the most suitable candidate for each office having been determined days ago. Only death can dislodge one. In that event, the office is apt to rotate for a few years until its predestined occupant is discovered, when it again becomes stabilized. The exception is the three selectmen, who, having the most to do, are most liable to censure. But we have a neat system to take care of that. To fill the three positions we have four suitable men. Each year the one in greatest disfavor at the moment is deposed, and the current spare elected to his place. By the following March his crime has been eclipsed by the blacker, newer indiscretions of one of the trio in office, and back he comes. It's a sort of political Musical Chairs. It works out very well.

This year Article 10 of the Warrant was the Fighting Article. We always have a Fighting Article. Once it was whether the constable should receive a salary of three dollars a year, or whether, instead, the town should buy him a star instead of making him furnish his own. One year it had to do with the licensing of a beer parlor. And once—oh, lovely year of which fables are still told and Rabelaisian quips repeated—it was whether or not the town should appropriate money to hire the services of a bull for the convenience of the cow-owning citizens. This year the Article read: To see what sum of money the town will grant and raise to purchase or repair snow-removal equipment. Snow removal—"breaking out the roads"—is an impressive item on a Maine town's budget. It costs more than the education of the young.

"Mr. Moderator."

"Mr. Hart."

"Look, I been running that damn plow for seven years, ever since we bought her, and she was second-hand then. She ain't going to go through another winter. She's all tied together with haywire, and every time I take her out, something new falls off. I'm sick and tired of the whole rig."

"I don't see where Bill's got any kick coming," a voice from the rear proclaimed. "He gets paid by the hour, whether he's plowing or tinkering. Far as that goes, he was hired with the idea he'd keep her in good shape, and if he ain't done it, that's skin off his own nose."

"God A'mighty, there's limits to what a man can do with a bunch of junk. If you or any of the rest of your shiftless tribe can do any better—"

"Shiftless! At least my woman makes her own bread, instead of traipsin' up to the store for it, like some I know."

"Address the chair!" the moderator shouted.

"We need a new plow!"

"We don't! We can send her back to the factory and have them undo the damage Bill's done her."

"*I* done her!" There was more to this speech, but no

one heard it, because a perfectly deafening uproar started outside one of the long windows. A lanky farmer looked out and turned to report.

"Hey, Bill, that spotted heifer of yourn's stuck in a drift outside, bellerin' her fool head off and doing her damnedest to break a leg. You'd better see to her."

"How in hell did she get out?" and Bill streaked for the door. The meeting waited until he got back. The battle with his live-stock in thigh-deep wet snow had improved his temper.

"Look, folks," he said reasonably, "why don't we buy a new snow-plow? We'd be money-in-pocket in the end. Patching up this one's just pouring cash down a skunk hole."

"Couldn't we appropriate some money and let the selectmen study into it and decide–" a mild little man suggested.

"No," one of the selectmen said with finality. "That's what was done fifteen years ago when we put in that cement bridge down by Durkee's. I happened to be selectman at the time and we built the best bridge we could for the money. A good sound bridge, too, 'tis. But there's talk about it to this day. So it's up to you folks to decide what to do, and us selectmen will see it's done."

Bill Hart said hastily, "I move we appropriate three thousand dollars and buy a new plow." His sister-in-law's husband seconded the motion and one of the Hart uncles-by-marriage called for a vote before the opposition could collect itself.

The votes were written on slips of paper brought from home–no sense in wasting the tax-payers' money on printed ballots–and a straggling procession started for the ballot-box, over which the moderator and clerk stood to insure an honest vote. The town half-wit cast his ballot with the rest, and as soon as his back was turned the clerk fished it out and pocketed it, a flagrantly illegal act condoned by everyone present on the premise that there warn't no need to hurt his feelings. It was a close matter, but the new plow won.

A weather-beaten man with a rather fine and intelligent face, who had been figuring feverishly on the back of an old envelope, rose to his feet. "Mr. Moderator, we hadn't ought to do this. It's going to raise taxes sixty percent. I got the figures right here. We'd ought to do a little more considering before we act."

There was a stunned silence, and then a roar. The moderator pounded frantically, and then cut loose with a bellow. "There ain't no use losing our tempers now," he pointed out, demonstrating the derivation of his title. "We voted the money, and it's too late to change our minds."

"Why is it, if we want to?" demanded some untamed spirit.

"I don't know. But seems like it's against the rules."

"Where's Cedric at? Get Cedric."

Cedric had gone over to his store, but when the summons went out, he came splashing across in the March mud and slush with his coat-tails flying. His bearing was rather that of a mother whose better judgment had been telling her all along that she shouldn't have left the children alone with the buzz-saw.

"I don't recall anything about that in the rules," he said when the problem had been put to him. "But I don't see why we can't rig it up. How many want to back water?"

The walls bulged.

"All right. If someone will put it in the form of a motion, just so's it'll be legal—"

The haste with which the matter was put through was indecent. Then the conservative sum of two hundred dollars was voted to repair the old plow, and the Fighting Article was history.

The women had withdrawn some time before, and now one spoke to the moderator from the doorway. "Lee, if you've come to a good resting-place, dinner's on upstairs."

Town Meeting dinner is an event in the year. The food is all donated, and the proceeds—the charge is thirty-five cents—go to the Ladies' Aid. Everyone puts her best culinary foot forward. There were ham and chicken, scalloped potatoes, salad, and hot rolls; the pies were cut in quarters, in the generous country style, and the layer cakes were laced with jam and topped with yellow whipped cream. The coffee was hot and clear. It was insulting to the committee not to have second helpings, and thirds and fourths were subtle compliments. At first everyone concentrated on the food, but after a while the talk broke out.

"—ain't layin' now. Guess I'll hire me a dozen Rhode Island Reds to see me through till spring."

"Extravagant! My land, you'd ought to take one look in her garbage pail!"

"—lost his shirt on that cut in the Diamond. Had to haul five miles—"

"Sure I hired out to them. When them crazy Democrats come around and shove money at me, what'm I supposed to do? Sit on my hands? But when it comes to voting for any such tom-fool notion—"

Maybe the effects of the meal were soporific. At any rate, the afternoon session was as calm as a Quaker Meeting. There was a little discussion about the appropriation for the Poor Account, which is our version of Relief. This was during the depression, so perhaps the argument deserves a note, as being unique. The customary amount granted is five hundred dollars, but since it is never wholly expended, the Poor Account was getting top-heavy, having reached a total of about a thousand dollars, which is MONEY in Upton. Someone therefore suggested that it would be a good idea to skip the Poor Account this year, and let it feed off its hump, so to speak.

The first selectman was doubtful. "I dunno. 'Course, we never do spend it all, but still, it's good to have a backlog, case of emergency. We could cut down, say, to two hundred—"

This was the year when Relief money was running out all over the country, and when food riots were common in the big cities, but that's what we did, all the same. And that doesn't prove, either, that New England didn't feel the depression. What it proves is that rural New England, with its starved farms and hand-to-mouth living, is chronically so near depression that a big slump doesn't matter much. It simply means pulling in the belt another notch, wearing the same clothes one or two or three more years, and going without butter. We don't get guns for our butter, either. We get something even more necessary to the safe-guarding of Democracy. We get self-respect and the right to spit in anyone's eye and tell them to go climb a tree.

And that about covers Town Meeting. Ralph goes every year, since he considers it his duty as a citizen. His sense of responsibility doesn't carry him to the point of taking office, though. It was suggested to him one year that he'd be a good Health Officer. He didn't see why, until his one very special qualification was pointed out to him. He lives a long way from the village. "No one wants the job," they said earnestly. "You're in trouble all the time. Folks

Pond-in-the-River Dam

A Use for Spare Time—Alec Bright and Ralph Shortly Before They Were Wrecked

get mad if you light into them about the way their outhouses smell, or where they dump their tin cans. Next thing, you may find the air let out of your tires, or a hole in your boat. Now living way off up there, you could come in every so often and raise hell, and then go back to the woods till it sort of blew over—"

P.S. He didn't take the job.

As a matter of fact, there's really no point in our going Outside since for three months of the year the Outside comes in here, in the form of guests at what we call the Hotel, but which is, as I have said, Captain Coburn's Lakewood Camps at Middle Dam. That's two miles away from us, and that's a good distance for it to be. We can see the Outsiders whenever we want to, but they don't cramp our style. If I want to wear shorts, which is an error no one over eighteen should commit in public, I can do so. I can also run my household as badly as I please, and our house guests can sun-bathe in the altogether without let or hindrance. It's ideal.

The Outsiders who frequent Coburn's are known, of course, as sports—even the fat lady who comes here against her will, because if she doesn't spend two weeks in summer here with her husband, he won't spend two weeks in Florida in the winter with her. She's quite a gal. She's down, but she isn't out. She'd much rather be home in the suburbs, but since she can't be, she does her best to bring the suburbs along with her to the woods. She wears spike heels and flowing lavender chiffon draperies, and gives bridge parties every afternoon, at which she serves the nearest a fishing camp chef can come to a dainty fruit salad. She herself supplies the cut-up marshmallow and maraschino cherries to top off this dish. She gives cute prizes. I find her very tiresome at close range, but at a distance I rather admire her spirit. And to be honest, she's just as much interested in maintaining this distance as I am. She finds me impossible, too.

One thing about living in the backwoods—You Meet Such Interesting People! Or else you meet so few, and have so much more time to talk with them, that they seem interesting. Maybe everybody is interesting, if you get a chance to hash things over with them while they're in their old clothes and have their mental hair down. I met a woman on the dam the other day. She was sitting in the sun, knitting, while her husband fished. If I had met her at a tea, she would have been wearing a rather dowdy beige lace, a harassed expression, and an unbecoming hat, and we would never have got beyond "How do you do?" because I would have been feeling inadequate and lacking in chic, too. As it was, we covered everything, finally getting around to methods of coping with insomnia.

I'm not an expert, being the kind that seldom remembers hitting the bed; but I advanced my formula. Lying awake in the dark, I plan a trip. It's usually to the West Indies. I start at the very beginning and go shopping. I buy everything, from toothpaste to the exclusive little model that's going to knock them dead at the captain's dinner. Then I buy the very smartest luggage and pack. In theory I also conjure up all the people I meet on the boat, and what we do and say to each other. Actually I have yet to stay awake long enough to get myself aboard.

Her method promises even more entertainment. She starts from the present and moves backward in time, remembering every dress she ever owned and the most important thing that happened to her while she was wearing each one. She says a lot of things come back to her that she had completely forgotten.

I can believe it. I gave the idea a trial spin while I was washing dishes. I remembered dresses I wouldn't be found dead in now. That black evening gown of 1930, for instance, with a hemline above my knees in front and down to the floor in back, forming a sort of show-case for my legs, which were modishly clad in very light stockings. (Why some of my friends didn't tell me?!) I broke my ankle while wearing that dress, which probably served me right.

Then there was a dress—about the only one I can still contemplate without writhing—made of men's heavy silk shirting, striped ivory-color. (Ralph says how can a solid color be striped, but that comes under What Every Woman Knows and means alternate dull and shiny stripes.) It was softly tailored and becoming and lucky, as some dresses are lucky. I first brought my golf score down into the eighties while I was wearing it.

When I get more time, I'm going to play this dress game some more. I still don't know the name of the woman who told me about it, but I owe her a vote of thanks. I collect one-handed means of entertainment. They come in handy in the woods.

There are a few things that sports do that make me mad, such as wearing smoked glasses the first time I meet them. I hate to talk to strangers in dark glasses. I can see the quirk of the mouth, but without the corroborative evidence of the eyes, I can't tell whether it's a friendly quirk or a cynical one. I feel like snarling, "Take those damn things off, so I can tell what's going on behind them."

It doesn't make me mad, though, to have them patronize and laugh at us quaint natives. They don't know it, but we're laughing and patronizing right straight back. They think our clothes are just too picturesque and amusing; and we think beach pajamas a hundred miles from a beach, and waders worn for boat fishing, and shorts and halters in black-fly season are amusing. (You can skip the "just too picturesque." We don't talk like that, and besides, I don't think we're supposed to know what picturesque means.) Their delight in our naivete can't exceed our delight in their gullibility. They ask us what makes the lake look streaked. All right, that's a silly question. Any fool should know it's the wind. So all right, it calls for a silly answer, and we have one all ready, because that's a stock question. "Oh, that's where the sled tracks cross the ice in winter," we say, and they usually believe us.

Pete and Ira Brown and I had a lot of fun with a whole porchful of sports one evening. Pete and Ira are two old guides, friends of mine. They were sitting outside the hotel with a dozen fishermen when Ralph and I arrived for the mail.

Pete said, "Hi, Louise. Been to B Pond lately?"

I said, "Yup. Gerrish and I went over Saturday."

"Catch any fish?"

"Nope. I don't think there are any fish over there."

Ira stated flatly, "You don't fish the right place. There are plenty of fish there."

"Well, I fished everywhere, so I must have been in the right place part of the time."

Ira squinted at me through a cloud of cigarette smoke. His eye had a warning gleam. "Bet you didn't fish under the island."

The silence on the porch was electric. Every eye was turned out over the lake, but every ear was cocked in our direction. I had to play this right.

"Why, no," I said uncertainly. "I forgot all about under the island."

Ira looked relieved. "That's where the fish are, this time of year. In them caverns. Last time I was over, I camped overnight on the island. Couldn't hardly get a wink of sleep from the racket they was making, feeding off the roots of the grass. You try there next time."

I couldn't take it any longer. I couldn't stand the bland expressions on the Brown brothers' faces, and the puzzled credulity on the sports'. I said hastily, "Thanks. I will," and went inside.

I love some of the sports. I used to love old Dr. Aldrich, who came up yearly to fish and play poker. He liked to fish, but he also liked his comfort. There's nothing very cozy about sitting on a hard cold rock, surrounded by a cloud of black flies and mosquitoes, so Dr. Aldrich didn't do it. Every evening he'd go down to Harbeck, a good pool just below Middle Dam, weighed down with impedimenta. First he inflated an air cushion, a process which left him purple of face and bulging of eye, arranged it on a rock, and arranged himself on it. Then he tucked a steamer rug carefully around his legs and placed a Flit gun beside him, its handle, like that of Lady Macbeth's dagger, to his hand. Then he was ready to fish. He'd work out fifteen or twenty feet of line and make a dozen casts. Suddenly he'd reel in furiously, lay down his rod, and snatch up the Flit gun. A fog of insecticide all but obscured him, and the black-fly corpses fell like rain. Then down with the gun and up with the rod, until dark. I used to walk clear up to Harbeck of an evening to watch Dr. Aldrich fish. It was worth the effort.

Something else that is worth the effort once—and it is an effort—are the National Championship White Water Races that are held here on the Fourth of July. I'm not awfully sure they are worth tagging along after more than once. After all, one guy getting dumped into the river is much like another guy getting dumped into the river, and this is one sport that is as hard on the spectators as on the entrants. Harder, maybe. All that can happen to a contestant is getting wet, getting bruised on rocks, and getting drowned. All these things can happen to the spectators, and in addition they can get bug-bites, heel blisters, scratched, sun-struck, exhausted, and lost. So I do my race-watching from my own front porch, knitting and dispensing food and drink to those of our friends who drop in in passing. But I am in the minority. People come from all over the country to spend three days chasing up and down the river.

The reason that these races are held on the Rapid River is that the flow of water can be regulated here. A flood or a drought doesn't matter. Renny Miller can just raise or lower a gate in the dam. And the river, while actually not navigable, is so nearly so that there is always the sporting hope that by some combination of luck and skill someone might get through in a canoe. Most of the races are not canoe races, though. They are run in fold-boats, which are exactly what the name suggests—light little collapsible boats built like kyaks. The frames are made of short pieces of wood with metal sockets on the ends and can be fitted together into the skeleton of a boat. Over this is drawn a rubberized canvas cover, which comes up over the bow and stern, leaving a cock-pit for the operator, who sits flat on the bottom, on a couple of slats, and wields a double-bladed paddle. A rubber apron buttons tight about his waist. With this apron it is almost impossible to swamp the boat. It draws so little water that it can slide over submerged ledges, and the construction is so flexible that it bounces off rocks instead of cracking up on them. So it is comparatively easy to run the river in a fold-boat. But only comparatively, you understand. I don't want to try.

What fascinates me is not the races themselves, although they are exciting, what with spills, hair-breadth escapes, and near-drownings. The real interest lies for me in what I will call the White Water Crowd. Travis Hoke, a friend of ours, is always talking about the various crowds—the Wedding Crowd, for example, college classmates who make a life work of attending each other's weddings, and whose conversation is filled with references of how stinko dear old Pinko got at Blinko's bachelor dinner. Or the Doggy Crowd, with their dead-serious discussions of that little bitch of the Squires', Faux Pas, by Social Climber out of Emily Post.

Me, I adore the White Water Crowd. All day long they slide down the river in their little boats, looking grim and desperate, and stagger back to Coburn's, battered and exhausted, to start all over again. They talk about haystacks when they mean swells, and about amazingly clever bow-work, and about Skowhegan Guide's Models, and they talk about nothing else. Tense and distraught, they come into the yard and ask to borrow some inner-tube patches and rubber cement, so they can mend their boats in time for the next race. They're so deadly earnest about the whole thing. I feel like saying, "Take it easy. It's supposed to be sport." But I know that would be considered a wrong attitude. I know the reason I'm no good at games is that I can never forget that they are games. It never seems very important whether I win or not, as long as I'm having fun playing. I spinelessly don't mind if someone else can hit a tennis ball harder and more often than I can. So I don't dare to suggest that maybe river running isn't exactly as important as they think it is.

They don't even slip into something loose and relax in the evening. Oh, my, no! When it gets too dark to risk life and limb any longer on the river, they trail back to Coburn's, take off their foot-ball helmets, life preservers, and sodden shorts and sneakers—regulation river-running costume—paint their wounds with iodine, and assemble in the lobby of the main lodge to look at each other's river-running movies. The movies are very good, actually. I like to look at them, too. But most of all I like to sit in the dark with all these hearty souls sprawled around me on the floor and hear them talk. I am sorry to say that I can never believe that floor-sprawling is anything but a pose; I have tried it, and it is *not* comfortable; but it looks well in the flickering fire-light, and is in good magazine-story tradition.

"That's Pussy on the Housatonic," someone will say of a fast-moving streak on the film. "Remember? That's the first time Pussy was ever in a fold-boat."

"Sure. But Pussy was always a good canoeman."

"Where is old Pussy now?"

"Pussy? Oh, Pussy's out on the Great Snake in Idaho, trying to make a record. Heart-broken not to be here, of course, but when this thing came up—"

"Ooooh, look! Ace, there's you. Look, Ace! I told you you were putting too much beef in your back-water. See what I mean now? See how your bow weaves and— Oh! Hey, can't we have that run over again? I want to show Ace—"

It all adds up to lunacy. And the lovely lunatic pay-off is that they do all this for a little bronze medal with a picture of a man in a fold-boat on the front and the date, place and occasion engraved on the back; and I, who never wet a foot or scraped a knee, I, with my wrong attitude, get one, too. I get one because Ralph was helpful about carrying them and their boats repeatedly from the finish back to the start in his cars. So when the Presentation of Medals came along, and they had one left over, they gave it to him, ceremoniously, to show their appreciation, which was very nice of them. And he came home to where I was sitting and reading and pitched it into my lap, saying, "Here, Mama. Here's something to add to that charm bracelet you've been claiming you're going to collect." Rubies wouldn't have pleased me more. I like a dash of irony in my dish.

So after all, why should we bother to go Outside? There would be only one reason, to see our friends; and our friends come here instead. We have swell friends, as I suppose everyone has, and we'd much rather see them here, undiluted by people we don't like, than Outside. So if they are willing to put up with my off-hand meals for the sake of lounging around in their oldest clothes and being free to do and say what they please; if they are willing to swap their own good beds for our not-so-good ones plus a lot of excellent scenery and fishing; if they want to take the long, involved trip in with nothing much at the end except us and the assurance that they are very much more than welcome, why, that's the way we want it, too. And that's the way we have it.

Once in a while the river gets to sounding like the wake of a steamer, and then I think maybe I'd like to go somewhere on a boat. I've only been on boats a little—one trip to Europe, long ago—and I love boats. But where in the world could I go to-day? Where is there peace and quiet and contentment? Where—except here.

XI

"*Is It Worth-while?*"

NOBODY EVER ASKS ME, "IS THIS LIFE YOU ARE LIVING worth-while?" That's a question that I ask myself, occasionally.

I ask it when I get up on a twenty-below-zero morning to find the kitchen stove in one of its sullen moods. Smoke oozes from every crack, but the top won't heat enough to melt the ice in the tea kettle. A cup of hot coffee is a long way in the future. I bang the oven door and the stove pipe falls down, raining buckets of soot over everything, including the butter that I have put on the stove shelf to warm to a spreadable consistency. Smoke pours out of the down chimney in clouds, and I have to open the door and all the windows, or suffocate. My eyes smart and run water, and my hands and feet slowly and painfully turn to ice, and the answer is, "No! Nothing is worth this!"

I ask it when, at the end of a long, hot summer, everyone in Middle Dam has used up his entire ice supply, and I want a glass of ice water. I can't have it. Moreover, the meat is going to spoil unless I do something about it at once, and the butter is unattractively liquid, and the lettuce has wilted, and the tomato aspic that I made this morning isn't going to set. I think of tall, frosted glasses, and salads that are crisp and noisy under the fork, and lemon sherbet, and decide I'd swap the whole north woods for one properly refrigerated meal.

I ask it when Rufus, all snowy and rosy, comes in from a day with his lumberjack pals and croons lovingly, "Mummy nice old son of a bitch." I ask it when I've got the lunch dishes done and the kitchen tidy and am all set for an hour's leisurely reading before going swimming, and a whole hungry gang drops in. Anywhere else, we could drive to the nearest hot-dog stand, but here I have to start from scratch and throw together another complete meal. I ask it when I look at the hands of Coburn's women guests and then at my own, with their short nails, calloused palms, and the burns from the oven door across the backs. The answer is always "No. It's not worth it."

You can't very well stop operations to ponder the problem of worth-whileness when you have a big salmon on the end of a light line. When the reel starts screaming and the rod bends into a vibrating bow and you suddenly remember that you meant to change that frayed leader and didn't; you have enough to think about. The fish starts away from the boat, and you burn your thumb braking the line. Then the water explodes fifty feet away, and you see him, a furious arc in the air, shaking his head viciously in an effort to dislodge the fly. He's a whale! He's easily the biggest fish that— He starts for the boat, and you reel in frantically. The sun is in your eyes, and the landing net is just out of reach—not that you'll ever bring him to the net; your arms are numb already—and then, abruptly, there he is, right up under the gunwale, just as tired as you are. You find that you can reach the net after all, and you ease it over the side, taking care not to hit the leader —and he's yours! He doesn't weigh the seven pounds you thought he did when you saw him break water, but the pocket scales say four and a half, and four and a half isn't so bad. You wet your hands carefully before taking him off the hook, and slide him over the side. You don't think to ask yourself then if that was worth-while. It's enough that it was fun.

"Is it worth-while?" is not a question that I think to ask myself when I am out in the middle of B Pond, watching the gulls inscribe their white scrolls against the sky. I don't ask it when I see a deer drinking at Long Pool, or hear a loon laugh, or when I compare Rufus with other children of his age and discover that he is two inches taller and five pounds heavier than most of them, and that he doesn't enter rooms with a piercing shriek of "It's Superman!" I don't ask it when I get a check for a story, or find that my $1.98 mail order bathing suit looks much nicer than the $15.00 model I saw on a woman up at the hotel—or does it only seem that way because I'm browner and thinner and can swim better than that woman? I don't ask it when friends have such a good time with us that they hate to leave as much as we hate to see them go; or when we all sit on the porch in the evening with our feet on the rail, and watch the tide of the dusk rise from the valleys up the hills and across the sky. The stars come out one by one, and the moon swings up above Pondy Dam, changing the river to a road of restless gold. It isn't a moment to be asking yourself questions. It's a moment to enjoy.

It amounts to this. "Is it worth-while to live like this?"

is a question that I never ask myself under fair conditions. I ask it only when exasperation or discomfort or exhaustion pre-determine *No* as an answer. That's about ten times a year. On the other three hundred and fifty-five days of the year, I don't question anything. Happy people aren't given to soul searching, I find. Revolt and reform, whether private or general, are always bred in misery and discontent. So now, sitting here quietly with nothing to annoy me and nothing to exhilarate me—except that I am at long last on the final chapter of this book I undertook so light-heartedly to write—I will once and for all try to find the answer.

Why did we come to live here in the first place? We thought it was because we liked the woods, because we wanted to find a simple, leisurely way of life. Now, looking back, I think that we were unconsciously seeking to find a lost sense of our own identity. Looking back through the telescope of the last six years, I can see myself as I was and realize how living here has changed me. I hope it has changed me for the better. Certainly I am happier than I was then. Certainly I am more at home in this world that we have created than ever I was in that vast and confusing maelstrom that we call civilization.

Here I dare to be myself. I don't see why it should ever again be important to me what I wear, or whether I have read the latest book or seen the latest play, or know the newest catch word. I don't see why I should ever care again what people think of me. It seems silly now, but those things were once important. I don't see why it should ever matter to me again who does or does not invite me to her house, who does or does not speak to me, who does or does not have more money than I have. Those things used to matter, though, because I had no identity of my own. I had nothing to go by but the standards someone else had set up. To define freedom, for which men and women and children are dying all over the world, in terms of indifference to clothes and social contacts and popular attitudes seems so trivial and irresponsible a thing to do that I am ashamed of it, as of a gross impertinence; but that is what living here adds up to, for me. I am free.

It adds up to more than that. All ordinary people like us, everywhere, are trying to find the same things. It makes no difference whether they are New Englanders or Texans or Malayans or Finns. They all want to be left alone to conduct their own private search for a personal peace, a reasonable security, a little love, a chance to attain happiness through achievement. It isn't much to want; but I never came anywhere near to getting most of those things until we took to the woods.

I have peace here. It may suffer surface disruptions when I forget to put my bread to rise, or Ralph discovers that Rufus has drained the radiator of the Big Green "Mormon" and poured the water into the gas tank; but the depths of that peace can't be shaken. We have a reasonable security. Sometimes we may have to figure a little closely to pay the taxes and outfit the kids and put the groceries in for the winter; but the things that matter—our feeling of entity, our sense of belonging—are never in danger here. Neither is the contentment that comes through accomplishment. What we have achieved isn't important to the world. No lives will be saved or unborn generations rise up to call us blessed for our six years' work here. All we've done is to take a little slice of wild land and force it to produce; to take some old ramshackle buildings and make them livable; to take land and buildings and two diametrically opposite personalities and make them into a home.

A great many people ask me if Ralph and I don't get on each other's nerves horribly during the long periods when we see only each other. That's a legitimate question. Everyone knows the corroding effect too great familiarity has on even the strongest attachment. It should have an even more devastating effect on me, as I am, I know, not quite normal in my loathing for having anyone crowd in on me, either literally or figuratively. I can't stand being jostled physically, and I can't stand having my actions questioned or commented upon. I could, quite literally, kill anyone who says to me, "A penny for your thoughts." I'm a New Englander, so I can't talk about love. The only way I can explain why I never feel like killing Ralph is open to unflattering misinterpretation; but I'll try to explain, all the same.

Emily Dickinson once said of a little niece who had been shut up in a closet as punishment, and was discovered there hours later, perfectly composed and happy, "But no one could ever punish a Dickinson by shutting her up alone!" That applied to Emily herself, and it applies to this obscure Dickinson. It applies to my ability to be contented here, away from the world, and to the truth underlying Ralph's and my relationship: that being with Ralph is just exactly as good as being alone.

Now that that's written, it looks terrible; and I meant it to be the nicest thing I could say!

And what about Ralph himself? Does he feel as I feel about our life here? I can't answer for him. No one can truly answer for another person's thoughts and feelings. I can only go by what external evidence I have.

Last summer a visitor, Barbara Wing, asked Ralph a purely hypothetical question, during one of those long rambling discussions that kindred souls get into: "If you had a million dollars left you to-morrow, what would be the first thing you'd do?"

Ralph thought for a long time, and I thought right along with him, wondering whether it would be an island in the South Seas—this was before Pearl Harbor—or a ranch in the Argentine. Finally he said slowly, "Well—that's a hard question to answer. I can't make up my mind whether a bathroom or a new roof for the woodshed comes first." He was serious, so we all laughed; but I don't worry any more about whether he really likes it here as much as I do.

I'd spend my million dollars on Forest Lodge, too, except for a fund I'd invest in letting the kids see the world. I'd send them everywhere and let them taste everything, so that at last they'd come to know what we have here to value. Discontent is only the fear of missing something. Content is the knowledge that you aren't missing a thing worth-while.

I know that many people—perhaps most people—couldn't feel that, living here, they held within their grasp all the best of life. So for them it wouldn't be the best. For us, it is.

And that's the final answer.

THE END

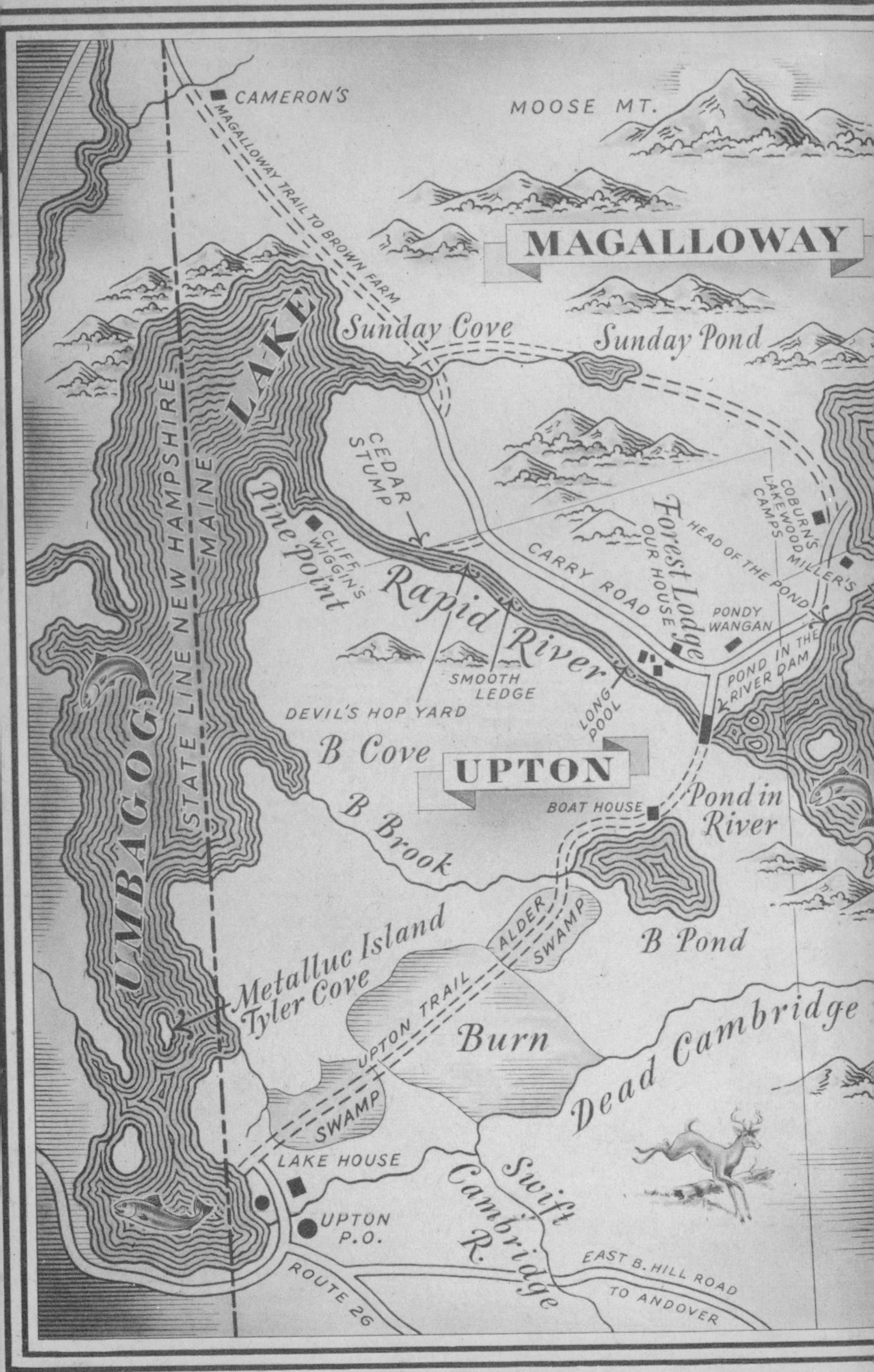
CAMERON'S
MOOSE MT.
MAGALLOWAY TRAIL TO BROWN FARM
MAGALLOWAY
Sunday Cove
Sunday Pond
LAKE
UMBAGOG
NEW HAMPSHIRE
STATE LINE
MAINE
CEDAR STUMP
Pine Point
CLIFF WIGGIN'S
Rapid River
CARRY ROAD
Forest Lodge
OUR HOUSE
HEAD OF THE POND
COBURN'S LAKEWOOD CAMPS
MILLER'S
PONDY WANGAN
POND IN THE RIVER DAM
SMOOTH LEDGE
DEVIL'S HOP YARD
LONG POOL
B Cove
UPTON
BOAT HOUSE
Pond in River
B Brook
ALDER SWAMP
B Pond
Metalluc Island
Tyler Cove
UPTON TRAIL
Burn
Dead Cambridge
SWAMP
LAKE HOUSE
UPTON P.O.
Swift Cambridge
Cambridge R.
ROUTE 26
EAST B. HILL ROAD
TO ANDOVER